IN THE
EYE
OF THE
STORM

IN THE
EYE
OF THE
STORM

Robert Thier

2016

First Printing: 2016

ISBN: 978-3-00-053262-7

This book is also available in eBook format. More information on this and any other subject connected with Robert Thier's books on: www.robthier.com

Dedication

This story is dedicated to all my fantastic fans and fiery little Ifrits! It is thanks to your fervent support that I have now been able to publish the second book of the *Storm and Silence* series!

Firstly, there are all those awesome people who have either supported my writing by buying the first book of this series (and actually bringing it onto a few online bestseller lists!) or are supporting my literary efforts by subscribing to my chapters on Radish Fiction. Thanks to your help, I've taken a big step closer to becoming a professional writer, and I'm deliriously excited!

Secondly, I would like to thank Grace Harris, who contributed to the *Storm and Silence* publishing campaign and didn't get mad at me for accidentally forgetting to include her in the last book's dedication. My sincerest apologies!

As with the last volume of this series, a big cartload of thanks goes to Iris Chacon, the wonderful editor who volunteered her time to edit this opus from front to back.

And finally, I wish to thank every other kind of fan under the sun: composers of *Storm and Silence* melodies, creators of awesome fan-art and fanfiction, writers of glowing reviews and readers who devour my writing – I love you all! (In a very platonic, non-schmaltzy way...) Thank you for being the world's best fandom! I look forward to scribbling many more stories for your enjoyment, knowing that you shall be with me every step of the way.

Contents

COLD AND HOT

My eyes roamed across the deck, searching. I spotted my victim about a dozen yards away, leaning against the railing. He was smoking a pipe, relaxed, quite unaware of what I had in store for him.

'Captain!'

My water-soaked boots squeaked with the kind of wrath possessed only by a girl who has just escaped drowning in the North Sea like a wet rat. He made the mistake of turning towards me with an ingratiating smile.

I wasn't really in the mood for smiles. My hand shot out, grabbing him by the collar.

'Captain, what is this I hear about you having given the order to stop searching and turn back? Have you found him yet?'

I knew he hadn't before the words were out of my mouth. That smile of his, as if he were dealing with a mentally incompetent damsel who needed to be treated with care so she wouldn't snap in half, told me all I needed to know.

'Miss Linton.' Reaching out, Captain Crockford patted my hand reassuringly – or at least in a manner he thought would be reassuring. 'We've already combed the ocean for Mr... what did you say his name was again?'

'Ambrose! Rikkard Ambrose!'

'We've already combed the ocean for Mr Ambrose for five days in a row. That's how long he's been out here, Miss Linton, five days! Even if he managed to crawl onto a piece of wreckage somehow, a human being cannot survive longer than three days without fresh water. And if he was just afloat in the sea... well, the cold water would have killed him in no more than two hours.'

'No! He must be alive! He must be!'

'Even if, by some miracle, he still is, it is not my responsibility to look for him.' For the first time, a note of annoyance crept into the captain's voice. I barely kept myself from trying to strangle him. 'True, the Waterguard[1] has always helped victims of shipwreck, but our main duty is and always shall be guarding Her Majesty's coast against smugglers, not wasting our time on fruitless searches!'

'I don't care about that, Captain! Keep searching!'

'I repeat, there's nothing alive to search for, Miss Linton. Your... what is he again to you?'

In spite of the intense cold, I felt my face flush.

Blast, blast, blast! Why do you have to blush? Nothing happened between him and you! Nothing whatsoever! Well, except for that moment, just before the ship went down...

No. That was nothing!

---

[1] The Preventive Waterguard, simply Waterguard for short, was the predecessor of Her Majesty's Coastguard, operating in Great Britain in the 19th and the early 20th century. Their main job was indeed catching those naughty people who smuggled goods into England and throwing them into the sea, instead of fishing people out who had accidentally fallen in.

'My cousin!' I lied.

'Your cousin, Miss Linton, will not be found alive. I'm afraid he is fish food by now.'

'No! Never!'

'Most regrettable, of course, most regrettable.' The captain puffed out a smoke ring. 'But you'll have to face the inevitable sooner or later. If you'd like to sit down and have a shot of brandy, I could...'

I told him where he could stick his brandy.

'Miss Linton! That's hardly appropriate! I...'

'Oh, to hell with what's appropriate!' Grabbing the man's collar more tightly, I shook him, trying to make him see with the sheer force of my stare. 'Have you got any idea whom you are about to doom to a wet grave, Captain? Any idea how important he is?'

The captain puffed out another smoke ring.

'Yes, yes, of course. I'm sure he was very important to you and you feel his loss greatly, Miss–'

'I don't mean important to me, personally,' I cut him off.

Although he is. Oh, how very much he is.

'I mean *important*. Think very carefully, Captain. Have you never heard the name Rikkard Ambrose before?'

The captain opened his mouth to blow yet another smoke ring – then he choked, and coughed out the smoke through his nostrils. Underneath the tan of his weathered skin, I could see the colour slowly drain from his face.

Ha!

'Y-you don't mean... You can't mean *the* Rikkard Ambrose? The financial magnate?'

As if there were any others like him!

I met the captain's gaze without flinching.

'That's the one.'

Captain Crockford's teeth clenched down so hard, they nearly bit his pipe in half.

'Well?' I raised a questioning eyebrow. 'Are you going to keep searching?'

~~**~*~*

Captain Crockford didn't just keep searching – he called in three more ships to help. I didn't see them at first, the white of their billowing sails almost invisible against the white cliffs of Dover. But when men on the other ships started waving signal flags, coordinating search patterns, I realized we were not alone any longer.

There are more of us now! And we're going to comb the whole breadth and width of the English Channel until we find him!

'Man overboard!' The cry from the prow of the boat sent me whirling around. 'Man overboard ahead!'

I reached the prow just as the dinghy was lowered into the water. The men began to row, and I looked around wildly, trying to see where they were going.

'Where is he? Where is he?'

The ship's lieutenant, who was standing beside me, also gazing after the departing men, pointed to a spot not too far away from the ship.

'There, Miss!'

I followed his outstretched arm with my eyes, and saw a man in a dark tailcoat floating in the water – floating facedown. Without warning, a feeling of nausea came over me.

Well, look on the bright side: if you're going to vomit, the ship's railing is just a few feet ahead. Do it over the side and nobody will care. You might just throw yourself over the side while you're at it, too.

I felt like laughing and crying and screaming my rage all at the same time.

Calm down! It's just a man wearing a dark tailcoat! Lots of men wear dark tailcoats. It doesn't have to be him.

No, it didn't have to be him. I kept telling myself that, over and over. But the question kept coming back: *what if it is?*

The men out on the water pulled the motionless body into their little boat and returned to the ship with swift dips of the oars. I stood motionless, awaiting their return. Awaiting my doom, or my salvation.

And since when have you been so bloody melodramatic?

The answer to that was simple. Since him, of course.

A rope was tied around the dead man's torso, and he was pulled up the side of the ship until he slid over the railing and landed on the deck with a wet *thwack.* I didn't look. I didn't dare to.

'Miss?' It wasn't the lieutenant's voice. Captain Crockford had appeared beside me, looking not half as relaxed and aloof as earlier. His face still was rather pale. 'Miss, I'm terribly sorry, but I'm afraid I'll have to ask you to identify the body.'

Somehow, I managed to swallow around the giant lump in my throat.

Get a grip and look! You owe him that. You would be dead if not for him.

'All right, Captain. Step aside, please.'

The captain did as I asked and offered me his arm for support, but I didn't take it. I was a wreck, but I would have to feel a lot worse than this to need a man's arm to stand upright. Lifting my chin, I forced my gaze towards the contorted figure on the planks of the deck.

'Thank the Lord!' I breathed in a sigh of relief so deep I could hardly believe my lungs had the space for all that air. 'It's not him!'

'Are you sure, Miss?' the captain asked, still sounding worried. 'I mean, with his face looking like that...'

'I'm sure!'

Even with his face swollen and horribly bluish, I could instantly tell that the man on the deck was not Mr Ambrose. In fact, it would hardly have been possible to find a man who looked less like Rikkard Ambrose than the pudgy individual with the sodden black moustache that lay there in front of me.

'Well, what does Mr Ambrose look like?' the captain asked.

A choked sob escaped me. 'Why? Are you expecting to fish so many men out of the sea that you'll have to pick and choose?'

'Just tell me, Miss Linton.'

With a shrug, I gave in. I didn't have the strength to resist right now. Following right on the heels of the relief that the dead man wasn't Mr Ambrose had come the horror of knowing that this was what he probably looked like now: blue, swollen, stiff and cold.

Well, he's always been stiff and cold, so at least that won't change, will it?

Another sob escaped me.

'Tell me, Miss Linton,' the captain insisted.

Oh, what the hell! If he thought it would help...

'He's tall, dark...'

...and handsome. So bloody perfectly handsome!

'...and, um, dark. Dark-haired, I mean.' I coughed, hoping that nobody was noticing my ears reddening. A drowned man was lying right in front of me, for Pete's sake! How could I think of something like that at a time like this?

'Beard, Miss Linton?'

'He hasn't got a beard. Not even a moustache.'

The captain's eyebrows rose. 'No beard?'

I shook my head. 'None at all.'

But a jaw you could break rocks on. And eyes, dark and coloured like the sea...

I shook myself. What bloody use was his eye-colour going to be to them for fishing him out of the ocean?

Focus, Lilly! Focus on what's important!

'Hm. No beard... He's not an old man, then, Miss Linton? I would have thought to have reached his position in life...'

'No. I don't know how old he is exactly, but no more than twenty-five, I'd guess. His face is as smooth as polished granite, and as hard and unmoving, most of the time.'

But his lips... They can be so very soft.

Blast! I was supposed to give a description here! Clenching my hands, I bit back the tears that were threatening to spill over and concentrated on one thing, and one thing only: Rikkard Ambrose.

'His figure?' the captain enquired, taking notes in a small notebook he had snatched out of his pocket.

'He's leanly built.'

But he has muscles, even though one doesn't see them at first glance. And you've felt every single one of them.

'His voice? Just in case we hear him calling for help?'

'Quite deep, but most of all curt and cold.' My lips twitched. *So curt and cold...* 'If you hear him calling, he'll probably not be calling for help but ordering you to come.'

What wouldn't I give to hear him snapping at me again, making demands, ordering me around. Before, it had almost driven me crazy. Now that he wasn't here anymore, I missed the bloody tyrant! I missed his eyes, his voice, his overwhelming presence. I even missed his stinginess and gruff, biting remarks. But most of all, I missed the knowledge that he was safe and well. I missed him. All of him.

Blast! That's all you need! After the way he treated you, you've gone and become fond of the bastard!

Although 'fond' might not be exactly the right word to describe the way I was feeling, I admitted to myself, my ears still burning.

'Miss Linton?' The captain's voice pulled me from my reverie. 'Miss Linton, are you all right? You look a little unwell.'

'It's just... seeing that poor, unfortunate soul,' I lied, gesturing to the corpse on the floor, from which any remnant of a soul already had departed.

'Oh, of course, Miss Linton. How thoughtless of me. Men, wrap him up and carry him away! Now!'

'I... I'm sorry, Captain. It's just... I've never seen a dead man before.'

My goodness, you're good at lying today, aren't you?

The captain made an impatient gesture. 'Lieutenant! Fetch a glass of brandy for Miss Linton! And signal the other ships to keep looking.'

'Aye aye, Sir!'

When the brandy came, I didn't say no. On the contrary. I tossed the whole contents of the glass back in one large gulp. When I lowered the glass, the lieutenant was looking at me, wide-eyed, as were all other members of the crew in the vicinity.

'What's the matter?' I asked. 'Never seen a lady take a sip of brandy before?'

'Not quite like that, Miss, no.' The lieutenant bowed. 'If you'll excuse me... I have to get back to my other men, to oversee the search.'

And so we continued around the white cliffs of Dover and past beaches and bays. For hours and hours and hours we scoured the water and the coastline, now and again exchanging flag signals with another ship, but mostly just staring into the water, searching, always searching. The monotony was almost as bad as the bone-deep fear.

And when the monotony was interrupted, that was even worse. Because the only possible interruption was another corpse.

'N-no. That's not him, either.' Shaking my head, I turned away from the dead form on the deck. 'Please... take him away?'

'Of course, Miss Linton. Remove that thing at once, men!'

'Aye aye, Sir!'

And again, hours of staring into the blue-grey sea would follow. If only the sea weren't exactly the same colour as *his* eyes. Maybe, just maybe that would have made it a little easier. That blasted man had to have eyes the same blasted colour as the blasted ocean he was probably drowning in at this very moment!

'Captain! Miss Linton!'

The shout from behind me made me turn. It wasn't the usual shout of 'Man overboard' that heralded the finding of another corpse. It wasn't even one of the search party who had called. No, the ship's signaller, brightly coloured flags in hand, motioned for the captain and me to join him.

'What is it, Watkins?' the captain demanded, marching towards the man. I was only a few steps behind.

'Signals, Captain! From one of the other ships! And not the usual signals about search patterns, either! They're sending a message!'

Shielding his eyes against the sun, the captain stared off towards the ship to which the signaller pointed. I, too, followed the man's arm with my gaze, and saw nothing more than a few spots of colour in the distance.

'What does that mean?' I demanded. 'I don't know flag signals!'

The colour in the distance changed. 'That's an M!' The signaller shouted.

'An M?'

'Messages are sent in colour-movement combinations. Every combination stands for a different letter in the alphabet. That's an A! And that's and N!'

M-A-N...

'Man! They're sending a signal about a man!'

Or maybe a mantis...

'What kind of man?' I demanded, telling my stupid inner voice to shut up. 'Is he all right? Where's the signal coming from?'

The signaller ignored me with the thoroughness of a man who does nothing but swing flags all day. Full of concentration, he stared into the distance.

'W!' he shouted. 'A-S-H-E-D...'

Man *washed*? What the hell...? Had Mr Ambrose had taken a bubble bath?

'A-S-H-O-R-E...'

My heart made a leap! *Man washed ashore!* Of course! Oh God... if he had been washed ashore, did that mean he couldn't swim by himself anymore? Did that mean that he couldn't move at all, that he was stiff and cold and...

No! Please, Lord, let him have escaped! He can't be... He just can't!

I was just about to open my mouth again, to demand to know more, when the signaller's next yelled letter hit me in the stomach like a sledgehammer.

'A!'

My mouth was open, but no sound came out.

'L!'

Oh God... could it be?

'I!'

Yes, please! Please let it be true!

'V!'

Yes! Yes! Yes! Just one more letter and...

'E!'

Yes!

'He's alive?' Crossing the distance between myself in the signaller in the fraction of a second, I grabbed him by his lapels and shook him. 'He's alive! Tell me, where is he? Blast you, tell me where he is!'

THE SISTER-COUSIN-FIANCÉE-SECRETARY-DOGSBODY

I reached the small village of St. Margaret's at Cliffe that same evening, just as the sun was setting. A dinghy set me ashore on the beach, beyond where the cliff ended.

'Are you sure you don't want us to accompany you up to the village, Miss Linton?' the captain asked. He had insisted on coming ashore with me. 'If the gentleman needs anything, or if you can't find the way...'

'No, thank you. I'll take care of everything myself from here on.'

'Well... if you're sure.'

'Absolutely sure, Captain.'

If it wasn't really Mr Ambrose who had been washed ashore, I didn't want the captain there to see me crumble. And if it *was* him... Well, I didn't want *anyone* around for *that* meeting.

'Very well.' The captain bowed. 'Farewell, Miss Linton.'

'You, too, Captain.'

Captain Crockford barked a few orders, and two sailors pushed the dinghy away from the shore. Not long after, it was moving back towards the dark shape of the ship, contrasted sharply against the flames of the sunset.

I didn't stay to watch the dinghy disappear. Instead, I turned and started marching up the beach towards the twinkling lights of the village. After only a few paces, I stopped marching and started trudging instead, the sand shifting and scraping under my thin, and still damp, shoes.

'Dash it all! Couldn't that arrogant son of a bachelor manage to be washed ashore on a paved stretch of shore?'

The night remained silent, unsympathetic to my trials and tribulations. The walking became easier once I was across the beach and on the path up to the village, but by that time my socks were already full of sand. Muttering a few more unladylike expletives, I considered how Mr Ambrose would react if I were to ask him for three days sick leave because of footsoreness.

Hm. Probably not a very good idea.

The village at the end of the path was tiny. It didn't take me long to find the vicarage, and after I knocked, it was only a few moments before the door swung open, and a portly little man with glasses blinked out at me, obviously confused at finding a strange female on his doorstep.

'Um... yes, my dear? How can I help you?'

'Are you Vicar Dawson?' I asked, although his white collar really made the question rather redundant.

'Um... Yes. I suppose so. Most of my parishioners seem to think so, at least.'

'Good evening, Vicar.' I made the best curtsy I could manage in a damp dress and sand-filled socks. Judging from the vicar's expression, my efforts didn't exactly come up to scratch. 'You found a man on the beach earlier today, I believe?'

'Yes, indeed, Miss... err...'

'Linton. Lilly Linton.'

'Yes indeed, Miss Linton. The poor soul was half-drowned and unconscious, clutching a piece of wreckage as if it were the railing of Noah's Ark itself.'

I stepped forward, eagerly. 'Did he wake up? Did he tell you his name?'

'Why?' the vicar asked, with obvious curiosity. 'Do you know him?'

'I can't very well say until I know what his name is, can I!'

'Oh. Of course. How silly of me.'

'Well? Did he tell you who he was?'

The vicar shook his balding head with regret. 'I'm afraid he did not wake up while in my charge, Miss, and since he's not in my house now, I can't say whether he might have woken up by now.'

'Not in your house?'

'I live alone, Miss, and am more used to taking care of souls than earthly bodies. So I gave the unfortunate man into the care of Mrs Fotheringay, a kind lady living just above the cliffs, at the edge of the village. She has a room where she takes in lodgers during summertime, and with true Christian charity she agreed to put the unfortunate gentleman up for a few days.'

'Where? Where exactly does this Mrs Fotheringay live?'

'You know him, then? The man who was washed ashore?'

'Yes, yes!' *At least I hope so. Oh God, please let it be him.* 'Tell me, where can I find this Mrs Fotheringay?'

Stepping out of his door, the vicar pointed down the village. 'Just go down the main street until you come to the big oak. Turn right and carry on until you see a red brick house with pretty green shutters. That's Mrs Fotheringay's house.' He gave me a kind smile. 'I hope your, um... friend is all right.'

'Thank you, Vicar! Thank you so much!' I had already started running down the street, when I screeched to a halt. Blast! Quickly, I turned around again. I had nearly forgotten to ask the most important question.

'Vicar, that room that he's in – will he have to pay for it?'

The vicar blinked at me, taken aback. 'Um... I don't think so, no.'

'Thank God!' A wide grin spread over my face. 'That means he really will be all right!'

If it's him, that is.

Not wasting another second, I went tearing down the street. Not even the sand in my socks could hold me back now!

The house was there, just as the vicar had described it: red brick and abominably pretty green shutters. It also had an ornate brass doorknocker, which I grabbed and smashed against the wood hard enough to crack the paint. After a while, hesitant footsteps approached from the other side, and the door opened a crack.

'Yes?'

'Mrs Fotheringay?'

At hearing that it was a woman outside, and not a mad axe murderer, the person on the other side widened the crack slightly.

'Yes. Who is this?'

'My name is Lilly Linton. The vicar gave me directions to your house. I'm here about the man you've taken in.'

'The castaway?'

I couldn't help grinning at hearing that term applied to Mr Ambrose. It made me think of some fellow in a Robinson Crusoe getup, with a huge beard, a jacket made from goatskin and an old-fashioned rifle over his shoulder. Just thinking of Mr Ambrose in that outfit made me want to burst into giggles.

But then I remembered that it might not be Mr Ambrose I was about to see, and my urge to giggle ceased abruptly.

'Yes. The castaway. Please, Mrs Fotheringay. I know it is late, but will you let me in? I... I was on the ship that went down, and have been searching for a man who was with me for five days now, and...'

My desperate pleas trailed off as the door swung open the rest of the way. In the doorway stood a crinkly little lady with the kindest smile I had seen since nearly drowning. Atop her brown hair, shot with grey, sat a homely-looking brown bonnet, and her shabby beige dress looked to me like the garment of an elderly angel who had retired to a nice cloud in the country.

'Oh, my poor dear! Come in! Come in, please!' I was grasped by both hands and pulled inside. 'You were on the ship when that dreadful accident happened?'

If it was an accident...

But I didn't say that out loud. Instead I just nodded.

'Oh, dear Lord! Come into the sitting room and have a cup of tea, my dear! We'll find you a nice place by the fire. You're shivering!'

'Perhaps later, thank you. Your guest, the man...'

'Of course, what was I thinking?' Squeezing my hand again, the old lady tugged me down the hall. 'I'll take you to him right now, dear.'

Letting myself be pulled down the hallway, I gathered enough courage to ask the question I really, really didn't want to ask.

'Mrs Fotheringay... What did he give as his name?'

Please, Lord, let it be him! Let it be him!'

Mrs Fotheringay gave a good-natured snort. 'He hasn't told us his name! In fact, the gentleman hasn't deigned to speak so much as two words strung together. When I asked who he was, he looked at me as if it were an insult that I didn't recognize him at first sight!'

'Well, that definitely sounds like the one I'm looking for,' I muttered, hastening my steps. *Please, let it be him! Please!* 'What does he look like?'

'Well, entirely too cool and collected for a man who had seaweed in his hair not half a day ago. He's tall, and dark, and... tall. Even when he's lying down, if that makes sense.'

'Handsome?'

'I suppose you could call him handsome, if you do not mind that cold glower following you around the room.'

Thank God!

My lips twitched upwards without meaning to. 'I don't think I'd mind.'

Opening the door at the end of the hallway, Mrs Fotheringay led the way into the sitting room, where to my surprise a girl, about my age, sat in an armchair. She was doing her needlework, and it took me only one glance to see that the work was perfect, and there wasn't a single bloody puncture wound in her fingers. I disliked her immediately.

'Miss Linton, may I introduce my daughter, Violet?' Mrs Fotheringay gestured to the girl with a smile. 'Violet, my dear, this is Miss Linton. She was on that ship that went under, and thinks she might know our guest. If she does, she's going to take him away with her.'

The girl's hands twitched, and her eyes flashed to my face. Oh. Apparently, my dislike was reciprocated – fervently!

I curtsied. Slowly, Miss Violet Fotheringay rose from her seat to return my curtsy, making it quite obvious she took pleasure in the fact that hers was about ten times as graceful as mine.

'So pleased to make your acquaintance, Miss Linton,' she lied.

'As am I,' I lied right back at her.

'Violet has been nursing our guest,' Mrs Fotheringay supplied cheerily, blissfully unaware of the lightning bolts crackling through the air in her sitting room.

Nursing him, hm? So that was it. I bored my gaze into the girl, trying to drill my way through her brain. *Keep your hands on your needlework, where they belong, Missy!*

'So...' Young Miss Fotheringay's eyes slid over me from head to wet toe, obviously not impressed by what she found. 'You want to take him away with you, do you?'

'Yes. And I will.'

She gave a condescending smile. 'Of course. Forgive me, I'm sure my mother mentioned it and I just didn't catch it, but... What is your connection to him, exactly?'

Her eyes drilled into me as mine had into her. Even Mrs Fotheringay looked at me with interest. My connection... My connection with Mr Rikkard Ambrose...

In the fraction of a second, myriad images flashed past my inner eye:

Mr Ambrose, glowering at me from across his desk. Mr Ambrose, threatening me. Mr Ambrose beside me, fighting, ducking gunshots in the dark.

God, what could I say to explain my presence here? That I was his dogsbody? His secretary? It was true, but I'd be damned if I let her look down on me!

Mr Ambrose glowering at me again, his eyes glinting with cold danger. Mr Ambrose rushing towards me...

Just for a moment, I considered telling them that I was his sister – but the moment the idea entered my brain, my mind, body and soul mutinied and kicked me in the metaphorical backside. No! No, no, no, no!

But why not? Why wouldn't I use a perfect explanation for being here?

Mr Ambrose's lips crushing mine while he pulled me against him...

I pulled a face. Probably *that* was why not. Blast that man! Why did he have to do that?

What if I told her I was his fiancée? But... I wasn't. And I didn't want to be, did I? Bloody hell, I was a proud feminist and a suffragette! I wasn't supposed to want or need any man, least of all a bloody chauvinist like him!

'I'm his cousin!' The words came out of my mouth before I knew what I was saying. A cousin. A relation close enough that it wouldn't be strange for us to have been travelling together—and distant enough to still make me competition for Miss Fotheringay.[2] The flash of hostility in her eyes told me she understood perfectly.

'Oh, his cousin?' Her eyes swept once more over my rather short figure, my brown, shoulder-length hair and equally brown eyes. Her lips twitched in a sarcastic smile. 'Of course! The family resemblance is *so* startling! I should have noticed it before.'

'What do you mean, Violet?' Mrs Fotheringay asked, confused, not noticing how I was trying to murder her daughter with my gaze. 'She looks nothing like the gentleman.'

Apparently, the daughter had not inherited that penchant for sarcasm from her mother. Her father must have been a nasty piece of work.

'He gets his looks from the other side of the family,' I told them both, not taking my eyes off the younger woman. 'Now, if you would be so kind as to take me to him...'

Mrs Fotheringay opened her mouth, but her daughter was faster.

'Of course! I'll take you.' She smiled at me, her teeth gleaming like razor-blades. 'I'm sure he will be glad to see me. He has grown quite fond of me over the last few days. I was the only one who was really there for him, you know.'

If I strangle her now, would that count as murder? Surely, English law would make an exception in a case like this.

Probably not. After all, the law had been written by men, and they hardly ever were reasonable.

'Lead the way,' I told her, returning her smile.

She led me down a corridor towards a room at the back of the house. Outside, I could hear the whisper of the wind and surge of the sea. We had to be close to the cliff's edge, here.

'Wait here, will you?' she told me with another smile. 'I'll go in first. Maybe he doesn't want to see you. He hasn't had long to recuperate, and it might not be good for him, seeing a strange face like that.'

Strange face? Who does this witch think she is? If anyone is the stranger here, it is she!

I opened my mouth, but before I could say a word she had already slipped into the room, leaving the door open just a fraction. Peering inside, I could barely see the end of a bed in which someone was lying. Part of me wanted to fling that door open – but another part shied away from it. What if it wasn't him in there? What if it was some total stranger?

---

[2] Back in Victorian days, people hadn't heard of DNA, or to call it by its full name, Deoxyribonucleic Acid, yet. So romantic entanglements between such close relatives as cousins were quite common. In Jane Austen's *Pride and Prejudice* for instance, both hero and heroine were intended for their respective cousins before they fell for each other.

'Hello, darling...' Miss Fotheringay leaned over the bed with a broad smile on her face. 'How are we this evening? Do we feel a little better?'

The only answer to this was silence. Icy silence.

Promising. Very promising indeed.

'Have we drunk the hot tea I made for you? I'm sure it would be good for us.' Her smile widened even more. 'And have we kept the hot water bottle on our feet?'

Hot water bottle or no, the silence on the other side of the door dropped another few dozen degrees in temperature. The smile on Miss Fotheringay's face flickered slightly, but she did her best to keep it intact.

'Well... um... listen. There is this young woman here to see us. I mean, to see you. There's no need to, of course. I can send her away and make you another cup of tea, and you won't have to worry about–'

Her voice broke off in the middle of her sentence.

'Um... All right. Maybe I should let her in.'

Two seconds later, she came marching out, her lips pressed tightly together.

'He wants to see you,' she informed me. Huffing, she stalked off down the corridor. I, for my part, reached for the doorknob.

Please, I sent one last, desperate prayer upwards. Blimey! I hadn't prayed this much in years! *Please, let it be him!*

Pushing open the door, I stepped inside.

SWEET REUNION ON THE ROCKS

The room was small and homely: a single window looking out over the cliffs, a gently flickering lamp on the bedside table, pictures of sailing ships on the wall and a four-poster bed with velvet hangings that had seen better days. But I didn't really take in any of that. I didn't even see the beautiful view of the cliffs and the sunset over the sea through window. Because in the bed, clothed in the tattered remnants of his black tailcoat, and with a bandage around his right leg, lay Mr Rikkard Ambrose.

He was not looking at me, but staring the other way, at the flowered wallpaper. This gave me a prime opportunity to study his profile to my heart's content. It was just as I remembered it: rock-hard, immovable and with power etched into every inch.

'Whoever you are,' he said to the wall, 'get on with what you've come here for and get out. I have no patience for time-wasters.'

'I know, Sir.'

My voice was nothing but a whisper – still, his head whipped around the moment I spoke. His facial expression didn't change when he saw me, but there was the slightest widening of his eyes.

'It's *you*!'

'Yes, Sir.'

12

Silence sank over the room. Mr Ambrose's dark, sea-coloured eyes bored into mine, but his lips didn't move.

Blast you, why can't you say anything? You had no problem yelling at me on the ship, during the storm! You didn't even have a problem with kissing me, for heaven's sake!

'It's really you.'

'Yes, Sir.'

Silence. More bloody silence!

Why can't you say something, damn you? And I mean more than just 'It's you!' You can! I know you can! Remember last time? Last time we spoke. Last time you held me. Last time your lips touched mine! Remember that? Why don't you say anything about that?

'I thought you were dead,' he told me. My breath caught. The words themselves were as cold and curt as any you could think of, but the tone... Had I really heard emotion there? Surely not.

'Well... I'm not, Sir.' Whatever was in his voice, there was emotion in mine sure enough. Blast it!

'I can see that. What took you so long?'

The corner of my mouth twitched up. 'I'm glad to see you, too.'

My feet suddenly started to move. Before I knew it, I stood beside his bed. My fingers reached out, and I took his right hand in mine. Closing my eyes, I squeezed, gently, letting the feel of him, smooth and hard, fill me up.

'What, pray,' came his cool voice from down on the bed, 'are you doing?'

'I'm holding your hand,' I murmured, basking in the feeling. He was real! He was real, and alive, and with me!

'I realize that. To what purpose have you initiated this superfluous form of physical contact?'

'Oh, shut up!'

There was a momentary silence.

'I beg your pardon?' His voice lowered to a dangerous level – but right now I didn't care. 'I am your employer! You will address me with respect!'

'Fine. Shut up, *Sir!*'

'That is not what I was referring to and you—'

'Blast you!' Wrenching my eyes open, I glared down at him. 'I thought you were dead, too!' *And I would have bloody missed you! Really missed you!*

He glared back just as fiercely. 'In that case, you should have ceased searching. No point in chasing something that is already lost. It would be a waste of mon–'

Quickly raising his hand in mine, I drew it to my lips and placed one, swift, almost imperceptible kiss on the inside of his palm. His voice cut off as if severed with a welding torch.

'I said shut up, Sir!'

Our eyes met, and there was silence again. But it was a different kind of silence. One I didn't mind at all. One that wasn't the least bit cold.

'It must really be you.' Shaking his head, he gazed up at me with those dark eyes of his. 'No figment of my imagination would dare to speak to me like that.'

Cautiously, I raised my free hand, and let it join the other one, enclosing his strong masculine fingers with my smaller ones.

'I'm always real for you.'

'More than just real. You're always you.'

'Glad to be of service, Sir.'

Raising his free hand, he crooked one finger. 'Come here.'

'For what?' I raised an eyebrow. 'Do you want to initiate a bit more superfluous physical contact?'

'Miss Linton?

My eyebrow rose even higher. 'What, not "Mr Linton?" I thought I would have to pretend to be a man while I work for you. I thought it would cause too big a scandal, otherwise.'

'Miss Linton? Close your mouth and come here. Now.'

'Yes, Sir! Right away, Sir!'

The springs of the mattress creaked as I sank down on it. All of a sudden, Mr Ambrose's face was very close, the planes of his perfectly sculpted cheekbones standing out sharply, his dark eyes like the sea itself. I felt something squeeze my heart, almost painfully.

'When I stepped on land, I thought I was safe from drowning,' I rasped. 'But when I look into your eyes, I'm not sure anymore.'

His eyes narrowed infinitesimally – the closest he ever came to looking confused. 'Is that supposed to make sense?'

'Not really. It's supposed to make you feel something.'

'Ah.' He gave a curt nod, and gently squeezed my hand. 'You will be pleased to hear, then, that the method seems to be effective.'

There was silence again. We looked at each other, I at him as if I had found everything I wanted, he at me as if he were lost. Lost in me.

Or... maybe just lost.

'You're supposed to say something, too, you know,' I pointed out, just managing to keep from smiling.

'Something like what?'

'Maybe something about what you feel.'

If I thought his eyes had been boring into me powerfully before, I was mistaken. It was nothing to what they now did, capturing me, holding me prisoner, drawing me closer.

'I would have thought that required no words. Is it not obvious?'

'Maybe. But I would like you to tell me anyway.'

'A waste of breath and time!'

'Yes. But a wonderful one. Please?' Cocking my head, I raised his hand to my lips again, not kissing this time, just skimming over the tops of his knuckles. 'Please, Sir?'

I heard his breath hitch, and saw the muscles in his jaw tighten.

'What,' he asked, his voice raw as a split iceberg, 'if I don't have the words? There are no words for how I feel right now. None that I know.'

Bloody hell.

I closed my eyes, letting joy flood through me. 'Those,' I told him, 'those were exactly the right ones.'

'But I told you I had nothing to say!'

'Yes, and you did it spectacularly. They were the best non-words ever not said.'

'You are not making any sense, Miss Linton.'

One corner of my mouth twitched again. 'It's not supposed to make sense. It's supposed to make you feel.'

Suddenly sitting up straighter, he gave a derisive snort. 'You want to know what I feel? I feel exceedingly aggravated. I have been forced to remain idle, lying in this infernal bed and simply wasting time by doing nothing, for the better part of the last two days. I could have been back to London by now, back to my business. I do not even want to think of the losses I incurred due to this inexcusable procrastination.'

Mr Ambrose lying down doing nothing? That didn't sound like the semi-human machine I knew.

'Why didn't you simply get up and leave if you felt like it?'

His eyes turned a shake darker. 'Because the wretched female who owns this establishment went behind my back and secured the services of a doctor. This medical gentleman told me that, apparently, wasting time by lying in a bed is an essential element in my convalescence.'

Doubtfully, I looked at his figure, lying as stiffly on the sheets as if the bed were a board with nails jutting out of it.

'I think when the doctor said you should stay abed, he meant stay abed and *relax*.'

'I cannot relax. I do not like beds.'

Idle banter. Are you truly making idle banter with Mr Do-Not-Waste-Time Ambrose, Lilly? Well, well. Miracles do happen.

'Oh really? You don't like beds? Then where do you sleep?'

Derisively, he looked down at the object he was lying on. 'On a bed. Cannot stand it. Get out of it as quickly as I can every morning. Wouldn't waste my time with it if I didn't have to.'

I hid my smirk behind my hand. 'Why do you have to? After all, if sleeping is such a waste of time, why not go without it?'

A muscle in his face twitched. If Mr Ambrose had been someone else, he would have scowled. 'I can't.'

He looked very displeased with the fact.

'Why not... Oh, blimey! Don't tell me you've tried!'

'Once. After four very productive days and nights without any sleep, I collapsed at one of my factories and nearly fell into a vat of boiling wax.'[3]

---

[3] This was actually tried once, and not by a curious scientist, but by a man who really thought that sleep was a complete waste of time. Frederick the Great, King of Prussia in the eighteenth century, was a renowned workaholic who only slept four hours a day, and once tried to stop sleeping completely. The experiment ended when he collapsed with colic after four days.

I shook my head. 'Such a shame you missed. You'd have made a charming addition to Madame Tussaud's.'

Judging from the look he gave me, Mr Rikkard Ambrose didn't appreciate sarcasm.

'This is not a joking matter, Miss Linton. Neither is my having to stay in this infernal bed! This place is as close to hell on earth as one can get. Besides the inactivity gnawing at my sanity, there's the mother, who keeps forcing a most disgusting hot broth down my throat. And she is nothing compared to the daughter. I believe that young female is not quite right in the head. She keeps asking me if "we" are feeling well – although it is perfectly evident that, besides her, I am the only person in the room. And she keeps making these strange, disturbing faces at me.'

I cleared my throat. 'I believe she's smiling at you.'

'Whatever for?'

'She likes you.'

He gave a sharp, derisive snort. 'Hardly. If the female had any positive feelings towards me, she would let me get up and leave, not keep me here and insist on my wasting time sleeping.'

Uncertainly, my eyes wandered to the bandage on his leg. I wanted nothing more than to have him out of this house and out of Miss Fotheringay's claws, but...

'Are you sure you should leave yet? Your leg–'

'Is of no significance. Now that you are here, I am determined to leave this place at the earliest possible moment.'

'But...'

'No buts, Miss Linton! Go and inform Mrs Fotheringay of our imminent departure. Find out when the next suitable transport leaves this place.'

Out of reflex, I opened my mouth to protest again. But on this subject, I didn't really need much convincing. Springing to my feet, I gave a mock salute.

'Yes, Sir! Right away, Sir!'

Before he could devour me alive or freeze me to a block of ice with his cold stare, I was out the door and down the corridor. I found Mrs Fotheringay in the living room, busy embroidering pretty birds on white linen.

'Mrs Fotheringay?'

'Ah, there you are, dear! Did you find the gentleman? Was he the one you were looking for?'

'Yes.' I felt relief flood through me as I said the word aloud. He really was alive, and safe. 'Yes, he was. He is.'

A smile spread over the old lady's face. 'That's wonderful, dear! I'm so happy for you.'

'Mrs Fotheringay, I'm terribly grateful for everything you've done for my, um... cousin. You probably saved his life. Now that we've found each other again, he shouldn't impose on your hospitality any longer. Do you know if a coach comes through this village?'

Mrs Fotheringay's hand slipped, and she almost stitched the beak of her pretty little embroidered bird shut. Staring up at me in surprise, she put the needlework aside.

'You mean you want to leave? But is he well enough?'

'Oh, yes, I think so. And a bit of exercise would do him a world of good, believe me.'

Besides, I won't rest easy until he's miles away from your charming beast of a daughter.

'Well, if you really think so, my dear, there's a coach leaving in two hours. It leaves every day at this time for Dover. And I'm sure from Dover you can catch a carriage to... where is it your cousin lives?'

'In London.'

'Ah, the metropolis.' Mrs Fotheringay gave a nostalgic sigh. 'I haven't been in London since I was a little girl. Does he have a house there?'

An image flashed through my mind of the monumental complex of stone and concrete with its great central hall, countless offices, and impressive view of the city of London that was called 'Empire House' – the headquarters of Mr Ambrose's business empire.

'In a manner of speaking.'

'A nice place?'

'Um... you could say that, yes.'

She might have asked more questions, but at that moment, the door opened and her daughter entered the room. Mrs Fotheringay turned to her with a bright smile on her face.

'Violet, my dear! Our guest is indeed the one the young lady has been looking for! They're happily reunited, and he feels well enough to return home to London! Isn't that wonderful news?'

Violet muttered something affirmative, but to judge by the way she was staring daggers at me, I didn't think 'wonderful news' were the words she would have chosen. I allowed myself a little self-satisfied smile at her, then turned and headed back to Mr Ambrose.

When I told him that we had to wait two hours for the coach... Well, let's just say he was not best pleased.

'Read an improving book for a change,' I advised.

'What would you suggest?' he demanded, glaring at the narrow shelf on the wall. '*Mrs McPherson's Book of Advice for Housewives? Dangerous Creatures of the Cold Sea? Cartwright's Collected Nursery Rhymes?*'

'Why not?' Shrugging, and giving him a meaningful smile, I picked *Dangerous Creatures of the Cold Sea* off the shelf. 'You never know where you might pick up a useful tip or two.'

I cuddled into a chair near the window and opened the volume in question. He remained lying on the bed, stiff as a board. Soon, we settled into a silence that was, to my intense surprise, quite companionable. Still, whenever I glanced up from descriptions of sea lions or whales, Mr Ambrose seemed tenser than the last time. Something was clearly on his mind – something besides wasted time.

The minutes passed by. I left behind whales and went on to sharks. More time passed, and nothing whatsoever happened. When the outburst finally came, it was out of the blue.

'You want to know what I felt?'

My head eyes snapped up from the book to stare at Mr Ambrose. It took me a moment to connect his words to our earlier conversation. He had picked it up as if no time had passed in between.

'Well?' he demanded. 'Do you?'

I was just about to make some teasing reply about him not having any words for feelings – but I caught sight of his face in time and stopped myself. Right now was not the time for flippancy. Instead, I just nodded.

'Yes.'

He looked away from me, shaking his head. 'I'm not talking about just now. I'm talking about back on the ship, when the storm hit.'

For a moment, I forgot to breathe. I remembered all too well what he had said and done – well, almost done – back on the ship. And Mr Ambrose was just like an iceberg: cold, hard, and only a tenth of him visible. The rest he kept well hidden. To imagine what feelings must have been raging inside him to make him act like that...

'I still want to know, Sir – if you want to tell me.'

He raised his eyes to mine again, his gaze iron-hard. 'I felt... desperate. I've faced death many times before, Miss Linton. But never once have I felt desperate before. Not once in my entire life.'

Desperate? That didn't make any sense. He hadn't seemed desperate to save himself at all, back on the ship. Quite the contrary. His only thought was getting me off that sinking death trap...

My thoughts tapered off into nothing, and my lips opened slightly.

Oh.

Maybe it wasn't himself he was desperate for.

The thought came out of nowhere, sweet, singing seductively to me, like a siren. It was too good to be true. But... what if it was?

'Why did you it?' I asked quietly. 'You're one of the richest men in the world, and strong. You could have tried to buy yourself a place in the lifeboat, or fought for one. Why did you make me go, and stay behind yourself?'

His left little finger twitched, the equivalent of an angry growl for Mr Rikkard Ambrose. 'I did a cost-benefit analysis.'

'A *what?*'

'A cost-benefit analysis. I weighed the cost of risking my life against the benefit of saving yours. To my not inconsiderable incredulity, the benefit outweighed the cost.'

Now it was really hard to keep the smirk off my face. 'Unbelievable.'

'I know! You are only a relatively insignificant young female with a bad temper, unpleasant relatives and an income so low you have to pose as a male to earn a living!'

'You really know how to give a girl compliments.'

'I, on the other hand, am one of the most influential and powerful public figures in the United Kingdom of Great Britain and Ireland, in the Empire, maybe in the entire world! I am clearly a much more important personage than you, ergo my life should be the more valuable thing to save.' His little finger twitched again. 'But... I found that that other factors entered into the equation.'

Leaning towards him, I put my right hand over one of his. 'We'll have to talk about those other factors, sooner or later.'

Underneath my hand, I felt his little finger twitch twice more. Dear me! He was practically an emotional wreck tonight!

Meeting my eyes again, he nodded, curtly. 'I know.' He held my gaze for a moment, and in his look lay a thousand unspoken words.

Or maybe there's not a single word in it, and you just have a much too overactive imagination.

All right, maybe.

'How long do we still have to wait?'

For a wild moment, I thought he meant until we could have our talk. Then I realized he wanted to know how long it would be until the coach left for Dover. Of course!

'Doesn't your pocket watch work anymore? Or did you lose it when the ship went down?'

'No. That harpy took it.'

'Miss Fotheringay?'

'Yes. She said it was bad for me, checking my watch every five minutes. She thought it caused overanxiety.'

'Don't worry. I'll get it back for you.' Patting his hand, I rose and made my way towards the door. At the door I paused and looked back with a grin on my face. 'Will you be all right while I'm gone? I mean, you're going to have to waste at least two and a half minutes waiting for me.'

Mr Ambrose gave me a cool stare. 'On the contrary. I shall not be wasting time.' He picked up an issue of *The Spectator* that was lying on the bedside table. 'I shall be finishing this. There are a few articles that I have not read yet. It is time to check up on what is happening in the metropolis.'

'Have fun.'

He ruffled the pages. 'Fun has nothing to do with it. This is information acquisition, Miss Linton.'

'Of course it is, Sir. I'll be back soon.'

Glancing back at him as I closed the door behind me, I caught a last look of him, lying in the bed, reading the magazine. It was a brief look, so I might have been mistaken, of course. But I could have sworn he was gazing after me with something almost akin to a smile on his granite face.

It didn't take me nearly as long to retrieve the watch as I'd feared. Miss Fotheringay had entrusted it to her mother, and the kind old lady had not only wiped it meticulously clean, but even taken it to the local watchmaker to have the mechanism inside cleaned, too. She didn't even mention money, for this or for the room Mr Ambrose had slept in. I would gladly have paid her out of my own purse – only, I had no purse, and certainly no money to put in one.

Letting the pocket watch snap open to check the time, I re-entered Mr Ambrose's room. 'Good news!' I announced. 'It's only half an hour now until the coach leaves. We should get going if we want to be there in ti–'

That was when I lifted my head and caught sight of Mr Ambrose's face. My voice abruptly cut off.

There wasn't even the hint of a trace of a fraction of a smile on his face now. It was as hard and cold as I had ever seen it. No, actually, it was a lot harder. He was holding *The Spectator* clenched in his fists as if it were a pamphlet demanding a pay rise for his employees. His eyes were boring into the paper with deadly, ice-cold wrath.

At the sound of my voice, he lifted his head and focused this look on me.

'*You...*' The word was spoken with so icy a threat, so chilling a power, that it made a shiver run down my back. '*You* did this!'

'D-did what?'

You're stuttering! He's just staring at you, and you're stuttering! Get a grip, Lilly!

'You did this.' Seeming not to have heard me, he flung back the blanket over his legs and rose with a sinuous grace that you would never have suspected from so stiff a man. He stalked towards me – that was the only word for it, *stalked* – without paying the slightest attention to his injured leg. His eyes remained trained on his prey – sweet little me! 'You did this! Oh... I'll make you pay for this!'

'Did what?' Was it only my imagination, or did my voice sound suspiciously like a squeak? I took a step back. And another. I was a feminist, I was all for standing up to men – but not this man, and not while he was in this mood! I took another step back, and my derrière bumped into the doorframe. 'What did I do?'

'Read this!' Giving me one more vengeful, dark glare, he shoved the magazine under my nose. I took it, and the heading jumped right out at me:

Scandal Around Financial Magnate

I tried to lift my hands, tried to take the magazine to read, but my arm wouldn't move. I was frozen in place by the ice in his eyes.

'Don't want to read it, do you?' he enquired, with an alarmingly soft voice. 'Don't feel like delving into the details? Don't worry. I'll read it for you.'

And he lifted the crumpled magazine to read, hiding his face. Part of me was glad I could no longer see him. But that just meant I had more attention to spare for the ice of his voice when he started to speak.

'Scandalous events often shake the newspapers these days, but seldom has the press of London had to report such an outrage as the writer of this article has now to reveal. Not long ago, at Speaker's Corner in Hyde Park, London, at a meeting of the esteemed Anti-Suffragist League of London, numerous important personages and a crowd of supporters came together to fight against those unnatural creatures who call themselves suffragettes and feminists and deny the fact that a woman's God-given place is in the home.'

The shiver that had run down my back earlier realized that its work wasn't done yet. Taking a run-up, it raced up my back again, leaving goose bumps in its wake.

Oh no...

'Among the gentlemen present,' Mr Ambrose continued without mercy, 'was Rikkard Ambrose, renowned financial magnate. However, Mr Ambrose's performance at the meeting did not at all reflect the power and position of his social rank.'

Blast, no! A curse on all newspapers and magazines! Please, let this not be what I think it is!

'Not that it was Mr Ambrose himself who caused an outrage: no, it was the behaviour of his secretary, whom he had brought along to the meeting, that was beyond all bounds of decorum – a young and still beardless young fellow people heard Mr Ambrose refer to as "Mr Linton".'

Blast!

Lowering the magazine an inch or two, Mr Ambrose's deadly stare burrowed into me. I swallowed, surprised I didn't drop dead on the spot.

'At this event,' Mr Ambrose continued reading, somehow managing to keep me pinned with his gaze while simultaneously looking at the pages in front of him, 'a rally held officially against the absurd notions of feminists and suffragettes, this Mr Linton dared to speak out in favour of such nonsense. His speech is re-printed in the section for jokes.'

His eyes fully focused on me now, and he cocked his head. 'There is an amusing caricature of the two of us, too. Do you wish to see it?'

I cleared my throat. 'Err... not particularly, no.'

'I see. Well, then let us relish the rest of this journalistic masterpiece, shall we?' With a hiss, he dived behind the magazine again.

Please God! Let me die now!

'Somehow, the impetuous youth managed to enthral the simple-minded people in the crowd. In the end, Mr Linton had to be forcibly removed from the stage to shouts of "Long live suffragism!".' Mr Ambrose's ominous voice reached me from behind the veil of paper. 'There is little doubt that he is a violent, unstable young man. And as for his employer...'

Please, God! Just kill me right now! It can't be that difficult! I don't need anything fancy. One lightning bolt will do!

'The writer of this article cannot but wonder how Mr Ambrose proposes to run a vast business empire if he cannot even control his own secretary. Also, if Mr Ambrose's staff is that unstable, what about himself? Are mental difficulties widespread in his circle? This casts a dark shadow of doubt on Mr Ambrose's abilities and the future of his business.'

Lowering the magazine once more, Rikkard Ambrose raised his eyes to me, and when I saw the expression in their bottomless depths, I had to swallow.

Oops...

Happy Homecoming

Mr Ambrose didn't say a single word on the coach ride to Dover – and he did it in a very scary way. Nobody could be silent like Mr Ambrose. It was a grand symphony of silence, punctuated with staccato stares and sinister drumrolls of finger flexing. In Dover, he sprang out of the rickety coach like a raven swooping down on his dead prey and stalked off, motioning for me to follow without a word. I did.

We ended up in front of a shop. In the shop windows, I could see displays of trousers and tailcoats. Over the shop, large metal letters proclaimed in cursive script: *Harris & White - Quality Tailors for Gentlemen.*

'Well, *Mister* Linton...' Mr Ambrose regarded me, his eyes glittering dangerously. 'Let's find you a pair of trousers.'

Let's just say that what followed wasn't exactly every lady's dream of a man buying her pretty clothes. When I left the shop half an hour later, clothed in a tailcoat and baggy trousers, and with three shocked sales assistants staring after us, I was feeling ready to kill. And I already had a victim in mind.

The only problem was... He looked just about as ready for murder as I did.

'How dare you!' I spat at him, as soon as we were out of hearing. 'How could you do that?'

'You're right,' he growled. 'I can't believe I paid for those clothes out of my own pocket. But I'll promise you, the sum will be deducted from your wages.'

'You...! I wasn't talking about bloody money! How could you do *this* to me?' Tugging at the fabric of the trousers, I took an enraged step towards him. 'I thought you had finally gotten it through your thick skull that I am a *girl*!'

'I know very well what you are! I'm simply doing my very best to ignore the fact – ignore it, and conceal it! If your little speech in front of the Anti-Suffragists was enough to cause such a sensation, do you have any idea what kind of scandal it would be if someone found out that a *female* is working as my secretary?'

'I don't care! How could you put me in these again? After all we've been through, how could you do that to me?'

'*I* did something to *you*?' His voice was as cold and distant as the peak of some lonely mountain. And yet... The mountain was grumbling. It might just turn out to be a volcano. 'You dare say that to me? *You* are the one who humiliated *me* in public!'

'I didn't humiliate anyone! I told the truth and fought for justice!'

Before I knew what was happening, he had gripped me by the arms and I was being swept backwards into a dark alley, until I was pressed against a cold brick wall. It was almost as hard as the feel of the body that was suddenly pressing into my front – the body of Mr Rikkard Ambrose. My heartbeat picked up, and not from fear. Not from rage, either. He was so close, every line of his perfect form pressing into me...

Get a grip, Lilly! You're furious, remember?

'Suffragism has nothing to do with truth or justice!' he growled, his strong hands like vices around my arms. 'Women aren't fit to vote, or work, or think for themselves! And the sooner you get that through your head, the better!'

'Men are a pack of arrogant, power-hungry jackals!'

'Better a jackal than a little, helpless puppy! At least jackals hunt for themselves! Women are too weak to do anything alone!'

My fist slammed into his chest with no effect whatsoever. Catching my other hand before it could hit him he forced it upwards, until I was practically dangling from my upstretched arm.

'Let go!' My free arm slammed my hand into his chest again.

'Make me let go, if you're so strong!' Catching my other hand in his iron grip, he pulled it upwards, too, joining my wrists so both of my hands were pinned against the wall by just one of his. 'What are you waiting for?'

'You bastard!' I writhed and pulled, but my arms wouldn't budge. All I managed to do was to press myself more tightly up against the hard barrier of his body, which didn't really feel like a bad thing, but didn't increase my desire to escape, either. Blast him! He was the greatest son of a bachelor south of the North Pole! Why couldn't I feel properly revolted and disgusted? Why did it feel so good to be held by him, even when I was trying to punch him?

'There, you see? You're the best proof!' His voice gripped me just as hard as his hands. It was the voice of someone used to command and being obeyed. 'Look at yourself! Look at the things you've achieved during your employ: getting drunk right before a fight, letting the file slip through your hands, humiliating me in front of all of London—'

'None of that was my fault! It just happened! Let go of me!'

'And as if that weren't enough,' he whispered, his cold voice sliding over me like iron fetters, 'you're so helpless, so weak that I have to rescue you from that infernal ship. *I* swam ashore alone, with my own two legs and feet. *You*? *You* had to be pulled out of the water like a drowning little puppy!'

'Let go, I said!' My knee jerked, trying to ram into him, find some vulnerable spot – but he was pressed too tightly against me. And, curse me, a part of me didn't want to fight! A part of me wanted him closer, harder, even now!

'Look at yourself right now.' The power in his voice made me want to bite him, strike him in rage – it also made me want to dissolve right into his arms, damn him! 'I need just one hand to hold you. You're weak and defenceless. Admit it.'

'No!'

'Resign your position as my secretary.'

'No!'

'You don't have the stomach for it, the strength, the tenacity. Resign, or you'll get hurt, sooner or later!'

'No!'

'That is an order!'

'I said no! I won't! You gave your word to keep me, and I will hold you to it, blast you!'

His free arm came up so quick I didn't even see it. A strong, hard hand gripped my chin and turned my head, forcing me to look into the bottomless depths of his eyes.

'Respect, Mr Linton. Show respect.'

'Very well – blast you, *Sir*!' I glared at him with fire in my eyes. If I couldn't get my hands free, I would burn him to ashes with the pure force of my gaze, melt that ice of his with the firestorm roaring inside me! 'So, finally I know. That's how you feel about me! That's why you saved my life! Because you think I'm weak!'

His left little finger twitched. Apart from that, he showed no emotion. 'Yes. That's it.'

'Well, do you know why *I* looked for *you* after the ship went down? Why I was hoping you would survive?'

'No.'

'Because I bloody well want my first pay cheque, that's why! If you croak, I won't get a penny!'

His eyes narrowed infinitesimally. 'Is that so, Mr Linton?'

Proudly, I raised my chin. 'Yes, it is!'

And it was true. Absolutely. Never mind the way in which his dark stare sent my heart hammering. Never mind how his hard body, pressed up so tightly against me, made me want to be closer still, to grab him, pull him down and...

Well, never mind all of that. Money! I was interested only in the money!

Tightening his grip on my wrists, he leaned closer until his forehead was almost touching mine. Bloody hell, his forehead wasn't the only thing too close! His eyes were two giant pools of sea-deep darkness, right in front of my face, and his mouth was so near I could feel his breath on my cheek.

'Are you sure about that?' The fingers of his free hand slid over my chin, upwards over my skin, sending a shiver through my entire body. 'Are you sure you want to be my secretary? Or do you want something else? Want to be something else to me?'

Something else? What in God's name does he mean? He can't be suggesting that we...? No! He can't. Most definitely not.

'I want to earn my money!' I growled between clenched teeth. 'The money to be free! Free of any man!'

'Free of any man?' He cocked his head a fraction of an inch. 'Except of me.'

'I only have to put up with you from Monday to Friday, 8 am to 8 pm, Sir!'

He regarded me for a moment, as if studying a strange and possibly dangerous specimen under the microscope.

'You don't belong in my office. I might have thought you'd do – but after that thing in *The Spectator*...' He let the sentence trail off ominously. 'You're a liability, Mr Linton. If you won't resign voluntarily, I'll have to make you. Be warned, Mr Linton – it won't be long until you will be begging to be sacked, and I'll be rid of you.'

Jerking my chin free of his hand, I raised it high in the air, facing him down. 'You can try!'

~~**~*~*

The drive from Dover to London wasn't much more chatty and cheerful than the previous one. This wasn't just because of the stubborn stone statue I had for a travelling companion. No, it had begun to dawn on me that my return might not be very warm and welcoming. Considering the fact that I had left my aunt and uncle's house supposedly for a brief stroll in the park, and had ended up on a ship that took me to a adventure on a mysterious island on the French coast involving danger, industrial espionage and near death, I thought they might be a tiny little bit upset with me.

Of course, neither my aunt and uncle, nor my five sisters actually knew anything about the adventure on the French island. I could just tell them I had lost track of time and my walk in the park had turned out to be a little longer than I expected. The only problem with that was that my aunt wasn't a very trusting woman. She might think that a weeklong walk in Green Park was a bit incredible.

Maybe you could say you went on a walk to Yorkshire and back, instead. That would fit the time frame much better.

It would also sound even more ridiculous.

'What excuse would you tell your family if you had to explain having disappeared for a week?'

I only realized that I had spoken out loud when the stone statue in the corner raised his head and looked at me.

'None,' Mr Ambrose told me.

I blinked, taken aback. I hadn't really expected an answer. So my next words popped out before I could really think about them. 'You'd disappear on your family for an *entire week*? Just like that? Without explanation? Have you done that? Left and stayed away for an entire week without sending word?'

'No.' He met my eyes coldly. 'I've left and stayed away without sending a word for approximately nine and a half years.'

I gaped at him. Ignoring me, he turned back to staring out the window. Well, well... so Mr Ambrose was not a family man, eh? What a surprise!

Which still didn't answer my question: what was I going to say to my family when I returned?

Well, why say anything at all? You could simply garb yourself in mysterious silence, like bloody Mr Ice-Cold Ambrose!

Yes, I could do that – if I wanted Aunt Brank to try and rip my head off!

Well, you'll simply have to let her try and hope it is attached firmly enough to survive.

Outside the coach, the landscape began to change. Gentle hills transformed into flat, monotonous country. After a while, it began to be dotted with a cottage here and there. More cottages came, then turned into houses. And before I knew it, we were rolling into London. The sounds of the city engulfed us, and the familiar smoky smell of the city crept into my nostrils.

Soon enough, the carriage was rolling down a familiar street – a *very* familiar street. Taken aback, I stared out of the windows at the neat, middle-class brick houses. Wasn't this...? Yes, it was! The street where my aunt and uncle lived! The street where I had lived, too, ever since my parents had died.

'What are we doing here?' I blurted out.

Turning his head just a fraction, Mr Ambrose deigned to look at me. 'You live here, don't you?'

'Yes, but...' I hesitated. How was I going to tell him I hadn't thought he'd care enough about me to care where he threw me out of his coach without sounding rude? It was impossible. But on the other hand, since when had I had a problem with sounding rude?

'I didn't realize you were providing cab services, for me, Sir,' I told him, one eyebrow raised in question.

'Don't get above yourself, Mr Linton. I just do not think you have the brains to find your way home alone.'

The arrogant...! Blast him! I could believe him, too, considering the way he was looking at me.

'Are you sure you don't want me to accompany you back to Empire House, Sir?' I said in the sweetest tone I could manage. 'Who knows, maybe you could use my help squeezing your head through the door, considering how big it has grown.'

'That won't be necessary.' He didn't even bat an eyelid. Curse him! Could nothing ruffle that son of a bachelor?

When we finally pulled up in front of my aunt and uncle's house, the coachman jumped off to open the door for me, but I was outside before his feet had even touched the ground.

'Do you have any luggage, Sir?' he asked, with a polite bow. 'Should I help you carry it in?'

'That all sank in the Channel,' I informed him. 'But thanks for the offer.'

Leaving a startled coachman behind, I started towards the door in the garden wall and the garden shed beyond, where I still had a secret stash of women's clothes tucked away. But after only a few paces, I stopped, half turned, and sent Mr Ambrose a bright smile.

'Looking forward to seeing you at work on Monday, Sir.'

He acted as if I weren't there. Clapping his hands, he motioned for the coachman to get back to work. Moving faster than should be allowed for a man who didn't have to work under the threat of slavery, the coachman jumped back up on the box and cracked his whip.

'Gee up!'

The horses darted forward and the coach was gone, a black streak that grew smaller and smaller in the distance. Only when it was already turning around a corner did I start to wonder:

Mr Ambrose had dropped me off in front of my house. But... how the hell had he known where my house was? I had certainly never told him! And if he knew my aunt or any of my sisters well enough to know where they lived, I'd eat my corset! He and my uncle might know each other from the annual meeting of the London Misers' Association, but I doubted it. My uncle never left his four walls except to go to work, and neither did Mr Ambrose.

So, that still left the question: how the hell did he know?

For a few moments I looked after the coach, biting my lower lip in thought. Then I shrugged, and turned back to the house. The Lord might move in mysterious ways – but he had nothing on Mr Ambrose in that department.

It took no time at all switching clothes. Ever since I had to do it on a sinking ship to save myself from drowning, I had gotten a lot quicker at lacing up a corset. Everything has its bright side, I suppose. Leaving the changing room (alias the garden shed), I made my way towards the back door and to my delight found it unlocked.

Huzzah! Fortune was smiling on me! Maybe I would be able to sneak up to my room and pretend as if nothing had happened. At least until the next morning.

I was about halfway up the stairs when a voice came like a whip crack from behind me.

'Lillian!'

Wincing, I stopped in my tracks. Apparently, fortune wasn't really smiling on me. It was just grimacing. Slowly, I turned and came face to face with Hester Mahulda Brank, my beloved aunt.

All right, the 'beloved' part might have been a lie. But judging by the death-glare she was shooting up the stairs at me out of those small, sharp eyes of hers set into her vulture's face, I wasn't particularly beloved by her either. More bedespised, if there was such a word.

'Lillian Linton! Tell me this isn't you, showing your face here after... after...'

'This isn't me showing my face here,' I assured her. 'It's not actually me at all. It's just a phantasm, some kind of ghostly image. So... why don't you carry on with whatever you were doing and let this phantasm go to bed? It is a really tired phantasm.'

'It is you! Nobody else would dare talk to me like that!'

Why was everybody pretending to recognize me by my insolence? First Mr Ambrose, and now her! It was really unfair! In reality, I was a quite nice, well-behaved, soft-spoken young lady. Yes, I bloody well was!

My aunt had started moving, stalking up the stairs towards me, her feather duster clutched in her right hand like a sword.

'You... you... ungrateful little brat! You disappear for over a week, and then you simply waltz back in here as if nothing had happened? Is that your thanks for the care I took of you all those years?'

You mean torturing me with etiquette lessons while you tried to marry me off to the first rich bachelor available? Yes, thanks so much for that!

But not even I was brave enough to speak that thought aloud.

'One week! One entire week!' She was nearly level with me now. I started to retreat, peering with trepidation at the feather duster in her fist. These things looked innocent enough, but who knew, maybe hers had a concealed blade or hidden spikes or something. I wouldn't put it past her. 'One week you disappear without a word! Do you have any idea how–'

...worried you've been for me? How many sleepless nights you've spent praying for my safe return?

27

'–many social events I've had to reschedule because of you?'

Oh, my dear aunt! It's so nice to know how deeply you care for me.

'Two balls, three dinner engagements, and one walk in the park with Colonel Spencer – all arranged for nothing! He's gone to India now, and he's such an old fool he might actually have taken you!'

Isn't it wonderful to have such loving relatives? They always give you such a warm welcome home.

Reaching the end of the stairs, she pointed the feather duster as if she meant to skewer me with it. I took a few more steps back.

'Such a pity,' I said, meekly lowering my head. 'I would really have liked to meet Colonel Spencer.' *Preferably with a large mallet in hand and no witnesses.*

'Oh, you would have, would you?' My aunt's eyes sparked. 'To think I might have had you out of the house by now, properly married and taken care of... And now you're back, costing me even more housekeeping money!'

'I'm really sorry. Truly, I am.' *A very, very large mallet.*

My back hit the door at the end of the corridor, and I was forced to stop. Moments later, a feather duster poked into my ribs. To my relief, there were no hidden spikes or blades.

'*Sorry?* That's not good enough, girl!'

'I'll do the dishes for a week aunt,' I promised.

'Not good enough!'

I bit my lip. What could be a worse punishment than doing chores?

'I'll go out every day to meet as many young men as possible! I'll attend every ball, every feast, everything there is. I'll practically throw myself at every young man I come across.'

'Still not good enough by half! You, young lady, are in need of a thorough dressing-down!'

My eyebrows shot up. Wasn't she already taking care of that? And most thoroughly to boot?

'Not by me,' she told me as if she had read my thoughts. Her voice had a coldness that almost rivalled that of Mr Ambrose. 'Turn around, girl!'

Reluctantly, I did as she said, and for the first time realized where my backward steps had led me: upstairs, at the very end of the corridor – in the forbidden zone. I stood right before the door that lead to the domain of the dread lord of miserdom, the gates to the lands of death and desolation and spanked bottoms for little five-year-old girls who had been so brazen as to peek inside.

I stood in front of my Uncle Bufford's study.

I tried to say something, but no more than a croak escaped my mouth. Half turning back to my aunt, I shot her a desperate, pleading look. But she looked back at me like a hangman escorting the prisoner to the gallows.

'I will see if he's ready to receive you, girl.'

The door to the study creaked ominously as she opened it to step in. With her inside, for a moment, I considered running. I could be out on the street and away from the study of terrors before anyone could say Jack Robinson. But... where would I go? I had no money to rent a place. I still hadn't received my first pay cheque. That happy event was still a few days in the future, and the thought that Mr Ambrose might give me an advance was too laughable to think about. And even if I'd had money... I was still a minor. They could haul me home whenever they wished.

'Girl!'

I jumped. Without my noticing, my Aunt had come out of the room again and was holding the door open for me.

'He's ready to receive you. Go in.'

Too late to run now. 'Aunt, couldn't you...?'

'Go! Now!'

Taking a deep breath, I straightened. There was no escape. I had to get a grip and bite the bullet, like any brave soldier faced by inevitable death and dismemberment. Raising my chin in defiance of the enemy, I stepped into the study.

A STUDY IN GOLDEN

At first, I couldn't see anything at all. Apparently, a love of money wasn't the only thing Uncle Bufford and Mr Ambrose had in common: a penchant for muted lighting was also on the list. Probably they thought it was wasteful, letting all that light into a room without enough eyes present to properly utilize it.

So I waited for my eyes to adjust to the gloom. And waited. And waited longer, while silence surrounded me.

Ah. So that would be *three* things they had in common: stinginess, darkness and taciturnity. I supposed I could expect as much from a man who had spoken to me and my sisters about three times in total since he adopted us over ten years ago.

So I waited some more. And more. The first thing I noticed when my eyes slowly got used to the dark was gold. Piles of it. Coins were heaped on the desk, on chairs, on and inside chests, even on top of the lamp in the corner. Bits of paper were almost as numerous as coins: they littered everything, everywhere, mixing with the coins into an ordered chaos that only one man's mind, I was sure, could understand.

'Step forward, girl!'

I flinched. The voice had come from a high-backed armchair that stood facing away from the door. Over the backrest I could just see what seemed to be the top of an oddly coloured cannonball. After a moment, I realized it was a man's bald head.

'I said step forward! By that I meant around the chair, so I can bloody see you!'

Ah. Another shared characteristic with Mr Ambrose: impatience. Maybe the two knew each other, after all.

Hurrying around the chair, I made a quick curtsy in front of the sitting figure. It wasn't until I straightened again that I got a good look at Uncle Bufford for the first time in years.

He wasn't a particular beauty, by conventional standards. His bald head was covered with brownish age marks, and so was the over-large beak of a nose protruding from his face. The deep-set eyes that were fixed on me flashed threateningly. His chin might have been firm and manly, but it was hidden behind a gigantic white beard that hung from his chin like an overgrown bush of white spirea. His bushy eyebrows were so large and his forehead so wrinkled that it seemed to be home to a permanent frown, and his bulky form was clad in a cheap tailcoat of a dirty grey-black colour. In short, he looked like Father Christmas after a very bad day full of blocked chimneys.

'Finished with your examination, girl?' he growled.

I flinched and reflexively folded my arms in front of my chest. On both sides of my head, I could feel my ears burning.

'Um... yes.'

Blast you! Don't sound so brazen! You may not like it, but this man could turn you out on the street with a flick of his finger! This isn't some adventure where you boldly stand up to any man you come across! This is real life!

'Sit down!'

Quickly, I sat on the only free chair in the room. There were other chairs besides that, but they were all covered in paper and coins.

Uncle Bufford fixed his penetrating gaze on me. It could not compete with Mr Ambrose in the category of utter, cool, dispassionate power, but had a way of winding around you like gnarled roots and holding you in place that was no less effective.

'You know why you're here, girl?'

'Yes.'

'My wife informs me you left this house recently.'

I swallowed and nodded. 'Yes.' Then, remembering his similarities to Mr Ambrose, I corrected: 'Yes, Sir.'

One of Uncle Bufford's bushy eyebrows rose. He showed no other reaction.

'She also tells me that you were gone for quite a long time. An entire week, in fact.'

'Yes, Sir.'

Uncle Bufford grunted into his beard. 'I suppose that is unusual for girls? How long are the free runs you're usually given? Do they take off your leashes at all?'

I blinked. Was he joking? He didn't seem to be.

'Um... we don't wear leashes, Sir.'

He shook his head. 'Pity. Education nowadays could learn a lot from dog training.'

Still, I was not sure whether he was joking. That gnarled old face gave away about as much as the trunk of an oak tree. Finally, I decided to assume for my own sanity's sake that he was, but outwardly, I had better act as if he wasn't. Just to be sure.

'I think leashes are not very fashionable, Sir,' I told him demurely. 'They would clash with ball gowns.'

My Uncle gave a derisive snort. 'Fashion! As if that counts for anything!'

Suddenly, in spite of the leash talk, he seemed a lot more likeable.

'I quite agree, Sir,' I told him, perfectly honest this time.

'Oh, you do, do you?' He studied me with those sharp eyes of his, and I couldn't help it. I raised my chin and met his eyes defiantly. Blast it! Why couldn't I be meek for all of five minutes? This man could throw me out on the street if I didn't behave!

'How would you liked to be leashed?' he asked, cocking his bald, bearded head.

'Not at all, Sir.'

One side of his mouth twitched up. 'Because it's not fashionable?'

'No, Sir! Because I want to be free.'

'Is that so...?' His eyes got even sharper. He was silent for a moment. Finally, he asked: 'Why?'

'Why what, Sir?'

'Don't play dumb with me, girl! Why did you run away?'

I swallowed. 'I cannot tell you, Sir. But it was important.'

His bushy eyebrows rose again. 'You cannot tell me?'

'Yes.'

'Cannot, or will not?'

'Both.'

'Was it a man?'

I nearly choked. 'No! No, no! It wasn't! It most definitely wasn't!'

His gaze wandered over my face for a moment. 'No, I didn't think so. So... what was it, then?'

'I cannot tell you, Sir. I'm sorry.'

His eyes narrowed. 'If this is all some sort of tantrum, a ploy to get me to give you more pocket money, you can forget it. I took you in for my sister's sake, God rest her soul, but I will not indulge your female extravagances!'

Female extravagances? My eyes blazed.

'No,' I told him flatly. 'It is not a ploy to get you to raise my allowance. In fact, since I'm already here, I want to use the opportunity to tell you that you can reduce it, if you want to.'

This time both of his eyebrows shot so high up, it nearly looked as if the bald top of his head had suddenly grown hair again.

'*Reduce it?*'

'Or forget about it altogether.' I made a dismissive gesture. 'From next week onward, I won't need it anymore.'

If he had been giving me searching looks before, it was nothing compared to how his eyes probed me now. There wasn't just determination in those eyes now. This time, there was genuine interest.

'You know, girl... my whole life I've had to deal with people badgering me to give them my money. But I believe you're the first one to ask to receive less of it than they're already getting.'

'I'm unique.' I gave him my brightest smile. 'Like a snowflake.'

That corner of his mouth twitched again. 'I think you're a little too fiery for a snowflake.' Then, suddenly, his mouth flattened into a grim line, and similar lines spread across his forehead. 'But we still haven't discussed that matter of you running away – and more specifically, how you are to be punished!'

Blast! And there I thought I would get off easily. As inconspicuously as possible, I looked around the room for carpet beaters and horse whips. True, I hadn't seen or heard from Uncle Bufford in ten years, but I had heard stories...

'Your punishment,' he proclaimed, his face sterner than ever, 'is to have your allowance cut. Not another penny you'll get out of me for dresses, or jewellery, or whatever frivolous things you girls buy nowadays, do you hear me? Not another penny!' Maybe I was mistaken, I mean, this was the terrible uncle after all, the figure that had haunted mine and my sister's nightmares as little children, but I could have sworn he gave me a small smile. 'I hope this terribly harsh punishment will be a lesson to you.'

I shot up from my seat and almost saluted. Instead, I gave a hurried curtsy. 'Yes, Sir! It definitely will, Sir!'

'Good! Now off with you, and don't bother me again unless the house burns down. I'm a busy man!'

'Yes, Sir! Just as you say, Sir!'

I hurried towards the door. Just in time before opening it, I remembered to let my shoulders sag and my lips quiver. When I stepped outside, and my aunt hurriedly straightened from where she had been trying unsuccessfully to listen at the thick oak door, she took in my woeful face with a nod of satisfaction.

'There! You see? That's what happens when you display a lack of respect for your elders.'

I nodded, meekly. 'Yes, Aunt. I'll remember, Aunt.'

'What did he say to you?'

'He... he said...' Making my lower lip tremble expressively, I trailed off into a sob-like noise. Now that was good acting!

My aunt gave another satisfied nod. 'There! I told you that you would regret what you did. Now, off to your room with you, and stay there until I call you.'

'Yes, Aunt. As you wish, Aunt.'

Hurrying off down the corridor, I managed to disguise my giggle as another sob. That must have been the best punishment ever! Reaching the door to my room, I pushed it open and sauntered in.

The room was just as I remembered it – except for one thing. My little sister Ella, the only one of my five sisters with whom I really got along and who by God's good grace happened to be my roommate, was lying on my bed, crying her eyes out.

My eyebrows rose. Even for Ella, who could be a bit sentimental and romantic sometimes, this was going rather far. Usually, she lay on her own bed, and went without the crying. In fact, at this hour of the day, she mostly didn't lie in bed at all, but was in the garden, conducting a supposedly secret and insufferably sappy romance with the neighbour's son.

It was only then that I noticed she was holding something. Curious, I stepped closer.

'Oh, Lill!' Ella said. Or to be precise, she didn't say it. She wailed it. Rather a curious way to say hello but, shrugging, I opened my mouth to respond with an, 'Oh, Ella,' when I noticed what the thing she was holding was: a picture of me!

'Oh, my dear, dear sister!' Covering her eyes with one hand, Ella let her forehead slump forward onto the picture frame. 'Oh, my dearest Lill!'

I closed my mouth. A picture? Where the heck did she get a picture of me? Had I ever sat down to have my portrait taken? Not since Mother and Father had died, surely! Uncle Bufford wouldn't waste a penny on something like that!

'Oh, Lill! Where can you be?'

I opened my mouth to say 'right behind you' – but Ella continued before I could get a word out. She seemed to be doing the dialogue fine without my help: 'Staying with relatives? No, no, we would have heard something by now. It has to be something else. Something sinister. Could it be... that man! That man she mentioned! He has abducted her and is having his wicked way with her!'

My mouth was already open, but that didn't prevent my chin from dropping down farther. Images flashed past my inner eye – images of Rikkard Ambrose having his 'wicked way' with me, whatever that meant exactly. They were highly illicit images not suitable for a young lady at all.

'Or... or someone has abducted her! To demand ransom!'

My eyebrows shot up. Demand ransom? From *Uncle Bufford*? Well, if something like that ever happened, the kidnappers would have another thing coming. But I had to admire Ella's imagination, at least.

'Or she's been killed by a serial killer! Oh, Lill! No! Please! Please come back alive and well!'

I felt this was the right time to announce my presence.

'Of course,' I told her, striding forward and patting her on the shoulder. 'Always happy to oblige.'

Ella stiffened. Then, very, very, very, very slowly, she turned around to look at me. I smiled at her. 'Hello, little sister? How have you been?'

Ella screamed. It was a high-pitched scream, almost worthy of a prima donna. Then the picture of yours truly slipped out of her fingers, and she fainted, falling back onto my bed. The bed I had been planning to use within the not too distant future!

I heaved a sigh. Really, did nobody in this house know how to give you a proper welcome home?

˷˷*˷**˷*˷*

Apparently, my aunt did. Only, she had her own ideas of what constituted a 'proper welcome home'. It seemed that about two minutes after she had found out I was back, she had hurried over to Mrs Fields, the wife of a rich merchant who often did business with Uncle Bufford, and told her some tale of how I had returned home after a long journey abroad. It only took a little skilful prodding to make Mrs Fields suggest: 'Why, we should give a ball to welcome her back home!'

My aunt reluctantly let herself be persuaded, and before you could say Jack Robinson, the invitations for a surprise ball the very next night had been sent out. A ball! In my honour! Torture like that should be prohibited by law!

'Don't you dare try to worm your way out of this,' my aunt hissed into my ear as she tightened the straps of my corset, caging me in as if she were putting full-body manacles on me. 'You promised!'

'I know,' I wheezed.

That in itself wouldn't have stopped me. I was really talented at breaking promises I had never meant to keep. But my aunt watched me with the eyes of a hawk and the determination of a starved hyena. If I managed to disappear, it would be a miracle.

'You will go to this ball, and you will spend your evening smiling and dancing if I have to drag you to it!'

'Yes, Aunt.'

'The coach is outside! You get into it right now, and don't stir from your seat unless I tell you too.'

'Yes, Aunt.'

'That goes for you, too,' my aunt snapped at Ella, who was helping to tie Elsebeth's laces. 'I want all of you out there in five minutes. It took a great deal of effort to arrange a ball at such short notice, and I won't have you being late!'

She rushed out, and I managed, in spite of my suffocatingly tight corset, to bend far enough down to pick up my dress from the bed.

'Here. Let me help you with that.' Slender white hands took the dress out of my rounder, tanned ones and slipped it over my head. When my head came free of the linen, I saw Ella, smiling a smile at me that was full of sisterly affection.

So, my little sister had finally forgiven me – *'I was so worried!'* – and decided that – *'I thought you were dead!'* – she no longer needed to pelt me with recriminations – *'You could have given me some warning at least!'* – every single minute of the day, had she? I did a quick calculation in my head. It had taken her nine full hours to forgive me. For her angelic nature, that was the equivalent of a year-long, festering grudge.

'You're talking to me again, I see?'

Ella's cheeks turned red. The look I had given her wasn't really that reproving, but Ella blushed at any and every opportunity she got.

'I never stopped talking to you!'

'Talking to me without trying to bite my head off, I mean.'

Ella's blush deepened, and she mumbled something about not knowing what I could possibly mean. With a wink and a sigh, I took her by the arm.

'We'd better go! If we aren't in the coach soon, Aunt Brank will have our heads on spikes.'

The coach ride to the ballroom Mrs Fields had rented for the night was quiet and uncomfortable. Being about as miserly as my uncle, her desire to save money only matched by her desire to gain social status, my aunt had rented a coach in which all seven of us would just about fit – if we were stacked on top of each other and holding our breath. By the time we reached our destination, I was already grumbling mutinously.

'Come on,' Ella said encouragingly, gently manoeuvring me towards the entrance. 'Let's go in. Who knows, it might even be fun.'

They were waiting for us at the door. The moment Ella and I stepped into the ballroom, three figures sprang out at us, barring my way. They were my best friends, Patsy, Flora and Eve. Though from the thunderous expression on Patsy's brick wall of a face, you might not have guessed the 'best friends' part.

'Where were you?' she demanded, waving a sausage-thick finger in my face. 'We don't see you for seven days, and then, out of the blue, Mrs Fields brings us the invitation to this ball and says it's to celebrate your safe return! What the devil have you been doing this last week?'

'Were you off on a Caribbean island, having a romantic adventure with some handsome, dashing hero?' Flora sighed.

For a moment I was tempted to say 'No, the island was on the French coast, actually' – then I remembered that as much as I might want to, I couldn't tell them anything about what had happened. Besides, even if I did have adventures, they were most certainly not romantic, and Mr Ambrose was neither handsome nor heroic! Not in the least, the blasted, beautiful son of a bachelor!

'Tell us right now,' Patsy growled, 'or I'll go through the ballroom telling every single gentleman here what a wonderful dancing partner and charming young lady you are!'

'You wouldn't!'

'Try me!'

I met Ella's eyes. 'Yes, I see what you mean,' I told her, my voice dripping with sarcasm. 'This will be very great fun indeed.'

Patsy was true to her threats. Two hours later, I had danced with more men than I cared to remember, and my feet felt about ready to fall off. Plus, I was aching all over from the tightly laced corset. I should never have let my aunt lace me up! My only consolation was that all the men I had danced with were surely nursing their wounded feet right now, suffering just as much pain as yours truly. I had made good use of the heels on my shoes in an honest attempt to produce a ballroom full of foot-puree. But that didn't stop new men from pestering me with invitations to dance.

Finally, I found a hidden spot behind some floor-length window curtains. As long as the bulge in the curtains, caused by my rather generous derriere, didn't betray my presence, no passing gentlemen suffering from sudden bouts of dancing mania could find me here. Taking a deep breath, I leaned against the wall.

'Finally!' I muttered. 'Safe!'

The words had hardly left my mouth when the curtain on the other side of the window jerked aside, revealing a man who had been hiding there, just like me, gazing out into the night. He stood there, staring at me. I stared back, in startled recognition.

'Miss Linton! Is that you?'

OH GENTLE LADY, SPARE MY FEET...

'Captain Carter?' I blinked up at the tall man with the mane of mahogany hair and perky little speck of a beard on his strong, otherwise clean-shaven chin. 'Is that really you?'

'In the flesh.' He swept me a bow just as snappy as the one I remembered from our first meeting. 'And blood and bones and earwax and other disgusting things I'd rather not mention, in fact.'

'I see you haven't become much more sensible since our last encounter,' I commented, a corner of my mouth involuntarily twitching.

'And you not much more ladylike. Isn't it wonderful how old friends never seem to change?'

'Old friends? We only met once before.'

'And you didn't try to strangle me, Miss Linton. That makes you an old friend in my book.'

The corner of my mouth twitched again. Captain James Carter was one of the few men whose company I could tolerate – maybe because most of the time, he didn't behave like a man, but like a naughty poltergeist trapped in the body of a British Army captain.

'I heard this ball was being given as a sort of welcome home to a Miss Linton.' He cocked his head. 'Is that you? Or one of your sisters?'

'Me, actually.'

'Ah! So you've been on holiday! Tell all. Which sunny shore has been graced by the radiance of your presence and your exquisite feminine essence?'

'Oh, shut up!' I mumbled, my ears glowing.

'I can't help it.' Theatrically, he placed a hand on his chest. 'In my chest, there beats a poet's heart! And my food is digested by a poet's stomach, and my drinking is dealt with by a poet's liver. So, where have you been?'

'France.'

What?! Why the heck did you just tell him the truth?

'*La France*,' he sighed. 'Did they try to feed you frogs and snails?'

'No. They shot at me.'

'The famed hospitality of the French!' He smiled at me, obviously not taking me seriously. Thank God! 'So, you're back now. Are you here with your aunt and sisters?'

'Yes. They're all here, dancing somewhere. And you? Did you come alone or–' I froze. A possibility had just occurred to me. 'Blimey! You didn't come here with your friend, Sir Philip, did you?'

'With Flip? No. Why?'

'Why? You ask why? Did you perhaps forget that he happened to fall madly in love with my sister Ella? A love which she, I might add, did not return in the least?'

He waved my concerns away. 'Ah, yes, but I told you, Flip falls madly in love with another woman every week. That's his thing, being madly in love. That, and flowers.'

'I remember,' I said in a dull voice, shuddering at the memory of the mountains of sunflowers, roses and carnations under which Sir Philip Wilkins had attempted to bury my little sister. He was a nice enough fellow, really, and quite harmless, but not the kind of person you wanted to fall in love with you or your little sister.

'I swear,' Captain Carter proclaimed, placing one hand on his poet's heart again, 'that Flip is not with me here tonight. And besides, he is currently madly in love with a Miss Eugenia Ficklestone from western Derbyshire. He is probably bombarding her with bouquets as we speak. So you see, your sister is perfectly safe.'

'Thank the Lord!' I hugged the curtain to me in relief. 'Not that I've got anything against your friend, mind, but...'

'You can't think of marriage and him in the same sentence without wanting to puke. I quite understand. I wouldn't like to marry him either.'

My elbow found his ribs and dug in. 'You! Why do you have to make a joke of everything?'

'Because life's much more fun that way,' he gasped, clutching his midriff. 'You have admirably sharp elbows, Miss Linton! Have you ever thought of a life as a professional tavern brawler?'

I harrumphed. 'You find the most curious things about women worthy of admiration!'

He shrugged. 'Any woman can have a pretty face. But with sharp elbows, you have to know how to use them. That takes talent. You are a dangerous young lady.'

'Lillian!' I suddenly heard a sharp voice from beyond the curtain. 'Lillian, where are you?'

'Speaking of dangerous women,' I whispered, 'here's one coming. Be warned! Hold on to your bachelordom with both hands!'

'What?' He blinked at me in surprise, but before I could elaborate, the curtain was ripped aside and there stood my aunt, thunder and death written all over her face.

'Lillian Linton! Where have you been? I've been looking all over for you! There are several young men who want to ask you to dance, and–'

It was only then that she spotted Captain Carter. Captain Carter, who, I now realized, had been standing in a secluded spot behind the curtains, rather close to my sweet little self. My aunt took in all six feet of his manliness, resplendent in his deep red dress uniform. The scowl was shoved off her face, and a smile sprang in its place.

'Captain Carter! How nice to see you! I didn't know Mrs Fields was going to invite you to this little festivity of ours!'

'It is my pleasure to see you again, Madam.' James Carter bowed, deeply. He could be perfectly well mannered when he wanted to. He just didn't want to very often. 'I was just having a nice chat with your lovely niece.' He winked. 'You understand?'

My elbow found his ribs again, but this time, the captain didn't even wince. He continued to smile brightly at my aunt, who returned the radiant expression, golden coins twinkling in her eyes.

'Of course I do! So you two know each other quite well, do you?'

'Sometimes,' he sighed, 'it feels as if I have known her all my life!'

My elbow lashed out again. 'We met for the first time no more than two weeks ago!' I growled under my breath.

'Really? It seems like an eternity to me.'

I was just about to shoot something back when suddenly, I heard the music of the dance around us change. Where before the stately tones of a quadrille had drilled their way into my ears, now, a frisky tune swept over the guests. It became faster and faster, and louder, too. All people over thirty hurriedly left the dance floor. The rest looked at each other with excited grins.

'Good gracious!' my aunt exclaimed. 'What is that they are playing?'

'A galop,' Captain Carter informed her. 'I hear it's all the rage in Europe.'

'Well, we are not Europe! Isn't that what the Channel is for?'

Ignoring her, the captain turned towards me and extended an arm. 'Would you do me the honour of dancing with me, Miss Linton?'

I hesitated. Dancing with Captain Carter was considerably less horrific than dancing with other people. Still, my feet hadn't yet stopped aching, and maybe I should refuse as a matter of principle. I didn't approve of the idea of having a man steer me across the dance floor.

'Well, I...'

'What?' my aunt interrupted. 'Dance to this frantic hick-hack? Surely, you are not serious, Captain Carter? My niece jumping about in an unseemly fashion? I forbid it! Do you hear me, Lillian? I forbid it!'

I heard her loud and clear. My hand shot forward and grabbed the surprised Captain Carter by the arm. My eyes flashed.

'Come along, Captain! You want to dance a galop? Let us dance a galop!'

'But Miss Linton, your aunt said–'

He didn't get another word out. In a flash, I had dragged him onto the dance floor and held him in a firm grip. He suddenly didn't look as if he wanted to escape anymore.

'So... how do you dance this?' I demanded.

His eyes widened. 'You don't know?'

'Of course not!'

'Then... blast! What are we going to do?'

'We'll just have to improvise.'

'And pray to God we don't crash into any of the other couples! Blimey... all right. Take your skirt in one hand and pull it up.'

'I get to pull my skirt up?' Grinning like a loon, I obeyed. 'Good God, my aunt will be furious!'

'Not that far! You don't want to show your unmentionables[4] to the entire ballroom!'

'How do you know I don't?'

'Well, maybe you do, but you shouldn't! Let your skirt down again, or I'll have to make you!'

I bowed my head in my best pseudo-ladylike submission. 'Like that?'

'Yes. Admirable.'

'Now, I'll put my arm around your waist, and take your hand with the other...'

'Seems like any other dance to me. What are the steps?'

'There are no steps. We don't step, we jump.'

The grin on my face widened. 'Now that's *not* like any other dance. How high?'

'As high as you want.' Seeing the gleam in my eyes, he added, hurriedly: 'Be gentle with me! I don't want to break a leg.'

'Can I start? Can I start? Please, please?'

'Wait for the music, will you? There we go. One, two, three, four... one, two, three, four... Now!'

The next few minutes passed in an ecstasy of stomping feet and flying skirts. I hardly felt my aching feet or my too-tight corset. Not once did I stamp on Captain Carter's feet. True, he was a man, but a sort of special case. There was no real reason to break his toes – not while I was having so much fun.

After the first galop, the musicians wanted to start on a quadrille again – but they were interrupted by the storm of mixed protest and applause from their audience.

'Bravo!' A girl from the crowd shouted. '*Da capo!*'

'Don't you dare play that stupid, sluggish muck!' I shouted. 'Or I'll come over there and ram your flute down your throat!'

Perhaps not so complimentary or diplomatic, but certainly effective. The musicians struck up another galop, and after that, another. Only when my feet would no longer support me did I allow Captain Carter to escort me to a chair in the corner. For the first time in my life, I didn't mind a man holding my arm to support me. He didn't seem to mind my having to support him right back, either. We were both a bit unsteady.

'My aunt was right!' I sank down into a chair, panting. 'This isn't dancing! It's wild jumping about!'

For a moment, Captain Carter looked concerned.

A broad grin spread over my face. '*Very* wild jumping about. I must say, I rather enjoyed it.'

His answering grin was brilliant. 'So, may I expect that you will do some more jumping about with me later tonight, Miss Linton?'

'With you, I'd even make cartwheels and jump about on one leg!'

---

[4] A Victorian expression for a certain part of the body. Can you guess which...? No, you don't even have to let your dirty little minds go so far. It's simply an expression for 'legs'.

'Ha! I doubt ballroom dances will develop so far as to include either of those. Though it is a pity.' His eyes, glinting with mirth, fastened on a particularly corpulent duchess dancing not far away. 'Cartwheels... that would certainly add considerable entertainment value to the average ball. It might be sufficient to draw away audiences from the music hall.'[5]

'We should do this again – not just tonight, but when the next ball comes along! I never before considered the possibility of actually having fun at a ball. I feel like a girl dying of thirst in the middle of the Sahara, in front of whom suddenly a hand appears with a glass of water and a voice says "Want a sip, dear?"'

Captain Carter grinned, but then he winced as if he had remembered something, and shook his head.

'I'm afraid I can't be your glass of water in the desert, Miss Linton.'

'Oh.' My face fell. I thought he had enjoyed our galoping just as much as I had, but maybe I had been mistaken.

He seemed to read my thoughts on my face. 'It's not that I don't want to. I'd like nothing better. But, you see, I'm leaving London in a few days. And I'm not likely to return for some time.'

'Really? Leaving? Why?'

He hesitated

'Is it a secret?' I teased.

'Well, yes, it is actually.'

'My lips are sealed. Well, actually they aren't, because I hate the taste of sealing wax, but you can tell me anyway.'

'Blast you!' He fought the grin, but it spread over his face anyway. 'I shouldn't even be thinking about telling you this! Why the heck am I?'

I waved my fan like I thought a proper lady would. 'Because I'm so irresistible?'

He studied my face for a moment. 'That must be it.'

'So, why are you going?'

'The fate of a soldier, I'm afraid. We're always going, going, going. Usually away from places where there are balls and pretty young ladies, and towards places where there are wars and people trying to stab you in the kidneys.'

'Is that so? And are your kidneys still intact?'

'Luckily, yes. But I don't know whether they still will be after this little adventure.' His face became uncommonly serious. 'We've had reports of a series of vicious attacks on traders in one of the eastern protectorates.[6] There's pressure on the Admiralty and the Commander-in-Chief to get quick results. The Navy has already dispatched several vessels, and if they can't root the bandits out from the sea, we'll probably be sent in.'

My eyes gleamed. 'That sounds dangerous!'

---

[5] A popular Victorian entertainment form, consisting of a mix of comedy, music and acrobatic acts.

[6] One step up from a colony. A protectorate is a foreign country that subordinates itself to a certain extent to a great power. Sometimes this might involve having to pay tribute, or relinquishing control over foreign affairs.

He looked at me, one corner of his mouth twitching. 'And that just makes you want to come along, doesn't it?'

'Why on earth not?' I demanded.

'Didn't you ever think about saying "Oh, that sounds terribly dangerous!" while clutching my arm in fear, staring deeply into my eyes, beseeching me to be careful and return to you in one piece?'

In answer to that, I stomped on his foot. Seeing as I had been restrained during the dance, I was entitled to give him at least one bruise.

'Ouch!' he laughed. 'You're no proper young lady, you little beast!'

'If I were a proper young lady I wouldn't have danced the galop with you,' I pointed out.

'True, true. Then, don't be proper, please.'

'That won't be a problem.' I rose to my feet and extended my hand to him. 'Since you'll be leaving soon, we have no time to waste. Would you do me the honour of dancing another galop with me, Captain?'

'I'm the one who is supposed to ask you!'

I grinned. 'Not a proper young lady, remember?'

He grinned back. 'Yes! I'd be delighted to dance with you.'

The rest of the evening passed in a whirl of flying skirts and disapproving glares from my aunt. And the best thing was: she couldn't even say anything! She had told me to spend my evening dancing and smiling, and there I was, dancing and smiling. The only thing was – I wasn't pretending.

When the evening finally came to an end, and people were rushing through the room, trying to say their goodbyes to everybody, I stayed beside the captain for a moment longer.

'When will you be leaving for your not-so-secret secret mission?'

He winced. 'Blast! I should never have told you!'

'Out with it! Or do you want an elbow in the ribs, or a smashed foot?'

'Please, gentle lady, spare me! I'll probably be leaving the day after tomorrow, if the ship is ready by then.'

Instead of trampling on his foot, I gave his hand a squeeze.

'I'll miss you,' I told him, and found to my surprise that I actually meant it. My arms reflexively crossed in front of my chest. 'You... well, you're one of the few men I don't actually despise.'

He swept a dramatic bow. 'Why, thank you! You really know how to compliment a gentleman, Miss Linton. May I say that I don't actually despise you, either?'

'You may.'

Bending still a little farther forward, he took hold of my hand and, before I could rip it from his grasp, pressed a kiss on the back of it.

'Goodbye, Miss Linton. Or should I say *au revoir*?'

My eyes narrowed. 'I prefer pip-pip, or cheerio.'

'Pip-pip, it is, then, Miss Linton.'

He turned and walked away. And I, for some reason, stood there looking after him long after the crowd had swallowed him, remembering the feel of his arms around me.

˷˷**˷*˷*

By Monday morning, I was no longer thinking about Captain Carter's arms – or his feet or nose, for that matter. In fact, any thought of any man existing on this earth had been expunged from my brain, excepting that one representative of the species *homo masculus masculus lentus*[7] that I would have to confront in no more than an hour.

It won't be long before you are begging to be sacked, and I'll be rid of you.

His words echoed in my mind while I got up and dressed. They still echoed when I went downstairs for breakfast. They hadn't faded by the time I got up from the breakfast table.

'Where are you going?' my aunt demanded, sharply.

'To the park,' I lied. 'For a rendezvous.'

Her face brightened. 'With that nice young man, Captain Carter?'

Somehow, she had been able to compartmentalize the events of last night in a way that allowed her to be furious with me because I had displayed such an atrocious lack of ladylike behaviour and spent the evening dancing frivolous dances, while she was simultaneously ecstatic about Captain Carter, although he had been the one to ask me to dance said dances. It was really amazing what levels of unjust nastiness an ambitious aunt could work herself up to if she put her mind to it.

'Yes,' I lied. Lying was such a useful skill.

'Excellent!' Her eyes narrowed in suspicion for a moment. 'There won't be any dancing, will there?'

'In the park? No, I don't think so.'

There! That one had even been true.

'Good. You may go. And see that you don't return before two pm. I don't want to see you near the house before then!'

'Don't worry,' I told her another very true fact. 'I think I'll be pretty busy all day.'

When nobody was looking, I slipped out of the back door into the garden and snuck into the shed. There, my new set of clothes was already waiting for me. During the last few weeks, I had been using my uncle's old Sunday best, which he hadn't used for years, but that had gone down with the Channel ferry. My new attire consisted of pretty much the same ghastly mixture of cheap trousers and tailcoat, only these weren't three sizes too large for me.

A few minutes later, I stepped out into the street, successfully transformed from Miss Lilly Linton, suffragette and part-time trampler of men's feet, into Mr Victor Linton, secretary to Mr Rikkard Ambrose of 322 Leadenhall Street, London. The new me gave the passing cabs a regretful glance – but I had just informed my uncle I didn't want an allowance any more, and it was still about a week until I would receive my first pay cheque. So this wasn't the time for

---

[7] I will leave you and your favourite Latin dictionary to figure that out by yourselves. Have fun!

42

luxuries. Straightening my shoulders, I started marching towards my goal, my feet already aching.

Not as much as they will be once he is through with you.

The thought came out of nowhere, like an adder in the grass. Sneaky! Blast, I wasn't going to surrender to *him* before I had even started.

It won't be long until you will be begging to be sacked – he said that. He meant it. You know he always does.

Yes, blast him! But so did I! I wasn't going to give up! Not ever!

What do you think he's going to do?

My foot caught on something, and I almost stumbled. Bloody hell! I should be watching where I was going!

Or even better: you should be thinking about whether to go at all!

Oh, shut up!

When I turned the corner into Leadenhall Street, I didn't waste a glance on the other buildings, not even on East India House, the headquarters of Mr Ambrose's main business rival and personal arch-enemy. My eyes were drawn to *it*, the largest building on the street, the largest building anywhere in London as far as I knew, with the possible exception of Buckingham Palace.

Empire House rose high, high into the air above the other buildings. Its size was not in breadth, but in climbing far above the other buildings, towards the sky. When first I saw the building, I couldn't think why. Now I felt sure I knew: it was cheaper to build high on a smaller piece of ground. Plus, I had to admit, it looked much more intimidating. And Mr Ambrose was as much into intimidation as he was into keeping his purse tightly closed.

Cautiously, I approached the portico. I half-expected him to jump out at me from behind one of the two gigantic support columns.

Don't be silly! Get a move on, Lilly!

Crossing the street, I climbed up the steps to the half-open door and entered the entrance hall. Immediately, I was surrounded by cool shadows and the patter of hundreds of busy little feet, coming from busy little clerks hurrying through the hall like ants through an anthill. The narrow windows let in only a few rays of sunlight, and the stone walls were completely bare of decoration.

I gave a happy sigh.

Home.

Except, of course, for the little fact that this was a huge stone monument to mammon, not a home. A monument of which not a single brick belonged to me. And in its bowels waited not a welcoming committee but a stone-faced madman who wanted to devour me for breakfast and spit me out again.

Don't be melodramatic, Lilly! At least not now! You can do that on your own time!

Fighting an urge to linger, I advanced towards the sallow-faced receptionist behind the desk at the back of the hall, and nodded a greeting.

Sallow-face nodded back. 'You may go up, Mr Linton. Mr Ambrose is expecting you.'

Oh, he is, is he?

I hardly noticed my aching feet while climbing up the stairs. My brain was too focused on wild, chaotic fears to have room for pain.

Blast, blast, blast! He's going to try to get rid of you again!

My feet touched the third landing. I hurried on without pausing.

Yes, he is. But what can he do? Make you carry more files than before?

Fourth landing... fifth... Outside, the bell of St Paul's Cathedral started to strike the hour.

'What can he do?' Did you really have to ask yourself that question?

Now I bloody couldn't stop imagining!

Sixth landing... just one more... seventh! Panting, I stumbled into the narrow hallway with doors leading off to either side that was the gateway to Mr Ambrose's inner sanctum. At the end of the hallway, Mr Stone, an astonishingly nice and unassuming man for someone working so closely with Mr Ambrose, sat at his desk, guarding the entrance like a timid Cerberus.

And behind Mr Stone... a door.

The door.

I started forward. The only sensible thing to do. But why the heck was I moving on tiptoes?

'Hello, Mr Stone.'

And now why are you whispering?

He smiled up at me. 'Welcome back, Mr Linton.'

I threw another glance at the door. 'How is he?'

Mr Stone cleared his throat. 'Um... not in a particularly good mood, I'm afraid. Here's his correspondence for the day. But if I were you, I'd avoid him until he has relaxed a bit.'

Mr Ambrose? Relax? Do you want me to wait a million years, or just ten thousand?

'Well, thanks for the advice,' I told him. 'I'll just go into my own office, then, and-'

'Mr Linton!' The cold voice from inside the head office cut through mine like a razor through rice paper. It sent a shiver down my back and made Mr Stone sit up straight in his chair. Then it came again. 'I know you're out there, Mr Linton. Come in here! We have work to do!'

Oh, bloody hell...!

TO WATCH FOR FAT AND GOLD

When I opened the door to his office, Mr Ambrose was sitting in his chair, glaring at a piece of paper on his desk as if he wanted to freeze it solid with his gaze. He didn't look up when I stepped in, but still managed to make me feel that the icy look was not for the paper alone.

'You are two and a half seconds late, Mr Linton!'

'Good morning, Sir. It's very nice to see you again, too.'

'Send a message through the tubes! I want to know if my new cane has arrived yet.'

'Your new what, Sir?'

'My cane! I tried to hold on to my old one, but it slipped out of my fingers while swimming ashore.' He sounded as if having survived the sinking of the ship was an insignificant event that could in no way outweigh the horrendous loss of his invaluable walking stick. 'I have to buy a new one. If things continue at this rate, I'll be reduced to beggary soon.'

'Yes, Sir.'

'And it's going to be infernally expensive! I have to have it custom-made, of all things! They don't sell them like I want them.'

'Really, Sir? I can't imagine why shops don't usually sell walking sticks with hidden swords inside. They're such a handy, everyday item.'

'Mr Linton?'

'Yes, Sir?'

'Get a move on and get me my cane!'

'Yes, Sir!'

While Mr Ambrose continued to shoot death-stares at the paper in front of him, I went into the office next door, to a spot where there was a hole in the wall, and beside the hole a number of levers and buttons. They gave me access to the system of pneumatic tubes that ran through the entire building. Shove a small cylinder with a message into one of the tubes and push the right buttons, and it would pop out at almost any place in the building, saving Mr Ambrose a lot of valuable time and my leg muscles from eternal cramp.

Dear Sallow-face...

My hand stopped writing, hovering over the little bit of paper. Hm... I probably shouldn't address him like that. He might be offended. Men were funny that way.

But I had such bloody difficulties remembering the man's name! What was it again? Parsnips? Pumpkin? No, Pearson! That was it, Pearson!

Dear Mr Pearson,

Mr Ambrose has requested...

I halted again. Then I crossed out 'requested' and wrote 'ordered' instead.

Dear Mr Pearson,

Mr Ambrose has ordered me to enquire with you if his custom-made walking stick has already arrived. You know, the one with the pig sticker inside?

Yours truly

Mr Victor Linton

The answer came back quickly and efficiently:

Mr Linton,

No.

Yours,

Pearson

Ah. Apparently the good Mr Pearson had embraced wholeheartedly Mr Ambrose's policy on quick and efficient communication in the workplace. Returning to Mr Ambrose's office, I handed him the slip of paper.

'Here, Sir! As requested, Sir!'

He threw a glance at the paper. He didn't curse – curses were a waste of valuable breath, after all – but the way in which his little finger twitched spoke volumes. Ones with lots of dirty words inside.

'I can't go without some protection,' he growled. 'Not *there*! Who knows what they might get up to?'

Shoving his chair back abruptly, he rose from his desk and marched out of his office into mine. A moment later I heard the rustling of keys and knew what he was doing.

What the bloody hell does he want in the safe?

'No, not that,' I heard him murmur to clanking and thudding. 'Not that either, and that's not right at all... Ah, yes!'

Seconds later he re-entered his office. And he had found what he'd been looking for. My eyes went wide! It was a massive wooden cudgel, painted lines drawn around the top, and the image of a very determined, very ugly demon's face carved into it.

'What the hell is that?' I blurted out before I could control myself. He gave me a look. One of *those* looks. 'Sir,' I added hurriedly.

'It is one of many trophies from my travels. Originally, I believe it had a ceremonial purpose. But it will suffice for what I have in mind.'

He gave the thing an experimental swing, and I jumped back.

'What in God's name do you need a ceremonial cosh for?'

Picking up the letter he had been staring at from the desk, he thrust it at me. 'Read!'

Carefully, not sure whether he would break out into any more sudden bouts of experimental stick-fighting, I took the piece of paper. Even more carefully, I lowered my eyes to it.

Sir,

A situation has arisen at factory number 12 in Soho, and requires your immediate attention.

Yours truly

Dennis Bradley

Factory Manager

Not far underneath that was scribbled in a rather hastier script:

P.S.: I resign.

'A situation?' My head snapped up to stare at Mr Ambrose. 'What kind of situation?'

'It doesn't say.'

'I know it doesn't say! That's why I'm asking you!'

'I regret to inform you, Mr Linton, that I am not omniscient.' His face stone-hard, he gave the cudgel another experimental swing. 'But I think it's best to go prepared for anything.'

Realization settled in.

'You... you don't mean that you are going to go there *by yourself*?'

'No.'

'Thank God!' I let out a breath of relief. 'I thought for a moment–'

'I won't be by myself. You shall accompany me.'

'*What?*'

His gaze was a lance of ice, pinning me where I stood. 'You heard me.'

'But... but... there will be dozens of men there!'

'No. Hundreds. Two hundred and thirty-seven, to be exact, not counting any females and juveniles.'

'So don't you think any trouble there will be dangerous? Whatever the trouble is, they'll probably be angry!' *Because you have a talent for making people heat to boiling point.*

'I expect so,' he told me, as cold as a cucumber in a barrel of ice at the North Pole. '*I* am certainly angry. They are lazing about while I pay them to work. And I intend to put a stop to that.'

'But... bloody hell, this will be dangerous!'

He raised the cudgel in his hand. 'Did you think I took this for decoration?' He took a step closer to me, cudgel still raised.

'Well...' Desperately, I floundered for something to say. On one level, I was excited. On another, I was something I would never admit being, even to myself. It started with a T, and continued with E, R, R, I, F, I, E, and D. 'Don't you have anything I could use as a weapon?'

'I have an African hunting bow. But I imagine that's not what you're looking for.'

'Not really, no.'

He shrugged. But... was that a satisfied glint I saw in his dark eyes? 'You'll just have to rely on your fists, if it comes to a fight, Mr Linton. After all, you are as tough as any man, aren't you?'

The bloody son of a...!

I opened my mouth to say something, but he was faster. He had crossed the distance between us with two long strides, and was suddenly towering in front of me, a column of iron encased in black cloth. His dark, sea-coloured eyes held mine captive.

'Did you think working for me would be easy, Mr Linton? Did you think I didn't mean what I said? This work is not for you! Or did you think being my secretary would mean sitting nice and snug in your warm office all day?'

I had difficulties holding that powerful, dark gaze of his. Still, the corner of my mouth twitched up in an involuntary smile. 'My office is freezing cold, Sir. All the rooms in the building are, because you don't want to pay for gas or firewood.'

His eyes narrowed infinitesimally. I could feel the tension in the air between us, crackling. 'Mr Linton?'

'Yes, Sir?'

'Be silent!'

'Yes, Sir!'

'And follow me!'

'As you wish, Sir!'

Going downstairs on Mr Ambrose's heels was always a remarkable experience. He was the only man I'd ever met who had mastered the art of striding arrogantly down a staircase. How he managed it without knotting his legs or breaking his neck was beyond me.

Today, however, I was more than a little distracted from the show by the fact that we were, very possibly, going to have our brains bashed in.

You're going to have another adventure! Admit it, you're excited!

Well, possibly, part of me was. Still, there was this other part that was the unspeakable T-word to which I would never admit.

Blast him! Why did he have to do this just to get rid of me?

But deep down, I knew he would do exactly the same if I weren't there. He was that kind of man: ruthless, and not afraid to march headlong into danger. Blast him thrice to hell and back!

Somewhere on the way down, I expected to be joined by others. If not by many people, at least by Mr Ambrose's personal bloodhound Karim. But no one came. Was Karim still alive at all? I realized I hadn't seen him since we had separated on *Île Marbeau*. I really hoped the grumpy bodyguard hadn't gotten himself shot or drowned or dismembered. I would miss his disapproving glares. They made such a nice change from the disapproving glares I got from Mr Ambrose.

But Karim was nowhere in sight. Mr Ambrose couldn't really mean for us to do this all alone, could he?

When we reached the bottom of the stairs, I couldn't hold it in any longer.

'Where's Karim?' I burst out. 'Isn't he going with us?'

Is he alive?

He looked over his shoulder, his cold gaze bored into me. 'Karim won't be coming. He is trying to clamp down on that scandal at Speaker's Corner, before any more rumours get spread all over London.'

He's alive! He's alive! He – wait! What did he say?

'Excuse me?' I pictured the huge bodyguard, nearly seven feet tall even without his towering turban, a mountain of muscle and armed with a sabre that could easily sever limbs. 'You employ *Karim* as your public relations man?'

'No. I employ him as the man who scares people into keeping their mouths shut.' And with that, he strode across the hall and out onto the street.

Outside, I stopped to wait for a carriage. Mr Ambrose, however, strode off down the street. After a moment, I hurried after him.

'Wait! Where's the cab?'

'Do you honestly think I would waste money on that?'

'What? You mean we'll have to walk all the way?'

Without turning back to me, he waved a dismissive hand. 'It's not far. And with the streets as crowded as they are we'll be faster on foot in any case.'

After about twenty minutes of brisk, silent marching, it had started to sink in that Rikkard Ambrose and I had very different ideas of the meaning of the words 'not far'. My feet hurt worse than after hours of dancing, but I trudged on without complaint.

You probably should be grateful he didn't make you walk back all the way from Dover!

Well, maybe so. But at the moment, gratitude was at the bottom of my things-to-feel list.

Around us, the city slowly changed. Men's and women's clothes grew shabbier. Fancy carriages were replaced by carts and wagons full of goods. Then, the goods became fewer and fewer, and after another few minutes there weren't even empty carts anymore. The smoke in the air grew thicker, and so did the crowds of people. Finally, we stepped into a street that was lined on both sides with large, flat buildings, their chimneys spewing clouds of black into the air. The high walls around them, some with iron spikes on top, didn't exactly make our surroundings any more inviting.

'Number twelve...' Mr Ambrose murmured, his eyes raking searchingly over the façades. The numbers were hardly legible from here. 'Which is number twelve...?'

'How about that one?' I panted, pointing to one of the walls, with the large red letters 'Freedom for Workers!' and 'To Hell with the Rich!' scrawled on the side.

'A reasonable supposition, Mr Linton. Let's go.'

The door in the wall of that factory wasn't closed like the others. As we approached, I could see it stood slightly ajar. Not just that, I could hear the murmur of voices inside. Voices – not the rattle of machines, even though it was the middle of a workday. My heart beat faster. Was this it? What was going on in there?

Mr Ambrose seemed to feel none of my hesitation. He marched towards the gates with iron determination. He was just six steps away from the entrance when something whizzed through the air above him and knocked his top hat clean off his head.

Mr Ambrose didn't yelp, or curse, or jump. Instead, he froze and slowly turned up his face. I followed suit.

On top of the factory wall – it was one of those without iron spikes on top – sat a small boy in grubby clothes and with a grubby face. He was grinning from ear to ear, and weighing a second stone in his hand. Immediately, my hands went up to clutch my hat.

Mr Ambrose sent the boy a look that by all rights should have frozen him solid and knocked him off the wall. The little twerp must have been a tough nut, though, because all the look did was make him lower the stone a little bit. Without taking his eyes off the boy, Mr Ambrose bent to pick up his hat. Carefully, he dusted it off and placed it on his head. Then, he focused his full intention on the miscreant again.

'You!'

Ignoring him, the little boy tossed his stone into the air and caught it.

'You, up there on the wall! I'm talking to you.'

'Get stuffed, you skanky tosser[8],' the youth replied merrily.

---

[8] British English insult, which means something like "badly smelling jerk".

'I shall most certainly remain unstuffed,' Mr Ambrose returned coolly. 'Taxidermists[9] charge insufferable fees, nowadays. Now, tell me what is going on in there, in that factory!'

The little boy beamed. Apparently, Mr Ambrose had hit upon his favourite subject.

'We're striking,' he proudly proclaimed.

'Striking?' Mr Ambrose's left little flinger twitched. His voice was as low and controlled as before, but that didn't fool me. 'Are you, now?'

'Yes, guv! We're fighting O-presh-ion and Ecs-ploi-tay-shion.'

'How fascinating.'

'Oh, yes, it is! We're fighting for our rights, you know, and for the first time really standing up to the bastard who owns this dump! Some rich bugger named Ambrose! 'e's been making us slave for 'im for years for a pittance, and in all that time 'e never once dared to show his ugly mug 'ere!'

Covering my mouth with my hands, I sent a prayer to heaven for the little boy who had just damned himself to a fate worse than death. Mr Ambrose cocked his head, narrowing his eyes.

'So you don't know what this Ambrose looks like, I assume?'

The little boy made a dismissive gesture. 'Ah, those rich buggers in their fancy clothes look all the same!'

'Indeed?'

'Aye. I'm supposed to keep watch out 'ere, you know, for when he arrives in his fancy carriage and drags his fat paunch inside.'

'Indeed?' Mr Ambrose little finger twitched again, and his eyes narrowed another micrometre. 'Well, why don't you keep on watching for Mr Ambrose's fancy coach? I'm sure he'll be along any minute to drag his fat paunch inside, as you so eloquently put it. Mr Linton and I will just go into the factory for a minute. We have a small matter to discuss with your fellow strikers.'

Without waiting for an answer, Mr Ambrose shoved the gate wide open and strode inside. I, bloody fool that I was, hurried after him.

Come on! Admit it! This will be fun!

Yes, if we didn't get torn to pieces...

The voices from inside the factory were louder now. They weren't murmurs, they were shouts and bellows and yells! Metal crashed against metal, and glass broke. Not far away, another boy darted over the courtyard. Raising a stone in his hand, he hurled it through one of the factory's upstairs windows. It shattered, and there was a roar of approval.

Mr Ambrose didn't slow his stride. He didn't even hesitate.

I swallowed. 'Um... Sir?'

'Yes, Mr Linton?'

'Don't you think it might be wiser not to go in there?'

'No, Mr Linton.'

'Oh.'

---

[9] People who stuff things, particularly of the dead animal variety.

He halted, then. He didn't turn around, but simply said: 'You can leave at any time, Mr Linton.'

My temper shot upwards. Against it, my good sense had no chance whatsoever! 'Not on your sweet life! And not on mine, either!'

'I see. Then let's stop wasting time.'

We had nearly reached the door of the factory by then. It was a rough thing, two raw and splintery slices of wood forming the wings of the gate under a brick arch. There was no telling what colour the wood or bricks had been originally, so blackened and stained were they by soot. On the steps leading up to the door, there was a smear of some dark red liquid. So, all in all, it looked extremely cheery. There was probably a party with tea and cake waiting on the other side.

'Death to the capitalists!' came a shout from inside, seconded by a roar of approval.

Mr Ambrose nodded, thoughtfully gazing into the gloom beyond the entrance. 'That would be me, I presume.' And with that, he stepped into the factory.

Bloody stone-faced son of a bachelor! Does he think nothing can harm him? Is his brain made out of stone, too?

For a moment, I hesitated – then I hurried after him. Huzzah! Apparently, both our brains were made of stone. How wonderful!

ONLY A FACTORY GIRL

Inside the factory, it was as dark as in a coalminer's unwashed pants, and it smelled nearly as bad. The thick mix of smoke, sweat and unidentifiable filth in the air made me cough and cover my mouth and nose with my arm. Mr Ambrose seemed to suffer no such problems. He strode directly towards the large crowd of factory workers – men, women and children – gathered at one end of the hall.

No, not a crowd – a mob. They had all the paraphernalia essential to the modern, self-respecting mob: torches, axes, protest signs heavy enough to bash people on the head with and, most of all, bloodlust in their eyes.

'...ain't gonna suffer under the yoke of oppression any longer!' one of the men who had climbed onto one of the machines was yelling. People all around him were nodding and cheering him on. 'The pittance that bugger Ambrose pays us ain't worth pissing for, let alone working!'

I winced.

The crowd cheered.

Mr Ambrose stared up at the man. Very intently. Very coldly.

'We'll have our due at last!'

More cheers.

Another wince.

More staring. Very, very cold staring. I wondered how the man was still able to move his arms. Hadn't they frozen yet?

'When that tosser Ambrose shows his bloody face here, I ain't gonna be afraid of him! I'll step up to him, and tell him to go bugger himself! Aye, I will!'

Oh dear...

There were more cheers from the crowd.

And then, someone cleared his throat. Technically, it shouldn't even have been possible to hear it. The cheers were as thunderous as a hurricane. But this was a very special cough. Not the kind of cough you make when you have phlegm in your throat, oh no. It was a cough as cold as a knife blade, and cut through the cheers with ease. Slowly, they subsided, and everyone began to turn towards the cough's originator.

Mr Ambrose met their gazes steadily. Somehow, he managed to twirl his exotic, demon-faced club as if it were nothing but a simple walking stick. Somehow, he managed to make that effortless twirl seem like the most dangerous movement anyone had ever seen. Not even blinking once, he bent his head a fraction of an inch.

'If I might introduce myself – Rikkard Ambrose, *not* at your service. You were waiting for me?' His eyes focused on the man up on the machine, whose mouth was hanging open. 'I believe you had something to say to me.'

The man's open mouth moved – but no sound came out. Mr Ambrose started forward, ignoring the mob. It parted for him, lowering torches and axes, some people trying to hide signs behind their backs. Mr Ambrose only stopped when he was standing directly in front of the man on the machine. Somehow, even though on his impromptu pedestal the worker stood far above his employer, it was Mr Ambrose who seemed taller.

'Tell me what you have to say to me. I'm most interested to hear it.'

Giving a little squeak, the man turned, jumped off the machine and vanished into the maze of mechanics behind him. I could hear the patter of his feet receding into the distance.

Nodding to himself, Mr Ambrose turned to the rest of the crowd.

'Now – does anybody else have something to say? What is the matter here?'

Some shouts rose again, particularly from the back of the crowd, out of sight of Mr Ambrose.

'Oppression! Against oppression!'

'Down with the capitalists!'

'Justice for–'

Mr Ambrose let the flood build and wash over him. Then, when it had reached its highest point, he stepped forward and plucked a man out of the crowd, hauling him to the front, where everyone could see him.

'Silence!'

It wasn't a roar, not even a shout, but Mr Ambrose's command had immediate effect. The crowd fell into silence, all staring at their employer and the man he had singled out at his victim. The man himself seemed to wish for the ability to crawl out of his own skin.

'You. Tell me what seems to be the trouble. Slowly and clearly.'

The man straightened. He didn't want to be out here, but now that he was, it was clear he meant to die bravely in the face of the capitalist enemy.

'We want more money!' he exclaimed. 'Sir,' he added as an afterthought. His demand was supported by shouts of 'Yay!' and 'Hear, hear!'.

Mr Ambrose cocked his head. 'If you want more money, why are you standing around idly? You should be working! You'll have to work at least two hours longer than usual to get more money out of me, and if you laze about now, you'll have to do overtime until one in the morning.'

The workers threw each other uncertain glances. Finally, the man facing Mr Ambrose gathered his courage. 'Err... No, Mr Ambrose, Sir. You don't understand. We want more money without doing overtime.'

Mr Ambrose's eyes narrowed infinitesimally. 'Do I understand you correctly? You want more money without working for it?'

Colour was beginning to rise to the man's cheeks. More people were beginning to lower their signs and hide them away. One man even tried to hide a burning torch behind his back, but stopped with a yelp when his trousers began to smoke.

'Um... Aye, Sir.'

'In case you haven't noticed, man, this is a *factory*, not a *charity*. In a factory, you work to earn money. That's what a factory is for.'

'I know, Sir.'

'Indeed?' Mr Ambrose clapped his hands. 'Well, then that problem is solved. Back to work, everyone!'

Again, the workers threw each other uncertain glances. Several of them actually turned and started back towards the machines. The voice of the man opposite Mr Ambrose halted them.

'Stop, everyone! Stop, you bloody buggers! You're not supposed to be working!'

'Yes, they are, actually,' Mr Ambrose contradicted him coolly.

'No, they aren't!' The poor man sounded almost desperate now. 'This is a strike! A strike for our rights, people, and you're just going to let him talk you out of it?'

'Much the more sensible option,' Mr Ambrose pointed out, his dark gaze sweeping over the hesitant crowd. His fingers flexed around the cudgel. 'You don't want me to have to do more than talk.'

'There! There, now 'e's threatening you! Are you gonna put up with that?'

Mr Ambrose's dark eyes returned to the man again, who had one trembling hand raised, pointing at him accusingly.

'That,' he said, his voice as cool as the winter night before a blizzard, 'was no threat. Trust me, when I threaten you, you'll know for certain.'

'We ain't gonna put up with your threats, you bloody bugger! We're free men, and we 'ave rights.'

'True. You have the right to work, and the right to get fired if you don't.'

'There!' The pointing hand jabbed at Mr Ambrose, as if pointing out the devil. 'There! That's what we're fighting against! Capitalism! Exploitation! We 'ave a right to fair wages! We have a right to shorter work hours! We have a right to protection from...'

It went on a while, like that. The list of rights workers had was long, apparently. Most of these rights I found very interesting, particularly because Mr Ambrose had shown no signs of extending these rights to me, or any of the other staff in his office. I wondered whether it might not be a good idea to join the strikers.

Then I looked at Mr Ambrose's face.

Hm.

Probably not.

'...we have a right to grngg–'

The man's long list cut off in a garbled choke when Mr Ambrose's hand shot forward and grabbed him by the collar. The other workers, instead of coming to their companion's aid, retreated a step or two.

'Listen to me very carefully,' Mr Ambrose said. His voice was low, but perfectly audible in the entire hall. 'I wish for you to go back to work. If you don't, well....'

Bending forward, he whispered something into the man's ear. The man's face paled, and his knees nearly buckled under him.

Pulling the fellow a little closer towards him, Mr Ambrose pierced him with lances of ice shooting out of those dark eyes of his. '*That* was a threat.'

The man nodded jerkily. 'Yes, Sir! I understand, Sir.'

'I want you to consider my next question very carefully, man. Think about what I just told you before you answer, and take a good look at me.' The lances of ice bored deeper. 'Now, the question is this: do you really expect to get more money out of me by *stopping* your work than by going on?'

'Err... no, Sir.'

'Ah. You're reasonably intelligent, after all.'

'Um... thank you, Sir.'

Letting go of the man's collar, Mr Ambrose wiped his hands on his trousers. He didn't take his eyes off the man. 'And since you are reasonably intelligent, can you tell me what you should do now?'

'Um... get back to work, Sir?'

'How perceptive. I'll leave you to it, then.' Swivelling around, he marched back towards the exit, parting the crowd of workers before him like Moses had parted the Red Sea – only that the fish in the Red Sea probably hadn't been so terrified of Moses.

I was just as flattened as the workers. He was past me before I realized.

'Come, Mr Linton!' came his cool command from outside, and I hurried after him.

'How...' I paused, fighting to catch my breath. He was marching fast, blast him! Why did he have to have such long legs? 'How the hell did you do that?'

He shrugged. 'It was my warm and winning personality, Mr Linton. Couldn't you tell?'

~~**~*~*

Over the following weeks, my dear employer, master and general tyrant took me with him on trips to a coal mine, a bank and several other business where he busied himself bullying and browbeating people. It didn't take long for me to realize what his strategy was: apparently, he reasoned that if I saw him being nasty to enough people, I would get so disgusted with him that I'd leave my job of my own free will.

However, in that, he had considerably underestimated both my tenacity and my own capacity for nastiness. The end of the month was approaching, and I was still his secretary. And do you know what that meant?

Well, I knew what it bloody meant, because I had been counting down to the end of the month by crossing out the days on my calendar at home. One after the other, the days passed, until finally, at last, the day of days had arrived! The day more important than a king's coronation! The day more important than Judgement Day itself!

Pay day!

That morning, I arrived at Mr Ambrose's inner sanctum ten minutes early. The broad grin on my face was probably not very wise, but I just couldn't wipe it off. Marching right past Mr Stone with a cheerful 'Good Morning', I knocked at Mr Ambrose's door.

'Good Morning, Sir,' I chirped. 'May I come in?'

'No!'

My hand froze on the way to the doorknob. When next I spoke, my voice wasn't quite so chirpy. 'I may not come in?'

'You're ten minutes early. Go away!'

I narrowed my eyes. 'I am not going anywhere! Today is the last day of the month, and you have to pay me, Sir!'

'Not yet, Mr Linton.'

'What's that supposed to mean?'

'As far as working hours are concerned, the last day of the month does not begin for another nine minutes and thirty-four seconds. Go, and return only when this time has elapsed.'

'You... you can't be serious!'

'Do I sound like I am joking?'

'You never sound like you're joking, you son of a bachelor!'

'How observant of you, Mr Linton.'

'Let me in!'

'Respect, Mr Linton. Remember to show respect.'

'Please, let me in, Sir!'

'No. Go.'

'I won't go!'

'Then remain standing outside my door. I don't much care, provided you cease to disturb me.'

'Do you honestly mean I have to stand here for another nine and a half minutes to suit your perverted sense of punctuality?'

'Nine minutes and three seconds now, actually.'

The truth hit me like a freight train. 'You just don't want to let me in there because you don't want to give wages to a woma– to me!'

'Still quite observant, I see.'

'This is ridiculous!'

'No, Mr Linton, it is not. Eight minutes and twenty-seven seconds...'

'You're right – it's not just ridiculous! It's unbelievably, bloody ridiculous! If I arrived early on any other day, you'd jump at the chance to drag me in there and make me slave for you!'

'You're not a slave,' the cool voice from beyond the door told me.

'You're damn right I'm not!'

'Slaves don't complain as much as you do. Besides, their fortunate owners are allowed to use whips on them.'

'You bloody bas...!' My voice failed me. This was too much! I should go and chuck everything... No! No, that was what he wanted. He *wanted* to make me angry, to make me quit. I would not!

'There's another reason why I'm not your slave,' I said, sweetly. 'Do you want to hear it?' Silence. A triumphant smile spread across my face. 'Unlike a slave,' I cooed, 'you have to pay me for my work.'

More silence. Ha! That had shown him!

I started to pace up and down in the hallway. From time to time, Mr Stone threw me a half-anxious, half-curious look. Out of the corner of my eye, I saw a cheque for two pounds and four shillings sticking out from under his paper-weight. Apparently, Mr Ambrose didn't make quite as much trouble before paying *him*. Ha!

Finally, I returned to the door, and knocked. Or maybe 'hammered' would be a better word.

'Let me in!'

'Four minutes and fifty-five seconds.'

'Let me in, blast you!'

'Four minutes and fifty-three seconds.'

'Gah!'

I resumed my march, my footsteps thudding a bit louder than before. Now and again, I muttered a few curses. If I only had a watch!

Well, that's something for you to buy once you have your money, isn't it?

Yes – once I had it! Which didn't help me much now, did it?

When I at last returned to the door, I tried to not use it as a punching bag. *Be calm*, I told myself. *Be calm. He wants to make you angry. Don't give him the satisfaction.*

'Sir? May I come in now, Mr Ambrose, Sir?'

'One minute forty-seven seconds.'

Be calm. Be calm. Be c–

Oh, to hell with it!

'Let me in, blast you! Let me in, or I'll beat this bloody door down!'

'One minute and forty-three seconds.'

I went back to my pacing. The rest of my waiting time I alternated between fantasizing about the things I would buy, and fantasizing about strangling Mr

Ambrose with a piece of washing line. In spite of these two very appealing scenarios, never had one minute and forty-three seconds felt so long. When finally I heard the bell of St Paul's Cathedral strike the hour, I was quicker at the door than a thirsting lion at a Sahara waterhole.

'Mr Ambrose, Sir, I demand that you–'

I was interrupted by the sound of the lock clicking. Slowly, the door swung open. In the doorframe stood Mr Rikkard Ambrose, his eyes as deep, cool and dark as I had ever seen them.

'Come in, Mr Linton.'

'Why, *thank you*, Sir.'

If he noticed the sarcasm dripping from my voice, he did not comment on it. He let me into his office and closed the door. Then he turned to face me.

'Are you sure about this, Mr Linton?'

'About finally getting money out of you? Hell, yes!'

'I mean,' he said, the shards of ice in his voice clinking threateningly, 'about being my secretary.'

'Ha! Did you think your antics would scare me off?' I snorted. 'Your scare tactics won't work!'

'I noticed.'

'You'll have to think of something better than that to get rid of me!'

'Will I, now?'

He regarded me for a moment. I resisted the urge to blink. Blast him! His stare could make a dead marmot uncomfortable!

I held out my hand. 'The money!'

He hesitated.

'You owe it to me! I've worked for it, and I want my money!'

His facial expression didn't change. Still, somehow he managed to look as if a tooth were being pulled from his brain while he forced himself to turn and walk over to his desk. Withdrawing a chequebook from one of the drawers, he sat down. Perhaps it was just my imagination, but I thought I could hear the sound of teeth grinding.

'The pen is there, right in front of you, Sir. Go on.'

Throwing me an icy glare, he picked up the pen. The movement of his arm towards the cheque looked as if he had to pull against a ten-ton weight of reluctance.

'From Rikkard Ambrose...' he growled. 'To... Mr Victor Linton...'

'Why not Lillian Linton?'

The next glare he threw me was dangerous.

'Be content I'm doing this, *Mister* Linton. Don't argue with me.'

On the whole, I decided it was better to keep quiet. At least I was getting my money. Mr Ambrose dragged the pen across the paper. It seemed to take an eternity, but finally he was finished and ripped the offending cheque out of his chequebook. Sliding his hand across the table, he shoved it towards me.

'Here!'

Snatching the cheque from his hand, I held it up to my face and studied it closely. It was well I did. My eyes fell on the amount, and widened in outrage.

'This cheque says one pound and two shillings!'

'Yes. And?'

'That's half of what you gave Mr Stone!'

'Certainly. After all, you are only half of what he is. He is real. You are only a pretender – or should I say prentendress?'

My mouth dropped open. He couldn't possibly be trying to...! Yes, of course he could. This was Rikkard Ambrose we were talking about.

'You're paying me less because *I haven't got balls?*'

'Language, Mr Linton.'

'I'll use any language I bloody well want, thank you very much! And I've got just as much balls as any man in this office!'

His left little finger twitched again. 'You are mixing anatomy and metaphor, Mr Linton.'

'I don't bloody care!' Marching forward, I placed both my hands, clenched into fists, on top of his desk and leaned forward until I was nose to nose with him. Being suddenly so close, I couldn't help notice the perfection of his chiselled features. And his eyes... they were so dark, so deep... deep enough to drown myself in...

Stop this! Get a grip! You're here to bang his head against the wall, not swoon over him, you blasted foolish female!

His eyes were angry. But was wrath the only thing that burned in their dark depths? Or was there hunger, too...?

Stop it!

'Tell me right out,' I hissed. 'Tell me that I haven't shown as much courage as any man in this building. Tell me that I deserve less, not because of what I am, but because of something you think I did wrong. Tell me that, and I'll accept half. Tell me!'

Silence. And more silence. Mr Ambrose's jaw worked as if he were chewing gravel soused in castor oil. His little finger drummed a *staccato presto* on the desktop.

'You can't, can you?'

More silence. The finger-tapping changed to a *staccato prestissimo furioso*.

'Write me another cheque! One for the full amount!'

Sluggishly, crawlingly, abominably slowly, as if he had to pull mountains with his elbows, Mr Ambrose moved his arms forward and once more dipped the pen into the inkwell. A salamander in the middle of winter moved more quickly than the pen did over the cheque in front of him.[10] I watched him with burning intensity. Finally, crunching a little more gravel with his teeth, he severed the cheque from the chequebook, and slid it across the table towards me.

I pounced! But before my hand could grab the check, Mr Ambrose's fist came down on one corner with a *thud*, holding the slip of paper in place.

---

[10] For those of my dear readers who are no experts in biology: salamanders are cold-blooded animals, which means they do not move in winter at all, or when they do, at a rate so slow it is imperceptible to the human eye.

'If you take this money,' he told me, his dark eyes capturing mine, 'If you really wish to be my employee, fully and completely, you'll have to accept the consequences. You'll have to do whatever I say, go wherever I command. Do you understand?'

I didn't hesitate, but snatched the slip of paper from his under hand.

'Yes!'

TRAVEL PLANS

Ding-dong...

The department store assistant looked up at the sound of the doorbell. Her usual bright I-have-things-to-sell smile wilted a little when she saw the shabby looking young man who had entered the premises.

'Sir? May I help you?' The unspoken words 'with leaving this place right away' were clearly attached to the sentence.

The shabby young man, i.e. me, didn't let herself be put off by that.

'Yes! I have some money with me, and I would like to spend it!'

The smile returned to the assistant's face in a flash. 'Really? Well, if that's the case, please follow me, Sir. What would you like me to show you?'

'Watches! I need a pocket watch. Nothing special, but it has to be reliable, and with a... oh, what do you call this fancy new invention when a watch makes "ding-dong" at a certain time?'

'Alarm?'

'That's it! A pocket watch with an alarm! I need to be at work every day at eight o'clock, punctually.' My lips twitched. 'Very, very, very punctually.'

'I see, Sir. Please come with me. I think I have just what you need.'

Following the assistant, I could hardly believe what was happening. I was buying something! Not just buying something, but buying it *with my own money!* I couldn't help a self-satisfied grin from forming on my face.

'Here, Sir... what do you think of this model?'

'Too flashy.'

'And that one?'

'That looks a bit too delicate. It has to withstand a lot of strain.'

'Like what, for example, Sir?'

I thought for a moment, memories flashing in front of my inner eye. 'Like a jump for a high wall, a fistfight, or a ride in a mine cart.'

The shop assistant blinked at me, taken aback. 'Um... what profession did you say again you worked in, Sir?'

'I'm a secretary,' I told her proudly. 'To one of the city's leading financiers.'

'Err... I see. The financial world must be an interesting workplace.'

'Indeed it is.'

'How about this watch, Sir? Sturdy, simple, and elegant.'

'Yes! That's exactly what I'm looking for!'

Snatching the item from the assistant, I let it snap open and shut. Walking to the nearest mirror, I put on a stony face, drew myself up to my full height, and let the watch snap open again.

'Knowledge is power is time is money, Mr Linton! Hurry up, Mr Linton! Bring me file XX322YZ4, Mr Linton! Right away, Mr Linton!'

Seeing the shopkeeper stare at me, I cleared my throat and closed the watch again. 'I'll take it.'

'Y-yes, Sir.'

'And there's another thing,' I added abruptly, glancing down at my clothes. 'I don't look particularly fashionable, do I?'

This time it was the assistant who cleared her throat – very diplomatically. 'Not as such, Sir.'

'Well, can you show me something better than what I'm wearing? Something appropriate for the city, but tough?'

'Certainly. Please follow me, Sir.'

Part of me was wondering why I was doing this, wondering why I didn't leave the shop but followed the assistant into the men's clothing department. I had never cared about how I looked. Not one bit.

Ah, said a tiny voice in my head, *but that was when you were dressed as a lady. A prim and proper lady only dresses well to impress men.*

But wasn't that still what I was doing? I remembered the contemptuous look on the faces of some passers-by and a few higher-ranking employees at Empire House. I wanted to wipe the sneers off their faces! I wanted to impress them!

Yes, you do. Think about the reasons why, though. When a lady dresses well it screams, 'Look at how pretty I am! I'm from a respectable family, so marry me, please!' When a man dresses well, it says, 'Look at me. I have money. I am strong and independent – so get out of my way, you bastards!'

A smile spread over my face. Yes, considered in that light, I had nothing at all against dressing well.

Half an hour later, I was standing in front of a mirror, dressed in a sleek black tailcoat and hat. And that wasn't all. Grinning, I regarded the waistcoat I had fallen in love with at first sight and demanded to have on the spot.

'What do you think of it?' I asked the assistant.

'Um... certainly very luxuriant, Sir. But... are you sure you wouldn't like something a tiny bit more restrained?'

'Whyever would I?'

'Well, excellent workmanship though your waistcoat undoubtedly is, it nevertheless has something about it that to some people might seem a tiny bit... ostentatious? The purple peacock pattern, for instance-'

'Exactly!' I gloated, turning from right to left to watch the peacocks dance. 'When he sees this, he'll go ballistic!'

'*He*, Sir?'

'I'll take it! I'll take the waistcoat.'

'Yes, Sir,' the assistant sighed, resigning herself to her fate. 'I'll wrap it up for you with the other items. Anything else?'

I hesitated. There was still quite a lot of money left. Amazing how far even a niggardly salary would go if you didn't have to pay things like rent, servants' wages and groceries.

'Yes,' I said, starting to nod. My grin became even wider. 'Yes, definitely. Do you sell solid chocolate?'

~~**~*~*

'Where did you get this?' Ella demanded. She, Patsy, Flora and Eve sat squashed onto one of the benches in Green Park, gazing with longing in their eyes at the box of sweets and treats I had brought along.

'That's a secret,' I grinned.

Patsy narrowed her eyes at me. 'A secret like where you disappeared to the week before last?'

'Oh, give it a rest, Patsy!' Eve's elbow dug into Patsy's massive ribs. The bigger girl hardly blinked. 'If I get solid chocolate out of it, I don't care if she's smuggling rum across the Scottish border!'

Ella stared from her to me in shock. 'Y-you aren't, are you?'

Rolling my eyes, I held the box of chocolates out to her. 'Here. Take one.'

Hesitantly, glancing around as if she expected a policeman to spring out at her from the bushes at any moment, Ella reached out and took one of the chocolates. With unusual restraint, I waited till all of them had taken one before I picked one for myself.

'Hm!'

'Mmm...'

Sounds of appreciation were coming from all around – except from Patsy. She was glowering at me, and pointed at the chocolate in her hand.

'This is bribery!'

'Oh, Patsy... now really. I was just trying to do something nice.'

'It won't make me forgive you, you know? I still want to know where you disappeared to! Friends don't disappear on each other. And if one does, that can't simply be erased by bribing with chocolate!'

'Just try it, will you?'

'As long as you understand that I won't forgive you–'

'Yes, yes, I understand. Go on. Take a bite.'

Throwing me another suspicious glare, Patsy cautiously raised the chocolate to her mouth and took a tiny bite. Her eyes closed in ecstasy.

'Mmmmmm...'

'Like it?'

'Hmm.... Yes! Yes, damn you!'

I took a bite for myself. The flavour spread through my mouth like ambrosia and nectar combined. I smiled at her.

'Am I forgiven?'

Putting the last bit of chocolate into her mouth, she hesitated. 'You said this wasn't a bribe!'

'I lied.'

Her eyes flew open. 'You little...'

'Well?' My smile widened. 'Am I forgiven?'

'Do I get another one?'

'Certainly.' Invitingly, I held the box out to her. 'Help yourself. If, that is, you...'

'Yes, yes, blast you! I forgive you!'

My grin threatened to split my face in two. 'You are the world's best friend, Patsy!'

'And you are a conniving little witch, Lillian Linton!'

'Thank you.'

'Now give me my chocolate!'

~~**~*~*

Needless to say, when I went to the office next time, I was in a very good mood. A mood that became even better when I passed Mr Ambrose on my way through the upper hallway, and he froze, his eyes bulging slightly at the sight of me.

Stopping, I proudly posed for him to show off my new attire.

'Is something the matter, Sir?' I asked sweetly.

His dark eyes, not bulging anymore, came up to meet mine.

'Nothing, Mr Linton. You have only just reaffirmed my conviction that females should not be allowed to have money of their own.'

'Oh, so you like my new waistcoat, do you? Aren't the peacocks pretty?'

'Mr Linton?'

'Yes, Sir?'

'Get to work!'

'Yes, Sir!'

I had just stepped into my office when, with a *plink*, the first message shot out of the pneumatic tube, landing on my desk.

Mr Linton,
Bring me file 37XVII197.
Rikkard Ambrose

'I haven't gone anywhere,' I called to him through the connecting door. 'I'm still here, in earshot. You could have just yelled through the door.'

With another *plink*, the next message popped out onto my desk.

Mr Linton,
This is still the most efficient method of communication. Now bring me the file.
Rikkard Ambrose

A snort escaped me. Efficient method of communication my foot! He just wasn't in the mood to open his mouth, that was all! But then, he had a perfect right to keep it shut, and, being my employer, he also had the perfect right to order me around to fetch files for him. So I rose to my feet and disappeared between the shelves. Once I had found the right one, I shoved it under the door to his office.

'Your file, Si–'

Another plink from the direction of the desk cut me off. I hurried back to open the message.

Mr Linton,

Bring me file 37XVI195.

Rikkard Ambrose

Blimey! He couldn't be that fast a reader, could he? No, of course he couldn't! I could see his game! He wanted to chase me around again, did he? Well then, let him chase me! I didn't mind sweating for my money!

Plink! Plink!

Message after message landed on my desk. They became faster and faster, shorter and less polite, if that was at all possible. From a shower of demanding little messages I stumbled into a rainstorm, and from that into a hailstorm!

I remembered the words I had flung at him not long ago – *You'll have to think of something better than that to get rid of me!* – and his soft *Will I, now?* in reply. It hadn't taken me long to realize that those three words had been a promise. He hadn't given up on forcing me to quit, not by a long shot.

But if this was his best effort, he truly would have to think of something better. Forcing me to carry files around? I had done that for him from the beginning! I could do it with my eyes closed, I could do it drunk, I could do it sleepwalking!

Bring me file 38XI199.

Bring me file 35IV150.

Bring me file 36VII176.

Thus it went on and on and on. I ran in a triangle between my desk, the shelves and Mr Ambrose's office door, hardly daring to sit down before with another *plink*, a new message popped out of the pneumatic tubes.

Plink.

Grab message, read.

Bring me file 35IV155.

Jump up, run to shelves, grab file, run to door, run back to desk.

Plink.

Grab message, read.

Bring me file 36VII174.

Jump up, run to shelves, grab file, run to door, run back to desk.

Plink.

Grab message, read, jump u–

I was already half-way to my feet when my eyes fell onto the piece of paper on my hand. I froze.

I had to read it twice before the message written there in Mr Ambrose's meticulously tidy hand reached my brain. Still, I did not comprehend it. I read it again. Slowly, the meaning of the sentence began to penetrate into my mind.

Mr Linton,

Tomorrow we are leaving by ship on a lengthy trip to Africa. Be at St Katherine's Docks at 7 pm sharp.

Mr Ambrose

~~**~*~*

I sat there for at least five minutes, staring at the message. I didn't have to consult my new pocket watch to know that it was at least that long. I just knew it. Maybe it was even longer. Ten minutes? Thirty? An hour? A year?

Finally, one thought managed to crystalize in my stunned mind.

Africa? Bloody Africa?

He had to be joking. Even if this was Mr Ambrose, he simply *had* to be joking!

Slowly, I rose from my chair and wandered towards his office door. I was already raising my hand to knock when the realization settled in:

He isn't joking. Bloody hell, he isn't joking!

My hand dropped and, instead of knocking, grabbed the doorknob. One twist, and I threw the door open with all the force I could muster. I crashed against the stone wall of the office with an unhealthy-sounding *crack!*

I held up the message.

'What is the meaning of this?'

Slowly, very slowly, Mr Ambrose raised his gaze from the file on which it had been concentrated. His dark eyes pierced me.

'I was about to ask the same of you, Mr Linton. Perhaps you are not aware of the subtleties of office etiquette, but you are supposed to knock your fingers against the door before you enter, not knock the door against the wall.'

'I feel more like knocking your head against the wall! What is this–' I brandished his message in the air, '–supposed to mean? Tell me!'

Leaning back, he regarded me coolly over long, steepled fingers.

'I should have thought the meaning was quite clear. We leave for Africa tomorrow. I have some business matters to attend to in Egypt and wish for you to accompany me.'

'*Egypt?* What the bloody hell do you want to go to Egypt for?'

His gaze cooled another dozen degrees. 'That is none of your concern.'

'None of my concern? I–'

'You took the money!' Suddenly he was on his feet and around the desk. It happened so fast I didn't even see him move. He was in front of me before I could blink, and I took an involuntary step backwards. 'You took the money, knowing full well what it entailed, remember?'

And I did remember.

You'll have to do whatever I say, go wherever I command. Do you understand?

Blast him!

'But... but I can't go to Egypt!' I protested. 'I got into terrible trouble for disappearing for just a few days! How on earth am I going to explain to my aunt that I'm going to be away for several weeks?'

'Months, probably,' he corrected, with a careless flick of his fingers.

'*Months?* She would go through the roof! That is absolutely impossible!'

'I see. Well, if you feel unable to fulfil the requirements of your position, I shall of course understand. Mr Stone will take care of the necessary paperwork. That will be all.'

My breath caught. I understood well enough – but I didn't want to.

'Necessary paperwork?' I managed. 'What paperwork, *Sir*?'

'Why, for your resignation, of course.'

'I have no intention of resigning!'

His dark eyes flashed. Taking two strides forward, he was in front of me in a moment, towering above me.

'Curious... You refuse to do your work, and still, you expect me to pay you? That, Mr Linton, is not something I tolerate in my employees.' Lowering to a murmur, his voice grew menacing. 'Either you do your duty and accompany me to Egypt, or your employment shall be terminated forthwith. It is your choice.'

Slowly, it dawned on me: this had been his plan all along. Burying me under a mountain of files for the day had just been a preliminary, a first stage to exhaust me and bring down my resistance. Now that I was weary from long day's work, he was launching his real attack.

Egypt! Bloody hell, I can't go to Egypt!

And he knew that. He had found the one crack in my armour I had not been able to patch up: keeping my work secret from my family. I couldn't disappear without explanation again – not if I wanted to have a home to return to. And if I tried to tell them why I had to go? That I was planning to go on a trip to Africa, dressed up as a man, to earn a living for myself? Ha! My aunt wouldn't just throw me out of the house – she'd throw me into a loony bin!

I glared at Rikkard Ambrose's cool, composed, stone face, suspicion burning in my gaze.

Does he have to go to Egypt at all? Or is it all just a trick to get rid of me?

Did it really matter? Either way, I was trapped.

Taking his pocket watch out of his tailcoat, Mr Ambrose let it snap open.

'Ten pm,' he announced. 'Apparently, it is time for you to get yourself home, Mr Linton. Your work is over for today.' Snapping it shut again, he stashed the watch away. 'In fact, your work here is over, period.'

'You... you...' I tried to think of something bad enough to scream at him, but I wasn't sufficiently well-versed in profanity. So I just glared up at his cool, chiselled, damnably perfect features.

'I shall expect your resignation on my desk tomorrow, or by the latest when I return from Egypt,' he told me, turning away and settling down at his desk again. Without even glancing at me, he resumed his paperwork. 'You may go, Mr Linton. Goodbye. I expect we shall not see each other again.'

Without a word, I whirled around and marched out of his office.

Well, I thought grimly to myself, *we'll just see about that, won't we?*

THE NICE OCEAN

He was standing near the water at St Katherine's Docks, looking out over the River Thames. The wind that was blowing grey, stormy clouds across the sky also gripped his black tailcoat and made it flutter around him like bat's wings. With his arms folded, glaring at the wide water as if he meant to conquer the river and all the oceans beyond, he looked like a darker version of Admiral Nelson, just before his triumph at Trafalgar.

It almost seemed a shame to ruin such a pretty pose. Almost.

I tapped him on the shoulder.

'Good afternoon, Sir.'

Mr Ambrose whirled around so fast he nearly knocked me over. His dark eyes were wide and, for once, I had the sublime satisfaction of seeing his mouth open with surprise. He had pretty nice teeth, incidentally. He should open his mouth more often.

'You... you...'

'Me.' I nodded and gave my best imitation of a salute. 'Mr Linton reporting for duty, Sir! Packed and ready to depart!'

'You can't be here!'

'Actually, I can. As far as I know, my presence at this particular spot does not violate any laws of physics or any moral standards. Besides, you told me to be here, didn't you?'

Slowly, his mouth slid shut until his teeth were hidden again, and his lips pressed into the usual thin line. To judge from the noises he was making, those nice teeth were being gritted. Poor darlings.

'Yes,' he informed me, keeping a tight leash on his voice. 'That does not mean, however, that I actually expected you to make an appearance.'

One of my eyebrows rose. 'What? You expected me to disobey you? Whyever would you think I would do something like that?'

More grinding noises. Dear, dear, those poor teeth...

'I thought, Mr Linton, that you mentioned there would be some slight difficulties regarding your accompanying me on this trip. Difficulties in respect to your family, if I remember correctly.'

'Oh, you mean my aunt?' I waved a dismissive hand. 'That was easy to take care of, once I gave it a little thought. I just told her that I would be visiting my grandmother in Northumberland to go man-hunting among the Northerners. The prospect of having me more than a hundred miles away combined with the possibility of my coming back with a husband or not coming back at all, soon won her over to the idea.'

His dark eyes sparkled, raking over me, then sweeping from left to right – looking for a solution, no doubt. A way out of this.

'And what will your grandmother in Northumberland say when you do not arrive?'

'Nothing. She doesn't know I'm supposed to visit her.'

'Indeed? That should cause something of a sensation when your aunt and grandmother next communicate with each other.'

I smiled. 'Not really. They *don't* communicate. They can't stand each other.'

'I see.' His eyes stopped roaming and focused on me again. 'I can empathize with the feeling. It seems you have everything quite neatly planned.'

'I have, haven't I?' Part of me had to resist the temptation to purr and stretch like a cat. This was as close to a compliment as Rikkard Ambrose had ever gotten.

'*Sahib*?' came a voice from behind a stack of crates and suitcases on the dock. '*Sahib*, I think we–'

A massive figure stepped around the pile of luggage and froze in mid-step, staring at me. I stared back. The last time I had seen Karim, he, Mr Ambrose and I had parted ways in the lair of the evil Lord Dalgliesh. True, I had known he was alive, since Mr Ambrose had said as much, but seeing him again in the flesh (and in a large amount of muscle and beard) was a relief.

'Karim!' I stepped forward, not knowing exactly why. Maybe to give the big brute a hug? 'So you got out of there alive, did you? Wonderful!'

The little black beetle eyes of the huge Mohammedan[11] bored into me. 'This creature! It is still alive? Why did you not warn me that it would be coming with us, *Sahib*?'

Oh. That's right. In my joy at seeing him alive again, I had completely forgotten for a moment that Karim and I detested each other.

'Excuse me?' My eyes narrowed. 'Did you just call me "it"? I do still have a gender, even if it's not entirely clear from my clothes which one, at the moment.'

'I didn't know he was coming,' Mr Ambrose told Karim. Both completely ignored me. I felt the strong urge to hit them over the head with a crowbar. What a pity there weren't any crowbars handy.

'My apologies, *Sahib*.' Karim bowed to his master. 'And my condolences for your continued misfortune.'

'Hello? Hello, you two, I'm standing right here!'

'You came to tell me something, Karim?'

'Yes, *Sahib*. The ship captain sent me to tell you we can start loading the luggage aboard.'

'Hello? Can one of you hear me?'

'I see. How long will that take?'

'No more than twenty minutes, *Sahib*.'

'Hello!' Stepping forward, I waved my hand in front of Mr Ambrose's face. 'I'm talking to you, with the stone face and the stuffed ears!'

'Adequate.' Ignoring me, he took his pocket watch out and let it snap open. 'Then we should be able to depart by seven thirty.' He wanted to put his watch away again, but hesitated. A muscle in the side of his face twitched. 'Or maybe it'll take a little bit longer than that.' With a cool glance at me, he added: 'It appears we have additional baggage to take aboard. We will be travelling with company. Bring the special suitcases out of my carriage.'

Baggage? I hoped very much, for his sake, that he was talking about suitcases, and not about me! I glared up at him.

'I have my own luggage, Sir, thank you very much!'

'Not the kind you'll be needing,' he told me darkly. 'Trust me.'

---

[11] I would like to point out, just because I have met with one or two people in the past who were offended by this term, that it is not at all derogatory. It is simply a term for Muslim that was predominant in the English-speaking world of the 19th century, and so I use it for reasons of historical accuracy. You can look its use up in original 19th century novels such as Rudyard Kipling's *Kim*.

Turning without another word, he marched off down the dock.

'What do you mean?' I called after him.

No answer.

'Hey! What the heck do you–?'

My voice broke off, and I forgot what I had been going to say. Eyes wide, jaw agape, I took in the vessel towards which Mr Ambrose was striding.

'*That?*' Panting in outrage, I ran to catch up with him. 'That's what we're supposed to be travelling on?'

'Indeed it is, Mr Linton.'

'Are you mad?'

'I suffer from no mental malady, Mr Linton.'

Well, if he thought *that thing* in front of us was going to make it through the Strait of Gibraltar[12] and the entire Mediterranean all the way to Egypt, I wasn't so sure about that.

The ship – if you could call it that – was large and sleek, granted, but it had ridiculously few masts. We would hardly be able to sail out of the harbour with those. In addition, the entire hull was a gleaming blackish-grey. I was no expert in nautical matters, but to me it looked as if the wood was covered with mould and rotting away.

'It'll break apart as soon as we leave the harbour!' I protested.

If we ever get that far...

'Hardly.' Marching up the gangway, Mr Ambrose stretched out an arm and knocked against the side of the ship. Instead of the wet thud I had expected, there came a hard, hollow *clank* that spoke of anything but rot.

'Iron?' I stared at the vessel. 'The whole ship is coated in *iron*?'

'Not coated in iron. *Built* from iron. Every last part of the hull.'

'In God's name, why?' I laughed. 'Are you expecting to sail into a war zone?'

'Yes.'

And with that, he left me standing and strode aboard.

'You might have mentioned that before baiting me into coming along,' I informed the empty air where he had been, then grabbed my suitcases and marched up the gangway. Not one of the sailors on deck jumped forward to help me carry them – one disadvantage of wearing trousers.

It's not a disadvantage! You're a feminist! You're supposed to love to carry your own luggage, and laugh haughtily at men who dare to offer to carry it for you!

All true. But that didn't change the fact that those suitcases really were bloody heavy!

Halfway up the gangway, I stopped and sat them down for a breather. My eyes fell for the first time on the name engraved on the prow of the ship.

Mammon

'The demon of greed.' One corner of my mouth twitched. 'How quaint.'

---

[12] For those of us who flunked geography in school: the Strait of Gibraltar is the name of the narrows that connects the Atlantic Ocean with the Mediterranean.

Rikkard Ambrose was standing at the railing, staring at the water again as if he had a personal grudge against it for being so wet. I marched up to him and prodded him in the ribs.

'Where is my cabin?'

He threw me a cool look. I sighed.

'Where is my cabin, *Sir*?'

If I have one, that is. If he doesn't expect me to sleep in the sailors' quarters.

He jutted his thumb towards the door leading down into the belly of the ship. 'Third door on the left.'

He really had a place for me? I was slightly taken aback. So instead of just going, I, like the dunderhead I am, asked the first question that popped into my mind.

'If you didn't think I was coming, why do you have a cabin for me?'

'I make it a point to always be prepared for the worst.'

Gah! Was it legal to try to strangle a man on a ship? After all, I wasn't technically on British soil anymore, so the Crown could hardly arrest me for murder!

The ship's captain, on the other hand, could, and probably would if I assassinated his employer. Besides, if I killed him, how would I get enough money to buy more solid chocolate?

Turning demonstratively to give him a good look at my new peacock waistcoat, I tightened my grip on my cases and marched off towards the ship's superstructure.[13] Inside, I found my cabin without difficulty, and was actually surprised at how exorbitantly luxuriant it was – for Mr Ambrose's standards. True, the space was miniscule, there was no furniture to speak of, and to fit into the bunk I had to bend myself like a banana, but there weren't any holes in the floor, and the walls looked freshly painted. I suppose even a man of Mr Ambrose's frugality realized that shoddy workmanship could lead to a watery grave at sea.

'And we wouldn't want him to die like that, now, would we?' I muttered, ripping open my first suitcase and starting to throw my clothes over the hooks on the wall. 'Oh no. That would mean we couldn't strangle him ourselves!'

A knock sounded from the door.

'What?' I snapped.

'Um... may I come in?'

'That depends! Who are you, and what the hell do you want?'

'My name is Coles, Sir. Charlie Coles, seaman apprentice aboard the *Mammon*. I'm bringing your suitcases, Sir.'

'I've already got them.'

'Well, apparently there are more, Sir.'

'More?' I frowned. Mr Ambrose had mentioned something about baggage... Apparently, he hadn't been referring to me after all.

'Yes, Sir. Um... quite a lot more, in fact. If you could open the door, please, they are not really very light.'

---

[13] The part of a ship that is built on top of the deck.

'All right, all right.' Sighing, I got up and strode to the door – if you can call taking one and a half steps forward across the miniscule cabin 'striding'. Pulling open the door, I revealed a scraggly young man with a boyish, freckled face, who was swaying like a landlubber under the weight of at least half a dozen suitcases.

'Good God in heaven! What's in there?'

'Stones?' the boy suggested. 'Anvils? Bricks?' He flushed. 'Begging your pardon, Sir.'

'I don't have any with me, so there's no need to beg. Come in, come in.'

Stepping aside, I beckoned him inside, and Coles staggered forward, depositing the cases on my bunk with a *thud*. Taking a deep breath, he straightened.

'Well, that's all of them.' He gave me a salute, in the process nearly banging his head into the low ceiling. 'If you should need anything else, Sir, please don't hesitate to send for me. Seamen Wood, Mason and I have been ordered by the captain to look after our passengers' every need on this trip.'

'Thank you,' I told the boy with a smile. He gave a little start, then saluted again and hurried out of the room. I stared after him for a moment, wondering about his odd reaction – then I remembered he worked for Rikkard Ambrose. He was probably not used to people in charge smiling at him.

Oh yes, Rikkard Ambrose...

'What the heck have you cooked up this time in that stony brain of yours?' I mumbled, stepping towards the suitcases. Narrowing my eyes, I pushed the lid upward. It didn't move an inch.

Locked! Blast him!

Well, if he was waiting for me to come running to beg to see inside, he would have to wait until he was blue in the face!

~~**~*~*

We were casting off. Sailors were hurrying over the deck, ropes in their hands, and commands were being shouted. Mr Ambrose stood on the quarterdeck, arms folded, face as stony as ever. Beside him stood the captain, and although he was the one shouting commands, there was no doubt who was really in command here.

'So, are you going to tell me now?' I demanded, taking my place beside the stony financial magnate.

'Tell you what, Mr Linton?'

'Why we are on this blasted cockleshell, of course! Why are we going to travel a thousand miles to Egypt?'

'Three thousand, six hundred and fifteen point one three seven six miles, actually.'

'Why the hell would I care how many miles there are? Just tell me!'

There was silence for a moment.

'Anchors aweigh!'

That didn't come from Mr Ambrose, but from the captain. I was still waiting for my answer. Finally, he unclenched his teeth.

'Fine!'

With a masterly flick of his hand, he motioned for the captain to move. With a prompt salute, the man stepped out of hearing range.

'You remember the plans that were stolen from my office?'

I cocked my head thoughtfully. 'The plans for that canal between the Red Sea and the Mediterranean that was supposed to give you control over most of the world's trade? The plans we risked our lives to retrieve? The plans that sank with that bloody ship that almost drowned us, too? Yes, I think I remember those.'

He threw me a dark look.

'The planning of that canal isn't my first attempt at establishing trade between the Red Sea and the Mediterranean. Years ago, I already established a caravan route across the Sinai Peninsula.'

I frowned. 'Then why build a canal at all?'

He threw another look my way. This was the arrogant look of a man who makes millions as easily as other people make breakfast, and expects everyone to have the same ability. 'Are you sure you have your brain switched on, Mr Linton? At the moment, my goods have to be unloaded from one ship in the Mediterranean, then packed onto camels and carried at a painstakingly slow pace all the way through the desert, only to be loaded onto ships again when they reach the Red Sea. The same goes for transporting things in the other direction. Something like that is only profitable or feasible for small, light luxury goods, not for heavy industrial goods, let alone raw materials.'

'Yes.'

'What do you mean, "Yes"?'

I raised an eyebrow. 'I mean yes, I do have my brain switched on, Sir.'

'Then use it!'

'I intend to. If your caravan route is already up and running, why are we going to Egypt?'

'That's just it.' Out of the corner of my eyes, I saw Mr Ambrose's hands curl into fists. 'It is *not* running. At least it does not seem to be at the moment. While we were away, trying to retrieve the plans for the canal from Lord Dalgliesh, this arrived at my office.'

Pulling an envelope out of his pocket, he held it up for me to see. The sharp wind blowing around us tugged at it, trying to pull it out of his hand. In spite of the paper's bending and fluttering, I could make out a strange, curly script all over it, and on the sheets of paper peeking out.

'What is that?'

'A letter from my agent in Alexandria[14], Mr Linton, telling me that my caravans across the Sinai Peninsula have recently been subject to raids.'

'Is that so?'

---

[14] The main port city of Egypt.

'Indeed it is. And not just normal raids, where the bandits grab everything they can and run. No, these were planned, coordinated and vicious attacks. Entire caravans were slaughtered – even the camels. And camels are expensive animals.'

I was gazing out over the ship at the bustling seamen. But I wasn't really seeing them. My brain was definitely switched on now, and the gears were whirring.

'Let me guess... your greatest competitor in the trade is Lord Daniel Eugene Dalgliesh.'

'Quite so. He transports the same goods I do, only he ships them around the Cape of Good Hope. A simpler process, but lengthier and more expensive.'

'What wonderful luck for Lord Dalgliesh that those bandits suddenly decided to have a go at your caravans, Sir.'

'Do you really believe in luck, Mr Linton?'

My lips twitched. 'No, Sir.'

'Neither do I.'

'So, what is the plan? We are going over there to make sure the authorities look into the matter?'

'No. We are going over there, and I am going to make *myself* the authority who looks into the matter.'

I turned to stare at him. It shouldn't have surprised me, I suppose. Rikkard Ambrose wasn't one to leave his dirty work to others. But still...

'*We* are going to hunt bandits?'

'Correct.'

'Just out of interest... How many of these bandits do you think there are?'

He gave an almost imperceptible shrug of his broad, hard shoulders. 'In each caravan, there were at least twenty men, quite used to fighting in the desert. They were slaughtered to a man, so I estimate that there must be at least forty raiders, maybe more.'

'Ah.' I tried to swallow. It didn't really work. A stubborn lump had suddenly appeared in my throat.

'We will be joined in Alexandria by a group of men who will assist us in our efforts. And several of the well-trained fighters I took on board in London will be accompanying us into the desert to lend us their weapons expertise.'

This made me feel a little better. I managed to get the lump out of my throat and speak again.

'So, once we have captured those bandits, what are we going to do with them?'

'Capture?' It would be too much to say that one of his eyebrows actually rose, but a sense of raised eyebrows definitely emanated from his unmoving features. 'What makes you think we are going to capture them?'

'Well, what else could you d–'

I broke off, as the answer abruptly occurred to me. Suddenly, the lump in my throat was back. It had gotten bigger on its short holiday.

'I don't have any use for bandits,' Mr Ambrose told me in that cold voice of his. Then he turned away, and marched towards the captain.

'What are your men waiting for, Captain? Tell them to get this ship out of the harbour! Now!'

Now? Most of me was still a bit numb from Mr Ambrose's casual revelation of our murderous plans. But another part of me couldn't help thinking: *How are we supposed to leave now? The wind is blowing in the wrong direction!*

The captain didn't seem to have noticed that, though. He saluted. 'Yes, Sir, Mr Ambrose, Sir!'

I expected him to cry out 'Set the sails' or something equally nice and nautical. But instead, he merely gestured to the nearest seaman, who opened a hatch in the deck and whistled, twice.

A shudder went through the entire ship, and suddenly I noticed black smoke rising out of one the things I had taken for masts.

'I'll be jiggered!' My eyes flitted to Mr Ambrose. 'That conniving son of a...!'

Over the next days, the constant *thump, thump* of the ship's steam engine became my constant companion. It was helpful in a way, distracting me from my own thoughts, except at night, when the bloody noise also distracted me from sleep. But even the Mammon's steam engine with its monumental powers of distraction could not pull my thoughts away from one thing:

The cases.

The suitcases which Mr Ambrose had had deposited in my miniscule cabin – without the slightest explanation! After three days of endless churning engines and watery waves, he still hadn't said a word about what was in them, the bastard! And I most certainly had not deigned to ask. Ha!

Of course, I had rigorously interrogated Seaman Charlie Coles. But even under the threat of keelhauling, he stuck to his story that he had only carried the cases, and never looked inside. Finally, I had pity on the young man and sent him off without any major mental scars from the inquisition.

What could I do? The days and weeks of the sea voyage stretched endlessly in front of me, with nothing to hold my thoughts but the contents of these suitcases. What the bloody hell could I do?

You can ask him, said a nasty little voice inside me.

No, no, no! I would not succumb to that! I would not be one of those spineless females driven out of her mind by curiosity! Not when he already thought the worst of women.

The only problem was: I *was* being driven out of my mind by curiosity. Blast!

Finally, I made a compromise with myself. I wouldn't ask. No, I definitely wouldn't. But I could mention it to him, and if per chance he happened to tell me something of his own accord – well, then everybody would be happy, wouldn't they? And I would keep my sanity!

So the next morning, when Mr Ambrose had taken up his usual position on the command deck, glaring at sailors in a way that made them work very, very efficiently, I carefully sneaked up behind him and insinuated myself beside his hard, unmoving figure, appearing calm and natural. Or at least I hoped so.

'Nice weather today, don't you think so?' I observed.

'No.'

Oh... well, to each their own opinion.

'But the sea looks nice in the sunlight, doesn't it?'

'No.'

All right, the conversation was started. It wasn't the most promising start, true, but you couldn't have everything. I cleared my throat.

'By the way... do you per chance happen to have the key to those suitcases in my cabin?'

'Yes.'

I waited for more. Maybe for an offer to give me the key. It didn't come.

'Well... maybe we could have a look inside, some day.'

That wasn't a question! It wasn't! I was not going to ask!

His dark eyes didn't even glance at me. 'You don't need the contents yet, Mr Linton.'

'Indeed?'

'You'll need it only when we arrive.'

'This... contents sounds mysterious, Sir.'

I waited again.

'Does it, Mr Linton?'

Blast, blast, blast!

'Well, even if I don't need the contents, Sir...'

I let the sentence trail off suggestively. There was nothing but silence in answer. Apparently, Mr Ambrose was immune to suggestively trailed-off sentences. So I started again.

'Even if I don't need the contents now, there is a possibility, you know, that a hypothetical person, who is most certainly not me, might be slightly interested in knowing what it is right away.'

'Indeed?'

'Yes, Sir.' I turned my head away, trying to avoid his eyes. 'You see, if this hypothetical person were trapped on a hypothetical ship, and had nothing to do all day but to think about the hypothetical contents of these hypothetical cases, this might result in a certain lack of indifference in this hypothetical person towards knowing what might be in these hypothetical cases.'

'Mr Linton?'

'Yes, Sir?'

'Are you curious about what is in the cases in your cabin?'

'What? Me? Oh, no, no, no, Sir!'

'I see.' His broad shoulders did another one of those almost imperceptible shrugs. 'If that's the case, I suppose I do not need to tell you.'

'You could, if you wanted to,' I quickly offered, with my usual awe-inspiring magnanimity. 'I don't mind listening to you. I mean, we haven't got anything else to do, have we?'

He shrugged again. 'Of course we have. We can enjoy the beautiful weather and watch the nice-looking sea.'

The bloody b–! Strangle him! Strangle him! Strangle him now!

~~**~*~*

'Tell me! Tell me now! I can't stand it any longer! Just bloody hell tell me!'

All right, as most of you will have guessed by my eloquent speech above, I finally broke down and, in a very polite and civilized manner (for me) enquired about the contents of the suitcases. It was a few days after we had watched the beautiful weather and the nice-looking sea together. Mr Ambrose was standing at the bow, and I approached him, posing my polite question.

'Tell me, or I'll shove you overboard!'

Slowly, Mr Ambrose turned towards me, his chiselled head cocked to one side, and in this very cool and detached and perfectly genuine voice said: 'Tell you what, pray?'

Is he serious?

Nonsensical question. This was Rikkard Ambrose. Of course he was being serious.

'Those suitcases! What is in them?'

He cocked his head the other way. In his sleek black tailcoat he looked like some great jungle cat contemplating the best way to slay and eat me.

'Strange. I distinctly remember you mentioning that you were not curious about this.'

'I lied!'

'Indeed? I would never have guessed.'

He is making fun of me! I know it! I just know it!

So how come, if he was making fun of me, his face was still absolutely straight, looking as if it had been carved from the heart of a mountain?

Because he's a bastard, that's why!

Not able to find any counter-argument to this, I simply kept silent, inside and out, staring doggedly at Mr Ambrose. I was not going to beg! No, I was not!

But he merely turned away and started watching the ocean again. I wondered what had ever given me the idea that it looked nice. It was grotesque! Hideous! Beastly!

'Well?' I demanded. 'Are you going to answer or not?'

He didn't look at me. 'That depends, Mr Linton. Will you ask?'

'I did!'

'I should perhaps have clarified: will you ask in a civilized, respectful manner?'

Blast him! Why did he always have to pick the things that were most difficult to do? I swallowed, gulping down a goodly portion of my pride along with my saliva.

'*Sir*, will you *please* tell me what is in those suitcases in my cabin, *Sir*?'

All right, all right, I did beg, I know! I was shameless! A disgrace to feminism!

'I will do better than that.' Stepping back from the railing, he turned around and started striding away. 'I will show you.'

I was after him in a flash. Disgrace to feminism be dashed! I wanted to know what was in those cases right now, or even yesterday if possible! My overactive mind had already started conjuring up all sorts of things.

Maybe it's weapons! Guns and grenades and God knows what else...

But why would he store them in my cabin? I highly doubted Mr Ambrose intended me to be the spearhead of our offence.

Who knows? Even a man like him might turn sensible someday.

Perhaps there was money in those cases. Money to bribe informants with, to find out where the bandits are.

Come on, do you really believe that Mr Ambrose would waste money on that? He would just glare darkly at any informant, and they would spill their guts without him having to spend a penny! Besides, if it is money, it still doesn't make sense for him to put it in your cabin, does it? It has to be something to do with you, specifically!

But what exactly? What?

We had reached the door to my cabin by now.

'You–' I began.

He pushed the door open and marched inside.

'–may go in,' I finished with a sigh. Why did I even bother?

Shrugging, I followed him in. It was a lot more difficult to fit into the miniature cabin now that, besides the giant stack of cases and me, there was also the tall figure of Rikkard Ambrose in there. I almost had no choice but to press myself up against him. I swear, it was completely incidental that I got squashed against his flat, hard front.

'Well...' I cleared my throat. 'Let's get this over with.'

Taking a key out of his pocket, he pulled one of the cases towards him. My eyes were drawn magically towards it.

What is in there? Weapons? Money? Bearer bonds?

As he leaned forward, he couldn't help but press more tightly against me. I could feel the hard, lean muscles of his arm.

Or are there maps in there? With secret, safe ways through the desert? Hm... by the way, his arm does feel rather nice...

Hey! What the heck was that thought doing in my head?

The lock snapped open. With a shove, Mr Ambrose pushed back the lid of the case and revealed the contents.

No weapons. However, it wasn't money, bearer bonds or maps, either. Oh no. It was something completely different. Nothing could have prepared me for the magnificent sight that actually met my eyes.

THE FEMALE MAN WHO IS A WOMAN

Clothes. That's what was in the suitcases. Clothes, clothes, and more clothes. And not just any kind of clothes. *Ladies'* clothes. And not just any kind of ladies' clothes, either, but the kind of ladies' clothes any girl would sell her soul for.

Any girl except me, of course! I'm totally immune to such things, being a feminist and all. I would never sell my soul for something as shallow as piece of oppressive fashion dictated to us by chauvinistic men!

Though, looking at those glamorous garments, I might decide to sell someone else's soul, if I could get away with it. Not the soul of someone I really liked, of course, like my little sister Ella. But I wouldn't really have minded handing my aunt over to the devil to get my hands on one of those dresses. If only...

Only then did it come to me:

These clothes were in *my* suitcases.

Well, not exactly my suitcases, since they had come from Mr Ambrose, but he had put them into my cabin. Did that mean...?

'Well?' I heard his cool voice coming from right beside me, and yet, somehow, from very far away. 'What do you think?'

Oh my God, oh my God, *yes*, it *did* mean what I thought it did! Yes! Yes! But... how? Where? When? And most importantly, *why*?

'I don't understand,' I said slowly, not quite ready to believe it yet. 'Why is there a case full of ladies' clothes in my cabin?'

'Not just clothes, Mr Linton.' Taking down another, smaller, case from the pile, Mr Ambrose opened it. My eyes nearly popped out of my head as the lid lifted and revealed a dazzling array of jewellery in all sizes, shapes and colours. Pearls, diamonds, sapphires and rubies mounted on rings, set in necklaces of gold and silver. I stared at Mr Ambrose, wondering whether this really was the same man I knew. Maybe it wasn't really him at all, but his generous twin brother. 'A-are you feeling all right, Mr Ambrose?'

'Of course! And if I let you touch those,' he said, gesturing to the jewels, 'be careful. They're only on loan. If one is damaged, you'll work the debt off till kingdom come.'

Thank God! Thank God, he's still himself!

Which left the question of what the heck was happening here. I watched in amazement as Mr Ambrose opened more suitcases, revealing handbags, fans, make-up, hand mirrors, parasols – everything a lady of high society could wish for to go out in style. But what I found most astounding were the clothes – *girls'* clothes!

'Do I understand you correctly?' My voice was weak. This had come as rather a shock. For weeks and weeks there had been tension crackling between Mr Ambrose and me because he did not want a female employee and had forced me to come to work dressed up as a man. And now this? I couldn't believe it. I just couldn't. 'These clothes are for me? When we arrive in Egypt, you want me to put them on?'

He nodded.

'You can put them on now, if you wish, Mr Linton. You'll have to, eventually, along with some of the rings and necklaces. But I would advise you to wait until we have reached coastal waters. The sea wind can be rather draughty in a skirt.'

Under normal circumstances, I'd have wondered how Mr Ambrose would ever know anything about how draughty a skirt was. But right then and there, I didn't care a penny. I was in shock – stunned by the sudden prospect of my approaching sex change. He would have to call me Miss! He couldn't call me 'Mr Linton' once I was in a dress, could he?

Don't bet on it, said a nasty little voice in my head, but I ignored it.

'You are serious? This isn't some stupid joke?'

He gave me a look. One of *those* looks. 'The dresses alone cost me fifty pounds ten shillings and two pence.'

Translation: It is not a joke.

'But... why? You've argued with me about this for over a month, never giving me an inch! And now this?' I gestured to the extravagance in front of me. 'Why?'

'For reasons of inconspicuousness, Mr Linton.'

'Inconspicuousness?' Tugging the embroidered lace hem of one of the dresses out of the suitcase, I snorted. 'Don't tell me this is inconspicuous!'

'It is in a way. Think about it, Mr Linton. Two men leave London – and who arrives in Egypt? A man and a girl. If there is somebody watching, somebody hostile, it is less likely the two events will be connected and conclusions drawn.'

I felt a sudden shiver go down my spine. 'Somebody watching?'

'Lord Dalgliesh,' Mr Ambrose told me darkly, 'has many eyes and ears.'

'Oh.'

That might well be true. And from what I had seen of His Lordship, it would be a very good idea to keep out of his line of sight. I still didn't really think putting me in a dress would help a lot with that, but for the moment, I shoved the thought aside.

'This is really going to happen?' I could hardly believe it. There were a thousand sensible reasons whirling inside my head why trousers were actually more practical to wear, but I couldn't ruin this with silly objections. Finally! He had caved in! Even if it was for some stupid reason, finally he was letting me be myself! 'You really mean this? You want me to dress as a woman? You want me to stop pretending to be a man?'

He stared at me, coolly, as if I had misplaced my sanity and he highly disapproved of my negligence. 'Of course not! You will keep pretending to be a man. Only as long as we are in Egypt, you will pretend to be a man who is pretending to be a woman.'

I blinked at him, not sure whether I was hearing right. 'What?'

'You heard me.'

'You... you are unbelievable!'

He nodded. 'I must admit, I have always thought myself that I am quite extraordinary.'

'That's not what I meant, blast you!'

'No?'

'No! You are a chauvinist son of a bachelor!'

His eyes narrowed a fraction of an inch. 'Show some respect, Mr Linton.'

'You are a chauvinist son of a bachelor, *Sir*!'

I don't know how he did it – the tininess of the cabin should have precluded any such movement – but somehow he managed to take a threatening step towards me.

'What is it you want, Mr Linton? Do you want to wear these dresses?'

78

'I want for you to not call me 'Mister' all the time! I want to be myself!'

'Does being yourself involve wearing women's clothing?'

'Yes, but–'

'Then I suggest you hold your tongue before I change my mind and take these back,' he told me, with a jerk of his hand towards the open cases. 'Do you understand?'

I opened my mouth to argue.

'*Do you understand, Mr Linton?*'

Slowly, agonizingly slowly, I forced my mouth shut again. 'Yes, Sir!' I managed to get out between clenched teeth.

'Adequate. I shall see you at dinner.'

And with that he whirled around – *How does he manage to whirl in a place that isn't big enough to scratch your nose in?* – and stalked out of the room.

I glared balefully after him. Then, deciding he was not worth my attention, I slammed the door shut and directed my baleful glare at the dresses instead. Dressing up as man who dressed up as a woman! Bah! How did he imagine that? Did he think I was going to walk around in the heat of the desert in women's clothes with a complete set of men's clothes underneath? Or did he just mean some sort of mindset, wherein I never forgot that although I was wearing girl's clothing, while I was in his employ, I was still technically a man?

Well, if that's what he meant, he could jolly well stick his opinions about gender where the sun didn't shine! I was a girl! *Basta!*

Maybe it's time to show him that.

My gaze focused on one of the dresses in particular, and turned from baleful to thoughtful. Should I? Should I not? Should I? Should I not?

I hesitated, gazing down at the fabulous dress. Then, suddenly, I dashed forward and grabbed it. Oh, to hell with Mr Ambrose and his breezy skirts! I was going to show him that a girl could fare just as well on a ship as man could!

I was just finished with dressing, and was gazing self-satisfactorily at myself in the mirror, when a knock came from the door.

'Yes?' I called. 'Enter!'

The door swung open, and a sailor stuck his head into the cabin. 'Mr Linton, Sir, the captain just sent me to tell you that dinner is almost ready and that–'

It was then that he noticed the lack of masculinity in the room. His eyes went wide. I turned towards him with a charming smile.

'That dinner is almost ready and that...' I encouraged him.

'Um... excuse me, Miss, I... I was looking for Mr Linton.'

'Yes.' I nodded. 'So now that you've found me, what is it?'

'Err... you are *Mr* Linton?'

The sailor was clearly having trouble rearranging his world view.

I shrugged and gave him another encouraging smile. 'In a way. Though it would probably better if you called me "Miss Linton" from now on.'

'Um, yes, Si– err, Miss.'

'Now, what was it the captain sent you to tell me?'

'The captain?' The sailor blinked. He had apparently quite forgotten the existence of his superior officer, and needed a moment to retrieve his memories.

'Ah. Of course. The captain. He wanted me to tell Mr Linton – you, that is – that dinner is almost ready, and he intends to open a box of his best Virginia Cigars today, if you would care to join him for one.'

In his frazzled state of mind, it took the poor man a moment to realize he had just offered a lady in silk and satin the opportunity to smoke cigars. When it dawned on him, he clutched the doorframe, and almost fainted.

'Oh my God, Miss, I... I'm so sorry, I... was supposed to tell Mr Linton, and you... well, and I... Oh God!'

He shot me a pleading glance. I took pity on him.

'Tell the captain I will be along directly,' I told him, curtsying. 'And tell him I will be only too happy to try one of his Virginia Cigars. I look forward to the experience.'

~~**~*~*

Have you ever seen the face of a sturdy, conservative ship captain watching a nineteen-year-old girl smoking cigars? No? And have you ever watched the twitching jaw muscles of a financial magnate sitting in the same room, staring so coldly at your cigar that by rights it should be extinguished and frozen? You haven't done that either? Well, then you haven't lived.

It wasn't just this evening that was quite amusing. The rest of the journey to Egypt in its entirety turned out to be rather entertaining, and all thanks to my new attire. True, the skirts were a bit draughty outside, but the sailors' faces as they tried to puzzle out the mysterious transformation of Mr Victor Linton more than made up for it. As did the look on Mr Ambrose's face whenever he caught his men staring at me.

'Land ahoy!'

The cry from the ship's highest mast came out of the blue. I was down in my cabin, and only heard it by luck because the engines were, for once, running at low steam to allow the men a chance to sleep. It took me about four and a half seconds to race up on deck.

'Where is it?' I demanded, materializing beside Mr Ambrose at the bow. 'Where is it, where is it?'

'Not in sight yet, from down here,' was his cool reply. 'If you want to climb up the mast in that dress, be my guest.'

'When will it be in sight? When?'

'I possess no accurate information on the matter.'

'Oh my God... I'm going to see Alexandria with my own eyes! *Alexandria!*'

'Yes.'

'And the pyramids? Do you think we could visit the pyramids?'

'I hardly think that the bandits we are looking for have their hideout in an ancient pharaonic tomb.'

'Not to look for bandits, of course! Just to see the pyramids!'

'What purpose would that serve?'

'It's sightseeing! It isn't supposed to serve a purpose, you do it because you want to soak up the atmosphere of a long forgotten and mysterious ancient world!'

'I am quite content with concentrating on the contemporary one.'

Despairing of the discussion, I leaned over the railing to peer more closely into the distance. And yes, through the morning haze, I could see something there. Or at least I thought I could. Maybe I couldn't. But then again, maybe...

It didn't take long for my indecision to become certainty. And then, it slowly morphed into awe.

'The Port of Alexandria,' I heard Mr Ambrose voice from my right. And I was so stunned by the sight before me that I wasn't even astounded about him voluntary unclamping his lips to offer information. 'One of the oldest ports in the world, maybe *the* oldest. The first facilities were probably built over four thousand years ago. There, do you see that stretch of land?'

'Yes,' I muttered, and indeed, I could see it. It was a faint golden line on the horizon. And behind it... No. That couldn't be ships behind the land, could they? Unless the Egyptians had decided to take the expression 'ship of the desert' to a whole new level.

'That's a peninsula,' Mr Ambrose explained as if having read my mind. 'It stretches out into the ocean, and then in a T-shape to both sides, protecting the harbour against the elements.'

I threw him a look. 'You're unusually chatty this morning, Sir.'

He caught my look easily, and hurled it back with double force. 'It's always best to know as much as possible about your surroundings when you're venturing into enemy territory. And make no mistake – this *is* enemy territory. Dalgliesh has a lot of influence here. We're not on a sightseeing trip.'

'Yes, Sir.'

'Once we land, if you possibly can, try to deport yourself like a proper lady.'

'I always do!'

In answer from him, there came only silence. A very meaningful silence.

'I *do*,' I repeated in an agree-with-me-now-or-I'll-bash-your-head-in tone. 'Always!'

'Hm. Well. Do your best. We don't want to arouse suspicion.'

'Yes, Sir.'

I did the best I could. I really did. I walked like a proper lady. I smiled like a proper lady. I even held my parasol like a proper lady, quite voluntarily, to protect myself from the merciless sun. But I couldn't keep my eyes from almost bugging out of their sockets. This was it! What I had been waiting for so many years! Adventure and excitement in a mysterious foreign country, far removed from the drab life of London, far away from balls and aunts and pesky suitors. As we sailed into the circular harbour, it seemed to welcome me with open arms. I took a deep breath of the sea air, filled with the smell of spices.

'Let's go!'

The moment we touched land, I was rudely awakened from my dreams. Mr Ambrose grabbed my arm and dragged me down the gangway to a waiting carriage. To anyone else it must have been looking as though he was courteously guiding me – but I felt the tightness of his grip and knew better. He wouldn't let go.

'Get in!' he hissed, under his breath. 'And smile! Pretend we are two happy people on holiday!'

'Is this really necessary?'

'There are three men in kaftans[15] watching us from over there. And another one is watching from the fishing boat to your left. Smile!'

I pulled my lips into a carnivorous grimace. 'How about this?'

'You'll need to work on it.'

'Why don't *you* smile, too?'

'I'm a man, in the company of a woman. Nobody expects me to.'

'*You arrogant, impertinent...!*'

'Smile, I said! And get into the coach.'

Reluctantly, I did as he said. Mr Ambrose climbed in behind me and thumped his new cane-and-sword against the roof.

'Drive!'

The coach jerked forward, and I shot him a mutinous look.

'I still don't see why you wanted me to put all this on,' I said, gesturing to my dress, made from the finest blue and red silk, with golden embroidery. The hands with which I was gesturing were bedecked with jewels. 'I mean... it's very flattering, but it's not really convenient for bandit-hunting.'

'I told you: it is more inconspicuous. A man with his secretary – that might arouse suspicion, particularly if agents of Dalgliesh are indeed watching, and they know of me. But a man and a girl...'

'...will be even more conspicuous. Conspicuous? Ha, what am I saying, it will be the biggest scandal of the city within a few hours! People will think I'm your mistress, or even worse, and they'll talk about it from sunup till sundown. It's not exactly considered decent or normal for gentlemen to travel with strange girls!'

'Not with strange ones, no.'

I blinked at him, but he didn't seem in the mood to explain his cryptic answer, so I let it rest. What did I care about my reputation in the city of Alexandria? I would leave this place again in a few weeks and probably never see it again.

The drive to the hotel was long and hot. To judge from the noise, the streets were as crowded as could be. I heard conversations, yelling and cursing in what I assumed to be Arabic, but I couldn't see a soul. Mr Ambrose had pulled the blinds down, and I was too apprehensive of the reasons to ask him to pull them up again.

Spies? Sharp shooters? Something worse?

Finally, the carriage came to a halt. Opening the door, Mr Ambrose revealed a staircase leading up to a... was it a royal palace?

---

[15] A full-length garment used by Egyptian men (similar to a coat). It often is often made out of bright, striped cloth.

It certainly looked like one, towering above us almost as high as Empire House, with finely crafted statues of ancient Egyptian kings decorating the façade and blooming gardens all around. But the words 'Luxor Hotel' over the entrance, and the uniformed porter already waiting to take our cases, indicated something other than a royal residence.

'You spent enough money to rent rooms in this place?' I raised an eyebrow at Mr Ambrose. 'Are you sure you're feeling well?'

Surprisingly, he didn't try to bite my head off. No, he simply nodded and said: 'It was necessary.'

Suspicion rose in me like a firework rocket. When Mr Ambrose deemed luxury necessary, something was fishy. 'Necessary? For what?'

'For our disguise. We have to fool Dalgliesh's agents, remember? We have to make them believe that I am not Mr Rikkard Ambrose, not the man they have been instructed to look for. Come.'

'I don't see what that has to do with–'

'Come, I said.' And taking me by the hand, he pulled me from the coach, steering me up the steps of the hotel. The driver was left looking after the luggage. We entered a luxurious lobby filled with marble columns and chandeliers, at the end of which stood a portly man behind a dark wood counter. He didn't have the same sallow expression as Sallow-face back home, preferring instead to pester the world with an ingratiating smile, but I immediately recognized him as a colleague of the sour watchdog that guarded Mr Ambrose's front hall. This was the head porter.

'Welcome to the Luxor Hotel,' he proclaimed, rubbing his smarmy little hands. 'Where we fulfil your every fantasy of an exotic holiday while providing every comfort civilized society can offer. Might I enquire after your name, Sir?'

'Richard Thompson,' Mr Ambrose lied with a cool ease that I just had to admire. 'There is a suite reserved in my name here.'

'Only one suite? To share?' The porter's eyebrows rose. 'Yes, there is a suite in your name reserved here, Mr Thompson, but... I hope you will not find it impertinent of me to ask what your relationship with this young lady here is.' He bowed to me, and his little pig eyes sparkled with curiosity for scandal.

I sighed. It was just as I had told Mr Ambrose. A man travelling alone with a girl? Such a thing was beyond scandalous, it was unthinkable! Unless of course the two of them happened to be...

I froze, horrified realization washing over me. My eyes flew down to the rings on my fingers – the rings Mr Ambrose had insisted I put on!

'This,' he said, taking me by the hand and planting a gentle kiss on my cheek, 'is Lillian, my lovely wife.'

The Art of Suggestive Name-calling

I showed admirable self-restraint. I actually managed not to kill him right there in the hotel lobby.

Be strong, I told myself, while a jabbering boy in hotel livery lead us through the hallways of the Luxor. *Brutus planned and schemed for months before finally killing Julius Caesar. If some measly Roman general can wait that long, you can keep a grip on yourself until we reach the hotel room and the door is shut.*

We reached a door made from the same dark wood as the front desk. A large and ornate number 79 shone on the polished surface. With more jabbering, the nervous boy opened the door for us and showed us in. I hardly glanced at the magnificent hallway of the suite. My focus was all on the man who had entered before me and was now turning to face me.

The boy said something else in Arabic. I didn't listen, but instead kept my full focus on Mr Ambrose.

'Send him away!' I growled at him. Maybe it wasn't the wisest thing to try and give Rikkard Ambrose orders, but right now I didn't give a penny about wise.

Mr Ambrose nodded to the boy and jerked his head, coolly. The youth didn't need any more encouragement. He was out of the door without even trying to get a tip.

For two or three seconds, there was a heavy silence in the room – at least ten tons and seven hundred and sixty-two pounds worth of silence. I stared at Mr Ambrose. Mr Ambrose stared at me.

'*Wife?*' I repeated.

He cocked his head, and shrugged.

Shrugged!

'I,' I repeated very slowly and clearly, 'am your *wife?*'

I do not believe I had ever managed to make my voice sound this deadly dangerous before. I was like a female tiger with fire in my belly! He didn't seem to notice or care, but simply looked at me with those cool, dark eyes of his.

'I told you, we have to be inconspicuous.'

'Inconspi–!' My voice failed me for just a moment. 'If I murder you and hang your body from the balcony, will that be inconspicuous?'

'You will do nothing of the kind. You are much too happy to murder anyone.'

'*Happy?*'

Was he delusional? Or on drugs?

'Of course you are,' he informed me in a tone as if he were explaining that one plus one made two. 'Deliriously happy. After all, you are on your honeymoon with the man of your dreams, my dear.'

'*Honeymoon?*'

I didn't seem able to do anything but incredulously repeat his last words. I should have thrown something at him, or slapped him, but all I could do was stare open-mouthed.

On your honeymoon... you're on your honeymoon with Rikkard Ambrose...

'Yes,' he told me, his face about as emotional as a slab of granite. 'We had what I believe is commonly referred to as a "whirlwind romance". Losing much of our sanity in the process, we fell passionately in love and got married in a small village near London not a week ago. We are a wasteful and completely irresponsible couple who actually went so far as to spend money on a frivolous pleasure trip called a "honeymoon". Although our marriage has already lasted more than a week, we are somehow, miraculously, still filled with love, tenderness, passion and similar superfluous emotions.'

'You've been planning this all along,' I whispered. 'If I decided to come along, you were going to use me like this from the very start!'

'Oh yes.'

'*Why*? Why this damn charade?'

He fixed me with his ice-cold eyes. 'Simple. You and I both know that the agents of Lord Dalgliesh are watching the port. They probably have been given my description, and yours, too. No matter how I disguise myself – as a tradesman, an army officer, a beggar – my disguise will be penetrated, and we will be hunted down. Even if I arrive as an oriental pasha with an elephant, ten peacocks and a horde of servants in tow, Dalgliesh will find out who I am sooner or later. He knows me too well. And precisely because he knows me well, there is only one thing he will never ever expect: me arriving in the company of a *girl*.'

He took a step towards me, his eyes boring into me.

'Especially,' he continued, his voice dropping to a murmur, 'a girl I am in love with.' Raising his hand, he stroked a finger down my cheek, once.

My heart stopped beating. Really, honestly, it did! Then it started up again, at twice its usual pace, doing its best to jump right out of my chest.

Love?

Suddenly, I realized how very, very close he was standing. His dark eyes were wide and stormy as the open sea. It felt as if I could fall right into them, and this time, I would not escape drowning. I would not want to.

Dark eyes. Deep eyes. Loving eyes?

Could it really be? My skin was suddenly tingling all over, the air crackling with expectation.

A girl I am in love with...

'So,' he told me, stepping back, his tone suddenly businesslike again. 'You see why we have to pretend to feel this ridiculous emotion towards each other, don't you?'

My heart screeched to an abrupt halt.

Pretend?

Of course, Lilly! This is all part of his scheme! Why the hell would you think that Rikkard Ambrose would ever be interested in marrying you? And, more to the point, why would you feel disappointed that he isn't?

Maybe because, as a wife, I would have prime murder opportunities? Yes, that had to be it! I could smother him with a pillow, or slip a little something into his nightcap, or... or... the possibilities were endless! If looks alone could kill, Mr Rikkard Ambrose would certainly have been nothing but a smouldering pile of ashes right now.

'Tell me,' I ground out between clenched teeth, 'that you aren't serious!'

He cocked his head. 'This continued insistence on your part that I am prone to jesting is getting out of hand. So far, have I displayed a tendency to pleasantry of any kind?'

'No.'

'There you are. I have explained my plan to you, and the reasons behind it. We have to hide from Dalgliesh's agents. So for now, to anyone who asks, we are Mr and Mrs Thompson, a happy couple of newlyweds from Hazlemere.'

'*Hazlemere?*'

'A picturesque little village in Buckinghamshire. Just the sort of place new-lyweds come from.'

'But... but...' I spluttered. 'I can't pretend to be your *wife!*'

He seemed surprised by this. 'Why not? All you need to do is wear a ring.'

'That's not what I meant, blast you! I meant I can't *pretend* to be *in love with you!*'

'Why?'

I stared at him in disbelief. Was he serious? God, why was I asking myself that? He was Rikkard Ambrose! Of course he was serious! He was also completely and utterly nuts if he thought I was going along with this!

'Apart from the fact that it was a dastardly trick of yours to force me into this without asking my permission first?'

He nodded, clearly impatient. 'Yes, apart from that, of course.'

My hands twitched, itching to reach for his neck.

Breathe, Lilly! Breathe deeply and slowly! Murder is probably against the law in Egypt!

'Well?' Mr Ambrose demanded, his gold gaze raking over me as if we were back in his office in London and I was taking too long with sorting through a couple of files. 'Why can't you pretend to be utterly and deliriously in love with me? It shouldn't be hard. I am me, after all, and you are female.'

My mouth dropped open. The arrogant son of a...! 'Why? Simple! Because... because...'

I hesitated.

Bloody hell, it wasn't so simple, after all. Why exactly couldn't I pretend to be in love with him? It wouldn't exactly be the first time I had pretended or acted a role. I had pretended to be a secretary in male costume for weeks now. After that, a bride on her honeymoon shouldn't be that difficult, should it?

There was only one problem.

I wasn't just going to be *a* bride. I was going to be *his* bride. The bride of Mr Rikkard Ambrose. Assumed name or not, he was still he. And I was I.

His eyes narrowed a fraction. 'Why?' he demanded for the third and, I could tell from his tone, very last time. There was thunder threatening in his voice.

'Because... because I can't stand you!'

He shrugged. 'Irrelevant.'

'Because I'm a feminist!'

'Also irrelevant. I pay you to work for me, not to hold absurd political opin-ions.' Taking a sudden step towards me, he forced me to retreat, his dark form towering above me. The aura of power radiating off his hard body was almost palpable. 'You will be my wife, Miss Linton – for the next few months. After that, you can feminise and frolic wherever and whenever you want. But for the next few months, *you are mine!*'

'No!'

'Yes!' I wasn't fast enough. He was already close enough for me to feel his breath on my face, the force of his dark, sea-coloured eyes pulling at my soul. 'You will.'

'N–'

Before I could finish my denial, his finger was at my lip, cool, hard, implacable.

'Think very carefully before you speak, Miss Linton.' There was a distinct note of threat in his voice. A shiver of mingled fear and excitement travelled down my spine. 'Remember your agreement, when you took my money. *Do whatever I say, go wherever I command...* Do you remember?'

Good God! Had he been planning all this even then?

What a stupid question. Of course he had.

I swallowed. 'I remember.'

'Well then?' He bent down from his towering height, until I could feel the hard muscles of his chest against mine, and his mouth almost brushed my lips. I could barely breathe, so thick with delicious tension was the air around me. 'What is your answer? Miss Linton, will you be my wife?'

'Yes.'

The word was out of my mouth before I even had begun to think. I stood there, dazed, uncomprehending.

Bloody hell, bloody stinking hell! How did that just come out of my mouth? And more importantly, *why?*

Maybe, suggested a nasty little voice in my head, *because he had phrased it just in that way – a way that almost sounded like a real proposal.*

No! That couldn't be the reason! Definitely not! Because that would mean I really wanted to ... that I would have said yes if he asked–

No, no, no! Absolutely not!

'Adequate.' With a cool nod, Mr Ambrose stepped back again, the pseudo-romantic tension in the air bursting like a bubble, leaving me reeling. 'Then we can get to the details of our disguise.'

'D-details?'

'Yes.'

Blast him! How did he manage to keep his voice so businesslike when mine felt like breaking any moment?

I cleared my throat. 'Details like what, Sir?'

'Like names and forms of address, of course. It is extremely unlikely, for instance, that a married couple would have enough sense to address one another by their surnames. And I doubt very much the female could be so well mannered as to address her husband as "Sir".' Reaching up, he stroked his chin for a moment – a gesture of contemplation I had never seen before. Was there a slight crease between his eyebrows? But... he never moved his facial muscles! What titanic struggle had to be taking place inside him?

I waited, my anticipation rising. Finally, he growled and jerked his head in annoyance. He looked as if he had just received news that he had to part with a thousand pounds on the spot.

'There seems to be no way around it. For the duration of our stay in Egypt, I give you temporary leave to address me by my first name, Miss Linton.'

I blinked at him. *This* was what had been causing his emotional turmoil? 'How... how very gracious of you.'

'Yes, I know. Married people really ought to have better manners. First names. Bah!'

'Yes – terrible! You might get the idea that they actually liked each other.' No reaction. Not for the first time I noticed that Mr Rikkard Ambrose was impervious to sarcasm.

'Probably using my first name won't even be enough,' he added sourly. 'Newlyweds are notoriously uncourteous and informal. You had better use an abbreviated form to give an appropriate impression of conjugal familiarity.' He considered the matter for a moment. '"Rick" would be an acceptable choice.'

I thought about it for a moment, rolling the name around my tongue. Then, suddenly, an idea came to me, and a grin spread over my face. 'I'm sure there are other abbreviations for your lovely name. How about "Dick"?'

He gave me a glare that sent shivers down my back. But my smile only widened. Inside, I was rolling on the floor with laughter, gasping for air. Ha! Payback time!

'It's "Rick", Miss Linton! No discussion!'

'Just as you say, ... *Dick*.'

His glare cooled another dozen degrees. 'I'm your employer, Miss Linton! You are obligated to follow my orders!'

In return for his ferocious glare, I gave him back a cheerful smile. 'Apparently, you're not my employer. You're my husband now, Dick. Haven't you heard?' My eyes were dancing. Good God, why had I been worried about this just a moment ago? This was brilliant! 'Wives lovingly tease their husbands all the time. It's their job. They also complain, argue and never shut up when they're supposed to. It's all part of the wonderful tapestry of married life.'

He took a deep breath. For a moment, I saw his little finger twitching – but then, in a movement so imperceptible you'd need a microscope to be sure it was there, one corner of his mouth lifted.

Dear God... What... That couldn't be a sm—

He moved before I could finish the thought. Suddenly, he was right in front of me, his ice-heart energy crackling in the air around me. His dark eyes were burning. 'Glad to see you're embracing your role so thoroughly, *Wife*.'

'Th-thank you.'

Damn the stutter! That didn't come out nearly as sarcastically as it was supposed to! I stared up into his eyes, and he stared back, implacable, cold and very, very determined.

'Do you know,' he murmured, slowly leaning towards me, 'what else is part of married life?' I started to back away, but he moved with me, coming ever closer.

'No. What are you talking about?'

He ignored my question, moving closer still. Blast, he was just a few inches away now – close enough for me to feel the heat of his skin and the freezing, calculating ice of his gaze, mingling in one irresistible maelstrom. Too close! Far too close!

'Do you know,' he breathed 'what a married couple does all the time? Especially newlyweds, who have just found each other and are still discovering all the enticing possibilities?'

'No!' I snapped. 'I have no clue what you–'

He went for me. I didn't have a hope of avoiding him. His arms were around me in a millisecond, caging me in, and then his lips came crashing down on mine. They were soft, oh so soft, yet somehow incredibly hard and demanding. They were exactly as I remembered from his last kiss!

Strange, considering you always thought that you hallucinated that one, right?

Well, apparently I was pretty good at hallucinating realistically! Bloody hell!

His mouth was voracious. It claimed mine in a race of burning need, sending shiver after shiver down my back – but shivers weren't strong enough for this! A shock followed in their wake, paralysing me, making me go limp in his arms. Arms that were drawing me closer towards him, holding me against his rock-hard body. My knees gave way, and spots danced in front of my eyes like sparkling snowflakes.

Blimey! Was I hallucinating again?

No, you idiot! You're not drunk this time!

Wasn't I? I *felt* drunk. Drunk with a delicious heat that filled my body from tip to toe, from lips to hairclips. I wanted more of it! More of *him*! Desperately! But how? *How?*

A strong, familiar hand slipped up behind my back, gripping my neck, holding it in place. His lips pressed harder against mine, forcing them open, and he plunged into my mouth with his...

Oh...

Oh God... so *that's* how!

His tongue was like a spear of desire, my mouth a gaping wound that wanted me to die from bliss. Around the clashing of our mouths, a little moan escaped me. His tongue stroked, caressed, kept in constant motion, never ceasing the attack on me. Meanwhile, his lips kept busy, holding me prisoner with a persistent, intoxicating rhythm that sent waves of delicious heat through my body.

How long did it go on?

Minutes?

Hours?

Years?

I didn't know, and I couldn't have cared less! I was in a daze. I felt like Tantalus must have felt when he pinched Ambrosia from the table of the gods to see what the heavenly drink might taste like. I couldn't do or say anything, until finally, out of the steaming hot fog of my mind, slowly a thought appeared:

What... what the heck is he doing?

I wasn't sure. It seemed, technically, as though he was kissing me, but... that couldn't happen in reality, could it? In drink-induced fantasies in which he and I temporarily lost our minds and forgot we hated each other's guts, maybe, but not in *real life*, for God's sake! That was impossible!

Well, judging by the way he's massaging your quail-pipe[16] at the moment, it is very, very possible!

Oh my God! He really was! He really was kissing me!

Yes, you silly tart! So you had better do something about it, and right speedily!

Of course! I had to! I was a thingummy, after all. A... what was it called again? With Mr Ambrose's lips devouring mine it seemed rather hard to remember...

Feminist! You're a feminist!

Right! I was a feminist, and I couldn't just let random men kiss me! No, I couldn't. No matter how nice it felt to have his hands exploring my...

My inner feminist screeched out in protest. *Do something! Now!*

Right. So... what to do?

Sliding my arms up, I pushed against Mr Ambrose's chest. It had no effect whatsoever. I pushed harder. Still, nothing happened. Except that is, for his tongue stroking over mine again, sending another wave of delirious heat through my body, making me shiver with...

Concentrate! Damn you, concentrate!

Um... on what did I have to concentrate again?

Getting away! You want to get away from that bastard who is using you!

Oh. That's right. I had almost forgotten that.

Once more, I pushed, harder this time. When that still didn't yield any results, I clenched my hand, and let my fist fly! It thudded uselessly against Mr Ambrose's rock-hard chest. Again, and again. I was pommelling him like a punching bag now, but his arms were still around me, and his lips, so soft, so seductive, still on mine. Damn him! He was as solid as a cliff, defying the waves of a thunderstorm. A cliff with a dozen splendidly naked male sirens on top, singing to me to come closer, to sink into the kiss, to stop fighting...

No! my inner feminist screamed. *Bloody hell, no! Do something!*

So I did. Reaching up, I slid my hands towards his head, grabbed hold of both his ears and pulled, hard!

'Arrr!'

To judge by the growl that escaped him, that seemed to work much better at getting his attention than punching him had. He lurched back, freeing my lips for the first time in I don't know how long. I sucked in a deep breath, in preparation for the insults I was going to fling at him. He deserved it! He deserved every bad name in the book! How dare he kiss me like that?

---

[16] A Victorian expression for 'tongue' – but, oddly enough, only a woman's tongue. I have no idea why. Maybe because the lady in question is literally smoking hot.

I opened my mouth to hurl the first expletive in his face – and then I was suddenly charging forward, kissing his face, his throat, his sculpted chin... every part of him that I could reach!

Good God! What the heck was I doing?

Good question, that! What about your feminist principles?

My hands slid up his hard body. For the first time since he had tackled me, I really had a chance to feel him, to explore the hard ridges of muscles under the black cotton. Blimey... To hell with my principles!

'How about this?' I whispered sweetly, letting go of his earlobes with my hands and taking one between my teeth instead, gently nibbling. 'Is this part of married life, too, *Dick*?'

'Do not,' he growled, his deep, ice-cold voice vibrating all the way through my body, 'call me that!'

I smiled against his skin, pressing a soft kiss on his earlobe. 'Just as you say, Dick!'

Suddenly, I was flying. In my shock I didn't understand what was happening, only seeing vague shapes of furniture rushing by, and only feeling his hands around my waist, lifting me higher and higher. A moment later, my back slammed into the wall, driving all the breath out of me.

'I told you,' he repeated, his voice even colder now, driving a hot surge of need up inside me, 'not to call me that. Understand?'

'Y-yes, Sir.'

His eyes blazed, flaming fires reflected on a stormy ocean. 'What is my name as long as we are here, Wife?'

'Richard!'

'Indeed it is. And for short?'

I contemplated the question for one breathless moment. Then, from between the wild strands of hair that had tumbled into my face, I grinned up at him, mischievously. 'Dick!'

He was on me in an instant. His tongue invaded my mouth, hungry and determined. I met it with my own this time, clashing, coiling, fighting for the right to rule. That didn't stop the hot waves of want from spreading down from my mouth all through my body. From the walls around us, the portraits of dignified Egyptian statesmen looked down at us disapprovingly. I couldn't give a flying fig for their opinion! Let them stare! I didn't even care for the moment that my inner feminist was swinging a protest sign. Later, I would care, I knew. Later, I would care like hell! But right now, he was kissing me and I was... floating. Blissfully.

My blissful floating was interrupted by the sound of the door opening. Ripping my eyes open – somehow, they had slid shut during the kiss – I saw the figure of a dark-skinned young maid in the doorway. Her eyes went wide at the sight of us. But nowhere near as wide as my eyes went at the sight of her seeing us!

'Oh.' A small smile spread over her face. 'Excuse, please, Lady, Sir. I not know anyone in here. Most sorry. I see nothing. Nothing at all.'

I opened my mouth to give some explanation, any explanation that would explain away my having my lips pressed to Mr Ambrose's lips that didn't involve a passionate kiss. Mr Ambrose was faster.

'No problem,' he said, with a dismissive wave, turning around, and bending towards me to place tender kiss on my cheek. 'We have all the rest of the day still left, after all.'

And then he winked.

Mr Ambrose. Mr I-am-a-block-of-stone Ambrose *winked*! Or at least he moved his eyelid. Maybe he was just getting rid of a speck of dust. But to the maid, it sure as hell looked as if he was winking. *Winking*!

The maid giggled and curtsied. 'Yes, Sir, Lady. I not interrupt again, Sir, Lady. I not see anything.'

And with that, she turned and hurried from the room, closing the door behind her.

I turned to gape up at the man beside. 'What have you done? Now the entire hotel will think we are... we are...'

'Married?' he enquired.

'Yes! No! I don't know!'

'Could you clarify that a little?'

'She's going to tell her friends, and they are going to tell their friends, and they their friends, and in half an hour it'll be all over the hotel that we are in here doing... stuff!'

He cocked his head. If not for the fact that this was Mr Ambrose, a man who had as much emotion inside him as a volcano had snow, I might have thought there was amusement in his eyes. 'Stuff?'

I felt my ears starting to burn. 'You know! Honeymoon stuff!'

'Which, considering the fact that we are *supposed* to be on our honeymoon, would be utterly scandalous, of course.'

My ears were in danger of spontaneous combustion by now. 'You're impossible!'

I tried to twist out of his hold, but his hands were too strong, blast him! Pulling me closer, he leaned down towards my face. His eyes darkened, and his lips opened a fraction.

'Don't you da–'

My protest was cut off by our mouths melding together. And I, instead of picking up the vase on bedside table beside me and smashing it over his rock-hard head, like I should have done, snaked my arms around his neck and pulled him closer.

God! What was wrong with me?

When we finally broke apart, I was panting like a panther. He, of course, was so cool and collected you'd think he was freshly imported from Iceland! His dark eyes bored into me.

'I think we have discussed the matter of convincingly acting the married couple thoroughly enough for today, don't you?'

His voice was just as cool as the rest of him, damn him! How was that possible? I was panting, burning up inside with a hot, persistent need to... do something, do anything! Preferably with him! And he – he just stood, there, gazing at me with those unfathomable eyes.

I raised my chin. 'I quite agree.'

'Adequate.' Raising one hand, he stroked one long, lean finger down the side of my face. 'It's quite late. What do you say to a romantic candle-lit dinner on the hotel terrace, my dearest love?'

I fancy not many people could manage to make the words 'my dearest love' sound like 'my obedient minion'. Rikkard Ambrose did it without the slightest problem.

I bridled. 'You can take your romantic dinner and shove it up your–!'

'Let me rephrase,' he cut me off. His arms were like a vice around me, holding me in place. 'We will go down and have a romantic candle-lit dinner. *Now!*'

I glared up at him, feeling sparks fly from my eyes. 'And we'll smile, and giggle and show everyone how very much in love we are?'

'That, and we will discuss how best to hunt bloodthirsty bandits in the desert.'

'How very romantic!'

'I always do my best.' Leaning forward lightning fast, he brushed his lips against mine – hardly a touch, nothing compared to what he had done before, and yet... It was a promise. A promise of things to come.

Good Lord... What had I gotten myself into?

Releasing me from his hold and stepping away, Mr Rikkard Ambrose marched over to the door, turned and held his hand out towards me. His dark eyes seemed to gleam in the failing light.

'Come, my love.'

THE PLIGHT OF MY PLIGHTED TROTH

Some things that happen to you make you feel *really* strange. You know the moments I mean – those moments where the world is standing on its head and everything suddenly seems unreal. Like, for instance, the time I discovered that my innocent little sister Ella had for years been conducting an illicit affair behind her family's back. Or the time a gentleman I had been dancing with at a ball complimented me on what good a dancer I was, after I had trampled on his feet the whole evening. Or the time my aunt actually, once in her life, said something nice to me in front of witnesses.

But none of these strange and mysterious occurrences, inexplicable and awe-inspiring though no doubt they were, could in any way compete with what was happening right now. None of these events had made me feel half as strange as I felt walking down the corridor of the Hotel Luxor in a dark red silk dress, a sparkling wedding ring on my finger and a darkly handsome Rikkard Ambrose on my arm.

Oh dear, merciful God... What is happening to me?

But if I had thought it would be strange to just be walking beside Mr Ambrose, I hadn't reckoned with the real trouble: having other people *see* me walk beside him. A *lot* of people.

After a few more yards, the corridor widened into a hallway. Passing a few potted plants obscuring our view, we stepped onto the landing of a broad, sweeping staircase that led down into a gigantic room, canopied by an ornate glass roof and countless palms, high ferns and papyrus plants, growing in gleaming copper bowls. In the gaps of the roof of green above, I could just make out a few stars twinkling in the slowly falling night outside.

It was when I looked down from the stars that I noticed the people for the first time.

Oh my God... Please, let me die! Let me die now!

People. Hundreds of them. And not just any kinds of people – high society, as high as you could get! Ladies in exquisite dresses, bedecked with jewellery, gentlemen in sleek black tailcoats, with golden watches and monocles tucked into their eyes. They were all sitting around tables, chatting, laughing, and... feasting. There really was no other word for it. The meals looked delicious. The platters, cutlery and glasses twinkled in the candlelight, shining with jewels and precious metals. If there had been a few camels and djinns, it would have looked like a scene from the Arabian Nights!

'How much did a reservation in this place cost, exactly?' I asked out of the corner of my mouth, my eyes wide.

'Too much,' came the dark reply from Mr Ambrose's direction. 'Don't remind me. Keep walking. And smile.'

I smiled as sweetly as a fairy godmother with a sugar addiction.

'Yes, Dick, my dear. Of course, Dick, my dear.'

A noise came from the back of his throat. It was somewhere between a volcano rumbling and a breaking iceberg. 'When this is all over, we're going to have a long talk, you and I!'

'I look forward to it, Dick, my dear.'

'Walk! And smile!'

We reached the top of the staircase. Talk down in the dining room sank to a murmur, and faces turned towards us. Only a few at first – but the moment the first female caught an eyeful of Mr Ambrose, her jaw dropped onto her plate. Without bothering to fish it out of her soup, she tapped her friend on the shoulder, and as she turned, so did the lady beside her. The ripple spread through the great hall. By the time we were halfway down the stairs, most of the women in the room were staring at us, and a goodly portion of the gentlemen.

The wedding ring on my finger was like a burning brand. I held my breath, waiting for someone to scream 'Imposter!' – but nothing happened. Well, nothing except most of the women in the room undressing Mr Ambrose with one look and wishing me dead with the next.

I leaned towards Mr Ambrose. 'Congratulations. So far we seem to be very inconspicuous. I think the entire room is staring at us, with the possible exception of that old lady in the corner, who is probably deaf and half-blind.'

'Lillian, my love...' The words were ice shards, his eyes threatening mael-stroms of dark colour. 'Hold your tongue and smile, will you?'

Why the heck did that make me want to grab him by the ears again and kiss him senseless?

'Why, certainly, Dick. Oh, by the way, my friends call me "Lilly". You may, too. We are married, after all.'

He cocked his head, and regarded me like a lion ready to swallow me whole. 'Thank you – Lillian.'

A waiter appeared in front of us, and bowed deeply enough for the Emperor of China.

'Welcome to the dining room, Mr and Mrs Thomson.'

Who the bloody hell was he tal–? Oh, right! *I* was Mrs Thomson! Straighten-ing, I clutched Mr Ambrose more tightly and lifted my chin in the air, trying to look as married as possible.

'Do you wish a particular table, Sir, Madam?'

Mr Ambrose gave a curt nod. 'On the terrace, if there's one free.'

'Certainly, Sir. Please follow me, Sir, Madam.'

Unbending himself, the waiter started across the dining room, weaving through the tables with ease. We followed, until we came to a large set of ornate double doors, opening on a luxurious terrace from which one could still see the sun, sinking in the distance over the ocean. The play of fiery colours upon the waves was a sight to see.

'Your table, Sir, Madam.' With a flourish, the waiter indicated a table right beside the railing, where the view was even more spectacular. Stepping up to the stone balustrade, I could see the lights of the ancient city of Alexandria glowing beneath me. History was thick in the air, an atmosphere that vibrated around us.

'Do you wish a menu?' the waiter enquired.

Mr Ambrose nodded. 'Two please. One each, for me and the lady.'

'Certainly, Sir. I won't be a moment.'

He disappeared, and Mr Ambrose stepped up to the table, drawing back a chair. I was still looking at the city, trying to make out the pattern of streets in the glowing lights. When I looked back at the table, Mr Ambrose was still stand-ing there like a statue, holding the chair.

I stood there, watching him.

He stood there, the back of the chair clutched in his hands, his eyes growing darker. I frowned.

What's the matter with him?

It was only then that I realized.

He's pulled the chair out for me!

Slowly but surely, a grin spread over my face. This 'being married' business might actually be some fun – for a while.

'The city looks beautiful, doesn't it?' I sighed, demonstratively leaning on the balustrade.

'I wouldn't know,' the cool voice of Mr Ambrose drifted to my ears. 'I cannot see it from where I am standing.'

'Really? What a pity.' I sighed again. 'Why don't you come over and see?'

His hands twitched around the wood of the chair. 'I can't. Wouldn't you like to sit down, my dear?'

'No, thank you, Dick. I'm fine where I am for now.'

'Indeed?'

'Yes, indeed. The sea is so beautiful in the sunset.'

I could almost feel his cold stare drilling holes in my neck. Acting as if it didn't bother me in the least, I took out my fan and began to wave it lazily, stirring up a breeze in the hot evening air. When I sneaked a peek at him out of the corner of my eye, he was still standing in exactly the same place, rigid as a column of marble, holding out the chair for me – the vision of a perfect gentleman.

I waved my fan again, just for the fun of it, and thought I heard a low growl from behind me, out of Mr Ambrose's direction. But maybe I was mistaken.

'Sir? Madam? Your menus.'

The waiter had returned, holding two leather-bound menus with golden cursive script on the covers. They already looked good enough to eat. Water ran in my mouth at the thought of what the actual food would taste like.

'What do you say, Dick?' Graciously wandering over, I gave Mr Ambrose one of my most charming smiles. 'Should we sit down to eat?'

His dark eyes met mine, and there was the promise of cold-blooded murder in them. 'I think that would be wise, love.'

'Oh, all right. If you insist...' Giving my fan another casual wave, I slowly sank onto the chair he was holding out for me, and he shoved it forward with enough force to squash my stomach against the table. How rude! I had to work hard to suppress a smirk.

'There! I hope you sit comfortably, my dear?'

'Why of course.' Pushing back, I rubbed my aching stomach muscles. 'Thank you! You are always so concerned about me, Dick, my dear. It's really touching.'

Folding himself onto the chair opposite me, Mr Ambrose met my gaze with cool, unfathomable eyes. 'Nothing more than what you deserve, my love.'

Taking a seat, Mr Ambrose held his hand out. The waiter reached out to both of us, wanting to hand one menu to Mr Ambrose and one to me, but Mr Ambrose snatched both away from him.

'We'll need a little time to decide,' he informed the man briskly. 'Come back in a quarter of an hour.'

'Um... Yes, Sir. Of course, Sir.'

Once the waiter had disappeared again, I nodded to the two menus. 'So hungry that you need two menus to decide, are you, Dick, my dear? You'll have to watch yourself so you don't gain too much weight. We don't want you coming back from our honeymoon looking all puffed up like a football, like you did that time you came back from Monte Carlo.'

Lowering the menus far enough so he could stare at me over the top he said, in an icy voice too low for anyone else to hear: 'What are you talking about? I've never been to Monte Carlo.'

I shrugged. 'Just keeping up the pretence, my dear. We are a happy married couple with a lot of history, after all.'

'And married people talk like that, do they?'

'So far as I know.'

His dark eyes bored into me. 'Then I am devoutly grateful that this is only a charade.'

I returned his dark look with a bright smile. 'A feeling which I sincerely return.'

Casting a quick look around to see if anyone was listening, I leaned forward and whispered: 'So, what are you doing with two menus?'

'This.' Sliding the menus off the table, he shoved them under the tablecloth. There was a rustling sound, and a moment later, the menus re-emerged. He handed one me one.

I frowned, turning it around. It looked exactly as it had before.

Hm...

Holding it up, I tapped on the side. Maybe there was a hidden compartment somewhere, or a latch, or...

'Open it!' came a low hiss from Mr Ambrose.

My heart made a leap. Had he hidden something inside? A secret document, maybe? Well, there was only one way to find out. With a cautious glance around to make sure nobody was looking, I let the menu fall open.

~ HOTEL LUXOR ~

Live Like a King on the Nile

List of Appetizers

By golly! Now that was some impressive secret document! I could see why Mr Ambrose would make such a fuss about this. What did we have here...?

Winter Salad marinated in French Dressing

Crab Puffs with Chives

Potato Salad

Cucumber Basil Sandwiches

Caviar on Toast

Cranberry Sauce

Cream Cheese

Oh my gosh! That was so... amazing! I hardly knew the words to express how impressed I was – *not*.

Looking up at Mr Ambrose, I raised an eyebrow. 'Yummy! I love cream cheese.'

His little finger twitched.

'Turn the page,' he growled, glaring suspiciously at an elderly couple who were passing not very far from us. They looked about as likely candidates for spies as Mr Ambrose did for a loving husband.

I turned the page.

'Seafood,' I read aloud. 'Lobster, crabs, oysters...'

'Again! Turn the page again!'

Rolling my eyes, I did as he said, and started to read aloud again. 'Map of the peninsula of–'

Then I realized what I was seeing. And the sharp kick from Mr Ambrose under the table a moment later brought it home with force. I glared at him.

'That wasn't necessary!'

'I'd say it was very necessary,' was his cool reply. 'Read. But *not* aloud.'

'Yes, thank you. I got that.'

I lowered my eyes to the menu again. There, nestled between two pages of the ornately printed lists of dishes, was another piece of paper. One that most certainly did not belong to the Hotel Luxor.

Under the caption *Map of the Peninsula of Sinai*, it showed a roughly triangular stretch of land, surrounded by water nearly everywhere, and only attached by thin strips of earth to the rest of Egypt in the west and Arabia in the east. Over the peninsula, snaky dotted lines wound from one end to the other.

I looked up at Mr Ambrose. 'The lines?'

'Caravan routes.'

I frowned. 'Why are they so roundabout? Why aren't they straight?'

'Because most men prefer to ride around mountains rather than to the top and down again, my dear. There's also the little issue of not dying of thirst. Oases seldom have the good manners to be arranged in a straight line.'

The arrogant son of a...! I was tempted to kick him under the table but, with admirable self-control, refrained from doing so. Instead, I looked down at the map again. There were dozens of crosses all along the dotted lines. What were those? Cities?

But then I saw the caption beside one of the crosses.

Robbery site

A cold shiver went down my back. So many... and at least twenty men dead for every cross on this map. This was going to be one heck of an adventure – more than I had bargained for.

'What are we going to do?' I asked, my voice unusually quiet.

'We'll be starting our enquiries tomorrow morning.'

'Enquiries?' I looked up. Mr Ambrose's face was hidden behind his menu. For anyone who looked over, it had to appear as if he was intently studying his choice of seafood.

'Yes, Miss Linton. You don't think I intend to simply charge off into the desert, do you?'

No. I hadn't thought that. There were always plans with him, and plans behind the plans.

'There are agents of Dalgliesh in this city, remember? If we can find one of them, maybe encourage him to talk...' One of his hands let go of the menu and, picking up a knife from the table, whirled it in a manner that said more than a thousand words. 'If we can find out where the bandits are operating, our task will become much easier. That is when we will set out eastwards.'

My eyes flitted across the map, confused.

'Why? Aren't we supposed to be going south?'

'Not from Alexandria, no. Most of my goods came in through another coastal city, Damietta. Since we want to retrace the caravans' tracks as closely as possible, that's where we're going to start out.'

Blimey! This was like half a geography lesson! I found the word Damietta printed beside a big fat black blob on the map. Most of the dotted lines ended there – or started, depending on your point of view.

'I see. And then?'

'We're going to follow the caravan how about the lobster, dearest? I thought you loved lobster.'

'*What?*' I stared at him, uncomprehending. 'We're going to follow a lobster through the desert?'

'Or the oysters,' Mr Ambrose continued, kicking me under the table. His eyes darted to the left, and only then I noticed the waiter who was walking past close by, a tray of caviar in his hand. He was well within hearing distance.

'Um... well, yes, I do like lobster. So much. At home, I eat lobster all the time, as you know. Breakfast, dinner, supper, – always lobster for me. Yummy! Lobster tastes so...'

Another kick hit my shin.

I glared at him. All right, maybe I had slightly overdone it, but that was no reason for domestic abuse!

'I like oysters, too. But tonight I would prefer something less slippery. What about you, Dick?'

Ha! Now the ball is back in his court! Let's see what he does with it...

'I think that I'll have crab puffs with chives for starters,' Mr Ambrose invented, effortlessly. 'And after that, maybe a route from Damietta southwards until we reach Ras Sedr.'

'Excuse me?'

Mr Ambrose gave me a look. One of those looks that said he knew perfectly well his intelligence was infinitely superior to mine, but did I *have* to demonstrate it *all* the time?

'I said, we're going to follow the caravan route from Damietta southwards until we reach Ras Sedr.'

Oh. Of course. The waiter was out of hearing range again.

'What in God's name is Ras... whatsit?

'Ras Sedr. An ancient desert town at the end of the Gulf of Suez.'

My head started to whirl from all the names. 'What's the Gulf of...?'

I bit my tongue.

No! You're not going to ask this time! You're going to find out by yourself!

Pulling myself together, I stared down at the map. There it was! The Gulf of Suez. It was a little patch of ocean: where the Red Sea met the southern tip of the triangle of land that was the Sinai Peninsula, the sea split in two, creating the Gulf of Suez in the west, and some other gulfy Gulf in the east. And there, right at the end of the Gulf of Suez, was the town of Ras Sedr, just as Mr Ambrose had said.

I traced a one of the dotted lines down from Damietta southwards to the other city. It seemed to be pretty much the shortest route.

'How long do you think it will take us to find someone who knows where the bandits are? When do you think we'll be able to leave?'

'That is difficult to say. Anything from the lobster is *really* delicious, darling! I tried it when I was last here, and I tell you, it was food fit for the gods!'

'Wha–? Ouch! Oh!'

I didn't need the kick on the shin this time to realize what was going on. Out of the corner of my eye, I saw our waiter, returned to take our orders, approach the table.

'Have you decided yet, Sir, Madam?'

'I, um... I...' Hurriedly, I tried to cover up the map with my elbow. But it was too bloody big! In desperation, my eyes flitted across the pages of the menu, looking for something to order. 'I, um... would like the potato salad, please, and a robbery on toast.'

Deathly silence descended over the table. My words echoed in my own ears, slowly sinking in.

'Caviar! Caviar on toast, I mean! Not the other stuff I said! That would be ridiculous, right? Ahahahah! Caviar. That's all. Caviar on toast, please!'

More silence. Slowly, I dared to look up. The waiter stared at me as if I had grown a second head. A green one, with horns. And as for Mr Ambrose... I did not even want to look around to see how he was looking at me.

'I,' I heard his voice, colder than the very heart of the arctic, burning into me like frostbite, 'will have toast, too, please. But without the caviar'

He closed his menu with a snap. As the waiter buzzled away, his dark, sea-coloured eyes found, me, and there was a storm brewing in them.

'We two,' he whispered, 'must have a discussion on how to properly act our roles.' His hand reached out, brushing against mine with a feather-light touch. 'A very detailed discussion.'

Oh dear...

In Dark Alleys

Caviar on toast didn't actually taste very well. A bit salty, and not more. But maybe the fact that I didn't enjoy my meal didn't actually stem as much from the meal itself, as from the fact that Mr Ambrose's frozen dark glare bored into me the entire time. It's hard to enjoy your food with that kind of evil force focusing on you. The minute I was finished with my meal, I sprang to my feet and began to hurry back to our suite. I wasn't going to stick around for wine and desert and give him a chance to glare at me some more!

Halfway up the stairs, a vice-like grip closed around my arm.

'Where are you going?' Mr Ambrose's cool voice said right into my ear. I hadn't even heard him approach!

'To bed! I'm tired!'

'How unfortunate for you. The night is not over yet. Not by a long shot!'

'What do you mean?'

Without a word, he began dragging me down the stairs again, and into a corridor leading out of the dining hall.

'Hey! Let go!'

'Act, Mr Linton, act. You're my loving wife, remember? Wives do not speak like that to their husbands.'

'And husbands don't manhandle a wife like this!'

'Actually, many of them do.'

My temper flared. 'Well, they shouldn't! That's outrageous!'

'Depends.'

'On what, pray?'

He gave me a look that froze my toes and set my heart on fire. 'What their intentions are. I might be dragging you off to a secret place for a romantic tryst.'

My eyes went wide. 'Y-you aren't, are you?'

'No.'

'Oh.' I felt relief flood through me – mingled with a tiny bit of disappointment.

What? What's disappointment doing inside you, Lilly Linton? You have no business being disappointed!

Clearing my throat, I hurried to get my thoughts back on the right path. 'So, where the bloody hell are you dragging me off to?'

Mr Ambrose halted abruptly. We were standing in the middle of an empty corridor. Throwing a quick look around to check for an audience, he whirled around to face me. Before I could move a muscle, he had picked me up right off the floor, pushing me against the wall. His hard chest dug into places on my body I couldn't mention in polite society.

To judge by the look in Mr Ambrose's eyes, he was not going to be polite.

'Damn you!' His eyes flared with cold fire, ferocity and... fear? 'Can't you act like a loving wife for two minutes in a row?'

An involuntary smile appeared on my face. I had no idea why! Shouldn't I have been afraid? Pressed up against a cold wall in a strange country, in the clutches of a ruthless man whose morals were more than questionable – yes, I should have been afraid. But with his strong arms around me, and his gaze burrowing into me as if it wanted to dig itself into my soul, all I felt was powerful. The feeling rushed up inside me like a hot geyser, and wouldn't be contained.

'That depends,' I breathed. 'Can you act like a loving husband?'

He surged forward. Pinning me to the wall like butterfly, he claimed my lips for one single, hard, ferocious kiss – and then pulled back.

'Loving enough for you?' he growled.

'It's a start.' My voice sounded strange in my own ears – full of a thousand emotions I couldn't comprehend, let alone name. Neither could he, to judge by the look in his eyes. For a moment, he just gazed at me, the silence between us stretching. Then, finally, he spoke.

'We are going into very dangerous territory tonight. If anyone there finds out who I really am, it is doubtful we will come out alive. You will need to play your role to perfection. If you can't,' he told me, his voice sinking to a low and dangerous tone, 'I will be forced to teach you a lesson. Do you understand?'

My heart jumped. A lesson?

No! I bloody well did not understand! What did he mean?

But, looking into his dark eyes, I was too afraid to ask. Slowly, I nodded my head.

'Yes, Sir.'

'What's that?'

'I mean yes, Di– Rick.'

He held my gaze for a few moments more – then nodded and let go. In a daze, I followed him outside to where the same coach in which we had travelled before was waiting for us. He held the door open for me.

'Come on, darling,' he hollered in a cheerful tone I would never have believed him capable of, for all the world to hear – and especially for any curious ears in the vicinity. 'It will be fun. We haven't seen anything of Alexandria yet except the hotel. And you wanted to go sightseeing, didn't you?'

I looked around. Several members of the hotel staff stood around, watching. So I smiled at him, and shrugged. 'I'd love to go! But I'm a bit tired. Don't you think we had better wait until morning?'

'No, darling, not at all.' He met my eyes. 'The city has a special atmosphere at night. We will enjoy ourselves immensely, trust me. There will be things to see we could never see in daylight, and maybe even more interesting things to hear.'

~~**~*~*

'Well, I agree with you so far,' I told Mr Ambrose, watching a half-naked woman contort her body into agonizing shapes. 'I'm seeing things I've never seen in daylight. Only I'm not too sure whether I actually ever wanted to see something like that.'

'Immaterial,' Mr Ambrose told me, pulling me past the contortionist to the entrance of a house in front of which another woman with even less clothes on her body was performing a dance that let everything about her jiggle. 'We are here for work, not for pleasure.'

My eyes swept over the parts of the woman that jiggled the most. The eyes of all the men in the vicinity seemed to see nothing else. Only Mr Ambrose's eyes were fully focused on the street beyond.

'Err... work, not pleasure? Are you sure we're in the right part of the city for that, my dear?'

'In this case, yes. Our work involves buying information. And in this part of the city you can buy anything.'

We passed another house from which hoots, whistles, and ecstatic moans were issuing in a cacophony.

I nodded, feeling a bit queasy. 'Yes, I can see what you mean, dear. I really must congratulate you. You pick the most fantastic places for sightseeing.'

Not deigning to respond to this, Mr Ambrose tightened his hold on my arm and pulled me farther on. We had been walking for some time now, having been forced to leave the carriage behind over an hour ago, when the streets had gotten too narrow for it to pass. At first I had objected.

'Won't we be conspicuous?' I had protested. 'This isn't the best part of town, to put it mildly. Wouldn't a gentleman and a lady in a fine dress stick out like peacocks in a henhouse?'

In answer, Mr Ambrose had simply pointed out of the carriage window. Following his pointed finger, I saw a man in what looked suspiciously like a French admiral's uniform staggering along the street, each arm thrown around the neck of a very pretty and very scantily dressed girl. Not far behind him came a party of three gentlemen and one lady, obviously all tight as owls.[17]

'Rich people come here to waste their money,' he told me, his tone indicating what he thought of people like that. 'There are places like this in any big city in the world. We won't even be noticed.'

And we were not. Apart from the fact that every five minutes somebody tried to sell us something, we were pretty much ignored. And when Mr Ambrose pulled me off the main street into a dark alley, even the hawkers disappeared. It became ever quieter the farther we ventured into the darkness. The figures that passed us now weren't wearing admirals' uniforms. Most of them kept their faces hidden.

Suddenly, I heard a noise behind us and swivelled my head around – nothing. The alley was just as dark as before. Shrugging, I let Mr Ambrose lead me further.

Tap... tap...

There it was again! Footsteps this time, definitely! Twisting out of Mr Ambrose's grip, I whirled around just in time to see a dark shadow press itself against the wall, melting into the gloom.

'Someone is following us!'

Mr Ambrose didn't even bother to turn around. Tugging on my arm, he dragged me along with him.

'Of course they are.'

'But all your talk about remaining inconspicuous and hidden... I thought we'd gotten away so far with being Mr and Mrs Thomson!'

'We have. Those men who are following us work for me.'

'For you?'

'Certainly. As do the men following them.'

'Wait a minute... you have men following us?'

'Correct.'

'Why?'

'To protect us, of course.'

'And you have men following the men who are following us?'

'Also correct.'

'For heaven's sake, *why*?'

'To protect the men who are following us, of course.'

'Do they know about it?'

---

[17] British English expression for 'very, very drunk'. Apparently, English owls like to party.

103

'Certainly not.'

Something in my brain made *click*. 'Just in case they turn out to be traitors and try to attack us instead of protecting us.'

'You, my dear,' Mr Ambrose told me, throwing me a look out of his dark eyes that made me shiver from top to bottom, 'are a wife after my own heart.'

Amazingly, he actually sounded like he *meant* it. And, blasted fool that I was, I couldn't help but grin with pride.

A wife after my own heart, he said!

Bloody hell, what was wrong with me? I was *not* married to him! I wasn't married to anyone, and certainly intended to keep it that way!

'And what if someone attacks us from the front?' I asked, forcing my thoughts back on the matter at hand.

'Then they will run into a group of energetic, knife-wielding individuals whom you have not noticed yet. Something similar would happen to anyone trying to attack our flanks. I know how to take precautions, *Wife*.'

'I can see that, *Dick*.'

His hold on my arm tightened.

'Do – not – call – me – that!'

I thought it perhaps wiser not to reply to this with a prim 'Yes, Dick.' Not in a dark alley where I could be strangled without anybody raising an alarm, anyway.

'And Karim?' I asked instead.

'He's not far. He never is.'

I believed that. Mr Ambrose's Mohammedan bodyguard was huge as a mountain and strong as a Titan, but he could move with the stealth of a little black kitten in the dark.

In front of us, for the first time in a long while, I heard noises. Laughter, to be exact. Not far away down the alley, light spilled from a doorway. At my side, I felt Mr Ambrose change his course slightly.

Ah. So that's the place we're heading for.

Not the most inviting of establishments, I had to say. But maybe the exterior didn't reflect the inside. Reaching the doorway, Mr Ambrose pulled aside the curtain that was half drawn across it, and led me inside. My mouth dropped open.

I had been right. The exterior did *not* reflect the inside properly. I didn't think there could be an exterior to a building that fit this atrocious interior and still was legal!

The whole place was half in darkness. The red and green paper lamps dangling from the ceiling cast only a murky light on the proceedings around me, and for that, I was profoundly grateful! In the gloom, I could see scantily clad bodies swaying from side to side. Men were sitting around on cushions, inhaling smoke out of strange, bubbling, water-filled contraptions, their eyes fixed on the spectacle in front of them. Somewhere in the background, a woman was singing in a throaty voice. Somewhere in the foreground, other women were doing... other things.

Unbelievable!

I was about to open my mouth to let loose a tirade, when I felt Mr Ambrose's hand tighten around my arm.

'We are here to do business,' his cold voice reached my ear. 'Not to hold a lecture against the objectification and oppression of womanhood. *Are we understood, my dear?*'

I took a deep breath. If I thought that would help me calm down, I was mistaken. I got a mouthful of the poisonous fumes emanating from the pipes, and felt the need to vomit. Clenching my jaws shut tightly, I nodded.

Hold it together, Lilly! You can do this!

'Adequate. Do you see that man over there?'

Following a discreet gesture of his with my eyes, I saw a fat man reclining on a pile of cushions in one of the more secluded corners. He was dark-skinned, but not nearly as much as some of the Egyptians I had seen. Also, the form of his face looked slightly different...

'That is the man we've come to do business with – Signore Bertolino.'

Ah, Bertolino... That explained his different looks all right.

'A Spaniard, or Italian?'

Mr Ambrose's eyes flashed coldly. 'A worm. But a useful one. He knows everything that goes on in this part of Egypt, at least in the disreputable quarters. If any of the bandits or Lord Dalgliesh's agents came into his domain to sell their stolen goods or buy supplies, he will be able to find out.'

Mr Ambrose started forward, and I walked beside him, towards the fat man. We stopped not two feet away.

'Signore Bertolino?'

At Mr Ambrose's words, the potbelly looked up. '*Si?*'

'My name is Thomson. I sent a man to you not long ago, hinting that I might visit you and that I was interested in buying something.'

'Mr Thomson...' The fat man's eyes narrowed. 'My congratulations, Signore. You are a most singular man. Many, many fellow Europeans have visited me here...' He gestured to the den of iniquity around us. 'As a friendly gesture, you understand. But none of them knew of my more delicate business dealings. You must have extensive contacts.'

'Sufficient,' Mr Ambrose allowed. 'May I sit?'

'*Ma certo!* Find yourself a free cushion. And the Signora, too.' He gave me a smile so oily it could have been used to free hinges of rust. 'Pick a cushion close to me, eh?'

Mr Ambrose folded his long legs with surprising agility. I gave Signore Bertolino a death-stare and sat down beside Mr Ambrose, as far away from the smarmy man as I could get.

'A pipe?' he offered, holding out one of the contraptions, from one of which he himself was smoking.

Mr Ambrose shook his head. 'No. I'm here for business only.'

The fat man gave a sigh. 'How sad. Well, what is it that you have come to buy, then?'

'Information.'

'Ah…' The potbelly took a deep puff of his water pipe. 'Information… A most expensive thing to buy. And most delicate. Too delicate for company. Leave us, my dear.' He slapped one of the cushions that was sort of draped around him from behind. 'Go on, *Vattene!*'

The cushion grumbled something. And then, what I had hitherto taken to be a skin-coloured cushion rose to her feet. The half-naked woman curtsied, and hurried away. I stared after her in horror until I could feel Mr Ambrose's grip around my hand tighten once more.

The fat man's little pig eyes landed on me. 'Perhaps it would be better if the Signora leaves, too. We wouldn't want any secrets to come popping out of that pretty little mouth of hers, now, would we?'

I opened said pretty little mouth to tell him what exactly I thought of him, and where he could stuff his water pipe, but the pressure of Mr Ambrose's hand stopped me.

'She stays.'

Ha! I had to work very hard to suppress a triumphant grin – and it still didn't work. So what? I *liked* triumphant grins on my face.

'Very well.' Bertolino shrugged. 'It is your funeral. Now – what is it that you wish to know, Signore?'

'I am looking for a certain group of men.'

The potbelly's mouth twitched. 'That should be no problem. Just give me their descriptions. I know every alley of this city.'

'Ah, but they are not in the city.'

'I see. That complicates matters slightly, Signore.'

'And what complicates them further is that I do not know their descriptions.'

'Their names?'

'I do not know those either,' Mr Ambrose admitted.

'*Maledetto!*' Again, that twitch of the fat lips. 'No names, no faces… How do you know they exist at all, these men you seek?'

'Because,' Mr Ambrose told him, his voice ice-cold, 'they have been killing people.'

The lips stopped twitching. 'Ah. An effective way of proving your existence to the world.'

'Indeed. And also a good way to interrupt business. The men I seek, they have been killing people who are transporting goods. Specifically camel drivers, and other members of caravans that take goods across the Sinai Peninsula, both from the Mediterranean to the Red Sea and vice versa.'

'Oh, those enterprising gentlemen?' One of Bertolino's eyebrows rose. 'Their deeds are well known to me. There have always been bandit attacks on caravans, but they… they are a different sort. They have made quite a reputation for themselves. You should tread carefully, Signore Thomson.'

Mr Ambrose met the small, mean eyes of the man head-on. 'So should they.'

Bertolino sat there and puffed on his pipe for a moment, sizing up the lean, hard figure opposite him.

'Yes, maybe they should.'

A man in fez and kaftan approached Bertolino, and bowed. The fat man's attention was distracted from Mr Ambrose, and he waved the newcomer closer.

'You there! What do you want?'

'A message for you, Signore.' Bending forward, the newcomer whispered something into Bertolino's ear. The potbelly nodded, and rose with a groan.

'Excuse me, for a moment, Signore Thomson, will you? There is a slight matter I must attend to. I won't be a moment.'

'Certainly, Signore. I shall wait here.'

I waited impatiently for the fat man to wobble away. The moment he was out of hearing range, a flood of words, kept at bay far too long, burst from my mouth.

'That... that man! And this place! Bloody hell, I've never seen anything like it! It's abominable! It stinks of chauvinism even more than it stinks of those blasted pipes! Have you seen the men staring at those women?'

'Yes.'

'And the woman beside that fat excuse for a man... she was hardly wearing a thing!'

Mr Ambrose gazed at me, his dark eyes unreadable. Was there a spark of amusement in there? There had better not be! 'I did not know you were such a staunch moralist, my darling.'

I glared at him. 'I'm not! It's not about what the women do – they have the freedom to do whatever they want! It's about the men staring!'

'Ah.' Mr Ambrose nodded. 'So in your view, women can take their clothes off in public all they want, as long as men don't pay them for it.'

Blast him! Put like that, it did sound rather silly. Which it wasn't! Not at all! It was a point of principle. I shot him another glare.

'It's not right! Women shouldn't be treated like this!'

Mr Ambrose ignored my glare as if it didn't exist. 'This place is called "Dark Nights of Delight", my love. What did you expect?'

'People with at least a little more clothing! And stop calling me "my love"!'

'Certainly, my love.'

That earned him another glare.

'The women... the addicts...' I threw another glance around, and shuddered. 'Do all Egyptian bars and pubs look like this?'

'Egyptian?' Mr Ambrose snorted. 'This place is owned by Signore Bertolino, who, in spite of his being a worm, is a bona fide Italian.'

'Oh.'

Mr Ambrose's face betrayed not a hint of emotion. Not even disgust.

'Believe me, he knows far better than any Egyptian what fellow rich Europeans *expect* Egypt to look like. Here they get the "genuine" oriental experience they've always dreamed of, without having to bother with what Egypt really looks like.'

'Well... well, then that's not just chauvinistic, it's chauvinistic trickery!'

He shrugged. 'Yes.'

'*Yes?* Is that all you have to say to it?'

'What else should I say, my dear? Ah, there comes Signore Bertolino.'

He did indeed, waddling across the floor towards us like an overweight gander. I tried not to shoot scathing glares at him, but it was very hard. Settling down again with a grunt, he picked up his water pipe and inhaled, deeply.

'My apologies, Signore Thomson. Business is business.'

'Of course, I understand.'

'We were speaking of bandits, I believe.'

'Indeed we were. So, Signore Bertolino, what can you tell me?'

'That depends. What price are you willing to pay?'

Mr Ambrose met his eyes coolly, evenly. 'None at all.'

There was a slight pause.

'*Scusi?*' This time, the Italian raised both his eyebrows. 'You have an interesting conception of "buying", Signore.'

'I've often been told that.'

'Now, seriously. What do you offer? How much?'

'Seriously – not a single penny.' Taking the water pipe out of the surprised Italian's hands, Mr Ambrose leaned towards him. 'But, if you tell me everything you know about these bandits, I shall keep my mouth shut about a few things that I know. For instance...'

He leaned forward even further, whispering something into Bertolino's ear which I couldn't hear. The fat man's face paled under his tan.

'H-how do you know about that?'

Mr Ambrose shrugged. 'I told you; I have sufficient contacts. Tell me everything you know, and the authorities will never need to hear of your little escapades. I know they turn a blind eye on your business here, but *that*...' He shook his head. 'That would be another matter altogether, wouldn't it?'

The Italian's venomous glare was answer enough. For a second, Bertolino's eyes flickered to the entrance, where two burly men stood guard. They shifted, no doubt reaching for hidden weapons.

'Don't even think about it,' Mr Ambrose's voice cut into Bertolino's contemplation. 'I have men outside. If I am not out of here in a quarter of an hour, they are going to the authorities. Or they might decide to take this place apart. They're loyal men, and very easily aggravated.'

The Italian's fat cheek twitched.

'All right, curse you! You'll get what information I have about the bandits. It's not much, but you'll have it!'

'Adequate.'

The fat man's little eyes burned with malice. 'But I warn you – you had better not set a foot into Alexandria again! For a clueless English honeymooner, you are treading in dangerous waters. I have eliminated far more dangerous men than you!'

Mr Ambrose's dark eyes sparkled, and I had to work hard to hide my smirk.

'Somehow,' he told the Italian, 'I very much doubt that. Lillian, my dear?'

'Yes?'

Leaning towards me, he whispered: 'Go outside, so the men will know that everything is going to be all right. We do not want them rushing in here.'

'But I want to stay and–'

'Do you really? Outside, the stench of chauvinism isn't nearly as overpowering, I think.'

This time, I couldn't keep a smirk from flitting across my face. 'Actually, you might be right there. Very well. See you outside – in one piece!'

'I shall do my best, my love.'

'Oh, keep a sock in it!'

Rising, I marched past the dancing girls, past the staring men, towards the exit. At the door I turned my head to look back at Mr Ambrose one last time – and that was why I didn't see the man coming towards me when I stepped outside into the street. I only realized he was there when I ran head first into his hard chest.

'Oumpf!'

'Ouch!'

'Hey!' I snapped. 'Watch where you're going, you bugger!'

'I'm dreadfully sorry, Madam,' said a strangely familiar voice out of the gloom. Strong hands gripped my arms to steady me. 'I didn't see you and...' The voice trailed off. But no matter. I had heard enough to recognize the shadowy figure.

But... that was impossible!

Nevertheless, I knew it was true.

'*Captain Carter?*'

'Miss... *Miss Linton?*'

GRANNYFAKING FOR BEGINNERS

Captain Carter took a step backwards, and the light flooding from the open doorway fell across his face. A handsome face, a roguish speck of beard, a mane of brown hair – it was indeed him, in the flesh.

He? Here?

How could he be here? He said he was going to...

Oh.

Of course! A memory of his words during our last conversation flashed through my mind.

'We've had reports of a series of vicious attacks on traders in one of the eastern protectorates. There's pressure on the Admiralty and the Commander-in-Chief to get quick results. The navy has already dispatched several vessels, and if they can't root the bandits out from sea, we'll probably be sent in.'

I stared at him in stunned realization. Of all the countries in the world he could have been talking about, it had to be this one! And I already had a good idea who had perpetrated those 'vicious attacks' he had mentioned. Talk about coincidence. Bloody hell!

The surprise must have shown on my face. But if *I* was surprised, it was nothing compared to the utter incredulity in his tone when he next spoke.

'Miss... Linton? Miss *Lilly Linton?*'

I gave him a smile I hoped was casual and relaxed. It probably wasn't. 'The one and only.'

'What in the name of all that is holy are you doing here?'

Looking from left to right, I desperately wrecked my brain for something to say. 'I, um... went out for a walk.'

His eyebrows, already quite high up, hastily climbed another few dozen rungs on the ladder of his face. 'From London to Alexandria?'

'No, of course not! I came here by ship! On my ho–' I bit down on my tongue just in time. Blast! I had just been about to tell him I was here on my honeymoon! That might lead to slightly awkward results, seeing as he knew perfectly well I wasn't married and that my last name wasn't Mrs Thomson. 'I, um... I'm here on a holiday.'

Quickly, I hid the hand with the wedding ring behind my back.

'*Here?*' Captain Carter looked around at the dark, dingy alleyway. Most windows and doorways were as black as pitch. The few that betrayed some sign of life echoed with raucous laughter, or the sound of fighting. Finally, his eyes settled on the doorway behind me, through which, I knew, the forms of half-naked women had to be perfectly visible. 'An, um... interesting spot for a young lady to spend her holiday.'

I rolled my eyes. 'Not here in this place, obviously. I mean I'm *here in Egypt* on holiday.'

'Oh. I see.' He still didn't seem very reassured. 'You're here all alone?'

No, of course not. I'm here with a chauvinistic businessman who is forcing me to pretend to be his wife so he can take his time finding and slaughtering a few dozen bandits.

'No, of course not. I'm staying at the Hotel Luxor, with my grandmother,' I lied. It seemed believable. There were plenty of old ladies back at the hotel, here in Egypt to cure their rheumatism or something. I could only hope to God Captain Carter would never come to the hotel and find out the truth.

'The Hotel Luxor?' He took another look around. 'That's quite a long way away from here, isn't it?'

I shrugged. 'Like I said, I went for a walk, and I must have lost my way a bit.'

'I'd say!'

My chin lifted. Enough with this inquisition! It was time to go on the offensive.

'Since we're on the subject, Captain, what are *you* doing here?'

The captain bit his lip. 'I'm not really supposed to say...'

I gave him my most charming smile, and even went so far as to bat my eyelashes. 'Oh, Captain! You know you can trust me, don't you?'

There were a few more seconds of hesitation – then Captain Carter released his lip with a sigh. 'Bloody hell! You're a dangerous woman, do you know that?'

'Yes.'

I waited, then batted my eyelashes again, just in case.

He sighed in resignation. 'All right! You remember those things I told you about my being sent after bandits?'

'Indeed I do.'

'Well, they're here. In Egypt. Egyptian, English and French trade routes are all at risk, so it will be a joint operation, with each nation contributing one task force. I'm in charge of the force the British Army sent to take care of those robbers.'

'Dear me!' I actually managed to sound surprised. 'And what are you doing in this alley, then? Shouldn't you be in the desert?'

'Not yet. First I have to find out where those criminals are.' Looking from left to right as if fearing someone might be listening, he leaned forward. 'Don't tell this to anyone,' he whispered. 'But I think I might have found a clue to the bandits' whereabouts.'

I did my best to make my eyes go big with girlish excitement. 'Indeed?'

'Yes. In that disreputable tavern behind you – which, by the way, I advise you *strongly* not to enter – is a man who, according to my sources, might know where they have their lair.'

'You don't say.' I stepped aside to let him pass. 'Well, it was nice seeing you, Captain. I shouldn't detain you any longer. You probably have to get on with your investigation.'

His mouth dropped opened slightly. 'What? You surely don't expect me to leave you behind in this den of iniquity, completely alone and without protection?'

I won't be alone. There are men in the shadows watching. And men in the shadows watching the men who are watching!

I managed to force a smile on my face. 'But surely, your investigation...'

'...can wait until tomorrow! I will escort you back to the hotel straight away.'

'Oh, Captain, that really isn't necessary.'

'Of course it is,' he told me sincerely, taking hold of my hand. 'There are all sorts of ruffians loose in this part of the city. I myself was nearly attacked twice on my way here. I am surprised that you've made it this far in one piece.'

Well, my secret legion of bodyguards probably helped.

'Really,' I tried one final time, 'You don't have to do this. I'll be fine.'

'Please.' Squeezing my hand, he gazed deep into my eyes. His shining brown eyes looked like chocolate: warm and utterly enthralling. I had never noticed before how beautiful they were. Blast! Why did chocolate have to be my favourite food? 'Please, Miss Linton, let me accompany you back. I couldn't live with myself if something happened to you because I wasn't there to prevent it.'

That was so typically male, chauvinistic, and... and... sweet. Sweet as chocolate.

I gave a little nod. 'All right.'

Blast! What about Mr Ambrose? If he comes out here and finds me gone...

I could imagine his reaction.

But I really, really didn't want to.

'Besides,' he added in a more cheerful tone, 'if I come with you, I can meet your grandmother. I'd be delighted to make her acquaintance.'

Oh – my – God...!

'Of course,' I said, wishing I could just disappear into the earth. 'I can't wait for you to meet her.'

The only problem being that she's back in England! What now? Crap, crap, crap...!

Oblivious to my panic, Captain Carter linked arms with me and started to lead me up the alley. Halfway up I turned my head to throw an anxious glance back at the tavern which still contained my dear employer, Mr Rikkard Ambrose.

What will he think when he comes out and doesn't find you out here? asked a nasty little voice in my head.

Nice, calm, relaxing thoughts, I hoped. But somehow, I doubted it.

Our walk back to the hotel passed quite eventlessly. Captain Carter commented once or twice with amazement on how much quieter and safer the dark streets had apparently become since he'd passed through. I mh-hmed and tried not to flush. Once or twice, I saw dark figures out of the corner of my eye, behind us, to our left, our right – everywhere. It probably wasn't the entire group of guards, but at least part had split off to see me safely back to the hotel.

I wasn't particularly reassured by this. My brain was whirring like a mad spinning wheel, trying to figure out a way to manufacture a grandmother within approximately five minutes. So far, I had come up blank.

We reached the hotel by just about eleven pm. At the bottom of the stairs, I turned to Captain Carter with a charming smile.

'Thank you, Captain. It was *so* nice of you to escort me this far. But you don't need to come inside, really. I can manage the rest of the way fine by myself.'

'But then I wouldn't meet your grandmother! I've been looking forward to making her acquaintance.'

Blast! May worms nest in your stomach and nibble at your insides! Why do you have to be so infernally nice?

'You're too kind, Captain,' I told him, and never had I meant anything more literally. 'Please come in. I'll introduce you.'

Cursing myself and the blasted goddess of fate responsible for bringing us together in that dark alley, I led him up the stairs and into the lobby. Desperately, I looked around for something, anything – and my eyes fell on my salvation!

'Grandmother!' With a fake smile on my face that hurt my cheeks, I scuttled towards the deaf little old lady I had noticed before in the dining hall. 'Grandmother, how nice to see you again!'

With bated breath, I waited for the axe to fall. I had a fifty-fifty chance...

'Eh?' Blinking up at me, the old lady raised a hand to her ear. 'What? You'll have to speak up, dearie! I can't hear you.'

Yes! Yes, yes, yes, yes, yes, yesyesyesyesyesyesyesyes! Deaf as a post! Yes!

'Captain Carter,' I said, gesturing him closer, my grin now a hundred per cent genuine as relief welled up inside me. 'Meet my grandmother, Frederica Linton. Grandmother, this is Captain Carter, a good friend of mine.'

'What?' The old lady leaned forward a bit more. 'Who has kept it harder?'

'*Carter*,' the captain said, in a slightly raised voice. 'Not harder. Carter. Captain Carter!'

'What larder, young man? What are you talking about? We're not in a larder! This is the lobby of a first class hotel, in case you haven't noticed!'

'Charming, isn't she?' I asked the captain with a smirk.

'Absolutely dazzling, Miss Linton. I hardly know what to say.'

'Pay?' the old lady demanded. 'What would I want you to pay for? I've got my own money and can take very good care of myself, you know! Young people nowadays...! Who are you anyway?'

'Carter, Madam. Captain James Carter!'

The old lady shook her head. 'No, we're *not* in a larder! How many times do I have to tell you that?'

Captain Carter and I had a nice chat with my 'grandmother'. By the end of it, he was completely exhausted, and the old lady had had a fabulous time explaining to us how frivolous today's youth was and saying 'What?' about three dozen times. Finally, Captain Carter decided to take his leave.

'You won't mind if I go already, Miss Linton? You see, I have a long way back to my own hotel. But if you think it would be rude of me to leave already I could–'

'Oh, no, no, nononono. Not rude at all! Put your mind at rest, Captain.'

'Well, if you think so...'

'Definitely!'

He smiled at me. A genuine, warm smile that made me feel a little guilty for how I had been trying to get rid of him. 'May I look in on you, to see how you're doing?'

Yes, of course you may. I'd love to see you, really. The only problem with that is that I'm staying here as a married woman, under an assumed name!

'I'm afraid my aunt and I will be leaving soon for a trip down the Nile, or some other expedition.'

'Oh.' He looked disappointed. 'Well, then... farewell, Miss Linton.'

'*Au revoir*, Captain.' Reaching out, I took his hand, and gave it a gentle squeeze. 'I look forward to seeing you again in London, and dancing our next galop.'

That brought a smile to his face. He bowed snappily and kissed my hand in farewell. I waited until he was out of sight, outside the hotel – then I let my held breath escape. Thank God! Major catastrophe averted! Secret identity saved! Not bad for one night.

A tickling sensation drew my attention then. Raising my hand, I watched it for a moment, as if it might bite. The spot he had kissed was still sort of tingly. Odd. That had never happened when some of my suitors smooched my hand. The only thing that made me feel was an intense desire for a towel, soap, and a bucket of water. Hm.

Taking a deep gulp of air, I turned and started forward, towards the reception desk. In a matter of minutes I acquired a set of keys from the night porter, and made my way up the stairs towards our suite of rooms. I was bone-tired. From the bottom of my heart I prayed that the bed up there was soft and had a nice, down-filled cushion.

Reaching the top of the stairs, I unlocked the door to my room, and was just about going to go in search of my nice, comfy bed when I noticed the figure standing in the middle of the room. A tall and leanly muscular figure in a black tailcoat, staring at me with freezing intensity.

'Well, my love?' Mr Ambrose's voice was so icy it made the hairs on the back of my neck stand up. 'Do you want to explain where you've been?'

SUSPICIONS

'Well?' Mr Ambrose's gaze drilled into me like a diamond drill into hot butter. 'Where were you?'

'I... um... I...'

Seriously – that was all I was capable of saying. *I... um... I...* – so pathetic! What business was it of his where I had gone, anyway?

'Do you have any idea,' his menacing voice drifted to my quivering auricula auris[18], 'what I thought when I left *Dark Nights of Delight* to find you had disappeared?'

'Um... "Thank you, God, thank you so much!"?' I suggested.

He didn't seem to appreciate my fine humour.

'You,' he told me, taking a step towards me, gliding through the shadows, 'don't just leave without my authorization. Without my permission, you don't even move a toe, do you understand?'

I opened my mouth to fire back a reply – but then I realized there was only one fitting reply to this, and it didn't even need words. Bending, I unlaced my shoe, kicked it off and stretched out my foot. Slowly and demonstratively, I wiggled my toes. All five of them. I grinned up at Mr Ambrose. Oh, how good it felt to stretch one's feet after such a long walk!

'You...!' In two long strides, Rikkard Ambrose had crossed the distance between us. Grabbing my shoulders, he pushed me backwards, away from my forlorn-looking shoe. I felt like Cinderella in reverse.

'Hey! Let go of me!'

'Not until I have proof that I've managed to instil some semblance of sense into that foolish female head of yours! Do you have any idea what could have happened to you out there in the dark alleys of Alexandria?'

'I'm a Londoner! We have street gangs that are ten times worse than anything they've got here,' I proclaimed with an unusual burst of patriotism.

'And how much of your time in London has been spent in the darker corners of the East End?'

'Um...'

About five minutes. And you were with me, then.

'Exactly!' His eyes glinted in the darkness. 'Any city in the world has its dark places! And they're all deadly to a defenceless girl like you!'

'Defenceless girl?' In an instant, my temper shot up to the boiling point. *Ha! I'll show him how defenceless I am!*

---

[18] The big, trumpet-shaped part of your ear around the opening that helps sound get in.

My knee surged forward and upward, right towards his crotch. But before it could hit its mark, his legs snapped closed, trapping me in between. I wriggled and writhed, but no matter how much I strained against him, I couldn't get free. My leg struggled inefficiently against the vice of his iron-hard muscles.

'Let go!'

'Yes,' he told me, tightening his hold. 'A *defenceless girl.*'

'Let go, I said!'

'So, what would you have done,' he enquired coolly, 'if a few of the ruffians who infest that part of the city had decided to try their luck with you?' Completely ignoring my attempts to get free, he leaned closer. Even in the darkness that had taken hold of the room, from this close I could see his eyes clearly now. They were dark pools, swallowing everything, demanding more. 'Well? What would you have done?'

'I wouldn't have needed to do anything! The guards were with me!'

'True. And what if Karim, in his commendable foresight, hadn't sent half of them with you?'

'I still wouldn't have been alone! There was someone with me who–'

My voice trailed off as the darkness in Mr Ambrose's eyes flared, and the muscles of his jaw tightened. I knew instantly that he had seen Captain Carter. I also knew that mentioning him had been a bad idea. A very, very bad idea.

Oops...

'Yes,' he said. His voice, only Icelandic so far, had moved to arctic temperatures. 'I noticed. Tell me, just out of curiosity... Who was that man?'

'What man?' I tried to play innocent. The only problem was I had never been particularly innocent.

'The man who brought you to the hotel. Tall, brown hair, a ridiculous speck of beard on his chin.'

'It's not ridiculous! And I don't know a man like that anyway!'

'Answer me! Who was he?'

I tried to shrug. This isn't very easy to do when both your shoulders are in the unbreakable grip of a muscular financial magnate, but I did my best.

'Just someone I know from London. We accidentally bumped into each other. Don't worry, he doesn't know we're staying here under false names. I took care of it.'

Mr Ambrose cocked his head. Shadows moved across his face, casting his already dark eyes into deeper blackness.

'Just someone you know?'

'Yes!'

'A mere acquaintance?'

'Yes, exactly.'

'Ah.' A pause. A very heavy, very dark pause. 'I didn't know it was common for mere acquaintances to kiss a lady's hand on departure, nowadays.'

Blast! He had seen that? I felt my face heat. Double and triple blast! Thank God my skin was so tanned and it was dark in the room!

What was I blushing for, anyway? If Captain Carter wanted to kiss my hand, he could do so all day long, and there was nothing Mr Ambrose could say or do about it!

'I didn't know it was common for people to spy on other people's farewells, nowadays,' I shot back.

'It isn't,' he told me coldly. 'That's just something I do.'

'You are insufferable!'

'Respect, my dear, respect.' His voice was silky, unusually soft with threat. 'I am your husband after all.'

'You? You are an arrogant, calculating bastard with an iceberg for a heart!'

'That, too.'

'Let go!'

'No!'

'I'm going to kill you!'

'You're going to try.'

Bloody hell! How can he still sound so infuriatingly cool?

'Let – me – go!'

'No.' He leaned forward until I could feel his breath on my face. For some inexplicable reason, my knees suddenly felt weak. 'Let's talk about that man, my dear.'

'Let's not!'

'Who was he, exactly, and what was he doing here?'

I glared up at him. 'He isn't coming back!'

'Indeed?' He cocked his head like a panther about to leap. 'That is satisfactory to hear. But it is not what I asked, my love. What is he doing here in Alexandria?'

'Go to hell!' I snarled – or at least tried to snarl. It somehow came out softer and breathier than intended. Darn!

I could have told him about Captain Carter and his mission, of course. I could have told him everything, and he'd probably have been content. But I would be damned before I answered the questions of a man who had dared to call me a *defenceless girl*! Worse, a man who had grabbed me, held me, and proved to me that in comparison to him, I *was* a defenceless girl.

Curse him! I'll be damned before I say a single word! No matter what malignant methods he'll use to question me!

'Did he follow you here? Did he follow you from London to Egypt?'

My mouth fell open in utter astonishment. The flame under my boiling pot of anger went out in a puff of smoke.

'*What?*'

'It's a simple enough question, Wife. Did this man follow you to Egypt? Is he after you?'

'After me?'

'Yes.'

'You mean...?'

Lightning flashed in the dark clouds of his eyes. 'I mean is he enamoured with you? Does he wish you to be his?'

My mouth dropped open a little farther. I didn't know it could open this wide. You never cease to learn, I guess.

'What business of yours would it be if he did?'

Mr Ambrose's eyes glittered darkly. 'None whatsoever – except for the fact that, for the next few months at least, you're already taken.'

'You don't seriously expect me to...'

'Yes, I expect you to!' He leaned closer, and I couldn't for an instant look away from his chiselled stone-hard face. Those eyes of his seemed to draw me in, threatening to swallow me whole, body, mind and soul. 'Here's how seriously I expect you to!'

His mouth was on me before I could blink. A wave of heat surged through me from my lips down to my toes the moment our lips touched. Suddenly, I didn't mind the fact that he was holding me tightly against him so much. I didn't mind it at all. My hands shot out, grasping his arms to pull him still closer. His lips moved against mine with enough force to shatter a mountain. Was I stronger than a mountain? I'd always thought so, but I felt ready to break into a thousand pieces of ecstasy any moment.

'While we are here,' his cold voice reached my ear, his murmur caressing my mouth, 'you're mine. Do you understand? Mine!'

'I'm not–'

Before I could say another word, he had caught my lower lip between his teeth, holding it prisoner.

'Let go! I ot anyody's!'

'What did you say, my dear, temporary love?'

'I said I ot anyody's!'

What I had been *trying* to fling into his face were the defiant words 'I'm not anybody's.' But it's difficult to fling words of defiance into someone's face while that someone is attached to your face by biting down on your lower lip. Particularly if his gentle bite is sending tingles through your entire body, making your knees want to give way.

What the hell is the matter with you? Where is your self-respect? Stand up straight! Fight that bastard off! That's what you want, right? Right?

Hm... maybe. But standing up straight seemed like such an exhausting thing to do right now. Besides, what could I do to fight him off, anyway?

You can give as good as you get! Bite him!

Slowly, my lips curved into a smile. All right. Let's show him who's in charge!

Snaking my arms up around his neck, I pulled him closer towards me. In an instant, he was on me again and was delving into my mouth, probing its depths. Trying to keep my knees from melting, I waited. I waited until he pushed his lower lip forward, gently massaging my upper lip with both of his.

Now!

My teeth came down.

'Arrgh!'

My grin widened – for about one millisecond, before he picked me up off the floor like a doll and surged forwards. I had hardly time to think *Bloody hell! What's this? He's supposed to let me go, not carry me to the... !* before he rushed through the door into the next room and flung me onto something soft and velvety.

'Ouff!'

Feathers creaked under me. The chaise lounge! Why had he thrown me onto the chaise lounge?

'I have a question for you.' His voice came drifting out of the darkness, somehow seducing me no matter how cold and hard it was. No... *because* it was. 'While you are here...'

I tried to drag a breath into my labouring lungs. I tried to see where he was, to scramble away. But the breath had been knocked out of me, it was pitch-black inside the room, and my limbs felt like putty.

'While you are here, Mr Linton,' came his voice out of the dark again, 'what are you?'

This was bloody ridiculous! He had just kissed me on the mouth, and now he was calling me *Mister*? I opened my mouth to protest.

The creak of the feathers was all the warning I got. I never sensed him above me, so silently and smoothly did he move. Trapping both my arms at my sides, he claimed my mouth with his again, cutting off my protest – in more than one way. His kiss didn't just keep me from rejecting him. It kept me from wanting to.

Dear God...

'While you're here,' he whispered against my mouth, his smooth, ice-cold voice burrowing into me like a frozen spear until it found my heart, 'what are you? Tell me!'

He released my mouth for just a moment. My eyes had gotten used to the dark by now, and I could see the faint outline of his face in the gloom. I could see his eyes, calling me, holding me more securely than his hands ever could.

The words escaped my mouth without thinking.

'Yours! I'm yours!'

~~**~*~*

Just to make sure everyone who reads this knows: there were two beds in the suite. *Two*. And we used both of them that night. *Separately*.

I just wanted to get that out there before anyone got any ideas. My behaviour in the recent past might have been a tiny bit erratic. Some might even use the word 'passionate'. But that was just the heat of Egypt affecting my delicate English nervous system. I was still a feminist! I thoroughly and totally despised men. Especially one particular specimen of the species!

Really? I heard a little voice every time during the next few days when our lips happened to touch, coincidentally. *You don't really act like you despise him.*

Emphasis on 'act'! I was *acting* a role. After all, he was paying me, at the moment, to pretend to be his loving wife. Nobody should be able to accuse me of not doing a thorough job!

Nice! The only problem with that argument is that whenever you are in company, i.e. whenever your acting skills are actually required, you behave like a vengeful harpy. It's just when the two of you are completely and utterly alone that you–

'Shut up!' I growled.

The hotel doorman, who was just holding the door to Mr Ambrose's coach open for me, stared up at me in surprise. 'Excuse me, Madam?'

'Nothing! I was talking to myself.'

And not winning the argument, by the way.

Quickly, I got inside and settled down beside Mr Ambrose. I didn't ask where we were going. For the last couple of days, a routine had established itself: in the morning, we would breakfast and then drive into the city, continuing our enquiries, since apparently whatever information Bertolino had given was not sufficient. At noon, we would lunch at some place where the entire city observed us being the happily married couple. After another round of investigating, we would finally return to the hotel for a romantic dinner on the terrace.

'Next time we sit down for dinner and I ask you what you would like to drink,' Mr Ambrose whispered, leaning towards me, 'do try not to answer "Your blood, with soda". It doesn't really fit the role of a loving wife.'

All right... maybe not all the dinners had been *that* romantic. But what did he expect? The stress of having to wear a wedding ring was straining my feminist limits!

'You want me to behave reasonably?' I demanded. 'Then stop opening doors and pulling back chairs for me!'

Admittedly, in the beginning it had been sort of fun – but it hadn't taken long for the chauvinistic implications to occur to me. I could open my own doors, thank you very much!

'I can't! I'm supposed to be a gentleman, and you my loving wife!'

'I'm not some useless appendage to a man, my dear husband! I have two arms and hands of my own – as you will find out to your detriment as soon as I get my hands on a knife at dinner!'

'You do understand the meaning of the term "loving", don't you?'

I chose not to dignify that with a response.

With a derisive snort, Mr Ambrose turned away from me and struck his cane against the roof of the coach. 'Drive!'

More days of secret investigation followed, coupled with more attempts to display our relationship in public. Needless to say, the attempts were not very successful. Once, when I was trying to smile at Mr Ambrose at a dinner in the hotel dining room, a concerned waiter who had noticed my expression came over to enquire if I suffered from lockjaw and needed medical assistance.

What I wanted to know was: *why?* Why was I so useless at trying to be Mr Ambrose's pretend wife? I was usually a pro at acting! I had played a lady in distress, a secretary to one of the world's most famous businessmen, even my own Uncle Bufford!

On that last occasion you were caught and arrested, though, weren't you?

Well, yes, but that wasn't the point! The point was that I was really good at playing a role – any role! Being the fake wife of Rikkard Ambrose should have been a breeze! All I had to do was dance, smile and giggle inanely. Instead, I scowled most of the time.

It had to be the feminist in me, protesting against this violation of my principles! Yes, that had to be it!

Really? Are you sure the real reason you're having so much trouble at being a fake wife isn't something else?

Of course not!

Indeed? Are you sure, for example, it isn't the little twinge in your heart every time you think about the word 'fake'?

'Shut the bloody hell up!'

It took me a few seconds to realize the effect my words had had. Looking around, I saw a stone-faced Mr Ambrose sitting opposite me at the dining table. Around him, at other tables, couples were frozen in mid-motion, their mouths hanging open, staring at me. It was very, very quiet.

'Um... I didn't mean you. Sorry. Continue, everyone.'

'Come with me.' I heard Mr Ambrose's low and very controlled voice. His hand fell on mine, holding my wrist like a vice. Looking up, I saw ice glitter in his dark eyes. 'Upstairs. We need to have a little talk about acting skills.'

We went upstairs. But as it turned out, we didn't talk much that night.

~~**~*~*

Yes, we used separate beds that night, too! I am a feminist, remember? Staunch and true!

At least that's what I kept telling myself.

'How long is this going to continue?' I asked, trudging down the dusty alley beside Mr Ambrose, trying to cover my face against the dirt with the hand I didn't need to hold up my dress. 'This sneaking into the ratholes of the city, asking questions no one wants to answer?'

'As long as it takes to find out the truth,' was the curt reply. 'Or until we're found out. It's only a matter of time until Dalgliesh's agents discover who we really are.'

A matter of a very short bit of time, apparently. Mr Ambrose's lips had hardly closed when a man stepped out from a doorway in front of us. He was wearing a cloth on his head that was twisted so it covered half his face, and his hand was clutching a dagger.

I stopped in my tracks.

Two more men stepped out of other doorways. All of them had their faces covered and were wearing weapons. Wickedly sharp weapons.

Blast! They're blocking the exit to the alley!

And did I mention yet that the alley we were in happened to be of the blind variety?

The men pulled down the cloths from their faces. All of them were smiling. I personally didn't feel a great inclination towards amusement.

'You have been asking a lot of questions around here,' the man who had revealed himself first said. He had the biggest dagger and the nastiest smile of the three – so he probably was the leader. 'Our master would like to know why, exactly.'

'Let us pass!' Mr Ambrose's voice wasn't cold as ice now – it was cold as iron, which meant it was far harder. I only wished he had a gun of iron as well as a voice. The sight of those daggers didn't appeal to me. 'Whoever your master is, we want nothing to do with him. Step aside!'

The leader shook his head. 'Not before you tell me who you are.'

'My name is Richard Thomson, and this is my wife–'

'Don't give me that Thomson nonsense!' The leader spat on the ground. 'Your name is not Thomson, and whatever you are here for, it is no honeymoon!' Lazily twirling his knife, the man took a step closer, his nasty smile wider than ever. 'Speak! And what you say had better be the truth, or I am going to make this charming lady squeal.'

He raised an eyebrow expectantly. But I didn't answer, and neither did Mr Ambrose. We weren't even watching the three men with knives anymore.

No, our concentration was focused on the man who stood on the roof behind them. There was a movement and a soft *thump*. More movement came, and more *thumps*. The leader of the knife-wielding ruffians narrowed his eyes impatiently, waiting for an answer. He hadn't noticed anything, and didn't look behind him. That was why he didn't see the mountainous figure of Karim straightening from where he had landed on the street.

'Well?' The leader raised his knife. 'Speak! Tell me exactly who you are and who you are working for, or I warn you, things will go very badly for you!'

There was a soft hiss as Karim drew his sabre. He stepped forward, and his huge shadow moved with him, falling into plain sight of the knife-wielder. So did the shadows of the men who followed him. There were quite a lot of them.

'How interesting,' Mr Ambrose remarked to the three ruffians, who suddenly weren't smiling anymore. 'I was just about to say the same thing to you.'

TRUE FAKE LOVE

'They're getting close,' Mr Ambrose said, the moment he arrived at our dinner table in the hotel dining room. I had waited in vain for over half an hour before finally ordering my dinner without him. And the knowledge of what he was doing, somewhere in a secluded space with Karim, his other faithful minions and the three ruffians they had captured last night, hadn't exactly improved my appetite.

All of which explained why, when Mr Ambrose said, 'They're getting closer', I snapped in a rather tart voice:

'Oh, are they?'

He didn't even lift an eyebrow. 'Yes. Karim and I questioned them, and it turns out they are indeed in the employ of a certain British lord, just as we suspected.'

'Gosh! What a surprise.'

'Yes. I do not think they've realized who we really are yet, but, to judge by what Karim and I have managed to make the three tell us, they suspect that we are not who we claim to be – which means that we have to put more effort than ever into our disguise.'

'Oh, do we?'

'Yes. We have to be the perfect image of two young and foolish people in the grip of a mixture of the following irrational emotions: devotion, passion, love, yearning, infatuation and attachment.'

Good God! He sounds as if he were compiling a shopping list!

'Didn't you forget amorousness?' I suggested sweetly. 'Also known as "lust"?'

'By all means, add it to the list.'

Bloody hell! Doesn't he even realize that was meant to be sarcastic?

Ignoring the glare I was shooting at him, he took me by the hand and pointed to my still half-filled plate. I had spent the last five minutes shoving the food on it from left to right in a listless manner.

'Are you finished with your dinner, my love?'

'It went cold long before you arrived!' I said, with another meaningful glare.

He apparently was impervious to those. 'I see. How convenient. Then I assume you do not need to eat it. Let's dance. And do your best to arrange your features in a way that suggests ardent devotion, passion, love, yearning, infatuation, attachment and amorousness.'

I raised an eyebrow. 'In that order? Or may I rearrange them alphabetically?'

His dark eyes swept over me, coolly. 'If you wish.'

Gah! He was impossible!

'And what about you?' I asked sweetly, as we rose to our feet and he more or less dragged me to the dance floor that was set up in the next room, accessible through three wide arches. 'Will you, too, be displaying feelings of devotion, passion, love, yearning, infatuation, attachment and amorousness?'

'No. But then, you're the female, so everybody expects you to be the emotional one.'

Oh really? Well, I was certainly feeling quite emotional at the moment! My emotions, however, little resembled devotion, passion, love, yearning, infatuation, attachment or amorousness.

The music started playing, and we started to move. Or rather, *he* started to move *me*. After a few moments, he said, so low only I could hear:

'This isn't working.'

'Really? Whatever gave you that idea?'

'The fact that you've stamped on my feet three times already points rather strongly in that direction.'

'Indeed?'

'Yes, indeed. Also, you're glowering at me like a vengeful fury from hell.'

'Ah, you've finally noticed that, have you?'

Shooting me a cold glare, he leaned closer.

'Remember,' he growled, 'we are in love, you and I!'

Something painful tugged at my heart. I clamped down on the feeling, hard.

'No, we aren't!'

'Oh yes, we are, my darling.' Spinning me around in time with the music, he pulled me close. His dark, sea-coloured eyes sparkled in the candlelight, and before I could prevent it, his lips met mine. There, in public, on the dance floor!

Dash it all! What is he up to?

I didn't know, not in the least.

And you don't really care, as long as he doesn't stop kissing you, do you? Lilly, what is happening to you?

Ineffectually, I struggled to get out of his hold, but it was no use. His arms held me tightly, preventing my escape. And then I felt something delicious and wet tickle my lips.

Oh no! He isn't going to... No, not here, in public! He can't!

Apparently, he could. Half a second later, his powerful tongue parted my lips, invading my mouth. For one moment, just one moment, I surrendered myself to the blissful sensation. For that moment, I was dancing threefold. I was dancing with my feet, hardly noticing it anymore. I was dancing in my mouth, a delicious dance that sent my blood roaring through my veins. And I was dancing in my soul, more gracefully than I ever had in real life.

Then I heard the giggles. They came from all around us – nasty, female giggles that made it clear what they all thought of me. I gathered all my strength and, finding that it was just about enough, wrenched my mouth away from that of Rikkard Ambrose. Slowly opening eyes that had slid shut during the kiss, I stared into his perfect face, only an inch away.

'Just relax,' he murmured against my lips. 'Remember, we're in love. People who are in love kiss each other all the time.'

'I don't want to kiss you!' I lied, my teeth gritted. 'I don't love you! I hate you!'

Something flashed in his dark eyes. 'Then I'd suggest you start pretending better!'

~~**~*~*

They didn't have solid chocolate in Egypt! Why? Probably because it melted too easily, or because that ingenious invention hadn't yet reached this distant corner of the earth. Sullenly, I slumped down on one of the chairs beside the refreshment tables and picked up a date from one of the plates. My gaze turned to the dance floor, where Mr Ambrose was waltzing away with the daughter of the French ambassador, who stayed here as part of an excursion up the Nile Delta. Pointing out to me that my way of dancing with him was likely to break his toes sooner or later, Mr Ambrose had suggested I sit down for a dance or two. So, now I was sitting and staring at the dancing pair, morosely.

'Blast!' I murmured. 'Why do the French have to have an ambassador in Egypt, anyway? It's not as though they import frogs or snails from here!'

Viciously, I bit down on the date, and winced. Not exactly my taste. What I needed to give me comfort right now was chocolate, massive amounts of chocolate, dark and sweet. But there was none to be had. I grabbed another date.

The music ended, and on the dance floor Mr Ambrose and the French girl parted. She smiled. He bowed to kiss her hand. She smiled more widely.

'Oh, sure,' I grumbled, stuffing another date into my mouth. 'You go ahead and leer at him! He's only *married* to me, so no problem. No, actually he isn't even married to me! But you don't know that, you little vixen, do you?'

Even from this distance I could see that the girl was very pretty. A small, delicate nose, dimples in her cheeks, the kind of eyelashes that seemed to have nothing to do but to flutter all day and a waist so slender Mr Ambrose could probably have reached around it with one hand.

Not that he had tried so far.

Good for him! So far, I had only been watching in silence, but that could change at a moment's notice.

Stepping away from the ambassador's daughter, he sat down at a distant table and ordered a glass of water – the only drink on the menu that didn't cost a single penny. His drink arrived. He took a sip. Then, as if sensing my gaze, he slowly raised his head to look over at me. Our eyes met. The meeting was quite a long one – at least long enough to sit down and have a nice discussion about recent politics and the weather. However, neither his or my eyes seemed seemed to be focused on such tame subjects.

'Ah! *Bon Dieu*, young *amour* is such a wonderful thing!'

My head snapped around. Sitting beside me was the Comtesse Somethingorother, a French noblewoman who was also staying at the hotel and to whom I had been briefly introduced the night before.

'I... I beg your pardon?' I stammered. My knowledge of French was a little shaky – all right, maybe 'non-existent' would be the better word – but still, I thought even I knew what that particular word meant. '*Amour?*'

The comtesse gave me a smile as warm as a pot full of cooked snails, and considerably more appealing.

'*Certainement, ma chérie*. How do you say again *en anglaise*...? "Love", is it not? Yes, that it is! Young love!'

I stared at her in perplexed amazement. 'Um... love?'

'But yes, *ma chérie*! It is blindingly obvious how much you are in love with your young man.'

As you all know, my cheeks weren't given to blushing. There was not much on this planet that could embarrass me, and two weeks in Egypt had given me an even healthier tan than usual. But right then, my cheeks ignored all commands of character and colouring and flushed a deep, burning red.

I, *in love*? And more than that, in love with *Rikkard Ambrose*? She had to be joking! It was all acting, and so far, I appeared to have made a miserable job of it!

'And he with you,' The comtesse added with a wink.

My jaw dropped.

That did it! I was decided – the old lady was off her rocker! The French government should really pay more attention to its foreign policy! First they allow their ambassadors to have daughters that are too pretty by half, and then they let crazy comtesses loose all across the world! That was simply irresponsible!

Mr Ambrose, in love with me? Yes, of course, he was madly in love with me! That was why he treated me with such kindness and respect! Ha! I might just as well believe that an iceberg could fall in love with a volcano.

Really? whispered a little voice in my head. *Cast your mind back a little to the tender feeling of his lips on yours, to the way he held you while you were dancing in the candlelight, and you weren't busy treading on his toes. Remember how he looked at you.*

He was acting! Of course he was acting!

Indeed? Do you think anyone could be that good an actor?

Yes! No! Oh... blast! I didn't know!

My eyes were drawn over to Mr Ambrose again. His dark, sea-coloured eyes had never left me.

The comtesse beside me chuckled and winked. 'What did I tell you, *ma chérie? Amour...*'

With that, she got to her feet and bustled off.

Unbelievable! There really should be an export embargo on crazy French aristocrats!

Mr Ambrose had nearly drained his glass by now. Taking a last swig, he placed it down on the table with a distinct *clink* I could hear even from where I was sitting, halfway across the room. Getting to his feet, he started towards me, his eyes full of ... what?

Devotion, passion, love, yearning, infatuation, attachment and amorousness, maybe?

Ha! Not hardly!

He walked in a dead straight line, not deviating an inch from his course at any time. Somehow he managed to walk at just the right pace to not collide with a single couple on the dance floor. Not once did he slow down. I straightened in my chair and hurriedly swallowed my last date.

'My dear Lillian.' Stopping in front of me, he bowed as coldly and precisely as a metal man driven by clockwork. 'Will you do me the honour of dancing with me?'

My eyes met his cold, hard ones. I? In love with *him*? Ha! Never! That old crone was off her rocker! I would show her!

'No, thank you.' I told him with a dignified inclination of the head.

The little finger on his left hand twitched. And twitched again. Oh dear, twice in a row? I must have really gotten his dander up.

Putting one hand on either arm of my chair, he leaned down towards me. He didn't stop moving when he invaded my personal space. I leaned backwards until I was pressed up against the backrest, but still he kept coming. He didn't stop until his face was only inches from mine. Then he unclenched his teeth and, in a very low, controlled voice, said:

'You are my loving wife, remember? That is not exactly compatible with you turning down my invitation to dance in front of the entire ballroom. May I enquire after your reasons?'

I met this old hag who propounded the most ludicrous theory - and I'll do my bloody best to prove her wrong! I'm not in love with you, do you hear? No, I'm definitely not!

'I, um... just don't feel like it.'

Mr Ambrose's voice lowered, to a level so dangerous it should have had a warning label on it. 'You *don't feel like it?*'

'Err... yep.'

'We are in a ballroom full of people, any number of whom could be Dalgliesh's spies, and you *don't feel like it?*'

'Yes.'

'Get up and get on the dance floor - now!'

In love? Ha! And double ha! Who could ever be in love with such an insufferable tyrant!

I met his cold stare head-on.

'I'm not in the mood to dance right now. Thank you for the offer. Maybe later.'

'There is no later. You will not ruin our disguise because of some senseless, irrational female mood!'

It isn't senseless, you granite-headed brute! I've just had someone tell me that I am in love with you! I need some time to recover from the shock! I mean... you? You are the most arrogant, opinionated, chauvinistic son of a bachelor south of the North Pole! That's like being told you love being hit over the head with a hammer and having your toes doused in boiling oil!

I raised my chin. 'One dance won't make a bloody bit of differen-'

I cut off in a yelp as Mr Ambrose snatched my hand and with one powerful tug tore me up out of my chair. His arm came around my waist like a snake, and in a moment we were whirling off, moving towards the dance floor.

Oh God... that feels wonderful...!

'Let go!'

Struggling against him, I tried to jam my heels into the floor - only to realize my feet were no longer touching the ground. Mr Ambrose was holding me up, effortlessly whirling me through the air. His face betrayed not the least exertion - as if he danced on air every day!

'I do not know what is the matter with you,' he growled into my ear, 'but get it under control now! I will not have this operation ruined. Not by you, and not by anyone!'

~~**~*~*

The next days showed me how serious he was. Occasional forays into the city were fitted in between hours of dancing, dining and hand-holding. I tried to do my best, I really did! Heck, I was being paid for this, after all! But...

But I couldn't banish that word from my head.

Fake. Fake. Fake. All of this was fake.

Yes it is. And why the dickens do you care that much?

That was a very good question. One I asked myself again and again over the next few days, but never found an answer to. My frustration grew, along with my tendency to act like a stubborn mule on union strike.

'This isn't working.' Mr Ambrose's voice was low and cold, like morning mist creeping over the ground on a winter morning. We were at dinner, and I had spent half my time stabbing at my food, the other half glowering at his impossibly perfect face. This was the first time the silence between us had been broken. 'At least try to be convincing.'

'I am!' I informed him serenely. If I weren't, my objects for glowering and stabbing would have been exchanged over ten minutes ago.

'Your last chance!' His voice... oh, why did that cold voice of his have to send such a delicious tingle down my spine? I ignored it – and him – and stabbed another carrot with my fork. 'Your very last chance, I'm warning you.'

I remained silent. Why? I had no idea. I could have smiled and laughed and danced like a good little secretary, I supposed. It shouldn't have been that difficult. It really shouldn't, but...

But there was that word in the back of my mind.

Fake. Fake. Fake.

And then there was the French's lady's voice, sighing *Bon Dieu, young amour is such a wonderful thing.*

For reasons I could not fathom, those words made me lash out. I knew that, for no reason at all, I was behaving like a complete shrew. No, worse – I was behaving like a wicked witch who hadn't had enough children to gobble up for a week. But then, I'd always had a thing for wicked witches, so I didn't feel a particular need to change my behaviour.

'As you wish.' Nobody could convey more quiet menace with these three little words than Rikkard Ambrose. They thrummed with a freezing force that even I, sunk deep in my strange and inexplicable mood, felt to my very core. Slowly, he rose to his feet. 'Finish your dinner, Wife.'

I looked up questioningly. His plate was still half full. 'You're already done?'

'I feel like retiring early tonight.' And with that, he turned and marched up the stairs.

I remained, my mouth slowly chewing the rest of my dinner, while my brain was busy chewing on my conflicting feelings. Let's just say that my mouth was vastly more successful in turning everything into an easily digestible mush.

Suppressing a yawn, I finally got to my feet. It had been an exhausting day. The forays into the darkest parts of the city, the constant fear of another attack and, worst of all, the need to try and pretend to be blissful all day was really getting to me. Stretching, I crossed the dining hall and started to climb the stairs to our suite.

The moment I approached the door I knew something was wrong! Noises were coming from inside. Not the noises of a fight, or the kind you'd expect a burglar to make, thank God! No, those were unquestionably moans. It sounded as someone was in mortal pain!

My mouth dropped open in horror.

Blast! Mr Ambrose went up early because he didn't feel well! What if he... if he...

I didn't even want to think of what could have happened to him. Horror-stories of a thousand tropical diseases I had read about in books or papers flashed through my mind. Rushing towards the door, I made a grab for the door-knob. If he was sick...

The door crashed open. I plunged inside – and froze.

It only took me one heartbeat to see that I had been mistaken. Mr Ambrose was not sick. In fact, he appeared to be very healthy and vigorous. And so did the girl clenched in his arms.

FAVOURS AND FIRES

It took the two of them a moment to notice me. Quite impressive, considering the noise I was making, stomping into the room. But then, they appeared to be busy. Very, very busy.

I cleared my throat.

Neither Mr Ambrose nor the female, who, if I wasn't very mistaken, was the daughter of the French ambassador I had seen him dance with not too long ago, paid me the slightest attention. Just when their lips were about to touch, I decided it was time for more drastic measures. Grabbing a nearby side table I pushed, hard, and it toppled it over. The table and everything on it landed on the floor with an almighty, satisfying crash.

Disengaging from each other, they both turned to look at me. The girl's eyes were blinking rapidly in confusion. Mr Ambrose, the devil curse him into all eternity, was looking just as cool and collected as if he had just been sipping tea!

'Hasn't your mother ever taught you to knock before coming in?' he enquired.

The girl looked from me to him and back again. 'Who is sat, 'enry?' she demanded in a heavily accented voice.

'No one of consequence, *chérie*,' Mr Ambrose assured her.

Chérie?

If it hadn't been before, that was the point at which my blood started boiling. Trying not to look at the two of them or at their rumpled clothes, I stepped forward and picked Mr Ambrose's tailcoat up off the floor.

'Here.' I hurled the thing at him. I was hoping it would hit him in the head, but he caught it, effortlessly. 'Put that on. And you...' Turning to the girl, I pointed a finger at the door. 'Out!'

She stared at me, then turned her gaze to Mr Ambrose. 'Who is sat?'

'I'm his *wife*,' I informed her coldly. Well, why not? It was true, damn it! Well, sort of.

That made her look at me again, longer this time. It also made her eyebrows shoot up in disbelief. She looked back at Mr Ambrose once more.

'Sis one? Your wife?

'She is,' he allowed. 'In a manner of speaking.'

'Oh. *Alors*, if sat is se case...' She untangled herself from Mr Ambrose, and curtsied to me. 'I 'ope I 'ave not inconvenienced you, Madame.'

My mouth dropped open, stunned. She didn't seem to suffer from any such problems in dealing with the situation. She just laced up her half-open gown and left the room, not without blowing a kiss to Mr Ambrose in parting.

When the door had closed behind her, I marched up to my so-called husband, who, I saw to my great relief, was completely dressed again by now.

'What was *that*?' I snapped.

'That? That was Mademoiselle Bertrand, the ambassador's daughter.'

I had been tempted to murder him before, but that was nothing compared to the temptation I had to withstand in that moment.

'I know who she is,' I whispered. 'I want to know what you were doing with her!'

'We were engaged in preparations for a process known, I believe, as "osculating".'

'*Osculating*? Indeed?'

'Yes. Though sometimes, in a less formal context, one might also use the term "kissing" or "smooching". In any case, the words all denote a common human mating ritual and precursor to congress.'

'You mean you were *whoring*?'

'Certainly not.' He almost looked indignant. Indignant! *He!* 'You have to *pay* a woman to be whoring. She didn't get one penny from me, I can promise you that. What do you take me for?'

I was shaking. I didn't even know why I was so angry – bloody hell, I had no right to be! I wasn't married to him; it was all just a disguise; one, moreover, that I had done my best to fight, subvert and shatter! But...

That was just the problem. But.

'What did I take you for?' My eyes were burning. 'I took you for an honourable man! Apparently, I was mistaken!'

He had turned to the nearest window, to straighten his bow tie in its mirror-like surface. His reflection looked at me, all cool arrogance with a hint of displeased surprise.

'Correct me if I'm wrong, but you do not seem too pleased at my plans to osculate with Mademoiselle Bertrand.'

'Pleased?' My eyes almost bugged out of my sockets. 'You expected *me* to be *pleased*?'

'Certainly.' He gave another tug to his bow tie, and nodded, satisfied. 'After all, I undertook the whole matter for your sake.'

'Maybe,' I told him in a voice that could have frozen lava, 'I'm not the most experienced person in male-female interactions, but I fail to see how you can please one woman by kissing another.'

'I should have thought it is quite obvious.' Finished with his bow tie, he now went on to straightening his shirt. He didn't seem to notice that, from behind, I was trying to murder him with my eyes. 'It was clear that you were not pleased at having to play my loving bride. I had to find a solution. Ergo, I set out to find another female to osculate. The girl I selected is an utter gossip monger, and the story of my extra-marital adventure will be all over the hotel in at most half an hour, thus providing you the opportunity to switch from the role of loving wife to boiling angry, jealous and cantankerous wife – a role to which I think you are eminently better suited. Our disguise will once more be perfect, and Dalgliesh's spies will have no reason to suspect we are anything else than what we proclaim to be.' Content with his appearance, he clapped his hands and turned towards me. 'Problem solved, to our mutual satisfaction. There, what do you say?'

I didn't say anything. My mouth was opening and closing, no words coming out.

'Hello?' Mr Ambrose took a step forward. 'Are you all right?'

In a small part of my mind, far from the boiling flood that filled the rest of me, I dispassionately noted that, actually, seen from a logical and unemotional point of view, his explanation had made perfect sense. The only problem was I wasn't very disposed to be logical and unemotional right now.

He took another step forward. 'Are you all right, my love?'

That did it. Those two little words at the end. My eyes, open in shock right up to that moment, narrowed, blazing with fire. I took a step towards him.

'I see,' I said, my voice mild. 'You did all that for my benefit. How thoughtful. So did you just want to let her spread rumours behind my back, or did you plan on me coming in and discovering you?'

He shrugged. 'Either would have sufficed. But I was hoping to draw the thing out until you came. I thought it would be much more effective, and help you more in acting your new role as a jealous wife. Are you pleased with the alteration to the plan?'

He was serious! He was actually serious! God! That man might be the most brilliant financier and businessman to walk the earth since King Croesus, but he had bricks for brains where women were concerned!

'What do you think?' I purred. 'Do I look pleased?'

He regarded me for a few moments. 'Oddly enough... no, you don't.'

'How very observant of you.'

'What is the matter? Do you think my idea won't work? That the Bertrand female won't spread rumours about our tryst through the hotel?'

My eyes sparked. 'Oh, I'm sure she's already at it.'

'Then don't you think that will be enough to distract any watchers who were suspicious of us before?'

'Of course it will.' The fire in my eyes felt like two stars now, burning bright hot. 'Your plan was very well thought out. I'm sure it will work beautifully.' Blast him, but it was! Still, that didn't mean I didn't want to take his head off for it!

'Then what's the matter?'

I was trembling. 'You... you...! Don't you realize? Don't you realize what you've done?'

'Certainly I do. I've made your life a whole lot easier. Next time when we are at dinner, you can snap and shout at me till your heart's content.'

'You bastard!'

His sea-coloured eyes flashed darkly. 'I don't particularly see why you are so aggravated. You are not the one who had to fondle that female.' Wiping his fingers on his sleeve, he shuddered. 'Can you imagine? She actually perfumes her neck with lavender! Bah!'

A muscle in my cheek twitched. It wasn't the one I used for smiling. 'You have my profoundest sympathy.'

'Thank you.'

He thought I meant it! He honestly thought I meant it!

I raised an eyebrow. 'And will you go to bed with her as part of your little charade, too?'

He cocked his head thoughtfully, as if this idea hadn't yet occurred to him. 'Do you think I should? If you believe it necessary, I suppose I could–'

What?

'Argh!' I gripped my head with both hands, trying to keep from pulling my hair out. 'You're impossible!'

'I take objection to that.'

'Oh, you do, do you?'

'Indeed. The matter under discussion has nothing to do with the plausibility of my existence. I am quite certain that I exist. As the philosopher Descartes said, "I think, therefore I am".'

'Well, think about that!' Grabbing an orange from a nearby table, I hurled it at him. He ducked, and the fruit bounced harmlessly off the wall.

He gave an approving nod. 'Quite acceptable acting! That's exactly the kind of attitude you need to project now, for your new role as jealous wife.'

'If you ever come near that hussy gain, I'll kill you, do you hear me? I'll cut off your head, fill it with ice cream and eat it for breakfast!'

He stood there, slowly stroking his finger along his chiselled chin, regarding me consideringly.

'You know, for someone who is only playacting, you are a quite extraordinarily convincing jealous wife.'

'Of course.' I flashed him my tigress smile again. 'After all, you pay me for it.'

'Indeed.'

'So... what now?' Slowly prowling towards him, I eyed his hard, cold figure. 'What do you expect a woman to do? Run off screaming into the night? Crawl away to weep in a corner?'

'Probably.'

My eyes narrowed into slits. 'Ah, but you see, a wife wouldn't do that. At least not one worthy of the title. No, I won't pretend to run off. Instead, since I'm pretending to be your wife, I ought to pretend to be very, very angry at you.'

He considered this for a moment. Finally, he nodded his agreement. 'Yes.'

'Good.'

The first vase missed his head only by inches, shattering against the wall.

'I'm so glad to have your agreement, my dear!'

Grabbing the second vase of flowers from the dresser, I hurled it at him with all the force I could muster, careful to take better aim. He ducked just in time. The vase crashed against a portrait and splintered into a thousand pieces.

Marching over to the table, I picked up another and flung it after the first two – but that one flew wide of the target, sailing over his head and out the window. It shattered with a distant, lonesome crash somewhere on the cobblestones outside.

I didn't give him time to recover. Dashing forward like a mad fury, I hurled myself at him and started pounding on his chest.

'I hate you! I hate you, I hate you, I hate you, I hate you!'

'Quite satisfactory,' his cool voice reached my ear, like silk sliding over steel. 'Your acting has significantly improved.'

'Thanks!' My next punch hit him in the stomach. Bloody hell! It was as hard as a slab of granite! I hit again, and satisfaction rushed through me as he uttered a small groan.

'Really, quite significantly improved!' he grunted.

'Here! Take that, you bastard! And that! And that!' His hands shot up, grabbing me around the wrists. 'Let go! Let go, you bloody son of a bachelor!'

'So you can continue to utilize me as your own personal punching bag?' His tone was as dry as it was cold. 'I think not.'

'You... you...!'

'I must say, I am quite impressed, Mr Linton. You play the shrew exceedingly well. One might almost think the performance were genuine.'

'I am just doing my job!'

'Very thoroughly, I must say.'

'Thank you so much, Sir.'

'By the way, you'll pay for that vase out of your wages.'

'I don't give a damn who pays for it! I'm staying here in Egypt as your wife! I'm finishing my job, do you understand?'

There was a moment of silence. He was still holding me in his iron grip, and we stared at each other over the small, insurmountable distance between us, hardly able to make out each other's faces. I was breathing hard.

Maybe a bit too hard for someone who's only pretending to be angry...

That inner voice of mine should really learn to shut up!

'Do you,' I asked taking deep breaths to calm myself, 'understand?'

Another moment of silence. Finally:

'Yes.'

'I'm staying as your wife?'

'Yes.'

My eyes narrowed. 'And you realize that, in that role, I'm going to pretend to hate you passionately?'

Slowly, very slowly, he began to remove his hands from around my wrists. I made no move to attack him again. 'Something tells me that will not be very difficult for you.'

My lips twitched. Upward? Downward? I had no idea. I didn't have a hope of understanding the emotions roiling inside me right now. 'That's what I thought, too. I mean... you are an arrogant son of a bachelor. Nothing should be easier than to hate you, and as your fake wife, that's all I'd have to do to play my role, right?'

His hands let go of my wrists fully, and he took a step back. 'Right.'

His voice was unusually hesitant. He seemed to know that there was something still to come.

'But then I thought...' I took a step forward, towards him. When he stepped back again, I stepped forward once more, following him across the room. 'I thought, since I'm pretending I'm married to you...'

'Yes?'

Another step back for him, another step forward for me. We were at the window now, his waist pressed into the windowsill. He couldn't step back any more, unless he wanted to start a new career as a gory stain on the cobblestones of Alexandria.

'Since I'm supposedly married to you, now matter how much I hate you, I would also have to pretend that I'm still in love with you!' My hands shot forward. Grabbing his collar, I pulled him down until he was on my level and I could glare right into his dark eyes. 'I'd have to pretend to tell you that you're mine, and I'll be damned if I let some French hussy steal you away from me!'

A low rumble erupted from his chest. 'Then I'd have to pretend to say: I don't need a French hussy! I don't want her! I don't want anyone but you!'

I pulled him a few inches closer. 'And I'd have to pretend to say: prove it!'

Maybe I should not have said that. Oh, all right, I *definitely* should not have said that.

Why?

Because he took me at my word!

In a fraction of a second, his hands were at my face, caressing lightly, holding tightly. His lips crashed down on mine, soft as a feather and hard as a mountain of stone. He invaded me, possessed me, took hold of me. Not just of my mouth, but of all of me. I could feel his hands letting go of my face, picking me up from the floor and carrying me away to...where?

I did not know. I didn't really care.

Through the daze around my mind, I heard a crash. My eyes, closed in bliss up until then, flew open to see the double doors to the master bedroom swinging loosely on their hinges. A moment later, I heard the creak of metal feathers from beneath me and felt something soft at my back. The chaise lounge again?

But... wait just a moment! There was no chaise lounge in the bedroom. It was a *bedroom*. There was only one thing with feathers in here, and it started with a b!

The realization flooded through me like a whole bucket chain of cold water. I was in bed! I was in bed with a man!

You're both still dressed, aren't you? What's the harm?

The harm? I was a feminist! I was supposed to despise men! *That* was the harm!

Well, you can despise him far better if you're up close, can't you?

Bloody hell, no!

Just relax. He's still dressed, you're still dressed - this is harmless. And oh... quite nice, by the way. Don't you feel that?

That was the moment when I felt Mr Ambrose's fingers at the buttons of my dress. They didn't seem to be there to check how large the buttons were. No, his intent was an entirely different one. Looking up at his dark form above me, I saw that somehow he had managed to remove his tailcoat again. His shirt was unbuttoned at the top, revealing the smooth, hard planes of his chest.

My breath caught.

'So far, your acting hasn't been bad, my love,' he murmured into my ear, his breath caressing my earlobe. 'But there's one marital duty you've not fulfilled so far.'

A shiver raced down my spine, delicious fear and terrifying wonder in one.

'Oh yes?'

'Yes. We are on our honeymoon, after all. We still haven't had our wedding night. Not a true one.'

His fingers opened the first button. My heartrate picked up, hammering a drumbeat of ecstasy against my ribs.

What was wrong with me? I should be screaming bloody murder! Instead, my heart was ready to explode, and the traitorous corners of my mouth were curving up in a smirk. Reaching up for his free hand, I led it to my lips and placed a single, nipping kiss on the tips of his fingers.

'Indeed? But why should we? After all, Dalgliesh's spies won't know what we do or don't do in private.'

His eyes caught mine and held them. 'They might. They could be watching us right now.'

Another exhilarating thrill went down my back. Not that I truly believed they were, but...

'Do you really think so?' My smirk grew a bit wider, and I gently bit on the pad of his forefinger.

Out of the dark, I heard a cold hiss. 'Definitely! We have no choice but to keep up the pretence, my love.'

'Oh, well, if that's the case...'

I was going mad – completely and utterly mad! That was the only explanation for the words that were coming out of my mouth:

'In that case you had better get on with it, *Dick*.'

This time, the sound that came out of the dark was an infuriated growl. 'I told you... *Do not call me that!*'

I laughed. 'Why not, Di–'

My words were cut off by his mouth sealing mine. I wanted to protest – it was bloody rude to interrupt a lady! But his magic tongue started working, and I soon forgot about rudeness, I forgot about the letter r, I forgot about the whole bloody world! What the hell did I care if he was rude, if he could make me feel like this? If he could send flames through my veins and set fire to my secret, hidden pyre?

Without any conscious command, my arms went up around him, pulling him closer until I could feel his rock-hard chest pressing into me. Some part of my mind, somewhere, kept wondering what exactly was going to happen. Truth be told, I had no clue what happened between a husband and wife on their wedding night. My mother had died when I was five, not exactly the right age to share that kind of information with a daughter, and I had never bothered to ask anyone else. After all, why would I? I was a dedicated feminist! I would never give myself up to a man like that!

Only... now I was.

His mouth moved away from mine, over my cheek and my chin, down to my throat. Wherever it went, it left burning brands of bloody unfeminist desire!

'I want you!' he growled out of the darkness.

'I want you, too!' I heard some female with a confoundedly weak and breathy voice whisper. Bloody hell! That couldn't have been *me*, could it?

Keep calm. It's all right. Remember: you're only pretending. This is all part of your job!

Oh, right. I had nearly forgotten that.

Mr Ambrose's mouth found the little hollow at the base of my throat, and he groaned as he reached it. 'You're so...God! I want you now!'

'Then stop wasting time! Knowledge is power is time is money, remember?' Grabbing the next two buttons, I fumbled, trying to get them open – and when they wouldn't open, just ripped them off! 'Show me your power! Go ahead!'

In a thin beam of moonlight, I briefly saw his eyes. They were burning with cold fire. Uttering a sound that no man, only beasts, should be able to make, he claimed my mouth again, and his hands went to claim the rest of me.

No! That's going too far! I shouldn't...! Should I...? No! No... no... n...... Y-yes... Yes! Yes, yes, yes, yeeees!

My hands slid up towards him and met with the unwelcome barrier of his shirt. Scowling, I gripped it at the placket.

He's not going to like this much, you know. He's going to make you pay for having the buttons stitched back on.

Oh, to hell with the buttons! I got a good grip and, with one tug, ripped his shirt open, surging towards him!

That was the moment when the wall exploded.

EXPLOSIONS AND ABDUCTIONS

Just to be clear: I'm not speaking in metaphors. I don't mean that an emotional wall between Mr Ambrose and me exploded and we were suddenly free to engage in unbridled lust. (Because that had, of course, already happened five minutes ago.) No, I mean that the wall *literally* exploded.

Which wall, you want to know?

To be honest, I'm not entirely sure. It's not very easy to register such things when you're thrown through the air by the force of a terrific blast. One moment, Mr Ambrose and I were clenched in a passionate (though, of course, fake!) embrace on the bed, the next we were hurled with passionate force against the nearest wall that was still standing, the bed raining down in splinters around us.

I hadn't even started to figure out which way was up and which was down when the first gunshot exploded through the night. Through the hole in the wall, I could see flashes from outside, and with a *thud*, something hard buried itself in the wall next to my head.

'Down!' Apparently, Mr Ambrose was quicker than me at figuring out the up-and-down thing. He knew which was which, and proceeded to demonstrate it to me by throwing himself on top of me and slamming me down onto the floor, squashing all the air out of me.

'Oumpf!'

'Stay down! They're firing!'

I opened my mouth to tell him I had noticed that, thanks very much, but I got a mouthful of mortar and wood splinters, and choked.

Crash!

The door flew open and Karim loomed in the doorway, his sabre in one hand, a gun in the other. He took in the scene with one fierce glare.

Roaring a guttural battle cry, he rushed forward and leapt through the hole in the wall without the slightest hesitation. From beyond the ragged opening came a scream. It wasn't his.

'That's right!' Shoving Mr Ambrose off me, I struggled to my feet. 'Show those bastards!' Grabbing the nearest thing to a weapon – a copper statue of the Egyptian god Ra with a wickedly sharp hawk's beak – I made to step forward. I wasn't going to be outdone by Karim!

'Not so fast!' An iron-hard arm encircled my waist, holding me back without the least effort. 'Where do you think you are going?'

'Let me go!' Struggling against Mr Ambrose's unbreakable grip, I tried to get nearer to the smoking opening in the wall. 'Let me go, I said! I'm going to show them! I'm going to–'

'...come with me without making any trouble.'

'No!'

'Yes.'

With a swift kick, he swept my feet out from under me. Giving a startled cry, I fell back, and he caught me, lifting me into the air.

'You bloody bastard! Let me down!'

'No.'

He started forward.

'Let me down, now! I will not be carried out of here like a damn parcel!'

'No, not like a parcel,' he agreed, his eyes burning with cold fire. 'Not at all.' And, bending down, he pressed a passionate kiss on my lips. By the time he released my mouth and I could remember how to breathe, we were already out in the hallway – over the threshold.

Only he didn't carry you into your new home, clad in a white dress. He carried you out of a recently exploded hotel suite with a dress that is practically ripped in half!

Well, a girl can't have everything.

'Let me down!' I commanded once more. 'I can walk perfectly well on my own, do you hear me? Let me down!'

Ignoring me, he started marching down the corridor, his eyes flicking from right to left.

'I said let me dow-'

A man with dagger in his hand sprang from a doorway to our left. Mr Ambrose's hands darted with admirable speed into his tailcoat and drew forth a pistol, which he cocked and aimed. There was only one problem. To use his hand to hold the pistol, those hands did first have to let go of me.

'-ooouuch!'

Bang!

The lifeless form of the attacker dropped to the ground beside me, a big hole in his blue shirt that was suddenly rimmed by red. Above me, Mr Ambrose checked to see if any more men were coming, then calmly started reloading his gun.

'You know,' I moaned from floor-level, rubbing my aching derrière, 'when I said "let me down", I meant *slowly.*'

'Indeed?' Pressing himself against the wall, Mr Ambrose spied around the corner, his dark eyes sharp and searching. 'I'll remember that for the next time we're bombed and shot at. Now, stay down and be silent!'

I didn't particularly care for his tone. But seeing as he was the one with the gun in his hand, I thought it for once wise not to argue. Crawling towards the wall and pressing myself as flat against it as humanly possible, I tried to slow my ragged breathing and listen. Out of the distance came the sound of men's shouts and ladies' screams. From a few rooms down the corridor we could hear the sound of something big snarling. That was probably Karim at work. I pitied the poor fools who got in his way.

Then, from around the corner, the sound of footsteps came. Hasty footsteps, hurrying this way. Taking a deep breath, Mr Ambrose shifted his gun until it was pointing straight forward, ready to shoot anyone who would come around the corner. I caught myself hoping that it would be Mademoiselle Bertrand.

Be reasonable! It was just a kiss! No, not even that much! You don't want the girl to die for that, do you?

No, that was right, I didn't. I wanted her to be poked with hot irons, subjected to Chinese water torture and forced to beg on her knees for my forgiveness. *Then* I wanted her to die.

Someone ran around the corner, and proved that there was no justice in the world: it wasn't Mademoiselle Bertrand. It wasn't even some equally shootworthy skunk, but a perfect stranger. A lanky man in Egyptian dress, who stopped dead when Mr Ambrose's revolver came to rest against his temple. Slowly, the man's eyes wandered to his right, trying to see, without moving, the barrel of the weapon that was threatening to blow his brains out. Instead, he caught an eyeful of Mr Ambrose.

'E-*effendi?*'

'Ah, Youssef. It's you.' Mr Ambrose lowered his gun. 'An explanation! How could this have happened? I hired you to guard us!'

The man winced. 'I'm sorry, *Effendi*! They tricked us! The men with the bomb, they did not try to sneak in, but came into the hotel as regular guests, and booked the room next to yours. They looked perfectly harmless! They...'

Another explosion went off somewhere. The ringing silence that followed was broken only by a gurgling sound that didn't sound very healthy.

'I think we should leave this place, *Effendi*,' the newcomer suggested.

Mr Ambrose nodded. 'Agreed. Lead the way.'

Putting two fingers to his lips, Youssef let loose an ear-piercing whistle. In a moment, more men had emerged from around the corner. They were a motley crew, everything from black over brown to white. Yet they all had the same sharp look in their eyes.

Youssef nodded to them.

'We're getting out of here. Jabalah, Tahir – you check the corridors to the left. Francois, Umar, you check to the right. Sango, you scout ahead!'

A brawny, pitch-black individual shot down the corridor in front of us, and four figures less well endowed with pigments immediately vanished down the corridors on either side.

'The rest of you, form a circle around Ambrose *Effendi. Yalla!*[19] What are you waiting for?'

In an instant, there was a protective wall of bodies around Mr Ambrose. The men were obviously experts at their work. It was all very impressive. There was only one problem: I was *outside* the wall.

Slowly, I rose to my feet.

'Um... excuse me?' I tapped one of the men on the back. Whirling around, he drew his knife and had it at my throat before I could blink.

'I wouldn't recommend that.'

The man froze. Both he and I looked to the origin of the voice. A gap had opened in the wall of bodies, and Mr Ambrose was regarding the knife at my throat with cold eyes. Slowly, his gaze rose to the face of the man holding it.

'The lady is with me.'

The knife clattered to the ground, falling from suddenly limp fingers.

'Come.' Jerking his head, Mr Ambrose indicated for me to step into the protective wall of bodyguards. For once, I followed his orders without hesitation. 'I think it's time we leave.'

We rushed down the hallway, I sometimes running, sometimes sneaking, Mr Ambrose keeping up a pace steadier than clockwork. More than once I heard a shout, shot or gurgle from outside the protective circle, but never once did I get to see their origin. Down the stairs and out into the dining hall we went. The place looked as if the last dinner guests had been a herd of loony elephants. Tables were turned over or smashed to bits, fans, handkerchiefs and bits of food cluttered the floor, and even one of the chandeliers had fallen, and crashed right through a table. Nobody was in sight – not a single soul.

'Where now?' I demanded, trying to peek over the heads of our bodyguards. I had only seen the dining hall while coming down the stairs, when the men in

---

[19] An Arabian expression meaning 'Hurry up!'

front of me had been two steps below, opening my line of sight. Now, with them towering all around me once more, I couldn't see a thing.

'This way, *Hanem*.'[20] With a slight bow, Youssef indicated the direction.

When we entered the lobby, our group of protectors split up. Half stayed around us, in a looser group, the other half darted through the doors out onto the street, knives and pistols at the ready. Dazed, I took a look around. The lobby, too, looked as if a tornado had swept through it. Everyone had to have fled in a rush when they heard the sound of gunfire. Wait, no!

Not everyone.

'Mr Linton? Stop! What are you doing?'

Until Mr Ambrose called after me, I hadn't realized that I had started moving, slipping out of the protective circle of men. But even as his voice reached me, I didn't stop, but instead strode directly towards my goal, a diminutive little figure snoring in an armchair in the corner of the room. Stooping down beside her, I gently shook her shoulder.

'Ma'am? Ma'am, I'm afraid you'll have to wake up.'

Raising her head, the drowsy figure blinked up at me. 'What?'

'You're going to wake up and come with us,' I said, louder this time. 'I'm afraid there's been a disturbance in the hotel! It's not safe for you here, at the moment.'

'What did you say, dear? Speak up, I can't understand you!' Then the old lady looked around and for the first time noticed the upturned chairs, dropped fans, and broken windowpanes around her. 'Goodness gracious me! Did those young people throw another of their festivities? Looks like they got a bit above themselves, doesn't it? I really wish someone would take these youths in hand. Young people nowadays have no discipline, that's the problem! No discipline, and no consideration.'

'I'm sure you're quite right, Ma'am, but in this case it's not really a festivity, you see, it–'

Somewhere above us, another ear-splitting explosion rocked the hotel.

'There you are!' Shaking her head, the old woman pointed a stick-like finger upwards. 'Drinking champagne, popping corks... I can hear it from hear! Disgraceful!'

'Um, yes, certainly, Ma'am. And I'm sure you'd like to leave such a disgraceful place, wouldn't you? Right now, as a matter of fact?'

The old lady blinked at me owlishly. 'What did you say, dear?'

'I said we ought to leave! *Right now!*'

'Show? Yes, you're quite right, my dear.' She patted my head affectionately. 'Somebody ought to show those rascals what is right! Someone ought to teach them a lesson.' Reaching for her walking cane, she slowly pushed herself to her feet and stood there, wobbling precariously. 'I suppose I'd better go and...'

---

[20] An expression equivalent to the English 'Ma'am'. Dear me, when I'm finished with writing this book, I'll be able to order breakfast in Arabic. That would be something, wouldn't it?

That was the moment when Mr Ambrose decided to intervene. Striding forward, he grabbed the old lady around the midriff and lifted her over his shoulder.

'Let's go,' he told an open-mouthed yours truly and turned to march out of the door, the old lady's walking stick thwacking repeatedly against his back in time to her shrieks of protest. I hurried after him, catching up only when he already was by the door.

'Do you... think this is... really the best idea?' I panted, pointing to the old lady over his back.

Thwack!

'Help! Help! I'm being abducted! Help me!'

Thwack! Thwack!

'I can leave her here, if you wish,' Mr Ambrose offered. He didn't break his stride once. He didn't even blink.

'That's not... what I... meant!'

Thwack!

'Help! Police! Arrest this villain!'

'Then what did you mean, Mr Linton? Do you wish to carry her?'

'No! I meant we should set her down and explain things to her!'

'By all means, try, if you want to stay here to get shot.'

Mumbling a curse, I suppressed my further arguments. He did have a point. The old lady didn't seem to be very receptive to any new concepts delivered without the help of a megaphone.

On the courtyard outside the hotel, a coach was already waiting for us. Mr Ambrose shoved the old lady inside with the sweet gentleness of a charging bull, then picked me up and threw me in after her.

'Hey! What do you–'

Before I could finish my protest, I landed solidly on the hard bench and got my breath knocked out of me. Mr Ambrose swung in after me and slammed the door shut. Through the open window, he shot a last look back at the hotel.

Another explosion made the ground shudder. The windows on the third floor of the hotel burst outward, spewing tongues of flame into the night. Sparks rained down upon the courtyard like a hailstorm from hell.

Mr Ambrose cocked his head thoughtfully. 'Well, I think our cover has been blown.'

I snorted. 'You don't say!'

'Kidnapper! Villain! Black-hearted rogue! Don't you dare to touch me!'

Grabbing his cane, Mr Ambrose thumped it against the roof of the coach. 'Drive! Now!'

~~**~*~*

I never learned where we spent the next night. After depositing the old lady at a suitable hotel with less chance of rooms exploding, Mr Ambrose muttered some unintelligible destination to the driver, and soon afterward we stopped in front of a dark building.

It was a large house, but considering that it had nearly no windows and most of it was filled with barrels that smelled strongly of fish, I didn't think it was usually meant for the purposes of habitation. There was a room in the back that had a fireplace, though, and a few blankets on the floor that served well enough for a bed, as tired as I was.

Youssef and the others never left. They took turns standing guard outside the door and in front of the small barred window.

'Won't the fellow who owns this place object to our being here?' I asked drowsily, my eyes already half-closed.

'I doubt it,' I heard Mr Ambrose's voice out of the darkness. 'It happens to belong to me – as do the four blocks of buildings around it.'

A smile tugged at my lips.

'Of course...'

And I drifted off to sleep.

The next morning, I was awakened by a rat nibbling on my shoe.

'Piss off,' I yawned, and kicked. Squeaking indignantly, the rodent scurried back.

'That is not a very polite greeting,' came a cool voice from the other side of the room. Rolling over, I saw Mr Ambrose standing near the small window, looking out between the bars into the street.

'I, um, wasn't talking to you.' I yawned again. It was astonishingly warm and comfortable in my little nest of blankets. Looking down, I saw that not just blankets were spread over me, but Mr Ambrose's cloak and tailcoat, too. He stood in the cold morning air wearing nothing but a shirt. A shirt, I noticed with some embarrassment, on which most of the buttons were missing.

'I see.' He still hadn't turned around, but kept looking out into the street.

Silence filled the room. Heavy silence. The knowledge of last night's events hung heavy in the air between us. Not the explosion, or the gunfire, no. They were insignificant compared to what had come before.

Hot skin on skin... mouths melding... whispered words in the darkness... a disguise carried a little too far. Far too far, in fact.

A ray of early morning sunlight jumped over the horizon, down through the iron bars into our little room. It made the dust motes dance a glittering jig in the air. Still, there was silence.

Finally, I cleared my throat.

'What now?'

The question had more than one meaning.

'Now?' At last, he turned to look at me. His cold, dark eyes regarded me as I half-sat, half-lay on the floor, the sheets draped around me. 'Now our cover is gone. Now we have only one choice. We go hunting for bandits!'

The steel in his voice sent a cold shiver down my back.

'That wasn't all I was asking,' I whispered, pulling the blankets more tightly around me. I couldn't help but be very conscious of the slivers of bare chest that peeked out through the gaps in his torn shirt. Even in the dim light that filtered in through the small window, his muscles seemed to gleam, smooth like stone.

141

Am I still 'married' to him? When I leave this room, will it be as Mrs Thomson, or will I be Mr Linton again? What fake identity will he make me use this time? And was what happened between us last night just as fake?

He regarded me for a moment, not saying a word. He might have said more, might have explained – but at that moment, someone knocked at the door.

Mr Ambrose turned away from me.

'Who is it?'

'It's Youssef, *Effendi*,' came a voice from outside. 'I've brought the clothes you requested.'

Instead of unbolting the door at once, Mr Ambrose first pulled his revolver and cocked it. Only then did he push the bolt on the door back. 'Come in.'

The Egyptian entered – only to find his head once more being touched by the barrel of a gun.

'I am alone, *Effendi*,' he said, perfectly unconcerned. I had to admire his composure. I knew that *I* would have been somewhat miffed if my employer went around waving guns at me! But Youssef seemed to consider it all part of the job.

'I see.' Mr Ambrose threw a look out of the open door, then gave a curt nod and put the gun away. 'I had to make sure. After last night...'

'No need to apologize, *Effendi*,' Youssef said with a bow. 'I quite understand.'

'He didn't actually apologize,' I pointed out, raising an eyebrow. 'Nor is he likely to, I fancy.'

Mr Ambrose shot me a dark look and, without saying anything, grabbed the packages Youssef was carrying. The smaller one contained a new shirt.

'What? You went to the expense of buying an entirely new shirt?' My other eyebrow shot up to join the first. 'Not just needle and thread to sew the buttons back on? You must be in a hurry!'

That earned me another dark look. Picking up the second, larger parcel, Mr Ambrose threw it to me, and I caught it in mid-air. My heart beat faster as I undid the string that held the wrapping together. From underneath the brown paper, I pulled not a shirt, nor a tailcoat, nor any other kind of men's clothes. Instead, I held a dress in my hands.

So... He wants you to continue to be a female – at least for now.

Slowly, I let the smooth material glide through my hands. With another shiver, I remembered his words to me, spoken in a moment of pretended passion.

While we are here, you're mine. Do you understand? Mine!

Apparently, he had meant what he said.

I heard a soft thud as Youssef stepped outside, closing the door behind him. Mr Ambrose rose, the new shirt in one hand, and before I realized what he meant to do, he pulled the torn one over his head. My mouth dropped open. He stood above me, gazing down at me with cool, sea-coloured eyes.

'Well? What are you waiting for? Get dressed.'

'Err... um...'

'Is something wrong, my love?'

'Well... err... I... um... err...'

Just in case I wasn't clear enough before, I'm going to repeat myself and make it explicit: he had pulled the torn shirt over his head – without leaving the room, stepping behind a screen, shrouding himself in magical mist or otherwise concealing himself – a shirt, I must emphasize at this point, under which there was nothing else. Absolutely nothing. *Nix. Nada.* At least nothing resembling clothing. But there was himself. A lot of himself, very firm, and hard, and *there.*

He cocked his head. It made certain parts of his neck and chest shift in an interesting way.

'Are you quite well, my love? There seems to be something wrong with your facial muscles.'

'I... um... err...'

'If you're ill you had better tell me right now. Once I start after the bandits I'll need to travel quickly, and I can't have you tagging along if you're going to hold me back.'

'I, um... no. I'm fine. Quite fine. Actually, I feel excellent. There's nothing wrong with me whatsoever.'

'Well, then get dressed.'

I took a deep breath.

Gather your eyeballs up off the floor and get your head straight! Just because he's so very... himself, that doesn't mean you have to act like a stupid damsel. You're a feminist and a suffragist!

Only, it was a lot harder to be a feminist with Mr Ambrose standing over me half-naked.

He made an impatient gesture. 'Didn't you hear me? Get a move on!'

'Certainly.' Raising my chin, I did the impossible and met his gaze. 'Just as soon as you get out.'

He blinked. Just once, like a lizard that saw a fly make a surprising twitch, but that still knew the fly was going to be eaten. 'Excuse me?'

I met his gaze head-on. 'You heard me. Get out!'

Stay strong, Lilly! Just because you were ready to rip his clothes off a little time ago doesn't mean he gets to stay to watch you take off yours! That was part of the job – this isn't! Stay strong!

We gazed at each other for one long minute, neither of us willing to break the staring contest. An impressively long time, considering how much Mr Ambrose despised all kinds of time-wasters. Finally, he jerked his head in a movement that could be seen as a nod, or maybe a headshake, turned on his heels, and marched out of the door, his upper body still conspicuously lacking in the clothing department.

That was close!

Letting out a breath of relief, I quickly slipped out of my old dress and into the new one. Already under normal circumstances I hardly ever noticed what colour or pattern a dress was, and right at the moment I had no attention to spare for fashion whatsoever. But what I did notice as I pushed my hands through the sleeves was the thing glinting golden on my finger. One of the rings Mr Ambrose had given me. The wedding ring of Mrs Richard Thomson.

Almost unconsciously, I took my left hand with my right, and examined it in the shaft of sunlight falling in through the window. The gold sparkled in the early morning glow. I felt an odd tugging sensation somewhere inside me.

Harrumphing, I let the hand drop. Probably indigestion!

Can you have indigestion in the heart?

Yes, you bloody well could! Determinedly not looking at the sparkling ring around my finger, I buttoned up my dress and yanked on my hair, in the hope to make it a little more presentable. Although, once we were in the desert, that would hardly matter.

Finished, I opened the door and stepped out. I hadn't been mistaken last night. It really smelled rather strongly of fish in this place. I had my suspicions about the contents of the barrels stacked up around us.

'I must commend you on your choice of accommodation,' I said with a smile and gracious curtsy to Mr Ambrose. 'You could not have found a more romantic location for our wedding night.'

I waited for him to snap at me, to insist on my calling him 'Sir' again – but it didn't happen. Instead he took a step closer and leaned forward, gently stroked one finger over my cheek and down the side of my neck, making me shiver.

'You're welcome, my love.'

While we are here, you're mine. Do you understand? Mine!

I swallowed.

'What next?'

'Well, it appears our ruse has been discovered. We have no hope of acquiring any further information here in Alexandria – at least not without having to dodge bullets left and right.' His eyes became hard – or perhaps I should say harder. 'I know Dalgliesh. He's not going to shrink from spilling blood – especially if he has the chance of spilling mine.'

'Why don't we simply go to the authorities?' I voiced a question that had been bothering me for quite some time. 'Surely, there's such a thing as police here in Egypt? If we tell them...'

'Tell them what? That Lord Daniel Eugene Dalgliesh, Peer of the Realm of Great Britain and Ireland, Member of the Most Noble Order of the Garter and one of the major foreign investors in the Egyptian economy is hiring assassins to eliminate business rivals? Tell me, what do you think they would say?'

'Well...' I tugged on my lower lip. 'They might be just a tiny bit sceptical.'

'Indeed. Do you know what the motto of the Order of the Garter is?'

'No.'

'It is *Honi soit qui mal y pense* – in English, that means *Shame upon him who thinks evil of it*. It could be Lord Dalgliesh's personal motto, in a twisted way. He might be evil as the devil, but his reputation is spotless, and his power immense.'

'But yours must be, too! You're nearly as rich as he!'

Mr Ambrose's eyes sparkled, coldly. 'Richer! *I* am the richest man of the British Empire, not *he*!'

'Yes, I'm sure you–'

'I surpassed him long ago! His wealth cannot compare with mine, do you understand? I am the first! I am the best! I am the stronger and the richer!'

'Um... yes, of course you are.'

Ouch! Apparently, I had struck a sore spot, there. Taking that into consideration, my next words probably weren't very smart.

'Um... how much richer, exactly?'

This time, his eyes flashed with lightning. 'Currently,' he said in a voice clinking with ice-cubes, 'I believe the difference between our fortunes stands at three pounds, twelve shillings and four pence.'

Wisely, this time I held my tongue.

'Unfortunately,' he continued, 'power isn't always measured in superior wealth. Lord Dalgliesh has political influence, built up over years of court intrigues, which I couldn't hope to gain in the short time since I've returned from the Colonies. And besides, there's the little fact of his private army to consider. Such things tend to impress foreign nations.'

That I could understand. I remembered all too well the men in scarlet uniforms at Lord Dalgliesh's command. As the main shareholder of the East India Company, he essentially had control over the army that company used to enforce its rule over the sub-continent. And he utilized this control freely, whenever and wherever it suited him.

'Well,' I repeated my question from earlier. 'If we can't go to the authorities, what then?'

'I shall take matters into my own hands, naturally. As I said before, we will leave the city. It is time to go bandit-hunting.'

'But... do we have enough information about their location?'

Most of Mr Ambrose's conversations with his informants had been conducted in foreign languages of which I understood nothing. He never seemed to feel it necessary to share the results with me, one of the reasons why I'd aimed frequent kicks at his feet whenever we had been dancing.

'Not enough to know where the bandits' camp is, exactly, no,' he admitted reluctantly. 'I only know their general area of operation, and that they have slowly been moving westwards, extending their raids farther and farther.'

'What use is that to us? We still don't know how to find them!'

So quickly I thought I might have imagined it, one corner of Mr Ambrose's mouth lifted up into what wasn't a smile, not even a half-smile, but a quarter-smile, at most. It still was more than you ever got to see from him... unless there was something very special ahead.

'I have a plan. If it works, we don't necessarily need to find them.'

I waited for further explanation – but I had forgotten with whom I was conversing. Turning away, Mr Ambrose gestured to Youssef.

'Youssef! Alert the men! We're going!'

My heart made a leap. I had known this was coming, but still... Last night had really driven home what I had gotten myself into. For the first time I had a real inkling of what our trip into the waste would be like. Deadly.

'We're going?' I breathed. 'Into the desert?'

'No. To the bazaar, to buy supplies and transport.'

'Oh.' I couldn't suppress my sigh of relief.

'That, and we'll make a short stop at the ship to collect something.' Pulling his pistol out of his tailcoat pocket, Mr Ambrose checked and reloaded the weapon. 'All in all, it shouldn't take more than an hour. *Then* we're going into the desert.'

BIZARRE BAZAAR

The bazaar looked nothing like what I had imagined. I had dreamed up palace-like constructions, glittering golden in the sunlight, where sultans and beautiful, veiled (and of course deplorably unfeminist!) women were carried around on litters by hordes of slaves.

The reality seemed to consist more of a labyrinth of small booths constructed from wood and striped cloth. There were no sultans to be seen anywhere. True, there were quite a lot of veiled women, but they weren't being carried around in litters, and to judge from the volume and vigour with which they argued with the red-faced merchants inside the stalls, they were considerably more forthright than I had expected.

And last, but certainly not least, there were camels. Dozens of them, even hundreds. And they were all extremely large, extremely loud and extremely smelly. I had my issues with animals at the best of times, but at least horses didn't stink like public privies or try to spit in your eye!

'Is it quite necessary to utilize these creatures?' Mr Ambrose asked Youssef, his eyes narrowed at the nearest camel in a derisive stare. The animal managed to return the look without blinking, which increased my already significant respect for the ugly beasts. 'I have observed their movements, and horses are considerably faster.'

'But horses wouldn't make it through the desert, *Effendi*. Do you see this?' Yousef pointed to the great hump on the camel's back. 'The animals use it to store water.[21] That way they can travel for up to three weeks through the desert without drinking a single drop of water.'

'Hm.' Taking a yardstick out of his pocket, Mr Ambrose unfolded it and held it against the camel's hump. The creature gave him another contemptuous look that clearly said, 'My hump is bigger than your hump, you hairless monkey!'

Mr Ambrose nodded. 'I see. An efficient storage method. That is acceptable.' Snapping the yardstick together, he put it away again. 'Acquire forty of these creatures for our expedition. Here is the money.'

---

[21] Actually, this is a common misconception. WARNING! Everyone who is no nature-geek, please stuff your ears. Camels' humps are not filled with water but with fat. This fat can be used to produce water, but the moisture that is lost during the breathing necessary to produce that water actually means the camel loses more moisture in the process than it wins. So, no secret store of water in the camel, sorry. What really helps the animal to survive in the desert is its extremely efficient usage of the water that it does have.

He handed Youssef a number of bank notes. The Egyptian's eyes widened. 'But... *Effendi*, this is no more than seven hundred pounds! That would make not even eighteen pounds for every camel!'

'And?'

The Egyptian almost seemed wounded. '*Effendi*, a camel is not a cheap thing to buy. A good camel is a precious and rare creature. One of these prized companions costs at least twenty-five pounds!'

'Well, we are buying forty of them, aren't we? They should be easier to produce *en masse*, so I expect to receive a bulk discount!'

Youssef rung his hands. 'But... *Effendi*! These are not shirts or saucepans produced by machine! These are beautiful and gentle creatures, reared in years of care and–' He suddenly cut off when he saw Mr Ambrose's expression, or perhaps I should say expressive lack thereof. Hurriedly, he gave a bow. 'Yes, *Effendi*. Bulk discount, *Effendi*. Of course, I shall do my best.'

And he disappeared into the crowd, muttering in Arabic.

With the air of a suffering martyr giving away his life's blood, Mr Ambrose started distributing more banknotes among some of the other men and instructed them about what to buy and how much to pay for it. The list included everything from water to woollen cloaks.

'Woollen cloaks?' I asked, stepping nearer as the last man was dismissed, his task before him.

'It can get cold in the desert at night.'

'So you've been into the desert before?'

'Not this place.' He eyed one of the camels distrustfully. 'I've only been to decent deserts, where there were horses to ride, and the provisions were a lot cheaper.'

I was aching to ask, to squeeze out of him what information I could get about his mysterious past. Normally, he was as tightly closed as an oyster suffering from lockjaw, and I should have used this rare opportunity. But something else struck me that was of more immediate importance.

'You gave your men long lists of things to buy.'

'Yes.'

'But...' I hesitated for a moment. 'There was one thing that wasn't on your lists.'

'Oh, and what was that?'

'Weapons.' Glancing around at the rifles and knives visible at many of the booths, I lowered my voice in an unusual bout of caution. 'You told none of them to buy a single weapon.'

'That's right.'

I waited for more. Naturally, nothing came but blasted silence!

'Well, what about it?' I hissed.

'What about what?'

'Weapons! Shouldn't you have bought some, at least, if we're going after dangerous bandits?'

'No.'

'Oh, really? Do you intend to fight the bandits with your bare hands, then?'

'Certainly not. I intend them to fight them with the weapons we already have.'

I blinked. 'Excuse me?'

He nodded magnanimously. 'You are excused. You may leave and join Youssef over there, if you wish.'

'That's not what I meant by "excuse me", blast you!' I growled. 'I want to know what you mean, *the weapons we already have*. What weapons do you have, except your revolver?'

'Several hundred rifles, a hundred pistols, a wagonload of knives and daggers, and various... surprises.'

I stared at him, as if trying to find all of the above items hidden somewhere under his tailcoat. 'Where, in God's name?'

He cocked his head, giving me a look so full of cool arrogance it made me envy the camels' excellent aim with spit. 'I told you we had to stop by the ship before we embarked on our expedition, didn't I?'

Of course!

'Why bring the weapons from England?' I demanded, stepping closer and lowering my voice even farther. A man to my right was eyeing me in a speculative way I didn't much like. 'Why not just buy them here?'

He shrugged. 'People would get suspicious.'

'Of someone who wants to buy enough weaponry to outfit a small army? I'll say! But why didn't the people who provided you with these weapons back in England get suspicious?'

'When the owner of the weapons factory you work for asks for samples, most people don't suspect he wants to use them to shoot people.'

'Oh.' I threw him a look. 'Weapons, eh? Is there anything you don't own a factory for?'

He nodded. 'Yes.'

I waited. Nothing came. I wasn't going to be content with that! For once, he was semi-talking about himself. That was a chance that had to be exploited!

'Well?' I demanded.

'Well what?'

I glared at him. 'Well, what is it? What do you not own a factory for?'

He considered this for a moment. 'Potatoes,' he decided, finally.

'Potatoes are vegetables! They aren't produced in factories!'

'That would explain why I haven't got one.'

All right. Maybe I had been wrong about his being willing to talk. I chose not to dignify his last remark with a response. If I wanted to probe him further, better to wait until the desert sun had thawed him a little, if it was able to manage that.

'Since we are on the subject of purchases...' A muscle in his jaw twitched reluctantly, and he glanced at me.

Can it be...?

Mr Ambrose pulled two more banknotes out of his pocket and handed them to me.

Yes! Yes, a miracle!

'I suppose you cannot very well ride on a camel in a dress. Purchase something more appropriate to wear.'

My lips twitched. 'Appropriate being a synonym for cheap?'

'Keep up this level of insight, and you might just keep your job.'

Curtsying, I took the notes from him. 'Always a pleasure to spend your money, Sir.'

His eyes flashed. 'Or maybe you won't keep it after al–'

Before he could finish, I had whirled and vanished into the crowd, two bodyguards trailing after me and a wide grin on my face.

~~**~*~*

Slowly strolling down the row of booths, I eyed each one closely. Many sold some kind of article of clothing, but I didn't really see anything that screamed 'Me!'. Then again, I couldn't expect any pirate costumes or parasols with spikes at the end at an Egyptian bazaar, could I? Not at any kind of bazaar, truth be told.

Wandering away from the booths selling clothes, I ambled towards the ones displaying rows of knives and other glittering instruments of death and destruction. Now, those appealed far more to me than the thought of buying a pair of trousers. Mr Ambrose had said he had plenty of weapons already, but I wasn't sure whether I would be given one, considering the fact of my femaleness.

Hm... maybe if I showed up in a suitably masculine set of trousers, he would at least let me have a small knife...

'Miss Linton!'

At the sound of that voice, I whirled around even faster than my two bodyguards.

Crap, crap, crap! Not he! Not here! Not again!

But all my silent protests went in vain. There he was: Captain James Carter, tall, red-coated and just as handsome as usual – but not as well in control of himself. His face was deathly pale under his tan, and his mouth was standing open as he stared at me. What was the matter with him?

He took an involuntary step forward. 'Good God! Is it really you?'

I shook my head, pointing upwards. 'Sorry, no. He lives up there.'

'Bloody hell, it *is* you! Only you would think of making a joke at a time like this!'

Crossing the distance between us with a few long strides, he grabbed me roughly by the shoulders, his hands sliding over me as if to check whether I was really there. I twisted out of his grip. I mean to say! I'm not fastidious about things like this, but he didn't exactly exhibit the behaviour a lady could expect from a gentleman!

'Captain Carter! Control yourself!' Stepping away, I raised my parasol threateningly, somewhat taken aback. My thoughts were in disarray. Had I misjudged Captain Carter all this time? Was he, in fact, one of these sinister individuals you read about in papers who dragged innocent girls into dark alleys to slash their throats while laughing mad, cackling laughs? 'What is the matter with you?'

'With me? *Me*?' His eyes bulged. I took another step back, just in case he was going to start cackling madly. 'It's I who should be asking that! What happened to you? I came by the Hotel Luxor this morning to visit you, just in case you were still there–'

Oh crap.

'–and the place was a smoking ruin!'

'Um. Well.' All right, that might explain his slightly irrational behaviour. If I had been wondering the whole morning whether one of my friends had been torn to bloody bits in a bomb explosion, I'd be a tiny bit surprised to see them strolling down the market, too. 'I see.'

'*I see*? What's that supposed to mean?' Breathing hard, he stepped towards me again and grasped me by the shoulders, hard. This time, I didn't twist away. I couldn't. Gazing up into his brown eyes, normally so cheerful, I could see they were filled with genuine concern. Maybe even with something more. 'How on earth did you get out of there unharmed? And your grandmother...'

'She's fine. We're both perfectly fine.'

'How?' he demanded, his hands still clutching my shoulders too tightly. Strangely, I didn't mind.

Oh, it wasn't that hard. We were escorted out by three dozen guards in the employ of my pseudo-husband.

'Well...' My brain scrambled for the easiest lie. 'Um... we... we weren't there when it happened. We were out, shopping for... fans. You know, because the weather is so terribly hot here.'

'Thank the Lord!' He let out a breath of relief and moved to enfold me in his arms – then realized what he was doing, stepping back a step, a slight tinge of colour in his cheeks. 'My pardon, Miss Linton. I was overcome at the joy of seeing you well.'

'Err... I'm flattered.'

And also very, very, very glad he had remembered himself before actually hugging me. If he had come that close, I think I wouldn't just have been flattered, but he would have been flattened. My bodyguards were staring daggers at him already.

'So... you've found a safe place to stay, Miss Linton?'

'Yes, Captain. My grandmother and I are perfectly safe, thank you. We're staying at a nice little hotel near the Nile and I'm just out on another shopping trip.'

Captain Carter smiled – then his eyes fell on the products of the booth beside me, and his smile became a bit strained. 'Um... you are, are you?'

Lowering my gaze, I looked at the impressive array of curved daggers in front of me. Some had ivory handles, some ones made from wood. Some were just slightly curved, others shaped in a snake-like pattern. But all had two things in common: a wickedly sharp edge and a deadly point at the end.

Ooops...

Quickly, my gaze darted around to the other booths, looking for a suitable product for a lady to buy. What I found were several dozen muskets, about ten rifles, one with a suspicious-looking dark red stain on the barrel, and hundreds more daggers and sabres.

'Ehem... well... Dear me. A minute ago I was looking at perfumes and handkerchiefs. I must have lost my way a bit.'

That excuse is really wearing a bit thin. Why don't you think of something new, for a change?

'Should I escort you back to the hotel again?' Captain Carter offered, his eyes returning to my face and staying there, the weapons forgotten.

'That will not be necessary,' a thickly accented voice said from behind me. I winced. Captain Carter's eyes flicked to the man who had spoken. For the first time, he seemed to notice the two large Arabs with their curved sabres, standing behind me like bodyguards. Which was, after all, exactly what they were.

'And who are you, pray?' he demanded, his eyes narrowing.

'They're men my grandmother hired to protect me,' I hurriedly constructed another ramshackle lie. 'She, um... knows a few people whom nobody wants to cross.'

'Your *grandmother*?' The captain's eyebrows shot up, no doubt thinking of the deaf little old lady he had met a few days ago. He eyed the bulks of my darkskinned bodyguards again. 'Um... an impressive old lady. I wouldn't have thought she'd have it in her.'

'She has hidden depths,' I assured him solemnly. 'And very powerful contacts. There's not a man in Alexandria who would dare to bring her wrath down on him.'

He eyed the bodyguards again. 'I can readily believe that. At any rate, I'm glad to hear that you're both well.'

'Indeed we are.'

'So... do you know what it was all about? The explosion and the fighting at the Luxor, I mean. Do you have any idea who was behind it?'

Oh yes, certainly. Lord Daniel Eugene Dalgliesh, Peer of the Realm of Great Britain and Ireland, Member of the Most Noble Order of the Garter, resident at East India House, Leadenhall Street, London. It's wonderful to have all-powerful enemies, isn't it?

'None at all, I'm afraid, Captain.'

'Strange... very strange...' For a moment, he looked troubled, thoughtfully stroking the speck of beard on his chin. Then he shrugged. 'Well, as long as you are unharmed – that is all that matters.'

'Yes.' Inside, I breathed a sigh of relief. The difficult part of the conversation seemed to be over. 'Enough about boring old me, Captain. How are things going with you? Was the man you were going to question as informative as you hoped?'

Regretfully, he shook his head. 'Unfortunately, no. I don't know what was the matter with him. When I arrived at *Dark Nights of Delight*, he was red in the face and shouting at his subordinates at the top of his voice about some fellow named Thomson. When I tried to approach him about the subject of the bandits, he cursed at me and ordered his men to chase me out of the building.'

I coughed delicately. 'Fancy that.'

'I imagine someone must have angered him for some reason, just before I arrived – maybe this Thomson. In any case, he wasn't very informative and, for some reason, neither were the other informants I have been able to find. They all seemed a little on edge.'

Probably a residue left over from our visit a day or two earlier.

'Strange. Very strange indeed.'

'Now there's nothing to do but to head out into the desert and find the bandits by good old tracking and searching,' he sighed, gazing around the bazaar. 'That's why I'm here, in fact, I and a few of my men. We have to buy supplies and camels for our journey into the desert.'

'No! Camels?' My eyes became huge with fake surprise. 'You can buy those creatures here in the bazaar, too? I never knew!'

'Yes, but don't get too close to one. They spit.'

'You don't say!'

From the distance, we heard someone shouting Captain Carter's name. Turning, we saw a young sergeant waving his hat above the crowd, pointing to a particularly disagreeable camel tethered right beside him.

'Sir! Captain Carter, Sir, I've found one for you!'

The captain sighed. 'Well, duty calls, Miss Linton. I'm going to have to leave, I'm afraid.'

'Oh, that's perfectly all right, Captain! You go back to your duties, and the best of luck to you. And to your French and Egyptian comrades, too.' The corner of my mouth twitched. 'Make the world a safer place for helpless maidens such as myself, will you?'

His eyes strayed to the two bulky guards behind me, their hands on their sabres, and his lips twitched, too. 'I'm not sure whether young maidens nowadays are quite as helpless as sometimes assumed. *Au revoir*, Miss Linton.'

And with a bow, he vanished into the crowd.

Breathing another sigh of relief, I turned back to the nearest booth. Behind it, a Bedouin man with a big dagger at his belt and an equally big paunch behind the belt, looked uncertainly from me to his deadly wares.

'You would, um, be interested in my wares, *Hanem*?'

'Depends. How much is one of those?' I pointed to a wickedly sharp dagger, at least as long as my forearm. The trader's eyes widened.

'Um... perhaps you'd find something more appropriate at another stall, *Hanem*,' he suggested. 'Maybe a trinket, or a nice lace handkerchief?'

I was just about to shoot him a dark glare when I noticed something right behind him. On a peg sticking from one of the posts of the stall hung a long, bright white garment. My eyes lit up. I was supposed to find something to wear, wasn't I? Well... maybe I had found just the right thing.

'Forget about the dagger. How much is that?' I pointed to the unconventional piece of clothing.

'What?' The man's eyes widened even more. 'This is not a clothes booth, *Hanem*!'

'How much would you ask for it?'

The trader drew himself to his full height, width and breadth. 'That garment belongs to my wife's grandfather, *Hanem*! It is absolutely non-saleable!'

'Now then, now then... what seems to be the matter here?' A woman peaked her head out from the back of the stall. 'Fazl, what are you doing? Are you scaring off the customers again?'

'Scaring off the customers?' the man demanded, his belly wobbling in outrage. 'Do you know what this young woman wants, Abda? She wants to buy your grandfather's *thobe*!'

'She does, does she?' Abda asked, stepping out of the shadows and up beside her husband. Her sharp, intelligent eyes landed on me.

'Yes. Of course, I told her it's not for sale.'

Quickly, the wife's eyes shifted to her husband, narrowing. 'You did, did you?'

'Yes, of course. I would never dishonour your family in such a way as to—'

He cut off with a garbled sound. To judge from the movement of Abda's gown, she had just stepped on his foot, hard.

'You are interested in buying this *thobe*, yes?' she asked me, swiftly taking it down from the peg and spreading it out on the counter. 'Very fine material, very fine. Of course, a bit used, but it hardly stinks of camel at all. I just washed it this morning.'

I gazed at the white garment and the coloured headdress that seemed to go with it. 'Yes. It looks quite interesting.'

'Abda!' her husband protested. 'That's not for sale! How can you—'

'Don't listen to the old *Moghaffal*[22], dear,' his wife cut in with a charming smile that revealed two rows of white teeth contrasting sharply with her dark skin. With an elbow that was no less sharp than the aforementioned contrast, she shoved her husband aside. 'Of course it is for sale. That would make twenty piasters, please.'

~~*~**~*~*

When I found Mr Ambrose, he was busy haggling with an Arab merchant over the price of a sack of grain. The poor merchant was already in a pitiable state. Mr Ambrose seemed to have slight difficulties with the concept of 'haggling'.

'Five hundred piasters!' the merchant exclaimed. 'That is my offer, *Effendi*! Take it or leave it!'

'One hundred,' was all Mr Ambrose said, his face stone-hard.

'Four hundred and eighty-five! *Effendi*, you are ruining me! You are robbing me! This is outrageous! I should call the authorities and have you arrested!'

'Please try. That will be interesting to see.'

'Four hundred and seventy-five, *Effendi*! I beg you, consider, I have three wives and seventy-five children...'

---

[22] The best way to render in western letters the word مغفـل, which is Arabic for the epithet bestowed by any loving wife on her slow-witted husband at some point: fool.

'And overactive loins, I imagine. One hundred.'

'*What?*' The Arab's eyes almost bugged out of their sockets.

'You heard me. One hundred piasters.'

'*Effendi,* you cannot be serious! Four hundred and sixty!'

'Perfectly serious. One hundred.'

'You... you...' The merchant waved his hands hysterically. '*Jamalick cil jahash!*'

Mr Ambrose remained perfectly calm. 'I do not have a donkey. And if I did, I certainly would not intend to lick any parts of it.'

'Four hundred and fifty!'

'One hundred.'

'Do you intend to destroy me? Four hundred and twenty-five, and that is my last word!'

'Then you won't sell any grain today. One hundred.'

'You... *Qad tamut w taefan fi alssahra!*'

'I feel in excellent health. It's rather unlikely that I will die any time soon to suit your wishes.'

'Four hundred!'

'One hundred.'

Giving a tortured groan, the merchant grabbed one of the supports of his stall to hold himself upright. He was swaying under the onslaught of his churning monetary emotions, his tender financial heart obviously pierced through with a poisonous dagger. Mr Ambrose stood like a rock, regarding him with a detached look.

Clearing my throat, I stepped closer to Mr Ambrose and, from behind, whispered into his ear: 'I think you are having problems bridging a cultural chasm.'

Mr Ambrose didn't turn to look at me. Which was rather a good idea, considering the way I was dressed. 'Cultural chasm?' he enquired coolly. 'This man for some reason seems to believe that I am willing to deviate in the price I am offering for his wares. That is incredible!'

'That's what I'm talking about. He expects you to haggle.'

'I am. He suggests a price, then I do, then he again, and so on, and so on.'

'Yes, but you see, I think for haggling to work you have to actually *change* what you are willing to offer.'

'There!' The merchant was suddenly upright again, pointing at me with a shaking finger. 'There, do you hear? Listen to her! The truth flies out of her mouth on wings!'

'Change my offer?' Mr Ambrose directed his gaze at the sack of grain. 'I see. If it will get this over with more quickly, I'll oblige you. You go first.'

'Thank you, *Effendi*! May shady palm trees turn your garden into an oasis, *Effendi*! Three hundred and eighty-five piasters!'

Mr Ambrose shook his head. 'No. Ninety.'

The merchant's jaw dropped. 'What?'

'All right, if you insist,' Mr Ambrose gave a shrug. 'Eighty-five.'

'You...! *Yixrib beitak!*'

'I have several houses that God could destroy. Which do you mean? Seventy-five piasters.'

'Um....' I cleared my throat again. 'I think you still don't quite get the principle of haggling. He's supposed to slowly lower his price, while at the same time you slowly change your offer – and by *change* I mean *raise*, not *lower*.'

'What?' Mr Ambrose blinked. 'You want me to offer him *more* money?'

'Yes.'

'Let us be very clear about this. I am conducting a purchase here. This... individual,' he gestured to the trader, 'is wasting my time by throwing ridiculous offers at me, trying to sell me his wares for a price far greater than their real value, and you want me to reward him for that by offering him *more* money?'

'Um... well, yes.' *How the heck did he manage to make that sound so unreasonable?* 'A bit more with every offer. That's how they do it at bazaars.'

There was a pause.

'At least that's what I've read in a book,' I quickly added.

'To your information, my dear...' He still didn't turn around. 'I am not a character in a book.'

'No, Sir! Of course not, Sir!'

Blast! Why did you say that? You're still pretending to be his wife! You should call him Dick, not Sir!

'And I do not have to conform to oriental customs. I am an English gentleman, and do not submit to foreign ways.'

'Yes, Sir! Of course not, Sir!'

Blast, blast, blast! Not again!

It just came so naturally. Mr Ambrose was the kind of man who could make you want to stand at attention just by looking at you.

'Especially if they are expensive.'

'Certainly, Sir!'

Mr Ambrose pointed to the sack of grain. 'Seventy piasters.'

The merchant was nearly in tears by now. 'No! No, you cannot do this! This is against all tradition! Something like this is not allowed in a bazaar! Here we honestly haggle and cheat each other! We do not simply demand to have something! That is not done!'

'Sixty-five piasters.'

Covering his face with one hand, the merchant slumped against a barrel of salted fish. 'This is torture! Inhuman torture! Go!'

'Can I take the grain?' Mr Ambrose probed. 'For sixty-two piasters?'

'Yes! Anything!'

'Anything? So I could take it for sixty piasters, too?'

'Yes!' Wailing like a wounded wolf, the merchant waved his free hand. 'Go! Just take the grain and go, you demon in human form! Do not plague me any longer!'

Depositing a number of coins on the counter, while the merchant was busy bewailing this smudge on his beloved commercial tradition, Mr Ambrose grabbed the sack of grain, swung it over his shoulder and marched off as if were no heavier than a feather. He didn't even bother to glance at me.

Which might not be such a bad idea right now...

Swinging the sack of grain onto the back of a camel, Mr Ambrose signalled to one of his men to come tie it down. Clapping his hands, he turned towards me.

'Well, I think that was all the grain we need. What about you? Were you successful in your search... for... clothes...?'

He saw me, and his voice slowly trailed off.

'Well?' I tried to smile. It didn't really work.

He made a strangled noise in the back of his throat.

'What do you think?' I did my best to make a twirl for him. The folds of my garment flapped in the breeze. 'Isn't it nice?'

'What – in – Mammon's – name – is – that?' He emphasized every word. Very slowly. Very distinctly.

Oh-oh...

'Can't you see what it is?' I demanded.

'I think I can. But my logical mind is refusing the evidence of my eyes. Are you or are you not standing there in front of me in the middle of a marketplace wearing nothing but a bathrobe and a towel around your head?'

'It's called a headscarf, thank you very much! And the garment you refer to as a bathrobe is called a *thobe*, I believe. It is not for the purpose of visiting the baths.'

'No?'

'No! And this overcoat is called a *kibr*, and the cloak,' I proudly held up the article in question, 'is called a *burnous*! The Bedouins and many other Arabs wear them all the time, apparently. I know it doesn't look very practical, but it's actually very cooling and comfortable.'

And very figure-flattering. You couldn't even detect a hint of my generously-sized derrière under the swirling folds of the *thobe*. But I wasn't going to mention that reason for buying it to him. Not in a million years!

'You,' he pointed out, his eyes still wide, his nostrils flaring, 'are not a Bedouin.'

I raised my chin. 'True. But you did tell me to pick something appropriate for the desert and for camel riding, didn't you? Well, what could be more appropriate than a Bedouin's dress?'

His left little finger twitched. 'I could think of a number of things.'

'Oh, don't be a spoilsport!' My lips twitched. The desperate effort he was putting into not exploding... It was almost comical. Slinging one of the long white folds of my gown around his neck, I jerked him towards me, until we were standing only inches apart. 'Well? Just tell me! What do you think?'

His slightly widened eyes contracted and cooled, their temperature quickly approaching arctic. 'What do I think?' he hissed, his eyes flashing dangerously. 'I think we need to get you out into the desert, where no one can see you in that thing except passing camels – fast!'

~~**~*~*

156

The remainder of our little shopping trip in the bazaar passed very quickly. Mr Ambrose practically browbeat the merchants into giving him their wares for free, so anxious was he to get me out of there. No wonder he was so rich, if these were his usual ways of negotiation.

Now and again, he threw dark glances at me and my 'bathrobe'. Every time I saw him do it, I gave my headscarf a determined tug. The thing was really coming in useful. I hadn't realized how much heat it would absorb! For the first time in hours I was resting in peaceful shade.

It was only when we all gathered around the camels and Mr Ambrose started giving his orders for our way to the ship that I realized someone was missing, had been missing, in fact before we even arrived. Blast! How had I not noticed this before? It wasn't as if he was hard to overlook or forget.

'Where's Karim?' I demanded.

Mr Ambrose froze in the act of reaching for his camel's bridle. He hesitated. 'He... couldn't come.'

A claw of cold apprehension gripped my heart. O God! Why hadn't I thought of this before? Karim had still been in our hotel room when we left! He had faced all those attackers alone! Had something happened to him?

Please let him be all right! Please!

Yes, the huge Mohammedan and I hated each other with a vengeance – but it was a quite chummy way of hating. I wouldn't like to have to look for someone new to despise. Not at all.

'Why?' I asked, my voice managing to remain steady. 'Is he injured?'

'In a way.'

'What's that supposed to mean?'

Mr Ambrose turned away, so I couldn't see his face, and started fiddling with his bow tie. 'You remember there was a fire in the hotel?'

'Yes! And? Was he burned?'

'Not really. He got half his beard singed off.'

For a moment I blinked into nothingness. '*What?*'

'His beard. Half of it is burned off. He seems to be very put out by it.'

Slowly, very slowly, a grin started to spread across my face. 'He is, is he?'

'Yes.'

'So, where is he now?'

'At a barber's shop, undergoing emergency surgical barbering.'

My grin widened. 'Oh dear. How terrible. I must remember to express my sympathy, the next time I see him.'

Mr Ambrose gave me a very level look. 'I'm sure he will appreciate that *very* much.'

And with that he started marching down the street, leading the camels behind him, his men swarming out in a protective circle. With his men forcing a path for us through the crowd, we reached the ship in record time. A man was standing guard at the gangway and saluted when Mr Ambrose approached.

'As-salamu alaykum[23], Effendi.'

'Are the weapons ready for loading?' Mr Ambrose demanded.

'Yes, Effendi. Karim arrived a while before you did and gave everything a thorough check. Then he went to scout ahead. He, um, seemed to be rather in a hurry.'

'Indeed?' The grin on my face widened. 'What a pity. I'm so looking forward to seeing him again.'

Mr Ambrose shot me a dark look. 'Good. Tell Youssef to start arming the men. Then return to your post. You and Hakim are to guard the ship until our return.'

'Yes, Effendi!'

As I watched, packages that even through their wrappings looked suspiciously rifle-shaped were distributed among the men. There were other packages, too, more curiously shaped and much larger. More men joined us, strolling towards us out of alleys as if they were just sailors come to chat with their friends at the harbour. I didn't believe it for a minute. These men were handed weapons, too, casually, unconsciously, as if nothing interesting at all was happening here. Soon, our number had swelled to over sixty, and I would be very much surprised if outside the city there were not more reinforcements waiting for us.

'So...' Holding the hem of my thobe up, I approached Mr Ambrose. 'Now you might as well tell me. You said you still don't know where the bandits are exactly. What is this mysterious master plan of yours to find them?'

He shrugged. 'Simple. We take the same route as all my caravans did...'

'And then?'

'Then we'll let ourselves be ambushed.' Grabbing his camel's reins, he started to pull the reluctant animal down the street. 'Let's go! We haven't got all day.'

HOT AND SWEATY

'What do you mean, *we'll let ourselves be ambushed*?'

It was the seventy-third time I had asked that question since we had set out from the ship - or maybe the seventy-fourth? I hadn't kept an exact count. I was too busy being furious at not getting an answer.

He shrugged. 'I mean exactly what I said. We'll let ourselves be ambushed.'

'But... but you can't mean for us to simply run into the bandit's trap!'

'Can't I?'

'You have to have some kind of plan!'

'I do, do I?'

---

[23] An Arabic greeting meaning 'peace be upon you'. A rather optimistic way of greeting Mr Rikkard Ambrose, all things considered.

'Yes! You're going to let them come close enough so they can't escape and then launch your attack first, aren't you?'

'Actually, no. The bandits will completely surround and disarm us. Then they will proceed to emptying our saddlebags and cutting our camels' throats.'

'And ours next, if I'm not mistaken!'

He shrugged again. 'If they're not prevented from doing so by some miraculous intervention... Yes.'

I stared at him suspiciously. His face was just a tiny little bit too calm, too stony, too unemotional. There was something going on in that cold, calculating brain of his, gears ticking away at lightning speed.

'You have a plan!' I accused him again.

'Interesting. How do you know that? I cannot remember mentioning it to you.'

'Gah! The devil take you!' Hastening my stride, I marched forward to walk beside Youssef instead of the insufferable man behind me.

We crossed the city quickly. Soon we reached the edge of Alexandria, and in front of us stretched a seemingly endless landscape of green-brown grain and reed, interspersed here and there with the sparkle of lake water.

'A surprisingly green sort of desert,' I commented.

Youssef shook his head. 'We're nowhere near the desert yet. We have to traverse the whole of the Nile Delta first.'

'Why did we land in Alexandria then, and not somewhere farther east?'

'Because Alexandria is the largest port in Egypt, the only one large enough for the kind of ship Ambrose *Effendi* uses for trade. Any spies of the bandits could only have been found here. And now that this first plan has failed, we have to use the same route as his traders, if we want to be taken for a merchant caravan.'

I threw Mr Ambrose a dark look. 'And of course we want that, don't we? I mean, who doesn't want to have their throats cut?'

'Have faith, *Hanem*.'

'Ha! In whom? God, or Mr Ambrose?'

He considered that for a moment. 'Both?' he finally suggested.

'Ha!'

'Time to mount up!' I heard Mr Ambrose's cold voice from behind me. 'We ride east!'

Youssef bowed. 'You'll have to excuse me, *Hanem*. I have to fetch my saddle.'

I nodded. Luckily, some considerate soul had already wrestled the saddle onto the back of the sweet little camel I was supposed to ride from now on. But that still left the actual riding to be done. Cautiously, I eyed the hunch-backed ungulate beside me. It was busily chewing on its reins, covering them with slobber.

Very well... I could do this. It couldn't be that difficult, could it?

'Hello there,' I said.

The camel very courteously stopped chewing, and spat at me in reply.

'That's a charmer,' I heard Youssef from behind me. Glancing over my shoulder, I saw him walk by with a camel saddle under his arm. 'What's his name?'

'He hasn't got one yet, I think.'

'So, what are you going to call him, *Hanem*?'

I turned back to the camel, meeting its cool, derisive eyes. For a moment, I considered – but there really was only one possible choice. 'I think I'll call him Ambrose.'

From behind me, there came the *thud* of a heavy camel saddle hitting the ground, and a strangled sound from Youssef. I smiled.

'Well?' Leaning forward, I ticked the camel below the chin. 'Do you like your new name, Ambrose?'

The camel spat at me again.

'There, you see? He likes it! He's downright enthusiastic!'

Grabbing the saddle, I tried to swing myself up, like I had seen horse riders do. All I managed, however, was to dangle from the camel's side like an over-ripe plum. No matter how much I pulled, I couldn't get myself up there!

Blast! If you weren't so heavy you could do this! It's all because your derrière is so f-

No! My derrière wasn't fat! Just generous. That was the word. Generous.

Behind me, Youssef cleared his throat 'You have to make the camel kneel down before you can get on, *Hanem*.'

'And how am I supposed to do that?' I growled, pounding on the beast's hairy side. 'Let me up, you smelly monster, you!'

Ignoring me, the camel went back to chewing on its reins.

Youssef regarded the camel cautiously. 'Um... well, actually they should be trained to kneel when someone approaches them.'

'In case you haven't noticed, that hasn't happened yet!'

Spitting out the reins, Ambrose turned his head and began chewing on the sleeve of my *thobe* instead. Ah! A gourmet camel, eh?

'Um... yes, *Hanem*. Well, in that case, you simply command him to kneel in an authoritative tone of voice. That should be enough.'

I filled my lungs with air. 'Kneel, you bloody flee-ridden beast! And stop chewing on my sleeve!'

Nothing happened. Youssef cleared his throat again. 'Well, you could try to...'

'*Kneel!*'

The cold, hard voice cut through Youssef's like a knife through butter. The camel's knees buckled and I yelped as my feet suddenly hit the ground. Quickly, I braced myself against it and scrambled up into the saddle. When I turned my head to look, I already knew whom I would see.

There he was: Mr Ambrose – the real one, not the camel – sitting in the saddle of his own mount as if it were the armchair in his very own office, his back ramrod straight, his gaze cool and assessing. Unlike all the others, who were all swathed in white Arabian dress, ready for the desert, he was still wearing his back tailcoat. Even his black top hat was still on his head.

'Thank you.' I gave him a nod.

He returned it, curtly. 'Let's stop wasting time.'

'Agreed.' I urged my camel forward. 'Let's go, Ambrose!'

'Excuse me?' My employer's eyes sparkled dangerously. 'Since when do you give orders to me?'

I gave him a charming smile. 'Oh... I wasn't talking to you.'

~~*~**~*~*

It didn't take Mr Ambrose long to discover the name I had given to my dear, trusted friend, the camel.

His reaction?

Well, let's just say he wasn't best pleased about it. Of course, he didn't throw a fit or scream at me or anything like that. Oh no. He was Mr Rikkard Ambrose after all. Words of anger were a waste of his precious time. Instead, he attacked and punished me with the stoniest, coldest, most absolute silence that ever refused to be heard by a human ear. All I got whenever I tried to make conversation was a baleful glare, so I mostly conversed with Ambrose (the one I was sitting on, I mean) instead. I didn't get any more conversation out of him, but at least he spat at me now and again, in quite a nice way, really.

The days dragged by. We followed a well-travelled road, crossing the arms of the Nile at several points, always travelling towards the sunrise. The air was incredibly heavy and humid, the ground moist beneath our feet. I tried to enjoy it as long as it lasted, knowing that all too soon the ever-present moistness would be replaced by dry, hot desert air. But the mosquitos that flew around and around me, attacking every inch of my skin, made enjoying the trip rather difficult.

Mr Ambrose's silence meant that any distraction was out of the question. I couldn't even get an answer out of him about what he planned to do when we ran into the bandits. The few times I tried asking, I was met with a wall of silent ice, and his men weren't much more forthcoming.

The one ray of sunshine in the whole situation was that after a few days journey, we were joined by our long lost companion, who had been riding ahead, scouting, and avoiding everyone in the hope for the miracle of accelerated beard growth.

'Karim!' My face lit up. The rider who approached us had his face covered against the mosquitos, but there was no mistaking that giant form, those massive shoulders, and the even more massive turban. 'It's a joy to see you after all this time! Come on, get rid of that rag hiding your face. Show your old friends a smile!'

Very, very slowly, the Mohammedan reached up and drew back the cloth that hid the lower part of his face.

Oh. Apparently, the hoped-for miracle had not occurred.

A word of caution about beards here. Everyone knows that a beard covers your face. But what most people who decide to grow beards don't consider, and what I learned only now, was that if you grow a beard, the upper half of your face will get a lot of sunlight, while the lower half will get none at all, causing strongly varying degrees of tanning. If then, at some later point, for whatever reason, you have to shave the beard off again, the result will look... interesting.

I stared.

'Ah. Oh.' I cleared my throat. 'Um... so good to see you got out of the fire without any um... major injuries.'

His bushy eyebrows drew together. A storm cloud seemed to appear over his turban, and his eyes flashed.

One word, those eyes seemed to say, *one word more and I'll...*

'Well... so good to see you again,' I repeated, smiling as broadly as I could, fighting to keep my face straight. 'So very good. I suppose you want to see the others now to, um... chat. Or whatever it is you men do in your spare time. Well... cheerio, then.'

His eyes flashed warningly one more time. Then he spurred on his camel – a monster of an animal that seemed just able to bear its enormous burden – and rode past me, towards Mr Ambrose. I waited until he was well out of hearing range. When he was, I waited five minutes longer, just to be sure.

Then I collapsed onto Ambrose's neck, biting on my *thobe* to conceal my laughter. 'Oh my God! His face! His bloody face! He looks like... he is so... Oh my God!'

~~**~*~*

That was just about the only noteworthy historical event during our expedition though the Nile Delta. The rest consisted of silence, stale bread and an occasional bowl of gruel around a campfire. We passed a few more crossings and a lot of peasants working in the fields. Finally, the vegetation grew sparser, and one day we were standing under a few lonely trees, looking out into the distance, and there were no more trees there, and neither were there bushes, grass, or any other vegetation. All there was were rocky crags, sand, dust and more sand, stretching to the horizon.

'The desert,' I heard a cool voice beside me. Looking over, I saw Mr Ambrose regarding the craggy landscape before us with narrowed eyes.

'Thank you,' I told him. 'I think I realized that much myself.'

No reply.

'Don't take that as a criticism, though,' I continued. 'Those are the first words you've said to me in more than a week. You're making progress. Now you've just got to remember that your vocal cords are actually good for something, and maybe we'll have a nice chat one of these days.'

No reply.

'Or not.'

Again, no reply. With a snap of his cane, Mr Ambrose spurred his camel forward, forging ahead, into the desert. His top hat didn't wobble in the slightest from the camel's march on the rough ground, but remained still and steady as a black marble tombstone.

'Beware of the sun!' he called over his shoulder.

'*Beware of the sun*,' I muttered. 'What helpful advice! Why, thank you for mentioning that before you force me to ride hundreds of miles through the desert!'

Sighing, I eyed the glowing, simmering landscape in front of me. Well... what was one desert? Just a stretch of land without trees, after all. It couldn't be that bad.

I spurred my camel forward.

~~**~*~*

'Please, please let me die!'

Mr Ambrose glanced over at me. 'Be my guest.'

'I wasn't talking to you!' I groaned, wiping the sweat from my forehead. Or at least one litre of it. Another six litres remained, stuck to the skin under the scorching sun. They felt more like glue than perspiration. 'I was talking to God!'

'I see.'

Blast him! How could his voice be this calm, controlled and, most baffling of all, *cool* in this abominable heat? Balefully, I glared at his face. His voice wasn't the only part of him that was cool.

'How is it,' I demanded, 'that while I'm quite literally sweating my guts out, there's not a drop of sweat on your face? Not a single blasted drop!'

He shrugged.

'You just bloody shrugged! That's no bloody answer!'

He shrugged again.

'Gah!' Grasping the hem of my headscarf I tried to pull it further down to get at least a little more shade, but to no avail. The sun had already heated up the cloth mercilessly. It was like a woven oven. 'Still, not a single drop of sweat! And you're not even wearing anything for protection!'

'Certainly I do,' he contradicted me, one long pail finger tapping the side of his black top hat.

'That's no protection against sunlight! At least it's not supposed to be! Why do you think the Arabs make all their clothes from white cloth? Because black attracts heat!'

'Does it indeed?'

'Yes!'

'I see...' He gave me a long, cool look. He didn't even have to speak the words out loud, I could hear them as clearly as if Moses himself had shouted them from the nearest mountain: *Then why are you sweating, and I'm not?*

I was damned if I was going to give him an answer! Especially since I had none.

'You should put on a *thobe* and headscarf yourself, or you'll get heatstroke!' I prophesied darkly, hoping to hell I was right.

'I don't think so.'

'You'll start sweating any minute now, I warn you! Not even you can stay cold as an iceberg in this heat!'

'Indeed?'

'Yes, indeed!'

A hot breeze picked up, blowing sand our way. I coughed, and buried my face in my camel's foul-smelling neck to avoid the worst of the dust. Mr Ambrose just sat straight in the saddle, ignoring the stinging grains of sand as if they didn't exist. When the breeze died down, he carefully removed his top hat, and began dusting sand off it. The sun now hit his perfect, sculptured face full-on, and he still didn't even blink.

'The heatstroke is coming!' I warned. 'Just you wait! In a few minutes you'll be dead on the ground. Don't say I didn't warn you!'

'If I am dead, I will not be likely to say much.'

'More than when you're alive, that's for sure!'

Silence. What a big surprise!

'Won't you at least try on a headscarf to protect you from the worst of the sun?' I grumbled.

'I don't think so. On the contrary, I think you should rid yourself of that bathrobe and the remainder of your current attire.' He sent a cold look at my form, bundled up in white linen. 'It is thoroughly un-English.'

'So is being a miserable skinflint,' I shot back. 'Are you sure you don't have Scottish blood in you?'

If it was possible at all for something already rock-hard to stiffen, then his posture did. 'Quite sure.'

His tone roused my interest from its siesta, providing the first distraction from the heat for hours. 'So... where *do* you come from, exactly?'

Somehow, I didn't know how, he managed to lower the temperature of his gaze below the freezing point – even here. 'That is none of your business.'

'It *is* Scotland, isn't it? I knew it!'

'No!'

The corner of my mouth twitched. 'Why would you want to hide it, unless it's really Scotland? Come on, admit it!'

'It is *not* Scotland,' he told me, his voice even stiffer and colder than before.

'Oh, really? Are you sure?'

'Quite sure. My home lies nowhere near Scotland!'

'Hm... how far away is it, exactly?'

The thin line of his mouth thinned into an even thinner line. 'Quite far!'

'Come on! How far, exactly?'

His left little finger twitched. 'If you have to know, three miles and one thousand and thirty-five yards from the southern Scottish border.'

'Oh, I see.' I tried to keep my face expressionless while I nodded solemnly. It wasn't easy. 'That's incredibly far away, of course. Nobody could ever take you for anything resembling a Scotsman under those circumstances.'

'Mr Linton?'

'I'm still wearing your wedding ring. I don't think you want to call me "Mister" in public – not unless you want to have some interesting explaining to do when we return to England.'

His eyes narrowed infinitesimally. 'Fine. *Mrs Thomson?*'

'Yes, Sir! Right here, Sir!'

'I have a very important order for you.'

'Yes, Sir! I will obey your every wish, as is my duty as your... what am I currently? Wife? Secretary? Dogsbody?'

'The order is,' Mr Ambrose said, ignoring me completely, 'Be silent!'

'Yes, Sir! Immediately, Sir!'

˷˷**˷*˷*

Did you ever hear the saying 'Be careful what you ask for, you might just get it?'

Well, I didn't. I had never heard of the damn saying in my whole life, but that didn't stop me from inventing it for myself the moment the sun began to sink behind the horizon.

The whole blasted day I had done nothing but pray for cold, cold, cold, cold... and now the desert was giving me exactly what I asked for, in concentrated form. The moment the sun's last, warming rays vanished below the earth, the warmth seemed to be sucked out of the barren landscape like the juice from an orange. My skin, heated just a moment ago, became cold and clammy. I started to shiver.

'W-what's this?' I demanded, wrapping my *thobe* more closely around me. 'What's the matter?'

'The matter?' Mr Ambrose cocked his head. 'Whatever can you mean?'

'The cold, of course! Why is it suddenly so bloody cold?'

'Why shouldn't it be? There's no vegetation to hold the heat. It just evaporates when the sun sinks.'

'And that doesn't bother you at all, does it?' I demanded, glaring at him. His Serene Mightiness, Mr Ambrose, still sat in the saddle like a stone idol of the God of Commerce, not even showing the slightest sign of discomfort.

'Certainly not. Why should it?'

But about ten minutes later, when he thought I wasn't looking, I saw him rub his hands together. Ha! He was mortal, after all!

'We'll make camp here!' came his order about half an hour later. I nearly dropped from my saddle in relief. For a moment I considered cuddling up to the warm form of the camel, but the stink of the creature would keep me at bay till I was at death's door from freezing. Anyway, there was work to be done.

'Pitch the tents! Cook food! Set guards!' Mr Ambrose's pelted us with orders, and we hurried to obey. Luckily, Youssef, and not I, got the task of collecting the camel shit to light a fire with.

'You there! Scout ahead as long as the moon is still up! I want to know what's out there! Be back in half an hour! And you, get my maps and instruments! I have to determine where exactly we are!'

Soon we were all huddled around a campfire that, while smelling rather peculiar, at least prevented our blood from freezing in our veins. There was warm food, companionship and even the occasional laughter. I didn't understand any of the jokes, since they were all in Arabic, but I laughed along anyway. Mr Ambrose, to nobody's surprise, did not laugh.

Finally, though, our evening's kettle full of warm stew ran out. Not long after, the day's camel shit ran out as well, and the fire began to die down. The men started to disperse, some gathering in groups around the warm, if stinking, forms of the snoring camels. Others with more sensitive noses just moved closer to the glowing remains of the fire and huddled together there.

This left only few solitary people: the guards surrounding the camp in a circle, and Mr Ambrose, and me, lying on the ground alone, separated by several feet of cold desert air. Shivering, I drew my *thobe* closer around me. Blast! I should have bought a woollen cloak, too!

I glanced over at Mr Ambrose. He was lying, stiff as a board, his arms folded in front of his chest as if daring the night to freeze him to death. I couldn't see his eyes – but I'd bet a month's wages on the fact that they were colder than the dark night around us.

Yes, his eyes might be cold. But the rest of him... Bloody hell, he has to be warm! Warmer than you, anyway!

I cleared my throat.

'Dick?'

No answer.

I sighed. 'Rick?'

Still no answer.

'Mr Ambrose, Sir?'

There was a moment of silence, then: 'Yes?'

'It's rather cold, Sir.'

He didn't move an inch, didn't even turn to look at me. 'I had observed that much for myself.'

'The others are all huddling together.'

'Indeed?'

'Against the cold, you know. Huddling together helps keep the cold away.'

'Is that so?'

'Yes.' I cleared my throat again, and waited for a moment, giving him the opportunity to continue. He didn't, preferring rather to lie stiff as a stiff and glare up at the stars. I cleared my throat for third time. It felt incredibly dry. 'So... I was wondering... why don't you?'

Now he did turn his head, very slowly, very deliberately. When his eyes met mine, I had to shiver again.

'Excuse me?'

I licked my lips. 'I said why don't you huddle together with, um... someone? Or cuddle, whichever you prefer.'

His eyes narrowed. 'I don't cuddle.'

'You don't?'

'Most certainly not!' he proclaimed to the night sky, his voice cold and powerful, as if he were sitting in his office at home, and not lying in the desert freezing his toes off. 'And I do not huddle either! I absolutely refuse to participate in such an undignified activity. The cold is not life-threatening. I shall not succumb to improper behaviour merely to decrease a temporary discomfort.'

Before I knew it, my hand had moved. We lay not far from each other, and it reached out, crossing the distance and coming to rest on top of his arm.

'Even with your wife?'

His arm shifted almost imperceptibly. 'You are not really my wife.'

'Do you mind keeping up the pretence until it's not so freezing anymore?' I lifted an eyebrow. 'Or would you rather that I go huddling and cuddling with one of the other men out there?'

His arm flipped in a startlingly fast movement, and his fingers closed around my wrist in an iron vice.

'Stay – right – where – you – are!'

No matter how icy his voice was right then, somehow it managed to make me feel warm inside, warmer than a thousand campfires. His eyes gleamed in the dark, sending a shiver down my back.

'Oh, really? What will you do if I don't?'

He moved. I barely had time to see his shadowy form rear up above me, casting a shadow worthy of a Titan, before he came down on me. His weight drove the breath out of me for a second, and that was all the time he needed. His arms encircled me, and we rolled to the side, wrapping us up in our blankets and clothes until they were an inseparable tangle. When we came to a halt at the foot of a small dune, I was still out of breath, and not just because of the impromptu wrestling match. My blood was pumping fast, and I felt tingly all over.

'Let go!'

'Why?' His cool voice slid into my ear, smooth and seductive. 'You wished to engage in huddling and cuddling, did you not? Well, we are.'

I tried to push him away – but his arms were so tightly wrapped around me, pressing my arms to my sides, that I couldn't even try. So I thumped my head into his chest instead.

'This isn't cuddling!'

'Why, my love?'

'Because I want to strangle you!'

'Let's say it is a new version of cuddling – modified and improved.'

'Blast you! Let go of me!'

'No.'

I began to fire a barrage of bad language at him, most of which I had picked up from Arabian sailors and traders in the bazaar, and none of which I actually understood. Mr Ambrose listened, not loosening his grip the tiniest bit. When I had finally run out of breath, he commented: 'You seem to have made a promising start learning Arabic. However, your vocabulary could be called somewhat one-sided.'

'You can take your vocabulary and stick it up a camel's...'

I might have gotten further had he not right in that moment covered my mouth with a kiss. Heat surged through me, my body instinctively moulding itself to his, growing softer, stopping to fight. No, that wasn't true. I never stopped fighting. But a moment ago I had been fighting to get away. Now I was fighting to get closer!

From somewhere, I heard a low growl. My eyes, closed in ecstasy, flew open to look for the hyena, or lion, or whatever was lying in wait in the dark night. Only then I realized where the growl had come from: my very own throat!

Slowly, my hands managed to crawl up his chest, until they had reached his face and could pull him closer. He made a low, masculine sound in the back of his throat, and an involuntary smile tugged at my lips.

'So...' he murmured against my mouth. 'About the effectiveness of my modified version of cuddling...'

'Yes?'

'Are you still cold?'

Cold? Is he kidding?

Cold was forgotten. The concept of cold belonged to another universe now.

'No! I'm not!'

'I didn't think so.'

'You... you...arrogant son of a bachelor! You *Ibn himar!*'[24]

'Not according to my birth certificate.'

'*Kol Ayre!*'[25]

'That would present slight anatomical difficulties.'

'*Kool Khara!*'[26]

'I do not like the taste of it much. Mind your language!'

My disgraceful language apparently didn't bother him too much, though – for the next thing he did was pull me closer and press another kiss on my lips. Rolling over, he placed himself so that one side of me was shielded from the bitter cold by the thickest wad of blankets, the other by his body, and, gently breaking our kiss, he pulled me against his chest. Sometime later, I drifted off into sleep, suppressing a grin as I snuggled into him.

~~**~*~*

Over the next few days, a tacit agreement developed between Mr Ambrose and me. We did our best to detest each other during the day, me flinging examples of my ever-growing vocabulary of Arabic swear words at him, he building up a thick wall of silence. But in the night...

In the night, different things happened.

We would lie down next to each other again, and he would fold me in his arms, creating a small cave of warmth for me amidst the cold desolation of the desert around us. The whole night he would hold me like this – and not just for warmth, either. The taste of his lips on mine... Up until then, I hadn't thought it possible for anything to rival the savoury scrumptiousness of solid chocolate. I had been mistaken.

When, in the morning, he returned to his usual cold, standoffish, silent self, I sometimes asked myself whether I hadn't simply dreamed up his night-time

---

[24] Son of a Donkey

[25] Eat my Dick

[26] Eat Shit

alter ego. But then the sun would go down, and the dark shadow of a tall man would stalk towards me.

'Lillian?'

'Yes?'

'Come to me.'

The nights passed. I supposed the days passed too, but recently I had started paying a lot more attention to the former than to the latter. We travelled at a slow crawl through the desert, or maybe we were whizzing through it faster than a racing horse. I didn't really know. In a landscape where everything always changed, blown away by the wind, it was hard to say where you were at any given time and how fast you were moving.

How many days passed before *it* happened, I didn't know. I only knew that it was an excruciatingly hot day, and the sun was beating down on our heads with red-hot, iron hammers. In other words, a day like any other. That was the day on which *it* happened.

We were just moving up the side of a dune. Unfortunately, it was the side that lay full in the sunlight. Ambrose was struggling, making grunting noises with every step. I supposed he was having bowel problems. He hadn't produced quite as much shit to burn yesterday as usual. Unfortunately, I couldn't very well ask his namesake to step into the breach.

Suddenly, Ambrose stopped entirely. Blinking, trying to rouse myself out of my heat-induced stupor, I saw something black right in front of me on the glowing sand. It looked like a cross between a crab and a giant spider, with a huge, sharp tail at one end. Wait a minute... I had seen something like this in an encyclopaedia once, hadn't I? What was it called again? A scorpion! Yes, that was it! A scorpion! Wasn't its tail...?

I frowned. Somewhere at the back of my mind I was sure there was *something* important I had to remember about that tail. But it just didn't want to come to me right then. Was it used in native medicine? Was it a delicacy in French restaurants? Yes, that was probably it! The French ate all kinds of weird stuff.

The scorpion clicked its pincers menacingly. Ambrose took a step backwards.

'Oh, don't be a chicken!' I told the camel. Leaning down towards the scorpion, I told it in a very loud and clear voice: 'Piss off!'

The scorpion hesitated for a moment – then turned, scuttled away and dived into a hole not far away.

'There, you see?' I patted Ambrose's neck. 'No need to get spooked. I'll protect you.'

Only when I reached the top of the dune did I realise that there might be plenty of reason to get spooked. I also realized that I probably hadn't been the reason for the scorpion's sudden retreat underground. Far, far ahead to the southeast I could see a yellowish something, like a sickly bank of clouds, hovering close above the ground. Far too close for it to really be clouds. At first I thought the thing wasn't moving at all, but then I noticed that the distance between it and a solitary rock ahead of us was slowly shrinking. Finally, it reached the rock – and swallowed it up.

I shivered.

'What's that?' I asked.

Youssef appeared next to me like a *djinn* out of a lamp. Only he didn't come to grant me three wishes. His face was grim. 'That's the devil's breath, *Hanem*.'

'Does it smell?'

'Worse. It bites, and chokes, and buries you alive. That's a sandstorm, *Hanem*. One of the worst I've ever seen.'

I eyed the sickly cloudbank doubtfully. 'It doesn't look like much.'

One corner of Youssef's mouth twitched in a humourless smile. 'It looks more impressive once you get closer, trust me, *Hanem*.'

Quickly, he turned and barked a few orders in Arabic. Hurrying to the top of the dune, men began to dismount and make their camels sit down. Several removed their headscarves and started pouring water over them, others quickly began erecting tents on top of the dune.

'What is this? What is going on?' Bringing his camel to an abrupt halt out of a gallop, Mr Ambrose slid down from the saddle and shot Youssef a menacing look. 'Explain yourself, Youssef.'

In answer, the other man simply pointed towards the sickly-yellow cloud. I realized that already it was not quite so distant anymore.

'Yes?' Mr Ambrose demanded. 'What is it about that thing?'

'It's a sandstorm, *Effendi*.'

'And?'

'We have to stop, *Effendi*. To seek shelter until it has passed.'

'Seek shelter?' Mr Ambrose's eyes narrowed a fraction of an inch. 'You do not honestly think that I will let this delay me, do you? That I will let a tiny bit of sand stop me from going on?'

The Arab sucked in a breath. 'A tiny bit of sand? *Effendi*, I...'

'We are going on, Youssef! Not another word.'

'But *Effendi*...'

Mr Ambrose raised one, long, extended finger, and Youssef fell silent immediately. Taking another breath, he bowed his head. 'Yes, *Effendi*. As you wish, *Effendi*.'

'Are you sure that going on is wise?' I dared to ask when we had started down the other side of the dune. 'If he really thinks it's dangerous, shouldn't we listen to him?'

He gave me a look. One of those looks. 'Do you know the size of an average grain of sand?'

'No,' I had to admit.

'It is between 0.0024803 and 0.08 inches. Now, think carefully for a moment. Do you think I am going to let myself be stopped by something smaller than the tenth of an inch?'

'Um... no.'

'Indeed, no.'

And that was all he deigned to say on the matter. Maybe he was even right. Maybe it was silly to get anxious just over a bit of sand. But whenever I looked down towards the increasingly fast-approaching clouds of dust in the valley below, I couldn't help getting the impression that it was more than just 'a bit of sand'.

We had just reached the bottom of the hill when the rumbling started.

'What's that?' I called, turning back towards Youssef. 'Thunder?'

'Yes, *Hanem*,' he replied grimly, glaring ahead. 'Out of a thunderstorm that doesn't need lightening to kill.'

The rumbling grew, and soon it evolved into a continuous roar, like the sound coming out of the maul of a dragon too hungry to ever shut its dreaded jaws. Wind began to slap and batter against my *thobe*, and I had to grip my headscarf to hold it in place. The wind didn't bring any relief from the heat. On the contrary, it was so hot it might make you think the gates of hell had opened.

'It doesn't seem quite so small anymore, does it?' I yelled over the racket. Mr Ambrose was riding only a few paces beside me, but still I had to raise my voice to make myself heard. The cloud in front us was growing larger by the minute now. From where we stood, it looked the height of a small house. A few moments ago it had only seemed to be camel-high. 'What did you say again? 0.0024801 inches?'

'0.0024803' he called back. 'Not 0.0024801.'

'Oh, of course, that makes a hell of a lot of difference!'

No answer.

'If you haven't noticed yet, there seem to be rather a lot of these 0.0024803-inch obstacles which you think are so easy to overcome. Maybe we should stop after all.'

No answer.

'You are a stubborn son of a bachelor!'

'I thought earlier you told me that I was the son of a donkey?'

'That was before I ran out of Arabic insults!'

He turned his head to look at me. I would have said there was a stubborn set to his chin – only, it wouldn't have been the truth. He didn't need to set his chin in a stubborn way. Its mere shape, hard and angular like a block of granite, was already more stubborn than others could ever hope to be.

'We can do this. No discussion. We're going on.'

A gust of hot wind struck us and ripped his top hat from his head. Shooting out, his hand grabbed it just in time before it was driven away over the dunes.

'Tell me...' The roar in my ears had reached such a volume now that I had to roar myself to be heard at all. 'Have you ever been in a sandstorm before?'

Silence. Or rather the absence of speech. With the storm winds wailing all around us, the very idea of silence was unthinkable.

'Well?' My heart started hammering faster. In front of us, the storm was towering higher than the tallest houses of London, now. It seemed like a cloud no longer, but a solid wall of sand, waiting to bury us. 'Have you?'

'No! But I've been in plenty of snowstorms.'

'Meaning?'

'Meaning that snow makes you freeze. Sand doesn't. So it can hardly be more dangerous.'

171

I threw another apprehensive glance ahead. Personally, I wasn't entirely sure about that.

We had reached the bottom of the valley beyond the dune now. In front of us rose a small hill, and down that hill the storm came, buffeting, bashing, slashing, thundering. To my left, I saw a column of sand roar past and swallow a cactus whole. It disappeared from sight, as if it had never been.

'Please, *Effendi!*' Youssef's voice was higher than usual, and scratchy, too. I realized that my own throat felt increasingly rubbed raw by the sand. Turning, I saw Youssef galloping towards us. 'Please, let us stop! We have to stop moving! The storm isn't dispersing, it's headed right towards us! We cannot...'

The storm bellowed, cutting him off. A moment later, a brownish cloud of stinging vapour drifted between us, and Youssef was gone. Frantically, I opened my mouth and tried to call out, but I caught a full mouth full of sand and choked. Coughing like a maniac, I collapsed over Ambrose's neck. The camel didn't seem bothered in the least by the raging torrents of sand around us.

'Blast! Ruddy stinking skanky hellhole of a...'

I coughed again, and had to close my mouth. Bloody hell! If you couldn't even curse out loud anymore, things were really going down the drain!

Pulling the neckline of my *thobe* up to cover my mouth and nose, I raised my head a few inches from the stinking camel's neck and tried to see where the others had gotten to. I blinked, thinking for a moment that there was something wrong with my eyes. The others weren't there anymore. Neither were the camels, the mountains, the dunes or even the ground!

Only a tiny circle of space around me had remained halfway visible. Beyond that, all had been swallowed up by a yellowish mist. A mist that was turning darker moment by moment.

Bloody hell? Where's the sun?

It wasn't there anymore. The storm had swallowed it up like everything else. Like every*one* else, too.

Oh my God... Everyone?

'Mr Ambrose!'

No answer. Wildly, I looked from right to left – if you could talk of directions in this semi-substantial world of swirling sand. Nothing. Not even the fluttering ends of his black tailcoat.

'Mr Ambrose! Where are you?'

No answer. There was the roar of the storm and, other than that, utter silence.

Curse him! If he's just keeping quiet to irritate me right now, I'm going to strangle him!

But what else could I do? How could I know for sure?

Well... there was one thing.

'Dick, my darling? Dick, my darling come to me!'

No answer.

All right, he *really* couldn't hear me. If he could, he would have definitely complained. Now, panic was really beginning to set in, and that didn't make the problem of breathing any easier. With my breath speeding up, more and more sand rasped down my throat.

'Ambrose! Ambrose, where are you, you bloody bastard!'

'Grumph? Grumph!' came the answer from underneath me.

I gave the camel a kick. 'Shut up! I didn't mean you!'

Taking my kick as friendly encouragement, Ambrose the camel hastened his steps. He seemed perfectly ready for a nice afternoon stroll through a stand storm. I let him go where he wanted. I was more than busy enough clinging on to him and trying to find something, anything in the darkening maelstrom around me that pointed to a sign of life.

Suddenly, there it was! A speck of black among the yellow-brown torrents.

'Mr Ambrose!'

Did I hear an answer? I couldn't be sure. Not over the roaring of the storm.

'Mr Ambrose, it's me! It's m–'

Another violent fit of coughing overcame me. When it was over, the spot of black was gone.

Bloody hell! You can't go on like this, Lilly!

No, I couldn't. But what else could I do?

You can stop and think for a second, dolt! Think about the men! What did they do when Youssef ordered them to prepare for the sandstorm?

Of course! Ripping my water bottle from the camel's saddle, I screwed it open and started pouring. In my haste, I wasn't careful: I emptied almost half its contents over the piece of cloth covering my mouth and nose before my sense returned and I remembered that I still had to have something to drink later on. But still, the relief was immediate: Instead of forcing its way through the cloth into my throat, tiny particles of dust started to cling to the wetness outside.

'Mr Ambrose!' With new energy, I started shouting, clutching the wet cloth over my face. 'Mr Ambrose, where are you?' Driving the camel forward, I raced further into the storm, to where I thought I had last seen a hint of his black tailcoat. 'Mr Ambrose!'

No answer.

Of course not! Why would he deign to say anything, when he is so well practiced at keeping his lips nailed shut? It's only his life that is in danger, after all! No reason to suddenly become unnecessarily vocal!

Then I saw it: a bit to my left, hardly visible through the roaring sands around me, a tattered piece of black cloth waved at me, like a black snake wagging the end of its tail. Did snakes have tails? This one did, anyway! One tail of a tailcoat!

There he was: Mr Ambrose, striding along as if the sandstorm blasting into his face were a mere annoyance. Somehow, he had managed to misplace his camel in the storm, but no matter. His powerful long legs were pumping, carrying him forward, his eyes were narrowed to slits, his top hat was somehow, miraculously, still on his granite head. He looked as if he could go on like this for hours.

And then he fell.

'Mr Ambrose!'

Whether he heard my cry I knew not. His knees gave way beneath him, and he slammed his hands into the sand, trying to hold himself at least half upright. His chest was heaving, racked with coughs I couldn't hear over the cacophony of storm and singing sand.

'Mr Ambrose!'

This time, he did hear me. Turning his head, he glared at me, as cold as he had ever done. I swear, for just a moment, particles of ice mixed with the particles of sand between us.

'Stay – where – you – are!'

For just a moment, his voice drowned out the thunder of the wind. The power of the command nearly knocked me backwards off my camel. Then I gritted my teeth, and glared right back at him.

Stay?

Ha! Not bloody likely!

I tried to spur my camel on to move faster. Anger flared in his eyes. He tried to push himself up, to get to his feet. He actually managed to raise himself up a few inches. For a moment, he remained like this, a fallen Titan rebelling against his fate, Prometheus about to be bound – then his strength gave way and he collapsed to the ground in a heap.

'No! Mr Ambrose!'

As if in triumph, the sand storm gave a ravenous howl, and a gust of sand blasted between us. His form faded into the whirling mass of 0.0024803-inch pebbles and vanished from sight.

TRAPPED

'No!'

My heart almost stopped. There wasn't a trace of Mr Ambrose left. None! The sickly, biting mist of stone around me, dark brown by now and getting darker by the minute, had swallowed him up completely.

Stay calm, Lilly! Think logically! He was just in front of you, right? So, if you keep going straight ahead, you should stumble over him sooner or later.

How wonderful!

There was just one problem: Where *was* straight ahead, exactly? And since we were on the subject of directions, where were left and right? All directions were swallowed by the roaring cataclysm around me. Just as *he* had been swallowed. Swallowed, chewed, and digested.

No! No, please not that!

Well... if he was chewed and digested, he had to be excreted again sooner or later, right? Maybe even in one piece?

And maybe you are taking this whole bloody metaphor a little too far, Lilly Linton! Get your butt moving!

So I got it. My butt moving, I mean. Or rather the camel's. It bleated in protest as I urged it to go faster, but we sped up, and a moment later I saw something in the sand right in front of me that made my heart jump: footprints! They were barely discernible, and disappearing as I looked, but they were there!

'Faster! Faster, Ambrose!'

Another few steps and bleats of protest later, and the sand parted, revealing a prone, black-clad figure, already half-buried in the sand.

'Mr Ambrose!' Slipping from the camel's back, I fell to my knees beside him. 'Mr Ambrose, Sir! Are you alive?'

'Go away,' he growled.

Yes. Definitely alive.

'Why on earth should I?' I demanded.

'It's not safe wandering around in this kind of tempest!'

'Oh, you've only just figured that out, have you?'

'I told you to stay where you were!'

'And I didn't listen. Now come, get over here.'

'Didn't you hear what I said? Go!' He tried to push himself up, to push me away, then sank back down with a half-groan, half-cough. 'Go, I said! My lungs are being shredded! You have a camel; maybe you can make it out of here alive. Leave me to die in piece!'

'Not a chance in hell! If you're going to die, I'm going to make sure your last minutes on this earth are as miserable as possible!'

'How very kind of you!'

I tried to tug at him, tried to pull him towards the camel, who was visible only as a dark form through the haze several feet away. But, opening his eyes, he stared up at me with those deep, dark, sea-coloured eyes of his and shook his head. 'No! Leave me! Save yourself!'

I narrowed my eyes. 'Are you being unusually noble, or do you simply not want a girl to save your stony behind?'

Silence.

Well, I guess I had my answer.

'So that's the way it is, is it? Well, I've got news for you, *Dick, my dearling*,' I told him, and tugged firmly at his arm again. He slid a few inches in the right direction. 'I've still got a wedding ring on my finger, and so do you, however temporary it may be. Do you know what that means? That means that right now I vow in the presence of God, a camel and a buttload of sand, to be your faithful partner in sickness and in health, in good times and in bad, in happiness as well as in sadness, and even when you behave like a bloody arrogant idiot! I promise to hate you unconditionally, to support you in your aspirations as long as you pay me for it, and to honour and respect you as long as I get a free day off every week. This –' I gave another tug, and he slid closer to the shelter of the camel 'is – my – solemn – vow!'[27]

'How moving.'

---

[27] WARNING! Do not use this vow in real life if you are planning to get married, no matter how much you may be tempted.

'You think it's moving? Then move your behind! We have to get over there, pronto!' I pointed to the dark outline of the camel, who was peacefully snoozing through the sandstorm a couple of yards away. 'At least Ambrose will give us some shelter from the storm!'

'You,' he rasped, staggering to his feet and stumbling over to my mount, 'are going to change that camel's name!'

'Oh, I am, am I?'

'Yes!'

'We'll just see about that.'

Both of us slumped to the ground next to the very, very aptly named camel. Ambrose was not paying any more attention to us than to the grains of sand battering his impressive rump. Instead – surprise, surprise – he remained perfectly cool and silent. Leaning over to the very, very, very, very, very aptly named camel's saddle bag, I pulled out a second headscarf, and poured some of my remaining water over it.

'Here!' I held it out to Mr Ambrose. 'Put that over your mouth and nose!'

'That is Arabian *women's clothing*! I will most certainly not–'

Smack! Even over the racket of the storm, the sound of the wet cloth hitting him in the face was satisfyingly audible.

'Leave it on if you do not want to choke to death! If you do, be my guest and remove it.'

'What was that about honouring and respecting me?' came a muffled voice from beneath the cloth.

'You remember the conditions, don't you? I haven't gotten a day off since we started on this accursed trip!'

Reaching up, he pulled the misused headscarf off his eyes, but still left it over his mouth and nose. Leaning towards me until our faces were only inches apart, he narrowed his eyes a fraction. 'Well, then I have good news for you.'

'Oh yes?'

'Oh yes, indeed.' He swept his arm around, gesturing at the raging tempest around us. 'I give you the rest of the day off.'

'Thanks *so* much, Sir! I'm going to the nearest café right away to enjoy a nice cup of tea and a piece of apple pie!'

'You're welcome! And don't forget–'

His voice was cut off by a bellow of storm wind and I felt a blast of sand hit me, almost hurling me towards him. Clutching at the straps of the camel's saddlebags, I caught myself just in time. Another blast of sand hit me almost immediately. Wide-eyed, I looked up. Something was happening!

Around us, the roaring had continued all the time without ceasing or abating once. But now... now, something altogether different was starting. All through the storm so far, directions had been swallowed, as had the landscape and any living being. But at least there had still been a sense of light, of existence, somewhere in the chaos.

Now, though, the dark brown haze around us began to darken further. The gale raged with renewed force, and I bit my lower lip to supress a cry of pain as the sand battered against my *thobe*, stinging even through the thick material. Wet cloth or no, it was becoming more and more difficult to breathe.

On the edge of my vision, things were going dark. Dimly, I wondered what was happening. Was I dying? Here, in this lonely desert, my only company a man who was as cold and hard as a block of ice?

No, that's not true. You've also got the camel!

Right! I was so lucky.

Are you sure you're dying? Because it looks as if things aren't just going dark at the edges of your vision. They're going dark everywhere.

Looking up, I sucked in a startled breath. Or at least I tried to. What I actually sucked in was a startled wagonload of desert dust.

'What in God's name...!' My voice was hardly audible in my own ears. The roar of the storm had reached new heights, battering my eardrums with primeval force. 'What is going on?'

Above us, the sky, or what passed for the sky in a sunless world of swirling sands, was growing dark. And I don't mean just dark brown. I mean dark. Dark like a night without stars and with shutters nailed over all the windows. Dark like a cup of Spanish roast coffee. Dark like the colour black before God thought it might be a nice idea to let there be light.

'Holy Moses and macaroons!'

From beside me, I heard Mr Ambrose make an indistinct noise. For once, he was not complaining about my language.

'What is happening?'

How he managed to hear me over the din, I didn't know. I certainly didn't catch a single one of my own words. The storm was raging like ten thousand mad dragons.

'The sun is dying,' he rasped.

'What?'

'Look.' Raising his hand, he stretched it out towards where the darkness was thickest. After only a few moments, his fingers were swallowed by the storm. Despite the heat, a cold shiver ran down by back.

'This... this can't happen! A storm can't block out the sun like that! It would have to be...'

'Several miles high.'

'No! No, that can't happen! It simply can't!' Panic rising inside me, I looked around. Things were quickly disappearing. Ambrose's head was already being eaten up by shadows. A moment more, and we would have a headless camel. And then... What then? 'No! This can't happen!'

'Apparently, it can.'

With horror, I watched the last vestiges of light drain away. I watched as my ability to watch was stolen. The roar of the storm reached new heights, ringing like the laughter of the devil himself, spitting hot sand and darkness in our faces. The wind tore at us with malicious force, tugging so hard it threatened to rip me off the ground and away into the blackness.

'Bloody hell! No!'

Reaching out my hand, I tried to grasp something, anything, to hold onto, but my hand was swallowed by a dark maelstrom of sand. The black nothingness closed in around me, swallowing me, smothering me. Coughing, gasping for air, I lunged again. This time my left hand managed to grab something.

'Ouch!'

Oops. That something apparently was alive.

A hand snapped around my arm, pulling me closer against something large and hot. I couldn't see what it was; the darkness was absolute now – but from the coarse, fury texture I assumed it was Ambrose and not *Mr* Ambrose. At least I very much hoped so.

The thing I still had hold of with my left hand, though... *that* felt like Mr Ambrose. It felt familiar, like something I had grabbed hold of before.

'I would advise you,' came a cool voice out of the darkness, 'to let go of my ear immediately.'

'Ah.' So that's what it was. 'Sorry.'

I let go, and he pulled me forward another dozen inches or so. Now I was pressed up right against the camel's fury side. Unfortunately, though, the fur wasn't long enough for my fingers to find any hold in. And Mr Ambrose had released my arm by now. I lay there, shivering in spite of the terrible heat, a terrible feeling coming over me in the darkness.

Loneliness.

Not loneliness like you feel it on cold winter evenings, when your little sister is visiting with friends, and none of the other people in the house have anything meaningful to say to you. Not the loneliness of wanting things other people didn't understand. No, this was worse. It was loneliness as if there were no other people at all, only darkness, and the heat of hell, and death.

The storm gave another bark of cruel, roaring laughter and buffeted me with sand out of the blackness. Again, it tugged at me ferociously, and I tried to bury my fingers in the sand in a useless effort to keep myself on the ground that seemed the only real thing in the world. From somewhere, I heard a low whimper.

That's you! It's coming from your own throat! Pull yourself together, Lilly!

'What's wrong?'

That voice... It sounded as if it were shouting. And yet, over the overwhelming racket of the storm in the background, it only amounted to a whisper. Whose voice was it? Surely not that of Mr Ambrose! He'd never waste his breath on a question like that.

'I... I'm alone.' I was shouting, too. But my voice, just like the other one, was barely audible.

'No, you're not. The camel is here.'

It *was* Mr Ambrose. Only he could think of saying something like that at a time like this.

'The camel hates my guts!'

'Intelligent animal.'

'You... you're doing this on purpose!'

'Doing what?'

'Making me angry!' I growled into the darkness. 'So I won't be afraid.'

'Is it working?'

'Yes, blast you!'

'Indeed?'

'That's all you've got to say? You are a bloody bank-vault-like, close-mouthed bastard!'

'I see.' There was a momentary pause. 'Or rather, I don't see. Anything, in fact.'

'Ha, ha! That's so funny!'

Silence fell between us. Or, at least, the absence of words. The storm raged on, gnawing at my shrinking courage, slowly suffocating me. Instinctively, my hand reached out, searching for something, someone to hold on to.

'Mr Ambrose?'

'Yes?'

I hesitated. Snarky comments was one thing, anger to drive the fear away was fine, but this, what I was thinking now... this was dangerous.

I cleared my throat. Not that anyone heard over the racket. 'I... feel alone.'

'Do you?'

'I don't want to be alone right now.'

Silence. He didn't say a single word. I didn't even have the help of seeing his face to read his expression. But then, with Mr Ambrose, what was there to read? Just this once, I simply had to take a chance. Cautiously, I reached out, and felt something smooth. Not skin. The fabric of his tailcoat, maybe. A sleeve?

He gave a slight twitch under my sudden touch. Not letting that deter me, I moved my hand up his arm, until my fingers came to rest on his hand. Carefully, I brushed away a few grains of sand and stroked the soft skin underneath.

The silence emanating from Mr Ambrose became silenter than silent. It seemed to last forever. When he finally spoke, his voice was somewhat hoarse – probably from all the sand. 'I thought that sort of thing between us was reserved for the dark of the night.'

I tried to wet my lips. But there was no moisture left in my mouth. 'It looks pretty dark to me.'

Yet another pause. Then... 'Yes. You're right, it does.'

A moment later, two strong arms came around me, pulling me closer.

~~**~*~*

Dark is a strange thing. In the dark things happen that you could never have imagined.

'What's that?' a voice asked. Or shouted. Or whispered. It was difficult to tell in this world of deafening, roaring silence. The voice sounded a little like my own.

'That's me. My neck.' Another voice out of the dark. Another shout. Another whisper. *His.*

My hands clenched tightly around his neck, pulling him close.

'No, I mean that smell. Has the camel had something bad for breakfast?' Although the odour wasn't actually that bad. It didn't smell of camel at all. A bit harsh, true, but also... interesting.

'I don't think so. That smell might come from the fact that you have your nose buried in my armpit.'

'Oh.'

A pause. The storm roared on.

'Um... It's a nice armpit.'

'Thanks.'

'Feels good.' The voice in the dark that sounded like mine hesitated. Then, lower, so low I almost couldn't hear it myself, it said: 'All of you does.'

Silence. But only for a moment. Then his voice came out of the black nothing.

'So do you.'

Suddenly, the unseen force of the black wind around us slammed a fist of sand into me. The voice that sounded like mine cried out, and strong arms tightened around me. I sagged back, breathing hot air and dust.

'Oh God... I... I'm scared!'

'So am I.'

Mr Ambrose? *Scared?* That couldn't be! Not to mention sweet little me! I was *never* scared, out of principle!

I knew there had to be something wrong! I knew it all along: these two voices whispering and crying in the dark – they couldn't belong to us! Not to Mr Ambrose, and certainly not to me! Someone else had to be saying all those strange things.

'Come here,' I heard the him that sounded like Mr Ambrose say. 'Let me hold you.'

Bloody hell! Now I was two hundred and fifty per cent sure someone else had to be talking! That could not, under any circumstances, in this or in any other universe, have been Mr Rikkard Ambrose talking!

'Yes! Please!'

And that most certainly could not have been me answering! And yet, I felt myself being pressed against a lean, hard body in the dark, felt my face glide over cloth and sand, until my cheek was touching another face. An angular face it was, chiselled and hard in some places, soft in others. Like his lips, for example. His lips were soft. Familiar.

But how could they be familiar? After all, this was not Mr Ambrose I was feeling against me, and this was not even me doing the feeling. Those were two phantoms in the dark who dared to say things we could never say, do things we would never do.

'Rick?'

'Yes, Lilly?'

'I'm glad you're here.'

Not me. Not me talking.

'I'm glad you're here, too.'

Not him talking either.

'Really?'

'Well...' A touch of sarcasm entered the voice of the phantom man. 'Not glad that you're here in the sandstorm, in imminent danger of suffocation, obviously. I meant here *with me*.'

'Yes. I meant that, too.'

'Good.'

'Yes.'

A moment of silence. A moment of roaring storm winds.

'Lilly?'

'Yes?'

'If we don't survive, I want you to know that I...'

And the storm gave another bellow, cutting the phantom short. Maybe it was better that way. It really did sound entirely too much like Mr Ambrose.

~~**~*~*

When the darkness began to lighten and, by some strange coincidence, I found my face – not the face of a phantom or doppelganger, but *my actual face* – tucked against Mr Ambrose's chest, I immediately flinched back from this suspiciously unfeminist position. He hurriedly opened his arms, which somehow had gotten tangled around me, and we slid back over the sand, eyeing each other cautiously, like a kitten and a dog caught in flagrante delicto.

The roaring of the storm subsided somewhat.

He cleared his throat, and sand landed in his open hand.

'Ehem. Are you well?'

'You mean apart from the fact that I'm bruised and parched and almost roasted? Yes, Sir.'

'Adequate.'

Now *that* was Mr Ambrose talking.

The dark brown haze around us lightened again, and we could see the faint outline of a human-camel hybrid a few dozen yards away.

'Youssef? Is that you?'

The human detached himself from his camel. 'Ambrose *Effendi*? You are alive?'

'Of course!' Mr Ambrose made a dismissive noise and waved his hand. 'I told you, a little bit of sand couldn't stand in my way.'

Youssef's eyes flicked from Mr Ambrose to me and back again. Underneath the sand-caped cloth covering his face, the Egyptian opened his mouth to say something – then closed it again, and bowed his head. 'Yes, *Effendi*. As you say, *Effendi*.'

Behind Mr Ambrose, I got to my feet and, pointing to him, rolled my eyes. Then I made a very expressive gesture involving my forefinger being energetically tapped against the side of my head. Youssef was still wearing a cloth over his face, but underneath, I thought I could see something twitch. The corners of a mouth, maybe.

'Wait until the sandstorm has died down, then send out scouts to find the others.'

'Yes, *Effendi*. They will not have gone far. They know that during a sandstorm, it is safest to stay put and seek shelter.'

I might have imagined it, but I thought there was just the tiniest bit of emphasis on the 'they' in that sentence. Before Mr Ambrose had a chance to comment on it, Youssef turned and vanished around a dune.

'And find that infernal camel of mine!' Mr Ambrose shouted after him.

It was only a quarter of an hour later that Youssef returned, all the men and camels in tow. They looked a little dusty, but none the worse for wear.

'All present and correct, *Effendi*,' he said, saluting. 'And there's one thing more.'

Mr Ambrose halted in the process of checking the saddlebags of his errant camel. 'Yes?'

'We spotted a troop of soldiers from afar.'

'Soldiers?'

'Egyptians and English, *Effendi*. Although there may have been some French, too. It was difficult to make out from a distance.'

English, French, and Egyptians?

I froze. Could it be...? No, it couldn't!

But it has to be! It has to be him!

So Captain Carter had set out into the desert after all. I didn't say anything, and was careful not to make any sudden movements. After all, Mr Ambrose didn't know anything about Captain Carter. And I didn't think right now would be the right time to inform him. Neither would next week be. Or next year. Or ever, to tell the truth.

Slowly, he turned towards Youssef. I only had to take one look at the cold glint in his eyes to know I had been right not to say a word.

'What are they doing here?'

Youssef shrugged. 'I couldn't say, *Effendi*.'

'How many?'

'At least a hundred, *Effendi*. Probably more in the surrounding countryside. What I saw looked like one detachment of a larger force.'

Without moving his head, Mr Ambrose threw a sideways look at Karim. 'Your assessment?'

The huge bodyguard reached up to tug thoughtfully at his beard – then grasped only air and scowled. 'They're here to take care of the bandits.'

'Yes... and probably not in the way I wish it to be done. Youssef? How much chance do they have of catching up with us?'

'None.' The Arab smiled a brilliant white smile, sharp and crooked like an ivory sabre. 'Some have camels, but most of the men are either on foot or on horseback, particularly the English. Those riders will soon be on foot, too, when their horses collapse from exhaustion and die.'

Oops...

I cleared my throat. 'But, um... the riders themselves, the soldiers I mean... they won't die, right?'

'Well, probably not.' Youssef shrugged. 'They have a few people who seem to know what they're doing, so some of them are probably going to survive.'

Great. Just great.

'The sun is already setting.' Shielding his eyes with his hands, Mr Ambrose gazed towards the horizon. 'We'll wait until it is dark and the stars are visible, so we can calculate our exact position. Then we'll go on. Hopefully, those soldiers will be roasted alive and won't get in our way.'

~~**~*~*

We marched on. When one day, the shadow of a craggy mountain fell on me, I realized the landscape had changed a bit. Why hadn't I noticed before?

Because you've been watching Mr Ambrose instead of hills, dunes and mountains, that's why!

Well, so what if I was watching him and trying to catch every word he said? It wasn't because I was interested in *him* in any way. Oh no, definitely not! There was a far better reason:

We were coming close to the area where the bandits were operating. He knew that, and so did I. And he knew that I knew that he still hadn't revealed even the hint of a plan of what he was going to do when the bandits attacked. Right from the beginning of our journey I had tried to worm information out of him and failed. That first time hadn't been the last. Here's how one of these conversations usually went.

Me: 'Dick?'

Mr Ambrose: **Cold Silence**

Me: 'All right, all right. *Rick!*'

Mr Ambrose: 'Yes?'

Me: 'You know how you said you were going to let us be ambushed by the bandits?'

Mr Ambrose: 'Yes.'

Me: 'Well... What about it? I mean... you can't really have meant that, can you?'

Mr Ambrose: 'No.'

Me: 'No as in "No, I can't really have meant that"?'

Mr Ambrose: 'No. No as in "No, I *can* have meant it, and did mean it".'

Me: 'But... we'll all be slaughtered!'

Mr Ambrose: 'Indeed?'

Me: 'You can't want us all to be slaughtered!'

Mr Ambrose: 'Indeed?'

Me: 'Tell me what your plan is!'

Mr Ambrose: **Cold Silence**

Me: 'You do have a plan, don't you?'

Mr Ambrose: **Cold Silence**

Me: 'Bloody hell, will you open your mouth for once in your lifetime?'

Mr Ambrose: **Even Colder Silence**

Now, taking conversations like that into account, is it surprising that I had a tendency to glare at him, and that I tried to listen in on every single word he spoke? I'm not a very self-centred person as a rule, but I like my neck uncut, thank you very much. And I wasn't about to let Mr Ambrose's stubbornness stop me from keeping it that way.

We were just riding through a shadowed valley between two bare hills when I decided to make another attempt at the fortress. Driving Ambrose closer to Mr Ambrose, I cleared my throat.

Nothing happened.

I cleared my throat again.

'Do you have a cold?' Mr Ambrose asked without looking at me.

If I had, it would be from your voice and not the climate!

'No!' I glared at him. 'I'm not putting up with this any longer! I'm not walking blindly into a trap! If you have got a plan, fine! Share! If you haven't got one, then at least admit it! After what you did back in the sandstorm, I wouldn't be surprised if you thought you could just march right through anything and anyone because you're so high and mighty! But at least admit it! And if you do have a plan after all, I want to bloody know what it is! I want to know what you plan to do when we meet the–'

'Bandits!' Mr Ambrose growled.

'Yes, that's exactly it.' I nodded. 'So are you going to tell me?'

But Mr Ambrose wasn't paying any attention to me. He turned around, signalling to Youssef. 'Bandits! There! Bandits!'

Slowly, the realization sank in: he wasn't talking to me anymore. Mr Ambrose raised his arm, and I followed it with my wide-eyed gaze. There, on top of the nearest hill, stood a figure, its silhouette sharply contrasting against the burning blue sky. My heart picked up the pace. More figures appeared, right and left, mounted and unmounted, until we were surrounded by a virtual forest of men.

'Oh.' I swallowed. 'I guess our talk will have to wait.'

Raising their sabres, the bandits gave a guttural war cry and charged down the hillside.

CAMELKABOOM

I expected Mr Ambrose to charge at the bandits single-handedly. I expected bullets to fly and gallons of blood to flow. I expected a terrifying battle. What I didn't expect was Mr Ambrose sliding from his camel, falling to his knees and throwing his rifle away.

'Please! Please don't hurt us! We are just merchants! We mean nobody any harm. Please don't hurt us!'

I stared at him open-mouthed.

The foremost bandit, the leader, to judge by the arrogant smirk on his face, pulled his camel to a halt in front of Mr Ambrose and spat on the ground.

'English pig! So much for your famous "stiff upper lip"! Tell your men to throw their weapons away!'

'Men!' Mr Ambrose called, his voice trembling, yes, actually *trembling with fear*! 'Throw your weapons away, immediately! These people won't harm us if we don't resist!'

The bandit laughed.

'I didn't say anything about that, pig! Out of my way!'

'But...'

Mr Ambrose didn't get any further. Driving his camel forward, the bandit leader rode directly at him, and Mr Ambrose had just enough time to throw himself out of the way. Riding directly into the centre of the valley, the leader raised his gun over his head and shot into the sky, silencing everyone.

'All right, men!' he hollered. 'Gather up the weapons! Drive the camels to the east of the valley, and those English pigs to the west!'

So far, I had watched the whole proceedings with mouth agape. But now my stunned brain jumped into action. I drove my camel forward and bent down to pick up Mr Ambrose's fallen rifle from the ground.

'Hey, you!' A shot rang out over my head. 'Stop that!'

I was just about to right myself and return fire – if I could figure out how a rifle worked in three seconds, that is – when a hard hand grabbed my wrist and pulled me down from the camel. A moment later I was flat on the ground, encaged in Mr Ambrose's arms.

'Forgive my wife!' he pleaded with the bandits. 'She's had a heatstroke. She's not right in the head!' And into my ear, he hissed in his usual, cold, commanding tone: 'If you don't keep still, I will knock you out, understand?'

I froze. That didn't sound like the voice of a defeated man. That sounded suspiciously like a man with a plan.

'Your wife?' The bandit barked a laugh. 'You've got one woman among you all, and she's the only one who is man enough to pick up a rifle! That is a good joke! So much for the famed courage of the English! Now, do as you're told! Get over to the west of the valley, or I'll shoot you down here and now!'

Rising to his feet and pulling me up with him, Mr Ambrose led me over to the west side of the valley, all the while keeping a tight hold on me. Bandits rode around us and all the others in circles, herding everybody off to the west, shouting 'Move! Do as we tell you, and you won't get hurt!'. Nobody was fooled by the show they were putting on. I could see it in my companions' faces: they knew what awaited them. All the previous caravans had been massacred. This one would be, too. The bandits were just dangling the possibility of life in front of us so we wouldn't resist. And so far, it seemed to be working.

Or was it?

I caught a glimpse of the cold, calculating look in Mr Ambrose's dark eyes, and suddenly wasn't so sure anymore. But then the look was gone again, replaced by abject terror and whining submission.

'Please!' he begged the bandits. 'Please don't take everything! I invested all my whole fortune into this caravan! If you take everything, you'll leave me a beggar! Please!'

The bandits roared with laughter. Not content with that, one of them stepped up behind my dear employer and booted him soundly in the behind. Flying forward, he landed face-first in the dirt.

My lips twitched. Well, now, even if I was going to die today, maybe it was worth it just for having seen this.

'Please!' Getting up again, he slipped through the row of bandits and hurried to one of the camels they had herded together. 'Please, don't take this one! Take all the others, but not this one!'

The laughter subsided. Suddenly, anticipation crackled in the air. All eyes flew to the camel beside Mr Ambrose.

'Why?' Brows furrowed, the bandit leader drove his mount towards my employer, stopping only a yard or two away. 'What's so special about this particular camel?'

'I... I... I don't know! Just please! Leave me just this one. You can have all the others, but please...'

'Is there a treasure in the saddlebags? Gold? Silver?'

Fear flickered over Mr Ambrose's face. 'No! No, nothing at all! The saddlebags are empty! Please, don't take it! Please, you can take all the others, but please...'

'Out of my way, you snivelling worm!' Sliding down from his camel, the bandit leader marched towards Mr Ambrose and shoved him out of the way. He was so intent on the saddlebags that he didn't notice Mr Ambrose crawling away rather fast for someone who, just a moment ago, seemed to have been determined to protect this particular camel. 'Now, let's see what's in here.'

Unfastening the buckles, the bandit leader opened the first saddlebag – and the camel exploded.

~~**~*~*

I must admit, it took me quite by surprise. I'm from Westminster. We don't often meet exploding camels in our neighbourhood. But, here in this place, things seemed to be different. Apparently, one exploding camel wasn't enough. The others wanted to join the fun, and the moment the fire of the first explosion reached the next bleating furry molehill on legs, it blew up too. In a few fiery seconds of chaos, the entire east side of the valley was blown to bits, including every bandit and camel in it.

A moment later someone shoved me from behind, and I fell to the ground. Looking up, I saw Youssef standing protectively over me, a rifle suddenly in his hand. Where the hell had he gotten that? Other men of our party were pulling out rifles, too, and aiming. Had they had hidden weapons all along?

'Attack!' His ice-cold command drew my eyes back to Mr Ambrose. He was rolling over and pulling out a revolver from his tailcoat pocket.

Bam!

The first bullet caught the nearest bandit in the head and hurled him off his camel. 'Attack! Get them, men! Kill them all!'

Hs men seemed more than glad to follow that order. Bullets whizzed over my head like a swarm of deadly bees. Screams rang out, and moments later, the half dozen bandits that had been surrounding us fell dead to the ground. Taking up a formation like a professional regiment, our caravan started firing at the rest.

Not that there were many left. Most of them, gathered around the camels when they blew up, had been ripped apart by the explosions. The few who were left didn't run, though.

'A trap!' shouted someone over the racket of the gunfire. 'It's a trap! Kill the English pigs, or Radi will have your head!'

I spat out sand and raised my head. 'Radi? Who the hell is Radi?'

Youssef grabbed me, shoved me down again and fired another shot at the bandits. 'How should I know? The chief leader of the bandits, maybe! Stay down!'

'Give me a gun, and I won't have to stay down!'

'The *Effendi* gave strict orders that you were not to be given a weapon under any circumstances.'

'Oh, he did, did he?'

Sooner or later, we were going to have a chat about that.

'Yes! And I agree! With the bandits, we have one deadly danger to face already, we don't need another! Now stay down!'

Bullets shot across the valley in deadly droves. From what I could see whenever I managed to raise my head long enough to catch a glimpse, the bandits were holding their own. Once, I saw Mr Ambrose at the other end of the line, commanding his men and shooting. But even his cold glare couldn't drive the bandits away.

'We aren't winning, are we?' I asked Youssef while he was reloading.

'Have patience.'

'That's all very well for you to say! You're not lying face-first in the dirt!'

'You won't have to lie down much longer! Look up!'

'You just told me to stay down!'

'Well, things are changing, *Hanem*. Look up!'

I did, just as the sound of more guns joined the cacophony of battle. Past all the smoke and shouting men and blazing guns, past everything up on the hills in the east, I saw riders appearing. A dozen? Two? No, soon there were more than that. They had to number at least a hundred, all sitting on camelback, and all shooting at our enemies.

'What in God's name is going on?' I yelled over the noise of gunfire.

'You didn't think the explosives in the saddle bags were just a trap, did you?' Youssef laughed. 'The *Effendi* never does anything for just one reason. The explosion was a signal. More men have been following us ever since we left Alexandria, far enough away so nobody would notice, but close enough to hear a herd of exploding camels! I was slightly worried for a time that they had lost us in the sandstorm, but then the scouts made contact yesterday.'

'He *knew*? He knew there were reinforcements, and he didn't tell me?'

'Yes.'

'I'm going to kill him!'

'Feel free to try, *Hanem*.'

As he spoke, more men started appearing to the west and the north. At a glance, I would have said they had to number at least three hundred. That bastard! That bloody, stone-faced, close-mouthed bastard!

Bandits were falling all over the place, shot in the back or in the sides. The ones left still alive cowered down in the sand, shooting wildly in all directions, their eyes wide with terror. For a supposedly timid caravan of traders, we were proving entirely too tough and nasty. Those who still had live camels underneath them kicked the animals into motion and darted towards the last few hills around the valley that were still free of attackers.

I scrambled to my feet.

'Bloody hell! We can't let them get away like that!' I glared at Youssef. 'Give me a gun!'

He shook his head. 'I'm sorry, *Hanem*. I have my orders.'

Shooting him another glare, I bent down to pick up a good-sized pebble from the ground. 'Good riddance!' I hurled it after a retreating bandit. It squarely hit his camel on the rump. 'Go bugger a banana!'

Only a few dozen yards away, I spotted Ambrose (the camel version), still loitering well away from the craters that had swallowed the fellow members of his species. The foxy old bugger! So he had survived, had he? Excellent! I started to run.

'*Hanem*! Wait!' a shout came from behind me. But I didn't listen to Youssef. I wasn't really in the mood to listen to anyone right now.

Just when I was about to swing myself up into Ambrose's saddle, a rider on another camel shot past me. I only saw him in a blur, but there was no mistaking that black colour. All the other men wore the white burnous. And there was no mistaking his voice, either.

'After them! Follow me, men!'

Cold. Hard. Commanding.

I pulled myself the rest of the way up into the saddle and urged Ambrose up and forward. It took me only moments to catch up to Mr Ambrose. When he glanced sideways at me, his face was still a kind of blur, constantly jerking around with the strange gait of the camel beneath him, but the ice in his eyes was clear enough.

'I said follow me, *men*! In case I wasn't clear enough, that didn't include you!'

My eyes narrowed. 'What do you want me to do? Stay back there?' I jerked my hand at the empty desert behind us.

'Yes. Right by that big rock.' He waved dismissively at a sandstone formation. 'We'll come back when the bandits are dead.'

Blimey. He was actually serious.

'Go to hell!'

'The road to hell, I'm told, is paved with good intentions.'[28] He gave his camel a kick, urging the animal to go faster. 'So it's very unlikely I'll ever find my way there.'

Picking up the speed with a protesting bleat, his camel shot forward. I urged Ambrose on to catch up again.

'Why didn't you tell me we had reinforcements? You could have let me know!'

'Knowledge is power is time is money.'

'So what?'

He gave me a look that clearly said he thought me very daft. 'Meaning that if I shared knowledge, that would be tantamount to sharing power or money.'

'Which you aren't willing to do?'

'Naturally. Especially not with you.'

My mouth dropped open.

'I hate you!'

'Indeed?' Raising his gun, he fired a shot at the closest bandit. More shots sounded from right and left. Without my noticing, the rest of our party, and the reinforcements, had caught up. Somewhere I saw Youssef's proud figure. Then I spotted Karim's turban, towering over the heads of the others. Oh, how many others! The masses of men and camels around us seemed endless, streaming down the hills from three sides, hot on the bandits' trail. I caught the eye of a bandit, looking around to see how close we were. His face paled, and a grin spread over mine. Grim satisfaction rose up in me, dispelling my anger for the moment.

'We're going to flatten those bastards, aren't we?'

'A slightly informal way of putting it. But, on the whole, you are correct.'

Another volley of gunfire went off, and several bandits dropped to the ground.

'Yes!' Not having a gun or a sabre, I thrust my fist into the air! 'Yes! Get the bloody bastards!'

The men behind me gave a cheer, and the next volley went off, felling another six or seven bandits. The remaining bandits pulled out canes and began to beat their camels furiously, forcing them to go even faster.

'Don't lose sight of them!' Mr Ambrose shouted a command. 'We have to know where they're going!'

'Don't worry, *Effendi!*' Youssef shouted back. 'Those are no racing camels! They cannot keep up that speed for long!'

And he was right. After only a few minutes, some of the bandits' camels began to falter and stumble. They slowed and slowed, no matter how many blows their masters inflicted on their rumps. A cheer went up from our men.

'Get them!' Cries rose up. 'Get them all!' Rifles were raised, and another volley of gunfire thundered over the noise of the running camels. We were so close

---

[28] The proverb Mr Ambrose refers to here – 'The road to hell is paved with good intentions' – originates from various sources, but in its most finished form appears for the first time in John Milton's Epic Poem *Paradise Lost*, where he says, 'Easy is the descent into Hell, for it is paved with good intentions'.

now, almost a dozen bandits fell to the ground, stricken. Out of all of them, only six were left now. 'Get them!' One of the men behind me shouted again. 'Get them all! Fire!'

Mr Ambrose opened his mouth. 'No! Don't–'

His voice was cut off by the gunfire. Five bandits dropped to the ground, dead. A last shot sounded, and the very last bandit slid out of the saddle, hitting the ground with a *thump*. His camel continued for a few more paces, then slowly came to a halt and sank to its knees, exhausted.

The men cheered. Gunshots were fired into the air. More cheers rose up, and more and more – until someone noticed the expression on Mr Ambrose's face. Well... if I was being honest, it wasn't an expression, exactly. It rather was what you would get if you deepfroze an expression and sprinkled it with promises of wrath and violence. Slowly, the gunshots stopped and the cheers subsided. When everyone, including, me, Karim and the camels, was absolutely silent and cowering under the glare of our employer, Mr Ambrose asked in a very cool, controlled voice: 'Who fired that shot?'

The men looked at each other, dumbfounded. Then one raised his hand. 'Um... *Effendi*? What shot?'

'The last one! The one that killed the last bandit!'

'Oh.' The hand sank down again, apparently profoundly grateful it wasn't attached to the guilty party. A few moments of deadly silence hung over the desert. Unbearably hot as it was, the desert air seemed suddenly ready to freeze. Finally, another hand, slightly trembling, rose from among the men. They parted like a bunch of chickens that had discovered a warthog in chicken costume among their number.

The man was of slightly less than average height, not dark-skinned enough to be an Arab – French or Spanish, maybe? – with a straight, rather short nose, and curly black hair that peeked out from under his headdress. At the moment, sweat was also trickling out from under there, down his forehead.

Mr Ambrose advanced towards him. His camel was slightly bigger than the other man's, not to speak of himself. He towered over the man in the burnous.

'Tell me,' Mr Ambrose asked, his voice deceptively low and smooth, 'what exactly were my orders?'

'To, um, get them all? All the bandits, Sir?'

'No. If you think back closely, you will remember that was what *you men* shouted. I want to know what *my orders* were.'

'Oh... um... well, Sir, I...'

'Since you are having difficulties with your memory, I'll tell you. My orders were, verbatim, "Don't lose sight of them! We have to know where they're going!".'

For a moment, heavy silence descended over the landscape again. Then, Mr Ambrose leaned forward until only a few inches separated his cold, hard face from that of his employee. 'Tell me: how exactly are we going to "not lose sight of them", how are we going to find out "where they are going", when they are all dead?'

'Um... well... I...'

'Do not be shy. I would be most interested to hear your opinion.'

'Well... I...I don't know, Sir.'

Shooting up, Mr Ambrose's fist clamped around the smaller man's throat and lifted him clean off the saddle. He dangled in the air, a few inches above the leather, fighting for breath.

'Neither do I!' Mr Ambrose hissed. 'Congratulations! I have crossed two oceans, survived explosions, assassins and the desert – not one of those things has been able to stop me from getting my revenge! And you have succeeded where all those things failed. Just a stupid little man who couldn't follow orders! What do you have to say for yourself?'

'Grrk! Grak! Rrrm!'

It seemed to me that with Mr Ambrose's hand clamped around his throat, the man didn't have much to say for himself, nor was it likely he would ever speak again if Mr Ambrose didn't let go. My dear employer didn't appear to have noticed that fact, though.

I cleared my throat. He didn't notice that, either. He was far too focused on the object of his ice-cold rage.

'Do you realize we will never find the rest of them, now?' he demanded, his voice like shards of ice piercing the skin.

'The rest of them?' The words were out of my mouth before I knew it. He turned just slightly to look at me. 'You think there are more bandits than the ones we killed, Sir?'

'Of course! The number of attacks on my caravans and the size of the raiding parties leave no other possibility. This was just one of three or four groups! The rest of them are still safe back in the bandits' hideout, wherever that is! And thanks to this gentleman–' He shook his victim like a ragdoll, eliciting more gagging noises, 'we will never find its location!'

Eyes glittering icily, Mr Ambrose glared up at the man. 'I wonder what would be a fitting punishment for you...'

'Rrrg! Mm Nnmh!'

'Silence! You have lost the right to speak!'

'Nhh Rmmgk!'

'Silence, I said! You will be sacked, of course... Maybe I should abandon you here. Or maybe I'll drag you before a magistrate, and have you held responsible for ruining this expedition. You can work off the cost in the next thirty years in some dusty coal mine. How would you like that?'

'Nnnmm!'

The man's face was turning blue now. I looked away, not particularly charmed by the sight. My eyes happened to stray into the direction where the camels of the bandits had stopped to rest.

They were no longer there.

Frowning, I looked around and spotted them a few dozen yards away. They weren't resting anymore. True, they were moving slowly, but they were moving. And what's more, they all seemed to be headed in more or less the same general direction.

'Or a quarry!' I heard Mr Ambrose from behind me. 'How would you like to slave in a quarry for the rest of your life?'

'Nmm! Nmm, pllsss!'

I cleared my throat again. 'Um... Rick?'

'Don't interrupt!' he snapped at me without looking. Then he returned to his prey. 'No, a quarry is too good for you! You might actually get to breathe fresh air! No, I'll put you in a match factory, where you will breath poisonous sulphur fumes until your lungs give up and...'

The camels were moving away faster now. 'Rick! I really think you should...'

'I said don't interrupt!'

They were definitely moving as a group, and they were almost over the first hill already! Almost out of sight!

'But I really think you should look at this!'

'What is it?' Exasperated, Mr Ambrose turned around. When I pointed, he followed my outstretched arm with his gaze.

'Yes? A few camels walking over a hill. So what?'

'It's obvious, isn't it? We follow them! We don't need the bandits to be alive. Their camels will lead us back to their hideout.'

'This is no time for ridiculous jokes!'

'I'm not joking!'

Turning his head slightly, Mr Ambrose pierced me with his gaze. 'Let me be clear... You want me to follow a group of beasts that smell like the doormat in front of a sewer entrance and look like the fury version of the Hunchback of Notre Dame into the desert, without knowing for certain that they are, in fact, heading anywhere specific?'

Swallowing, I held his gaze. 'Yes.'

'And this wild idea is based on...'

'Call it female intuition.'

Mr Ambrose muttered something too low for me to hear. From the look in his eyes, though, I gathered it was something not very complimentary about female intuition in general and the people who had them in particular. Meanwhile, he was still holding his victim up by the throat. The man's eyes had begun to roll in a rather unhealthy-looking manner.

'Excuse me, *Effendi*, but she does actually have a point,' came unexpected help from Youssef. 'Camels are herd animals. If there are more bandits as you say, they are sure to have more camels, and they will probably belong to the same heard as these ones.' He gestured to the bandits' camels that were almost out of sight by now. 'A riderless camel's first instinct, apart from spitting you in the eye, is always to find its way back to the herd.'

'Gnnk!' the man on the end of Mr Ambrose's arm pleaded, adding his support for the idea. 'Lnnk! Rrgg!'

Mr Ambrose sat absolutely still for a moment. His eyes flicked between me and the disappearing camels.

'You really believe this will work, Youssef?' he asked, finally.

'Yes, *Effendi*. It certainly cannot hurt to try.'

'All right.' Mr Ambrose opened his hand. Gasping for breath, his victim slammed back into the saddle. 'We've wasted enough time! Let's go!' And he drove his camel forward.

We didn't have to ride long. After only about half an hour, we reached a broad plain of dirt and sand, stretching out in front of us. At the end of the plain, a rocky cliffside rose up out of the ground, its impenetrable wall broken only by one single gorge, right in the middle. The camels were heading directly towards it.

Even from this distance, we heard surprised shouts out of the gorge as the first riderless camel entered. Then, muzzle flashes lit up the shadowy gorge, and the shouts were abruptly replaced by gunfire.

'We've been seen!' Karim roared. 'Men! Weapons out!'

What? I thought they already had their weapons out! Everyone had a rifle in his hand. But, at Karim's order, they threw open their saddlebags and removed other objects that looked far more sinister. Some round, some cylindrical, but far too large for an ordinary rifle. All were made of dark, shiny metal the look of which sent a shiver down my back.

A shiver of excitement!

The gunshots in the distance had ceased. I guess whoever had shot had realized by now that we were still out of range. But, to judge by the look on Mr Ambrose's face, that would soon change. We were going into battle! And I didn't intend to sit back idly!

'Give me that,' I told one of the men who had exchanged his rifle for a new weapon, pointing to the rifle. After all, he didn't need it anymore, did he?

The man hesitated, his eyes flitting to Mr Ambrose.

'Absolutely not!' my dear employer snapped. 'Have you lost your mind?'

'No, it's still in my head, just as usual.'

'You don't even know how to shoot!'

'It's never too late to learn, is it?' Grabbing the rifle, I pulled it from the man's unresisting hands. 'Where do you put the bullets in?'

'You're insane!' Mr Ambrose hissed. 'Put that down at once!'

'No!'

'You won't need it anyway! You're staying here!'

'In your dreams!'

Driving his camel forward, he was suddenly beside me, his hand reaching up. But other than with that poor man earlier, he didn't grab my throat. He grabbed my chin, pulling me towards him. 'In my dreams,' he told me, his voice still as hard and cold as an iceberg, 'more interesting things happen. Things that involve the two of us.'

I swallowed. Just this once, with his dark, sea-coloured eyes boring into mine, I had no words.

'Stay here!' he ordered.

I shook my head.

Youssef's camel skidded to halt beside us.

'*Effendi*, we have to go! We have already lost the element of surprise! If we delay much longer, they will have reinforcements at the entrance to the gorge, and we won't be able to take it!'

I felt Mr Ambrose's fingers clench around my chin almost painfully tightly. A muscle in his jaw twitched. He didn't take his gaze from me, almost not seeming to notice the commands shouted at the distant entrance of the gorge.

'There's nothing I can do to make you stay, is there?'

'No,' I vowed. 'I'm coming with you!'

Before I could so much as flinch away, he was on me. His arms came around me, almost lifting me off my saddle, pulling me so tight against him I felt every crease in his tailcoat, every line of his hard body, every grain of sand between us. Our lips collided like two opposing armies, ready to die and love it.

'*Effendi*! We have to...'

I didn't hear the rest of Youssef's words. My ears were ringing, my body was on fire. Dimly, I wondered whether one of the bullets had hit me. But this felt entirely too sweet for that.

When we finally broke apart, I was panting for breath. Mr Ambrose, of course, was as cold and collected as ever. Well, almost.

'Stay safe!' he ordered, pressing his forehead to mine for just a moment. Then he wheeled his camel around and raised his rifle into the air. 'Attack!'

THE ART OF LOSING YOUR WAY

It wasn't quite the attack I had imagined. I had expected a brave rush towards the entrance of the gorge, waving our rifles in the air and firing the occasional well-aimed shot at the bandits.

Reality was somewhat less heroic. We hunkered down behind a few rocks some distance away from the entrance of the gorge. While bullets were flying over our heads, I watched with increasing puzzlement as several of our men put up three of the large cylindrical objects they had brought on tripods. At one end, the objects had a barrel, like a rifle. At the other, something that looked like handle stuck out of it.

'What's that?' I demanded, pointing to one of the objects that was sitting a few rocks away from us.

'One of my prototypes,' Mr Ambrose answered, curtly.

A shot rang out, and I hurriedly snatched my hand back from over the rock, staring at him in disbelief. 'We are being shot at by blood-thirsty bandits, and you want to *test some new gadget*?'

'Yes.' He gave a signal to one of the men around the cylindrical thingamy, and the fellow grabbed the handle, directing the barrel-shaped protrusion directly at the entrance of the gorge. One final time he looked up, searching for final approval from Mr Ambrose. Mr Ambrose nodded. 'Fire!'

The handle began to turn – and the world turned into fire.

A roar went up the like of which I had never heard before. It wasn't an explosion. No, it was a never-ending series of explosions, battering the ears with incessant noise. Agonizing noise. I couldn't help uttering a small cry of pain. Then, suddenly hands were covering my ears. Looking up, I gazed in Mr Ambrose hard eyes.

'It takes some getting used to!' he shouted over the racket. He didn't seem to be bothered by the ear-splitting roar in the least.

My fingers trembling just a little, I pointed at the thing that was spitting bullets faster than lighting.

'What kind of hellish machine is that?'

'The killing kind.'

Blimey, was he right about that! Three of the things had opened fire on the entrance of the gorge now, and shots from there had halved in a few moments! Not that I could hear them over the din of the killing machines. But the muzzle flashes grew fewer and fewer by the second. Only a few more moments, and they ceased completely.

Something flashed in the corner of my eye, and my gaze darted to the left, then to the right. Ha! From both sides of the cliff, our men were slowly approaching the gorge entrance. They had to have taken a roundabout route to stay out of the line of fire, and were now sneaking up on the enemy without the bandits being any the wiser. If there were bandits left at the gorge entrance at all, that is.

The men on either side of the gorge raised their hands in what had to be a signal. Abruptly, the noise of Mr Ambrose 'prototype' cut off, and safe from fire, the men darted into the gorge. A few lone screams rose up into the air, then silence fell.

Letting his hands fall from my ears, Mr Ambrose stood up. 'Forwards, men!'

Some mounted their camels again. Others, whose animals had been hit by one of the enemy's bullets, simply ran forward, ready to hurl themselves on the ground the moment the enemy started firing again. But no shots came. We arrived at the entrance of the gorge, all unhurt and hardly out of breath. We were greeted by cheers from the men who had taken down the first line of bandits. Littered on the ground lay the bodies of their vanquished foes, the red bloodstains contrasting sharply with the white burnouses.

'Dismount!' Mr Ambrose called. 'The gorge is too narrow for camels! We go on foot from here!'

He was right: the cleft in the rock was hardly wide enough for one man to walk through, let alone a camel. The bandits had chosen their hideout well. I didn't know much about strategy, but under normal circumstances, this place would probably be as easy to defend as it would be impossible to take.

My eyes flitted to the massive prototype guns, and from them to Mr Ambrose. Circumstances, it seemed, were not normal today.

'Youssef, know the desert mountains best.' Mr Ambrose gestured for the Egyptian to squeeze past him. 'You take the lead!'

'Yes, *Effendi!*'

Pressed against the stone wall, rifle at the ready, Youssef started to edge down the gorge, Mr Ambrose right on his heels.

'*Sahib*, wait!' Karim called out. 'I should go next, not you!'

'Not this time, Karim.' With a menacing *ka-klack*, Mr Ambrose reloaded his weapon. 'I want them myself!'

And he slid into the shadows of the gorge.

Cursing in his native tongue, Karim dashed after him, and I followed suit.

"Blast and double blast that man! Does he think he's invincible?" Gripping my rifle more tightly, I ran after my dear granite-head of an employer, my eyes firmly on his bodyguard's back. I muttered a few more choice curses, but my efforts sounded pitiful next to Karim's. I really had to make him teach me a few of his home-made curses! They sounded too interesting not to be sprung on London's unsuspecting society.

Well, I could try to finagle them out of him – if we all got out of here alive.

Men pressed forward around me, sliding past me even though I ran at full speed. Whether it was because they had longer legs or were more used to moving in a burnous than I was, I didn't know. But by the time gunfire started up ahead, I was already somewhere at the back of the line. Cursing, I redoubled my efforts to go faster, and was just about to slide past the man in front of me, when I saw something out of the corner of my eye.

'Duck!'

The men didn't react in time, and one of them went down with a bullet in his shoulder. Whirling around, I raised my rifle to a ledge, about ten feet up the side of the ravine, where a bandit had stepped out of some sort of cave entrance.

Please, God, I prayed. *Please let that thing I'm about to squeeze be the trigger!*

Bam!

Apparently, it was. The barrel in my hands spat fire and smoke, and the bandit twitched back, ducking his head. Then, as he realized my shot had gone wide of the mark, he rose again, grinning – and a volley of bullets from the men behind me caught him full in the chest.

'Get up there!' I shouted. 'Check where that cave leads!'

'How about this, instead?' One of the men pulled something from his pocket. I only saw something round and shiny glint in the sun as it flew towards the cave entrance, then an explosion ripped apart the air, followed by the sound of stone crashing down. When the dust had settled, all that remained of the cave entrance was a pile of rubble.

'That was spiffing!' I grinned at the man who had thrown the explosive. 'Can I have one of those?'

'Only if you promise me not to blow yourself up.'

'Done!' I lifted my rifle. 'And can someone show me how to reload this blasted thing?'

We started down the gorge again, more careful this time about watching our backs. No ridges or openings appeared behind or above us. But after only a few minutes, the gorge started to widen, and suddenly we stepped out into a small valley with steep walls on all sides. The moment we were in the open, the noise of the fight assailed us.

'Bloody hell!' I sucked in a sharp breath. 'I guess Mr Ambrose was right. There are more bandits!'

A lot more. They were swarming out of cave openings all along the opposite end of the valley. Dozens of them! Hundreds! Opposite them stood our band of fighters, which no longer seemed so insurmountably strong as when they had come storming down from the hills. From what I could see, we were evenly matched in numbers.

Without hesitation, I ducked behind a rock, laid the rifle atop, aimed, and fired. The recoil, which I had hardly noticed the first time, with a thick mass of men right behind me, now almost knocked me off my feet. But I didn't give in! I reloaded and fired again. Not that I knew whether I actually hit someone – I was about as good a shot as Mr Ambrose was a conversationalist – but I couldn't just sit here and do nothing!

'Fire!'

That single word out of Mr Ambrose's mouth was all the warning I got before the roar I had heard only once before rose up again, straight out of hell. It was just as frightening as last time – only now Mr Ambrose wasn't here to hold me. Covering my ears, I peered past my rock, to where the three sinister guns had been set up, facing towards the entrances of the caves. The bandits in front of them were suddenly falling like flies. Those who somehow, miraculously, hadn't been hit yet, scrambled to get back in, bashing their own comrades over the head if necessary.

Glancing from left to right, I saw several of our own men on the ground, their hands stuffed into their ears. Apparently, they hadn't been fully prepared for Mr Ambrose's little surprise, either.

Knowledge is power is time is money. Meaning that if I shared knowledge, that would be tantamount to sharing power or money.

I snorted, remembering his words.

'One of these days,' I growled, fixing my eyes on Mr Ambrose's straight, black-clad back, 'your boarded up mouth is going to cost you dearly!'

But then – maybe spreading the word about weapons like these wouldn't be a good idea either.

Forcing my hands away from my ears, I hurriedly stuffed the edges of my burnous into my earholes to muffle the torturous noise. Once it was bearable, I picked up my rifle, which had fallen to the ground, and resumed firing. Not that my help appeared to be needed. There was hardly a bandit alive outside the cave anymore. When the last of them finally limped into the darkness, the roar of the guns ceased, and I dared to lower my rifle.

'Karim!' Mr Ambrose made a gesture to his bodyguard. 'Most of them went into these three big caves! That one, that one, and that one!' He pointed them each out in turn. 'You take fifty men and one of the prototypes and go down the left one. Youssef will take the right, and I the middle! Ten men stay outside to block up all the smaller exits with explosives! If the stone turns out to be too solid, stand guard outside the exit and shoot anyone who comes out that is not me or one of my commanders!'

'Yes, *Sahib!*'

'Yes, *Effendi!*'

In moments, the well-trained fighters split up into three main groups. But those moments were enough for me to slide out from behind my rock and join the middle one.

'Ready and reporting for duty, Sir!' I said, giving a mock salute.

Mr Ambrose didn't return it.

'What are you doing here?' His eyes flashed with cold lightning. 'I told you to stay safe!'

'And I told you I'd be coming with you!'

'A battleground is no proper place for a lady!'

My eyes narrowed. 'It's not, is it?'

'No!'

'Well, in that case I'm definitely coming with you. I love improper places.'

Mr Ambrose's left little finger twitched, twice, betraying a roiling thunderstorm of emotion inside his stony form.

'Fine! Stay behind me and do as I say!'

I gave him my demurest smile. 'Don't I always?'

Not deeming that worthy of a reply, he turned and headed towards the cave, surrounded by dozens of men bristling with weapons. Passing the prototype gun, he saw that one of the men in charge of it had been shot and lay dead on the ground.

'A volunteer!' he called. 'We need a volunteer to help carry and fire this!'

My hand shot up in the air.

'Not you! I order someone else to volunteer!' His glare raked the assembled men. More than a hundred hands shot up into the air immediately, and I lowered mine, pouting.

'You there!' He gestured at the lucky winner, and the man hurried towards his assigned post.

Motioning forward with his head, Mr Ambrose led us into the cave. Several of the men pulled out lanterns and lit them without having to be ordered. Orange light flickered on bare, craggy stone walls.

'Use only the rifles and other guns while we're in here,' Mr Ambrose ordered in a low voice. 'Not the explosives. We don't know how secure this place is, and we don't want it to come down on us.'

Muttered 'Yes, Sir's and 'Yes, *Effendi*'s came from all directions. We walked through the dark until we came to a bend in the tunnel. Behind the bend, I could just make out the tunnel splitting off into two directions.

'What now?' one of the men whispered.

'Give me that.' Shoving one of the men aside, Mr Ambrose took hold of his prototype. Without setting it on the ground, he started to turn the handle. Ear-splitting thunder echoed from the cave walls, and the prototype gun spat a lance of fire into the darkness. Other than that, nothing happened. Quickly, Mr Ambrose swung the gun around to face the other tunnel, and turned the handle again. Once more, thunder split the air. But this time, it was accompanied by a shrill scream from somewhere down the dark passage.

Mr Ambrose lowered the gun, pointing in the direction from which the scream had come. 'We go that way.'

And he started forward.

The tunnel was long and winding. Every time we reached a bend, Mr Ambrose gave a silent sign for us to stop. Then, the men with the prototype gun marched forward, held it around the corner and started firing. Almost every time we turned the corner, we came across blood-spattered corpses. After the latest such bloodbath, I turned to Mr Ambrose and whispered: 'You say this is a prototype? Still in development?'

'Yes.'

'How much money do you mean to ask of the government for one of these things when it is finished?'

He gave me a cool look. 'You don't honestly think I'll be selling a weapon like that to anyone, do you, let alone a government! It's far too powerful a thing for politicians to play with!'

'Why, Sir, you almost sound like a man with a conscience!"

'*Au contraire*, Mr Linton. I sound like a man who prefers to have the biggest gun himself, instead of giving it away.'

Well, that was certainly one way of looking at it.

Shrugging, he marched over the corpses on the floor, not bothering to step around them. 'Maybe in twenty years or so, once I have a better model for myself, I'll find a front man and sell these somewhere where the government is not quite as inane as in Great Britain.'[29]

Finally, we reached the last bend in the tunnel.

How did I know it was the last?

I couldn't see around it, of course. But we all could hear the bandits' hushed, angry voices, and see the light of torches and lamps flickering on the walls. They were not far ahead, and they had nowhere else to flee to.

'Has someone got a mirror?' Mr Ambrose asked, his voice almost inaudible.

Nobody spoke up.

'A mirror? Anyone?' His gaze drifted to me.

'Don't look at me! Do you think that just because I'm female, I'm carrying mirrors and fans and lace handkerchiefs around with me wherever I go?' I snapped.

'It certainly would come in handy.' He let his eyes wander over the rest of us. 'Anyone?'

Finally, a cautious hand rose from the back. One of the prettier men in the company apparently did carry a hand mirror around with him wherever he went. So much for gender roles.

'Hand it over.' Mr Ambrose held out his hand. Taking the mirror from the reluctant dandy, he cautiously slid it around the corner of the tunnel. It barely

---

[29] My apologies to Richard Jordan Gatling, the American inventor who in 1862, about twenty years after the events of this novel, invented the Gatling Gun (the first real machine gun). I'm sure that in reality, he was not a front man for a incredibly wealthy, stubborn, close-mouthed and good looking British financier by the name of Rikkard Ambrose. No, definitely not.

protruded a few inches past the stone, but suddenly there was a shout, and shots rang out.

'Idiots!' Mr Ambrose hissed, and pulled back the mirror with a jerk. We heard a strange, harsh *ping* sound, followed by a scream, and curses.

'Listen up.' Turning towards us, Mr Ambrose fixed us with those dark eyes of his that seemed even darker and more threatening in the gloom. 'I got a glimpse around the bend. There's a cave there, fairly round, with all sorts of crates and bags, probably the bandits' plunder. The bandits are scattered throughout the cave. Once we go around the bend, we can't use guns anymore. Not the prototype, not rifles, not even revolvers. The cave is too small. The bullets will ricochet off the walls, and they might be as likely to hit any of us as our enemies.' He jerked a thumb towards the cave, from which we still heard curses in Arabic. 'I think the bandits found that out just now, too. So it'll be one on one in there, close combat. Does everyone still have their blade?'

Shouldering their rifles, the men pulled scimitars, daggers and sabres. Suddenly, the light of the lamps was illuminating a forest of wickedly sharp steel.

'Good. That's everyone.'

I cleared my throat, meaningfully.

'Everyone but one,' he amended, and with a glare handed me a small knife from his belt.

'Is that a joke?' I looked at the tiny thing with distaste. 'That's not big enough to cut my toenails with!'

'Then you must have impressive toenails. Forward!'

And he charged into the cave. Not waiting to be outdone by one of the men this time, I dashed after him. I skidded around the corner, my dagger half-raised – and ran straight into one of the bandits. And by 'ran into him' I don't just mean we knocked heads. I really mean 'ran into him'. The tip of my dagger was just about belly-high. We collided, and there was strange, wet *thud*, like a blade being slammed into a soft sheath.

Only – the sheath was a man's belly.

'Mmpf!'

'Arg!'

We both toppled over, rolling across the floor, blood streaming over us. For a moment, I didn't know whether it was mine or his, then I felt him twitch under me, caught in his death throes. Above me, I heard yells and the trampling of feet, and I pulled in my head just in time. A boot stomped down where it had been a moment ago. Man after man jumped over me in the rush to storm the cave. I growled. I didn't like men going over my head, whether metaphorically or literally.

'Ouff!' A boot hit me in the side, and all the air went out of me. Another boot hit. And other. 'Ouch! Careful! Live one down here!'

Another boot hit.

'This is all your fault!' I growled at the man beneath me. 'Couldn't you have gotten out of my way in time?'

The corpse stared up at me with glassy eyes, not appearing in the mood to reply. Another boot hit me in the side, this time so hard that I rolled over and came to a stop with the dead bandit on top of me.

'Yuck! Get off me!'

I pushed, but nothing happened. The corpse only lifted a few inches, then smacked back down on top of me. That made me angry. Really angry. I pushed again, with all my might, and the corpse slid off me and onto the floor, leaving me panting, with a bloodstained dagger clutched in my hands.

If only Aunt Brank could see me now...

Not too far way, a scream sounded. It tore me from my paralysis. Bloody hell! I had to get off this floor, or I would soon join my friend, the disgusting corpse, in the underworld!

Rolling around, I pushed myself to my feet and steadied myself against the cave wall. Quickly, I looked around the cave to see what was happening.

It was mayhem. Utter and complete mayhem. Throughout the cave, bandits and Mr Ambrose's men were duelling with daggers, scimitars and sabres. Every now and again, a small explosion would light up the cave, and I knew that someone had thrown an explosive or dropped a lamp. The smells of sweat, blood and burning oil filled the room.

'Him! Over there! Get him!'

My eyes flicked to the origin of Mr Ambrose's voice. There he was, pointing to a big, bearded man, who, standing atop a ledge, seemed to be commanding the bandits. He was all the way across the cave, too far for Mr Ambrose or me to reach – but not for someone else.

'Jita la'il'

With a bestial war cry, a huge figure darted out of a second cave entrance halfway across. I needed only a glance to recognize that massive mountain of a man, even without the beard. If his stature had left any doubt, the turban would have clinched it.

'Karim!' Mr Ambrose bellowed. 'Get him! Get that man!'

The bodyguard's eyes flicked from Mr Ambrose to the big Egyptian atop the ledge, who had to be the bandit leader. Karim's face twisted into a fierce scowl. Roaring like a lion, he leaped forward, catching hold of the ledge and pulling himself up. The bandit leader's eyes went wide, and he hurriedly stepped forward to tread on his approaching assailant's fingers, but Karim was already up and storming forward. The Egyptian had just enough time to pull his scimitar free, before Karim brought down his own weapon.

Blood spewed up, and I hurriedly averted my eyes. But in the rest of the cave, the fight was just as vindictive. Mr Ambrose was duelling with two opponents at once, swinging his sabre with a deadly precision that spoke of years and years of experience. I looked down at my measly little dagger.

'One of these days,' I growled, 'I'm going to beat him into showing me how to use a proper weapon!'

I heard footsteps approach from the right, and whirled around just in time to see someone rush towards me, a metallic glint in his hands. I moved instinctively, throwing myself to the ground and rolling over. The sabre pierced the air above me, and the man stumbled over me with a foul curse. Jumping up, I whirled around again and swung the dagger.

There was a wet *thud*, and the bandit went rigid. Slowly, he slid to the floor.

'Well, well, well...' I murmured, staring at the dagger in my hand. 'Maybe this isn't so bad after all.'

'*Hanem*! What are you doing?'

Turning, I saw Youssef gaping down at me from an opening in the wall above me.

'Stabbing people,' I called up to him. 'What does it look like?'

Muttering a curse, the Egyptian swung himself down. The rest of his men were right behind him, bloodstained but alive.

'The *Effendi* told you to stay safe!'

'That's what I'm doing,' I told him, wiping the dagger on my burnous. 'By killing all potentially unsafe people.'

He rolled his eyes, and waved at three of his men. 'You three! Stay with her and guard her! If anything happens to her, the *Effendi* will have our heads on a platter! The rest of you, come with me!'

With that, he dashed off into the fray.

'"If anything happens to her, the *Effendi* will have our heads",' I mimicked, scowling after him. As if Mr Ambrose cared one bit what happened to me! He was a cold, hard, feelingless, arrogant, infuriating...

Well, it didn't really make much sense to finish the sentence. The list of bad adjectives would take up three good-sized pages.

'Get them, men!' I heard Youssef shout from not very far away. 'Kill them all! This time, it's an order!'

And I watched as they set upon the bandits. It only took minutes for the shift in the balance of power to show. Where before the fight had been slowly swaying back and forth, now the bandits were steadily being pushed back, until they were pressed in a line against the back of the cave. One after the other fell, staining the cave floor with his blood. No quarter was being given, and none was fool enough to ask. The bandits knew they had killed every single member of the caravans that had come through the desert. They knew what to expect in return.

It was a bloody business, and strangely, brutally beautiful. In another age, another place, this is what justice would have looked like. Today, it was revenge, pure, simple and unapologetic. Finally, the last bandit dropped to the ground, dead.

Well, nearly the last one.

'Move, you piece of scum!'

Holding the man's neck with one huge, muscled paw, Karim shoved the disarmed, battered and bleeding bandit leader down off the ledge. A fist in the back sent him stumbling forward towards Mr Ambrose, who stood, not even breathing hard, gazing down at the body of the last man he had killed as if he were looking at a rotting cockroach.

'On your knees, worm!'

Giving the bandit leader another shove, Karim forced him down on his knees in front of Mr Ambrose and placed his sabre at the last surviving bandit's neck.

'One wrong move, scum, and you are dead!'

'Your threats are meaningless!' growled the prisoner. 'You will kill me anyway!'

'True.' Bending forward, Karim hissed into his ear: 'But if you're not careful, I might just take my time and make your final moments very special.' His scimitar grazed the man's throat, drawing blood.

Mr Ambrose was still looking at the dead man at his feet. Slowly, he bent and gripped the corpse's burnous. A quick flash of steel, and part of the burnous was in his hand, cut clean off. He used it to methodically wipe the blood off his sabre. Only when the weapon was pristinely clean did he turn towards the man Karim had in custody.

'Your name is Radi?'

The man spat on the ground at Mr Ambrose's feet. Mr Ambrose didn't even blink. He motioned to Karim, who grabbed the man's arms and twisted. A scream echoed through the cave. When it had subsided, Mr Ambrose repeated, his voice still as cold as ice: 'Your name is Radi?'

'Yes! Yes, it is, curse you!'

'You are the leader of the men who have been attacking caravans?'

'Yes.'

'And on whose orders did you do this?'

The bandit laughed. It wasn't a humour-filled laugh. '*Him*? What makes you think an old desert dog like me would know the name of a man like that?'

'Then what does he look like?'

'Tall. Blonde. A nose like hawk's beak and eyes that can burn your soul away!' He laughed again. 'By all means, go after him! You haven't seen what he's capable of. He'll cut you down like a thin little reed. You have no idea who you're dealing with!'

'On the contrary.' Mr Ambrose cocked his head. 'I know him better than anyone alive.'

'Is that so?'

'Oh yes.' Mr Ambrose nodded. 'And you are going to take a message for me. A message to my old friend, to your employer.'

Impossible hope flickered in the man's eyes. 'You're going to send me to him? You're going to let me live?'

'No.' With a movement so quick I almost missed it, Mr Ambrose raised his sabre, and let it swing down again. There was a *thud*, as metal met flesh, and another, softer, one, as the bandit leader's severed head fell to the ground. Not even glancing at the corpse sprawled on the cave floor, Mr Ambrose wiped his blade again. 'Leaving you alive would send quite the wrong message. Dead you'll do fine.'

For a moment, everything in the cave was still and silent as a grave. Even the blood seemed to stop dripping for a moment. I looked around. Men were staring at Mr Ambrose, the expressions on their faces inscrutable. I guess even if you were a mercenary, or whatever most of these men called their profession, you didn't see someone decapitated in cold blood every day. Some part of me wondered whether I shouldn't feel horrified. After all, the man had been defenceless. But then, so had the hundreds of caravan merchants he had killed.

Putting away my dagger, I stepped forward and marched over to Mr Ambrose. Without asking, I slid my hand into his – the one that was still holding the sabre – and squeezed.

He glanced down at me, coolly. 'Why are you applying pressure to my fingers?'

'It's a thing some people like to do. It's called "comforting".'

His fingers opened slightly, letting me in, and squeezing back. Then, seeming to realize what he was doing, he hurriedly let go.

'Well, cease it immediately,' he ordered. 'It is a waste of valuable time.'

I couldn't help smiling, just a little.

In that very moment, a shrill whistle sounded through the cave. Everybody whirled around, bringing up their rifles to where the sound had come from.

'Stop!' Youssef shouted. 'Stop! It's one of my men!'

And indeed, up in the high tunnel entrance from which Youssef's troops had come, I could see an anxious face, clearly not an enemy.

'I posted him up there to warn us if any more bandits came down the tunnel,' Youssef explained. 'We didn't know if any of them might still have been outside somewhere.'

'A reasonable idea.' Mr Ambrose nodded, then gestured at the lookout. 'And? What did you see? Report!'

'Men, *Effendi*. A lot of armed men!'

'Bandits?'

'I don't think so, *Effendi*. They are wearing uniforms in red, blue and white!'

Red? That had to be the English! I knew that French uniforms contained a lot of blue, and the white had to be the Egyptians. They'd know how to dress sensibly for the desert.

'Can we get out back through the gorge without them seeing us?' Mr Ambrose demanded.

'No, *Effendi*. They are already in the gorge and marching towards the valley outside the cave.' The man hesitated. 'But there is another tunnel forking off from this one. It's very narrow, but big enough for a man to crawl through, and I see light at the end. I think it comes out at the back of the mountain.'

'Another way out?' I frowned, disbelieving. 'Why didn't the bandits use it, then?'

'If it's as narrow as he says, they would have had to leave their plunder and supplies behind,' Mr Ambrose dismissed my objection. 'No sane man would put his life above his money.'

I exchanged a look with Youssef. Mr Ambrose and we probably had different views of what a sane man was. But who knew, perhaps the bandit leader had shared his opinion?

'Karim, get up there!' Without hesitation, the Mohammedan followed Mr Ambrose's command. Leaning down out of the hole, the man up in the tunnel grabbed him by the hands and pulled. With some effort, he managed to pull the bodyguard's huge form up far enough for him to grab the edge and pull himself up the rest of the way. The two of them up there were not able to fit side by side into the tunnel at the same time, so the lookout scrambled back into the passage.

'Go down the tunnel!' Mr Ambrose ordered Karim. 'When you've gone through with no problem, we'll know it's large enough for the rest of us. Give us a signal, and we'll know it's safe to follow.'

Karim did his best to bow without ramming his head against the floor in the narrow space. 'As you command, *Sahib*.'

Minutes of tense silence followed. When Karim's shout of 'Follow!' finally came, we breathed out a collective sigh of relief. All of us except Mr Ambrose, of course. He would never waste breath in such a pointless manner.

'Move!' He gestured to the men to start climbing up. They rushed past him, one after the other being pulled up to the hole. Not one was tall enough to reach it by himself. When Youssef was about to go past, he stopped in his tracks.

'What about you, *Effendi*? You should go before me.'

'On the contrary. I am in charge. I should go last.'

'But *Effendi*...'

'That is an order, Youssef! Move, I said!'

Reluctantly, Youssef let himself be pulled up into the tunnel. We had about half the men safely on their way, when I thought I heard something.

'Stop!' I raised my hand.

Everyone froze.

'In case you have forgotten,' Mr Ambrose told me with a cold glare, '*I* am the one in charge here. Move, men!'

'Just stop and listen for a moment! Do you hear that?'

We all listened, and then we heard it: The *thud, thud, thud* of marching feet, coming down the big tunnel.

'As I said,' Mr Ambrose repeated, his voice even colder and harder. 'Move! Now!'

Everyone started running. Men almost ripped their arms out of their sockets trying to lift the ones behind them up as fast as possible. More and more men scrambled up the wall towards freedom, and all the while, the sound of marching feet came closer and closer. Finally, there were only two people down there.

'You first,' Mr Ambrose told me in a voice that brooked no argument.

Well, frankly, I didn't give a damn[30] what his voice brooked or did not brook!

'No! You go first!'

'I gave you an order!'

---

[30] In case any of you are wondering if this curse is a bit too modern for a historical novel, it is not. It actually has a very interesting history. When the British invaded India, the Indian currency was called "dam". It was worth so little compared to a British Pound, that if a British soldier in India wanted to say he didn't care about something, he'd say, "I don't give a dam". The saying travelled, and the spelling was wrongly altered to "I don't give a damn". Subsequently, it was made famous by its use in the famous American novel *Gone with the Wind* by Margaret Mitchell, where the hero charmingly says to the heroine: "Frankly, my dear, I don't give a damn!" That's a gentleman for you.

'And I don't bloody care! Look at these!' I lifted my arms, then gestured at his tall form. 'I'm flattered that you think so highly of my strength, but do you honestly think I'll be able to lift you up there?'

'You won't need to. He will.' Mr Ambrose gestured to the man waiting at the hole in the wall, his hands outstretched.

'Once I'm up there, he won't be able to get around me! The space is too narrow!'

'He could... I could...' Mr Ambrose trailed off. His eyes flicked from me to the hole in the wall and back again. 'I can't leave you down here to be the last one! You have to go first!'

'Why? Because I'm a girl?' I put my fists on my hips. 'This isn't the right time to be a chauvinist! Get your stony butt up there right now!'

'Watch your language!'

'And you stop wasting time!'

That did it. Faced with the truth of the terrible accusation of wasting even one precious moment that was equal to power and money, Mr Ambrose whirled and ran towards the tunnel opening. Just a foot or two away from the wall, he jumped. The man up in the tunnel grunted as he grabbed hold of his hands and pulled. Mr Ambrose wasn't nearly as bulky as Karim, but as I knew first hand, he had quite a lot of muscle hidden under that tight black tailcoat of his. It took several moments for him to be pulled high enough so he could grab hold of the stone edge and swing himself into the tunnel.

All the while, I stood, transfixed, listening to the approaching sound of marching feet. They were much closer now. It sounded as if they were just around the bend.

The man who had helped Mr Ambrose scrambled off up the tunnel. Mr Ambrose himself turned and held out his arm.

'Move! Take my hand!'

I was already running, when suddenly, there was burst of sound behind me: the stomping of feet, the scrape of metal on metal, the squeak of hard leather – the soldiers had entered the cave!

'Hey, you there!' I heard a shout from behind me. 'You there, in the burnous! Stop!'

I didn't stop. I sped up, focusing all my energy on reaching Mr Ambrose's outstretched hand.

Just a few more seconds, I prayed. *A few more seconds, that's all...*

'Stop or we'll shoot!'

I froze.

'Put your hands over your head and turn around!'

Slowly, I lifted my hands until they rested on top of my head. Looking up at Mr Ambrose, I hissed: 'Go! They might not have seen you yet!'

He said nothing. But his hard, hungry gaze yelled *no* for him so loud it almost hurt my ears.

'Go! If they catch you, they'll kill you! I'll be all right. I'm...' I swallowed back bile before saying it out loud: 'I'm a lady. They won't harm a lady.'

'Turn around, I said!' bellowed the voice behind me, much closer now.

I threw one last, desperate, pleading look at Mr Ambrose. 'Please! Leave! For me!' Then, without waiting to see what he would do, I turned to face the British Army officer who was pointing his gun at me. He was a young man, tall and muscular, with shoulder-long mahogany hair and a roguish speck of a beard on his chin. Besides being quite handsome, he also happened to be quite familiar.

I smiled, and curtsied as best I could while dressed in a burnous and holding my hands over my head.

'Hello, Captain Carter. So nice to see you again.'

His mouth fell open. Taking that as a sign that he wasn't going to shoot me on the spot, I lowered my hands, surveying the ranks of troops flooding into the cave behind Captain Carter. Then my gaze dropped, sweeping around the empty cave, strewn with wreckage, broken blades, and hundreds of dead, blood-soaked bodies.

I cleared my throat. 'I think I might have lost my way a bit again. Tell me, do you by any chance know how to get to my hotel from here?'

COMMUNICATION PROBLEMS

Captain Carter was a real gentleman. Yes, a real, true-born English gentleman. And I don't just mean that he helped me into the saddle of his own camel when we left the cave, or that he gave me a drink from his water bottle. No, those were just trivialities. A girl can only tell that a man is a real gentleman if he does something very special for her – such as not ask her how she happened to get 'lost' several hundred miles away from her hotel in the middle of a desert cave full of bloody, mutilated corpses.

Now, *that's* what I call a real gentleman.

I could tell from the way they screamed at Captain Carter, that the captains of the French and Egyptian detachments would have been only too happy to question me on the subject, and maybe encourage me a little if I didn't answer right away. But Captain Carter barked a few clipped words at them in French and Arabic, and they went away, grumbling.

I was burning to know what had happened to Mr Ambrose and the others. But I kept my mouth shut. Captain Carter might, for some unfathomable reason, want to protect me, but I very much doubted he would extend the same courtesy to Mr Ambrose and a few hundred mercenaries. So I mounted Captain Carter's camel and let myself be led back towards Alexandria like a good little girl, all the while nearly bursting with the need to run and find *him*.

Finally, weeks after we had set out from the mountain cave on the Sinai Peninsula, we saw the houses of Alexandria rising out of the mist.

'What are you going to do now, Miss Linton?' Captain Carter asked from beside me. He had been marching beside my mount nearly all the way, repeatedly gazing up at me with a mixture of puzzlement and fascination. 'Continue your, um... holiday?' One of his eyebrows went up, silently adding: *And maybe finding a few more blood-spattered caves to get lost in?*

'No.' I shook my head and gave him a demure smile. 'I think I've been lazing about long enough. Time to end the holiday and get back home. I will be leaving on the next ship.'

If he is still here. If he waited for me.

In all probability, he and his ship had left long ago. Knowledge is power is time is money, after all. The marriage sham was over, and he no longer needed to pretend. He wouldn't waste any time for me.

'And your grandmother?'

It took me a moment to understand what the captain was talking about. Then, I remembered the little deaf old lady and the web of lies I had come up with.

'Um... well, she will be coming home with me, of course.'

He frowned. 'Nobody else?'

'No.'

His gaze grew more intense, and he took an abrupt step forward. 'What? The two of you don't seriously intend to travel all the way back home to London alone, do you?'

No, I was actually thinking of travelling in the company of a ruthless financier and three hundred bought cutthroats.

I raised my chin. 'Yes, of course we do!'

'Miss Linton, please! I know your independent views, but I can't let you do this! Two women travelling alone on a ship, one of them an old lady who can't hear and is hardly able to stand? You don't even know whether you can trust the captain, and even if he is an honourable man, anyone else could take advantage of you easily.'

I opened my mouth to protest but, in a totally unexpected gesture, he reached up and cupped my face in his hands. I was so taken aback, my mouth remained open, unprotesting. His hands on my face felt so soft, so strong, and as he looked at me, his warm eyes shone like polished mahogany. 'No sense in arguing, Miss Linton! You are coming back with me.'

'With *you*?'

'Certainly.' His grip tightened, tenderly. 'Since the bandits are dead–' he sent me a searching gaze, which I chose to completely ignore, 'my mission here is complete. I'll be returning to England in any case. There's a Royal Navy vessel, the *HMS Morning Star*, anchored at Alexandria, and there is more than enough room on board for you and your grandmother.'

What could I say?

I'm sorry, but I can't, because that old lady isn't really my grandmother, and besides, I'm not really here with her but with a man who is pretending to be my husband but really is my lecherous, miserly employer, and he is going to go all frosty on me if I don't get back to him presto!

Yes, that would probably go over really well.

So I said nothing. Captain Carter dragged me to the hotel where the old lady was staying, and with the authority born of years of military command, simply packed her up and loaded her on his ship. The old girl's only comment to having her vacation abruptly cut short was 'What? What did you say, dearie?' Apparently, her hearing hadn't improved since we last met.

It was the evening of the same day we had arrived at Alexandria. The HMS Morning Star was preparing to cast off. I had taken a last walk around the harbour, in the hope of seeing a certain familiar ship somewhere, but to no avail. I was just about to step aboard the Royal Navy vessel, when I saw something that froze me in place.

There he was!

His ship was nowhere in sight. But he stood not ten yards away at the edge of the wharf: Mr Rikkard Ambrose, his black tailcoat fluttering around him like torn bat's wings.

He looked just the same as ever: hard, distant, towering in his cold splendour over all passers-by like the Colossus of Rhodes over ordinary humans. Our eyes met. Neither of us moved, neither of us said a word. We just stood there and stared into each other's eyes. Could it be that just a short while ago, I went around pretending that this perfect, god-like granite statue was my husband? That I, Lilly Linton, convicted feminist, had actually come dangerously close to showing emotion for one of the most detestably chauvinistic members of the male species?

I suppose there were unlikelier things in the world but, offhand, I couldn't think of one. Still... for some reason, it had happened. And, for some reason, I couldn't stop looking now. And neither could he.

Why don't you go to him, you dolt? Why just stand here like an idiot?

Yes... why not? I could go to him! I could–

'Miss Linton?'

The voice from beside me made me jump. I hadn't noticed the sailor's approach. He saluted, and gestured to HMS Morning Star.

'We're ready to set sail, miss. Would you please come aboard?'

'I... well...' Licking my lips uncertainly, I glanced again in the direction where I had seen him. But Mr Ambrose was gone – vanished into thin air. Maybe he had never been there at all, and I had simply been dreaming.

'Miss? Please?' The sailor gestured again.

'All right. I'm coming.'

It was when I stood at the railing of the HMS Morning Star, the old lady who still was my pseudo-grandmother beside me, sitting in a deck-chair and knitting, that I saw the proof: I had not been dreaming. In front of me, from behind the hull of a massive trading vessel, emerged the sleek black form of the Mammon. At the prow stood a tall, dark figure, that, even from as far away as I was, could not be mistaken. The ship passed us and turned, sailing around the harbour and out of sight. The last thing I saw was that tall dark figure, still seeming to stare at me out of the immeasurable distance.

I raised my fingers to my lips, where, if I let myself fall into memory, I could still feel the burning pressure of his last kiss.

'Bloody Hell,' I whispered. 'What am I going to do now?'

Beside me, the old lady ceased her knitting and blinked up at me, owlishly. 'What? What did you say, dearie?'

~~**~*~*

Theoretically, the return journey should have been much more enjoyable than the one to Egypt. I was actually quartered in a comfortable cabin – one of cabins usually reserved for important travelling dignitaries and diplomats – with a spacious, soft bunk to sleep in. Plus, Captain Carter, considering his cheerful disposition, should have been much better company than Mr Rikkard Ambrose.

Theoretically.

In reality, the return journey had one big drawback: I was alone with my thoughts of *him*.

'It can't have been real! No, it simply can't have been! Why would he...? It's impossible!'

I was in my cabin, with the old lady for company. While keeping one eye on her knitting, she watched me marching up and down, agitated, clearly curious about why I was trying to stomp grooves into the floor.

'It can't have been real,' I chanted. 'It was pretence. Everything was pretence. You have to remember that. You have to...'

I caught sight of my hopeful expression in the mirror on the wall, and groaned.

'Don't you dare look so damn girlishly excited?' I growled, pointing an accusing finger at my mirror image. 'Don't you have any shame? You're a feminist, remember! Any small hint of positive feeling you might have felt while he was... doing things with you that he shouldn't have been doing – all that was simply a result of bodily fluids malfunctioning! Understood?'

My mirror image shook her head.

'Gah! How can you be so stubborn!' Picking up a pillow from my bunk, I hurled it at the mirror.

The old lady paused her knitting for a moment and looked at me, interested. 'Something wrong, dearie?'

'Yes!' I groaned. 'I have been molested by the richest, best-looking, most powerful, chauvinistic, annoying and ruthless man in the entirety of the British Empire, and I don't know whether it was just pretence for an ulterior motive, which would be horrible, or whether he means to seduce me into a depraved, immoral affair, which would be even more horrible although part of me actually thinks it might be sort of interesting, or, worst of all, whether he might actually have meant the things he said and did, in which case I... well... I want to die! Or not! I don't know!'

'I see.' The old lady nodded, philosophically. 'That's nice.' She cocked her head. 'Could you maybe just repeat it a bit louder, dearie? I don't think I caught everything.'

I opened my mouth and took a deep breath, preparing to shout 'I have been molested and seduced!' at the top of my voice when, from outside, there came a knock at the door. Deciding that it might be better not to shout after all, I opened it. Outside stood Captain Carter.

'Good evening.' He bowed, smiling. 'I wondered whether you two ladies might want to join me for dinner this evening.'

Over my shoulder, I took a look at the mirror on the wall and the pillow on the floor. 'Yes,' I breathed. 'Thank you. I think I could use some company.'

Dinner that night was quiet. In fact, dinner every night was pretty quiet, except for the creaking around us as the ship was gently tipped this way and that by the ocean's waves. Captain Carter studied me a great deal, but didn't say much. Most of the dinner conversation was provided by the old lady, who seemed just as skilled at not needing other people's talk as she was at not hearing it.

The days drifted by. I had several more, long, exhausting arguments with my mirror image, stubborn wench that she was! My pillow saw a lot of wear. Captain Carter kept watching me, his expression alternating between pensive and a secret, dreamy little smile I didn't know how to decipher. Finally, the call came from the highest mast:

'Land ahoy!'

I could hardly believe it when we finally drifted up the Thames, and London's houses and towers slowly rose above the horizon. This was the real world. I was back. I was awake again. The fights, the tantalizing touches, the heat, the darkness of the sandstorm – everything that had happened in Egypt suddenly seemed only like the faint echo of a dream.

Almost involuntarily, my hand rose to touch my lips.

Well... maybe not *everything*.

Only a few minutes later, it seemed, the gangplank thudded onto the wharf. Captain Carter escorted my 'grandmother' and me off the ship. Once on solid ground, he stopped and smiled down at me this faint, dreamy, rather intense smile I didn't know how to read.

'Well, goodbye, Miss Linton. As always, it has been very... interesting, meeting you. I hope our paths will cross again, soon.'

I smiled back at him. It seemed the right thing to do. Besides, smiling at Captain Carter was easy. He didn't have an invisible sign taped to his forehead saying 'Smiling Forbidden!' like some people I could mention.

'So do I, Captain.'

'Will you find your way home from here safely?'

'Yes. Thank you for all your help.'

'It was my pleasure. Until we meet again, Miss Linton.' He leaned forward to bow – or at least that was what I thought! But instead, he took my hand and pressed a gentle but firm kiss on its back. I stared at him, flabbergasted.

Smiling, he nodded one last time, then turned and left. I stared after him in silent amazement until he had climbed into a waiting coach and vanished around a corner. Then I shook off my paralysis.

'Mental,' I muttered, wiping my hand on my skirt. 'Completely mental!'

Taking a deep breath, I banished all thoughts of Captain Carter from my mind, and the tingling echoes of his kiss from my hand.

'Come on, "grandmother",' I told the old lady on the wharf beside me. 'It's just you and me now. Let's get you home, wherever that is.'

The old lady bent towards me, cupping a hand behind her ear. 'Sorry, dearie? Could you say that again?'

~~**~*~*

It took me some time to extract her home address from the old lady and drop her off at her – quite surprised – relatives' house. Having thus successfully rid myself of one pseudo-grandmother, I turned my steps towards home.

Before I even knocked at the front door, it flew open and Ella came rushing towards me. A moment later, her arms were around me, crushing me with a force I wouldn't have thought my wisp of a little sister capable of.

'I missed you so much, Lill!'

'I've noticed,' I wheezed. 'Can you let go now?'

'Sorry.' Blushing, she eased her grip a little. 'So... How was grandmother?'

'Fine. A bit hard of hearing, these days, but there's plenty of life in the old bone yet.'

That moment, my aunt stepped out of the door to see what the commotion was about. The moment she caught sight of me, her eyes narrowed. 'Oh. It's you. And? Did you meet any eligible bachelors while you were at your grandmother's?'

I shook my head, grinning. 'No. There was this one man I spent rather a lot of time with, but he was already married to a very stubborn and possessive young lady.'

Harrumphing, my aunt turned on the spot and marched back into the house gain.

'I'm so glad you're back!' Ella repeated.

The welcome from the rest of the household was about as expected. Gertrude gave me a simple but sincere hug. Lisbeth smiled non-committally and said hello. Anne and Maria lost no time in pointing out how dreadfully tanned and ugly I had gotten while being away. Leadfield, our faithful aged butler, bowed so deeply he almost toppled over. My uncle kept his study door closed in a slightly more welcoming manner than usual.

It was all a sort of blur to me. Yes, I was glad to be home, but...

But what about *him*?

Don't think about him! Don't think about him! You're a feminist! Thinking about men is out of the question - except if you're thinking about grinding them into tiny little pieces!

Well, grinding sounded sort of nice...

Not that kind of grinding! Stop this at once!

But I couldn't stop. I couldn't keep the same questions from forcing themselves into my mind over and over again: *What is he thinking right now? What will he say when you arrive for work tomorrow? More importantly, what will he do?*

'Lilly!'

I was ripped from my thoughts by the door to my room bursting open and Patsy, Flora and Eve storming in. They bore the expressions of fierce amazons

212

on the hunt for gossip. 'You're back! So, what have you been up to while you were away?'

'Um...' Cautiously, I licked my lips, while trying to think of a way to describe to my friends what had happened in Egypt. 'I, um...'

They waited, their faces eager.

'I did... um... I...'

I went to bed that night, after some very inventive lie-telling, my head still filled with the same thoughts.

What will he say? What will he do?

I watched the handle on the bedside clock move from ten pm to eleven pm. It didn't seem inclined to answer my silent question.

Bloody, hell! What will he say? What will he do?

Eleven thirty. Still no answer.

It took me rather long to fall asleep that night. When I finally dozed off, I dreamt of the Sphinx chasing me through the desert, trying to kiss me. Apart from the fact that its nose was missing, the lecherous stone beast looked suspiciously like Mr Rikkard Ambrose.

AMBROSE

I woke up in the morning and thought *Oh God! It is Monday!*

It was sort of a déjà vu, exactly like the first time I'd had to go to work. But in a way, it was even worse now, because this time I had to deal with... certain things.

My lips tingled, and I clamped my hand over them, trying to rub the traitorous sensation away. Bloody hell! Stuff like this shouldn't happen without my express permission!

As fast as I could, I jumped out of bed and started dressing.

Keep busy, I told myself. *Keep very, very busy, then you won't have to think about what you are about to do. About what is going to happen.*

In quick succession, I threw on my petticoats, a corset and a dress. It was agonizing, knowing I would have to take all this stuff off again in a minute anyway, when I changed into my male work clothes in the garden shed.

No matter! Just keep busy, and don't think!

With flying fingers, I laced up the front of my dress, took a deep breath – and then made the mistake of looking in the mirror to check my appearance. I caught sight of my half-terrified, half-hopeful, half-angry expression. Can something have three halves, or is that impossible?

Oh, to hell with mathematics!

I could read the questions in my reflection's eyes as clearly as if they were printed on the mirror's surface: What will he say? What will he do?

Don't think, damn you! Keep busy!

Whirling around, I marched to the window, threw it open and climbed down the ladder I had placed there last night before going to bed. I guess I could have

213

gone out through the front door, but today I wasn't in the mood to waste any time. I was heading straight towards what I was both anticipating and dreading more than anything else in the world. Putting it off would make it worse.

Two minutes in the garden shed, and I emerged in my work clothes, out onto the street. Hailing a cab, I swung myself up inside and sank into the upholstery.

'Where to, guv?' the cabby called.

'Empire House!'

'In Leadenhall Street? The place where that posh bugger Ambrose lives?'

'Yes. That's it, exactly.'

The whip cracked, and we shot forward. Only minutes later I climbed out of the cab in Leadenhall Street, the bastion of British commerce, Empire House rising right in front of me. Never had its huge portico, supported by two massive columns of grey stone, seemed less inviting than today.

I raised my chin.

'You don't scare me,' I told the building.

Maybe it was just my imagination, but I thought I heard a faint answering growl.

Ignoring my thumping heart, I marched up the stairs, right towards the maul of the beast. I arrived on the top step and pushed, forcing open the monster's jaws, also known as doors. Cool, emotionless air with a familiar lack of smell drifted out to greet me. I swallowed and stepped in.

The hall inside was just as I remembered it, and yet... different. More intense. Had there been quite so much activity when I had last been here? Hundreds of busy feet were pattering through the cavernous space. People were carrying files, delivering messages, and most of all, sweating their guts out for fear of the great master upstairs.

I noticed everything with an almost supernatural focus. Sweat beaded on hundreds of foreheads. Dust motes danced through the air. Flies copulated on the ceiling, while trying their best to keep away from cobwebs. Atoms bumped against each other everywhere.

I noticed all this, and yet, the details passed me by, like water flowing around a rock in a river. The only thing I could think, was: *Oh my God! Oh my God, he's right upstairs!*

And all that lay between him and me was the hallway. Oh, and the information desk. And the stairs. And another hallway. And a door. And then... then...

Him!

In person!

Together with me!

All right, I told myself. *You are calm, Lilly. Calm and relaxed! You are a strong, sensible woman, and you will not lose your nerve simply because of some man.*

Him! Together with me!!!

All right... maybe I was not quite so calm, after all.

Gathering all my courage, I fixed my eyes on the opposite end of the hall and took one step towards the stairs. And then I took another. And another. Damn, why were there so many steps between me and that staircase? And how many had I already taken? I didn't know. I had forgotten to count. I was too busy thinking *He kissed me! On the lips! And now I'm going to see him again!*

What the bloody hell was going to happen? What was I going to do? And, again, the most important question: what was *he* going to do? He couldn't possibly...?

Oh my God, yes, he could!

If he wanted to.

But was he going to?

No. No, of course not! I mean, doing something like *that, here*... that would be totally... No! Of course he wasn't going to do *that*!

With the slow steps of a doomed woman, I continued through the hall. The dust motes fluttered out of the way for me, and the flies stopped copulating to watch me pass. Even the spiders stopped spinning their nets for a moment. Finally, I reached Sallow-face's desk.

'Good morning,' I said.

He inclined his head about a quarter of an inch.

'Good morning,' he said. His left eyebrow twitched suspiciously.

Blast, blast, blast! Could he see on my face that I'd been snogging his employer? I bet he could read it on my forehead! Rushing past him, I stepped into the separate hallway that led to my destination. I looked up and saw the steps leading up and around the walls, all the way to the top of the building, steps even steeper than the ones outside.

Dong...

The ominous sense of déjà vu overcame me again, even stronger than when I awoke. I turned my head westwards. There, a small window stood half open, just like it had been on my first day at work, letting a bit of light fall into the stark stone hallway. And, through that window, there now also came the sound of a bell. A deep, reverberating sound that chilled my bones.

Time for work. Time to meet my fate.

Dong...

But was this truly déjà vu?

Dong...

Admittedly, as I panted, desperately running up the stairs, some things were the same. Like my thinking *Oh my God, Oh my God, I'm going to be too late!* for instance.

Dong...

But on the other hand, some things were different.

Dong...

For instance, on my first day I had not been thinking *Bloody hell! He kissed me! He actually kissed me!*

Dong...

But then... that fact wasn't so very significant, was it? Oh no, of course not! I was a feminist! Why would it matter to me that some chauvinistic son of a bachelor pressed his lips to mine?

Dong...

He did! He really did! Crap, crap, crap!

I almost wished myself back at that moment, back to when life had been so uncomplicated, without kisses and caresses and confusing feelings. But then I thought of the look in Mr Ambrose's dark, sea-coloured eyes just before our lips met...

No! Don't think! Go on! Run!

Dong...

By the time I reached the sixth landing, I was ready to collapse. *Go on!* I screamed at myself. *Just a few steps more, and you're there!*

Dong...

Wheezing, I staggered onto the top landing and grabbed the brass doorknob. Turning it, I shoved open the door and stumbled into the long, narrow hallway at the end of which stood the desk of Mr Stone, the upstairs receptionist. I waited just a moment, until I was sure my heart wasn't going to burst from overexertion. Then I straightened, tugged at my clothes to get rid of a few creases, and walked forward as nonchalantly as I could. Maybe, if I just walked past in an innocent, everyday manner, Mr Stone wouldn't notice me. Maybe I would get into my office without–

'Good morning, Mr Linton.'

Wincing, I halted at the sound of the familiar voice. I inclined my head at the young man behind the desk in front of Mr Ambrose's office door. He was quite a friendly young man, actually. It wasn't his fault that, from my viewpoint, to-day he had the job of Cerberus, guardian of hell.

'Good morning, Mr Stone.' I said.

That seemed to exhaust our conversational possibilities. Longingly, I glanced towards my office door, and inched a step closer. But Mr Stone's next words froze me in place.

'Mr Ambrose would like to see you.'

My fingers clenched into fists, automatically.

'Oh, he would, would he?' I took a step away from Mr Ambrose's office door, and towards my safe haven. 'Perhaps later. Right now I have...'

Mr Stone gave me a look that was not without compassion, but still firm. 'Perhaps I should rephrase. Mr Ambrose *demands* to see you. Right now.'

All colour drained from my face. Then it rushed back again with a vengeance.

Damn!

'Oh.' Swallowing, I nodded. 'I see.'

Taking a deep breath, I stepped past Mr Stone and towards my employer's office door. The door creaked open as slowly and menacingly as the gateway to Pandemonium – or maybe just like the door of a man who was too stingy to buy oil for the hinges. Inside, it was dark. The curtains were closed, letting in only a thin lance of light that sharply silhouetted the dark figure of the man sitting behind the massive desk.

I gulped.

Broad shoulders, short, elegant and precise black hair, a chiselled face, a posture as stiff as a rod of iron – even if anyone but him would have dared to sit behind that desk, that dark silhouette left me in no doubt whom I was facing.

Gathering all my courage, I stepped forward until I was right in front of the dark figure. His face was cast in shadow, so at first I couldn't see what kind of lack of expression was on it at the moment. Only when my eyes got used to the gloom did I see the darkly motionless, beautiful mask which he called 'face'.

He stared at me in silence.

I stared back at him in silence.

We stared at each other in silence.

Then we stared at each other in silence some more.

I cleared my throat.

He remained silent. And stared at me. Silently.

I stared back. And I did it in silence. We stared. At. Each other. In a long, silent silence. Full of silentness.

All right... maybe it's time for someone to say something.

You remember that I mentioned my courage? The one I had been trying to gather? That was all gone now. Faced with the stare of his deep, dark, sea-coloured eyes, I had no courage of my own left. Oh, what the hell! I could always pinch some from someone else!

'Mr Ambrose?' I took a step forward. 'You asked for me, Sir?'

He continued his stare for a moment longer. Would it surprise you to hear that he did it in silence?

Then...

'Yes, I did, Mr Linton.'

More silence.

I wet my lips.

'So... What do you want from me, Sir?'

God, if he says come here and kiss me, I'll—

I cut off the thought before it could really form. But... what if he *did* say that? What if he demanded it, in that voice of his that brooked no argument? What would I do?

Would I run?

And, more importantly, would I run towards him, or away? My throat suddenly felt very dry.

'What do you want, Mr Ambrose, Sir?'

He leaned forward, until both of his powerful fists rested on the desktop, knuckles down. 'I want...'

'Yes?'

'I want file 38XV180!'

I blinked. 'What?'

He cocked his head, questioningly. 'Are your ears malfunctioning, Mr Linton?' Leaning forward a little more, Mr Ambrose fixed me with one of the superbly cold glares that were his speciality. For some reason, it filled me with a warm and fuzzy feeling. 'Bring me file 38XV180! Now!'

Thank you, God! I shot the words silently towards heaven as relief flooded through me. *Thank you so very much! The world is back to normal!*

I snapped to attention. 'Yes, Sir!'

For some reason, a wide grin spread over my face.

'Stop wasting your muscle energy on useless facial contortions, Mr Linton!'
My grin got even bigger. 'Of course, Sir! Just as you say, Sir!'
'Now bring me the file!'
'Yes, Sir, Mr Ambrose, Sir!'
'And be quick about it! I don't tolerate tardiness!'
'Yes, Sir! Right away, Sir!'
And I danced from the room, happier than I had ever been in my life.

THE END

Two chapters from

Mr Ambrose's Perspective

'Cold and Hot' & 'Hot and Sweaty'

CHAPTER TITLES ARE A WASTE OF INK

I woke up to the sensation of being tortured. You want to know what it felt like? All right. Prepare yourself.

I was lying on a bed. A *soft* bed, that smelled of *flowery perfume*. With a mattress that had *feathers* inside. The thick blanket on top of me was intolerably *warm* and *comfortable*, and someone had actually deposited a *pillow* beneath my head!

Whoever did this should pray they paid for these useless luxuries out of their own pocket. If they didn't... if they had even dared to touch one single penny in my purse—

My thoughts abruptly cut off as something soft touched my cheek. God! Not another pillow!

But... no. This wasn't nearly big enough. And it almost felt alive. Like a hand. Why in the name of King Midas would anybody dare to touch my face with their hand? This was intolerable!

'There, there,' a sickly-sweet voice whispered somewhere above me.

A woman? A *woman* was touching my face? Scratch intolerable. This was outrageous!

'There, there...'

There? Where, exactly? And what was supposed to be there? What was this female prattling on about? I tried to open my eyes, but they felt as if they had been glued shut with molten tar. I croaked, trying to speak.

'There, there, my little honey-bunny. Don't strain yourself.'

Honey-bu... This woman was out of her mind! I had fallen into the hands of a crazy person! I had to get out of here before she tried to smother me with another of her cushions.

'Violet?'

Another voice. Thank God! Someone who could rescue me from the madwoman.

'Yes, mother?'

Or maybe not. Mothers were notorious for their disinclination to put their daughter in a straightjacket.

'How are you getting on?'

Terrible! Horrifying! Gruesome!

'Simply wonderful, Mother. He's such a dear.'

Interesting. I wonder how she was able to come to that conclusion while I was unconscious. From the nice way in which I breathed, or the sympathetic way my head lolled to the side?

'And so handsome, too,' sighed the mother.

Apprehension gripped me. I recognized that tone. It was the voice of a mother in matchmaking mode. Normally, this wouldn't concern me. I wasn't like the other rich bachelors of London society who were hounded by a pack of salivating mothers, their supposedly eligible daughters in tow. Normally, one cool glance from me was enough to send them scurrying away. And if it wasn't,

I'd make a gesture to Karim, who would promptly scowl threateningly and put his hand on his sabre. That impressed upon most mothers how very unsuitable I was as a potential son-in-law. But right now, neither of these defence strategies were open to me. My eyes remained stubbornly closed, and Karim was God—or Allah, in his case—only knew where!

'So handsome...' Another sigh from the mother. She put a hand on mine, and I tensed. What was she doing? Was she planning to slip an engagement ring on my finger while I was sleeping? I wouldn't put it past her. If my experience in the colonies had taught me anything, it was that mothers were more ruthless than the most murderous cutthroats or savages.

'Do you suppose he's a gentleman?' the daughter enquired. I could practically hear the hunger in her voice and tried to raise my hands in preparation to defend myself. But they wouldn't move! 'Someone with a fortune? A position?'

'I don't know...' The mother sounded doubtful. 'I mean, look at his clothes. They were damaged by the shipwreck, yes, but they were practically second-hand rags before that.'

What?

'No gentleman would walk around in tatters like that, Violet.'

No gentlem... The impudence! I would make clear to this lady exactly what kind of 'gentleman' I was—the moment I got that infernal voice of mine back!

'But don't you remember this, Mother?' There was a soft metallic scrape. 'See? His watch has a coat of arms on the lid. Looks really fancy, too.'

'Maybe he stole it.'

Of all the insolent...!

'A man like that wouldn't have to steal, Mother.'

Ah. For once, a true statement.

'With a face like that, he could become an actor any time. People would pay gold to see him as Romeo.'

What?

This was becoming too much. I had to get out of here. Out of this madhouse, out of the clutches of these harpies!

With all my might, I tried to lift myself off the bed. I had managed about three inches, when female hands that were a lot stronger than they should be clamped down on my shoulders.

'Now, there! Don't move! Don't hurt yourself. You should be resting.'

I opened my mouth, trying to fling something vile at my torturers. A soft but determined finger pressed down on my lips.

'Psht! No need to thank us. Mother will get you another blanket, and I will make you a nice, warm bowl of broth. How does that sound?'

It was official. I was in hell.

~~**~*~*

Before I had decided that it was mostly waste of time, I had attended school like every other proper English gentleman's son. From my Eton days, I vaguely remembered that whenever people described hell, be they Dante, Blake, or Milton, they generally emphasized things such as fire, devils tweaking unfortunate souls with glowing tongs, and people forced to roll rocks up mountains over and over again.

There was none of that for me. The only heat I felt was that from smouldering under a heap of too-soft blankets. There were tongs, but they were of the sugar variety, and only employed at teatime, when the creature called 'Violet' asked me in that sickly-sweet voice: 'One lump or two, honey-bunny?' And as for rocks... The only one I ever felt was the one in my stomach when I was forced to look at that female. What had God been thinking when he took that rib from Adam?

No matter the lack of fires and devils: I knew what the worst circle of hell was, and I was right inside it.

If only I had been able to flee! But first my legs refused to move, and then the doctor came, telling me that if I did not rest, I might have a relapse. The thought of breaking down again and having to stay here even longer than was absolutely necessary kept me abed, my limbs turned to stone. Days, seeming like months, passed in an agony of torture. It was one afternoon, after the mother monster had just forced me to gulp down an entire bowlful of foul-tasting broth, that the doorbell rang.

Faint hope stirred in my despairing mind. Could it be the doctor? He wasn't scheduled to come, but maybe he had decided that I was well enough to leave, after all.

Footsteps approached down the corridor outside. Soft footsteps. Feminine. My hope evaporated. So, it wasn't the doctor after all. It was one of my torturers.

Grimly, I stared at the gruesomely flowered wallpaper.

The door creaked open. There was a moment of silence. What were they waiting for? Usually they were on me the moment the door was open.

'Whoever you are,' I told them, 'get on with what you've come here for and get out. I have no patience for time-wasters.'

'I know, Sir.'

The voice was soft and feminine, and yet utterly unlike Violet's. Violet's was the screech of a hellish harpy. This voice—this voice was a balm, a light at the end of the tunnel, promising rescue from my prison of comfort and care.

I whipped around, and there she stood: Lillian Linton. She was still wearing the same dress I had forced on her aboard the ship. It was stained now, and ripped in several places, but I didn't care. She might have worn rags and would have been more beautiful than any queen in golden robes to me! I had never particularly noticed her resemblance to an angel of light before, but right now, it was suddenly self-evident.

Particularly if she was here to get me out of this hellhole!

'It's *you*!' The words were out of my mouth before I could stop them.

'Yes, Sir.'

Silence descended over the room. My eyes bored into hers.

Why doesn't she say anything? Why doesn't she do anything? We have to get out of here, and she's just standing there, staring at me! Why is she staring at me?

'It's really you,' I said again, just in case I had been mistaken. My eyes might be playing tricks on me, and this might, in fact, be another hellish creature, come to torture me in a clever disguise.

'Yes, Sir.'

No. This was no hallucination. It was she. Only she could say the word 'sir' like that – like a call for rebellion. But why was she just standing there?

For the first time in my life I found myself in a position where I had to perform one of the most onerous duties imaginable: get a conversation going.

'I thought you were dead.'

There. That was a good start.

Strange, though. Why did my words sound that... rough? My throat had long since recuperated from all the saltwater. There was no reason to speak strangely. And there most certainly wasn't any reason to keep staring at her!

'Well... I'm not, Sir.'

Whatever my throat problem was, she seemed to suffer the same complaint. Her eyes didn't leave my face, either. What was going on here? Why weren't we escaping from this accursed place? Why were we just staring at each other?

Irritation made my next words cool and brusque. 'I can see that. What took you so long?'

The corner of her mouth twitched up. She was *smiling*? Why in King Midas's name was she smiling?

'I'm glad to see you, too.'

What was that supposed to mean?

Suddenly, she started moving towards me. Before I could move a muscle, she stood at my bedside, looking down at me with a very different expression from the one the harpy had borne. For some reason, it made the lump in my throat grow thicker. Damnation! Was I getting sick again?

Her hand—so small, so soft in comparison to mine—reached out and gripped my fingers with a fierce demand. Instinctively, I squeezed back gently.

What the...!

Since when was applying pressure to a female's paws something instinctive for me?

'What, pray,' I enquired, making sure to keep my voice cool and smooth as ice, 'are you doing?'

'I'm holding your hand,' she informed me simply. Her tone was unexceptional, but her eyes... Oh, her eyes! There was a light dancing in them. A light that made me want to reach out and—

Stop! Stop this at once! What are you thinking?

'I realize that,' I stated coolly. 'To what purpose have you initiated this superfluous form of physical contact?'

'Oh, shut up!'

The room was silent for a moment, while my brain ran over the sentence my ears had received, double-checked that I had heard correctly, and slapped a big red label on it saying *INSUBORDINATION!*

'I beg your pardon?' My gaze bored into her like an iron drill – she didn't seem to care. 'I am your employer! You will address me with respect!'

'Fine. Shut up, *Sir*!'

Correction: she *definitely* didn't care.

'That is not what I was referring to, and you—'

'Blast you!' Her eyes flamed, melting the iron in mine along with the ire in a millisecond. 'I thought you were dead, too!'

In that gaze of her, worlds of words were contained that didn't need to be spoken. She *did* care. Oh yes, she cared very much. Just not for courtesy. The soft hand in mine suddenly felt like a burning brand.

'In that case,' I managed, 'you should have ceased searching. No point in chasing something that is already lost. It would be a waste of mon–'

A tug on my hand cut my words short. Before I could protest, before I could even blink, she had raised my hand to her lips and...

Something touched my palm.

Soft.

Ethereal.

Like the touch of a butterfly's wings, or maybe a rose petal. Only – a rose petal I could have easily brushed off. This touch, I knew deep down, I would remember for the rest of my days. It was burned into my skin, and....

...and since when have you become so mind-numbingly poetic?

I was going insane! That was it. The two harpies' madness was rubbing off on me. I had to get out of here *now*!

'I said,' she whispered in a low voice that I would have heard through a hurricane, 'shut up, Sir!'

Our eyes met, and there was silence again. But it was a different kind of silence. One unlike any I had ever experienced. Silence had always been a tool for me: calm silence to think in, cold silence to let people sweat, dark silence to make them beg for mercy. This one wasn't cold, or dark, or anything but she and I, together.

'It must really be you.' Shaking my head, I looked up at her, my eyes unwavering, intent. 'No figment of my imagination would dare to speak to me like that.'

I watched as she raised her free hand and, with uncustomary caution, let it join the other one, enclosing my long fingers with her smaller ones as best she could.

'I'm always real for you.' The words tugged at something in my chest. Probably a muscle I had pulled while being shipwrecked.

'More than just real. You're always you.'

'Glad to be of service, Sir.'

Raising my free hand, I crooked one finger, in a gesture she had better not deny. 'Come here.'

She raised an eyebrow. 'For what? Do you want to initiate a bit more superfluous physical contact?'

'Miss Linton?'

She raised her eyebrow even higher, as surprised as I was at my sudden use of the female address.

'What, not "Mr Linton"?' she enquired. 'I thought I would have to pretend to be a man while I worked for you. I thought it would cause too big a scandal, otherwise.'

So did I, for that matter. But I suddenly didn't care anymore. A strange, almost drunken feeling had gripped me in its hold, and from one moment to the next I didn't care about a lot of things that had seemed important a moment ago. In contrast, I suddenly cared about other things quite a lot more.

'Miss Linton? Close your mouth and come here. Now.'

What was I doing? Why was I acting so bizarrely? Had the harpies put a gallon full of brandy in my broth?

'Yes, Sir! Right away, Sir!'

She crossed the last little bit of distance between us. A moment later, the springs of the mattress creaked as she sank down on it. Suddenly she was there, right in front of me, her warm, chocolate-brown eyes lit by an inner light, her impudent little nose seeming to defy me just by existing. So why the hell couldn't I stop looking at her?

'When I stepped on land, I thought I was safe from drowning,' she whispered. 'But when I look into your eyes, I'm not sure anymore.'

How do you think I feel when I look into yours? Drowning is one thing - burning quite another.

I tried to shake off the thought that seemed to have invaded my mind without asking my permission. Narrowing my eyes infinitesimally, I stared up at her. 'Is that supposed to make sense?'

'Not really. It's supposed to make you feel something.'

'Ah.' That tug in my chest again. Damnation! How did she do that? 'You will be pleased to hear, then, that the method seems to be effective.'

There was silence again. We looked at each other, I at her as if she were the key to the vaults of the Bank of England, and she at me as if... as if...

Well, I wasn't really sure what she wanted most in life. But she looked as if it might be lying in this bed.

It can't be... No! It can't possibly be me, can it?

'You're supposed to say something, too, you know,' she pointed out, the corners of that devious little mouth of hers twitching.

I almost frowned, before I remembered it was an unnecessary waste of energy on facial muscles. 'Something like what?'

'Maybe something about what you feel.'

Feel? Since when were my feelings of any significance? More to the point, since when was I supposed to have any?

I opened my mouth to give a cutting reply, but apparently my mouth had other ideas.

'I would have thought that required no words. Is it not obvious?'

Did that hoarse voice really belong to me?

Still, there was that devious little smile on her face. No matter how much I tried, I could not wrest my eyes away from her face. 'Maybe. But I would like you to tell me anyway.'

'A waste of breath and time!' I snapped.

'Yes. But a wonderful one. Please?' Cocking her head, she raised my hand to her lips once more. Again, I felt that flutter of butterflies' wings on me. It sent a torrent of sensation up along my arm, unlike anything I had felt before. 'Please, Sir?'

My breath caught.

'What if I don't have the words?' My voice sounded distant in my own ears. 'There are no words for how I feel right now. None that I know.'

She closed her eyes, and I felt her hand tighten around mine almost painfully. But somehow, I didn't mind. 'Those,' she told me in a whisper, 'were exactly the right ones.'

THEY STILL ARE!

The first inkling I got that something was wrong, came when Youssef started shouting orders in Arabic.

'Get off your camels, now! Put up the tents! Rags in front of your faces, all of you. And hurry! We're camping here!'

Camping here?

It wasn't just the order he gave – it was the fact that he dared to give it without my permission that made me turn and urge my camel back towards him, my eyes hard and flinty. Was there a reason for stopping, or did Youssef have a death wish?

By the time I reached the main body of men on top of the dune, most had already dismounted. It was the middle of the day, with dozens of miles still before us till dusk, and they were settling down their camels, putting up tents and chattering like old women! Some of them, I noticed, had even taken off their headscarves and started pouring water all over them. Had they lost their wits?

'What is this? What is going on?' Bringing my camel to an abrupt halt, I slid down from the saddle and shot Youssef a look that, under the circumstances, was quite benign and understanding. It didn't promise to kill him on the spot, at least. 'Explain yourself, Youssef.'

In answer, he simply pointed off into the distance, in the direction where we had been heading. Following his outstretched arm with my gaze, I spotted a sickly-yellow cloud, slowly approaching.

'Yes?' I demanded. 'What is it about that thing?'

'It's a sandstorm, *Effendi*.'

'And?'

'We have to stop, *Effendi*. To seek shelter until it has passed.'

'Seek shelter?' I felt my eyes narrow. So that was his excuse for dallying, was it? 'You do not honestly think that I will let this delay me, do you? That I will let a tiny bit of sand stop me from going on?'

The Arab looked at me, appearing offended. As if I cared! 'A tiny bit of sand? *Effendi*, I...'

'We are going on, Youssef! Not another word.'

'But *Effendi*...'

I raised a finger. That was usually all it took, and in this case, too, the method did not disappoint. Youssef fell silent immediately. Taking a deep breath, he bowed his head. 'Yes, *Effendi*. As you wish, *Effendi*.'

'Are you sure that going on is wise?'

Oh no. I knew *that* voice. Glancing sideways, I glimpsed *her* out of the corner of my eye. She was looking back and forth between Youssef and the sandstorm. 'If he really thinks it's dangerous, shouldn't we listen to him?'

I gave her a look. Usually, that was enough to make people back down. Actually, it was usually enough to make people beg and whimper in fear. Not with her, of course. 'Do you know the size of an average grain of sand?'

'No,' she admitted, rather grudgingly, obviously not knowing where I was heading with this.

'It is between 0.0024803 and 0.08 inches. Now, think carefully for a moment.' Leaning forward, I gazed into her eyes, letting her see all my iron determination. 'Do you think I am going to let myself be stopped by something smaller than a tenth of an inch?'

'Um... no.'

'Indeed, no.'

Ha! If I had not been opposed on principle to the activity of laughing, the idea would almost have made me laugh out loud. Stopping for a few tiny bits of sand? Ridiculous! Disdainfully, I glanced down at the approaching cloud of dust in the valley. Granted, it looked somewhat bigger than before and was moving rather fast, but still....

Shaking off the strange feeling, I gave my camel a whack with my cane, wishing I could do the same with lazy employees. 'Forwards!'

We had just reached the bottom of the hill when the rumbling started.

'What's that?' I heard her voice from behind. Not talking to me, I surmised. She knew I wasn't likely to answer. 'Thunder?'

Youssef's reply was lost in the growing rumble.

Even I began to be curious. What in Mammon's name was that? Surely, it couldn't be...

I glanced at the distant cloud of sand again, feeling a little uneasy for the first time since spotting it. It wasn't a feeling to which I was accustomed. Gritting my teeth, I shoved it aside and continued on. Around me, the rumbling grew into a continuous roar, like the sound coming from a mob of discontented factory workers. Wind began to slap and batter against my face, and I had to grip my top hat to keep it from flying off. The hot wind bit into my face with glowing fangs, but I ignored the pain, like I had always ignored anything that didn't suit me, and whacked my camel's arse with the stick again.

'Move!'

But although I continued on without letting up, I couldn't help my eyes straying to the approaching storm now and again.

'It doesn't seem quite so small anymore, does it?' Came a sudden, all-too-familiar voice from beside me. I glanced to the side, and who should it be but my dear, lovely and *very temporary* wife. 'What did you say again? 0.0024801 inches?'

'0.0024803' I corrected. 'Not 0.0024801.'

'Oh, of course, that makes a hell of a lot of difference!'

I didn't deign to answer that.

'If you haven't noticed yet, there seem to be rather a lot of these 0.0024803-inch obstacles which you think are so easy to overcome. Maybe we should stop after all.'

Gritting my teeth together, I kept silent.

'You are a stubborn son of a bachelor!'

Ah, the sweet endearments of married life... It was really quite charming. 'I thought earlier you told me that I was the son of a donkey?'

Out of the corner of my field of vision, I saw her eyes flash from between the folds of her burnoose. 'That was before I ran out of Arabic insults!'

I turned to look at her. She was looking at me unlike any woman had before. All the other women I had known had either tried to smile at me, or had turned tail and run. She did neither. She met my gaze head-on, as if her harebrained notions were true and the two of us were indeed equals. So I injected an extra dose of steel into my voice when I said: 'We can do this. No discussion. We're going on.'

A bloody insolent gust of hot wind struck me in the face and ripped the top hat from my head. Before it could get farther than a foot or two, my hand shot out and grabbed it. Hm... with this so-called storm approaching, the wind really was getting somewhat stronger.

'Tell me,' she shouted. 'Have you ever been in a sandstorm before?'

I didn't reply. What was the sense? She would question me no matter what I said or did. It was her favourite pastime.

'Well?'

I had to admit, she was insistent. I would have admired that trait, if she hadn't been a woman.

Glancing up, I watched the storm with narrowed eyes. It had grown some-what since my last inspection. And the way it looked, it was still growing, at a rate of approximately fifty-one per cent per minute. Too bad it was a storm and not my annual profits.

'Have you?' demanded a certain persistent female voice from beside me.

'No!' I told her. 'But I've been in plenty of snowstorms.'

'Meaning?'

'Meaning that snow makes you freeze. Sand doesn't. So it can hardly be more dangerous.'

Even if the storm is now growing at a rate of sixty-four per cent per minute?

I clamped down on that thought and continued on.

Soon, we had reached the bottom of the valley. In front of us rose a small hill, and down that hill the storm approached with a velocity that, even though I would never have admitted as much, was beginning to worry me. A blast of sand shot past us, swallowing a withered desert plant. It disappeared from sight, as if it had never been.

Maybe we should turn and...

Nonsense! Get a grip! You didn't get where you are today by being afraid of a little bit of sand!

'Please, *Effendi!*' At the shout, I glanced around to see Youssef galloping towards us. To judge by the look on his face, he didn't share my determination. 'Please, let us stop! We have to stop moving! The storm isn't dispersing, it's headed right towards us! We cannot...'

Cannot?

Cannot?

That word did not appear in my vocabulary. Turning to face the storm again head-on, I urged my camel forward, heading straight for the heart of the howling maelstrom of sand.

~~*~**~*~*

Darkness.

Absolute darkness, and roaring, tumultuous silence.

Hot sand was burning my face. And my hands. And other places. Around me, devils were dancing in the wind, spitting fire, laughing at me. Faint images danced in front of my inner eye. Water, shimmering in the distance. A maul with great fangs, opening, ready to swallow me up.

Memories? Visions?

I had no idea. Right then and there, I didn't care.

'Mr Ambrose!'

That voice... that face. I might not be too sure about everything else, but that face was no figment of my exhausted imagination. Never in my life would I dream up a female this tenacious, stubborn, and... beautiful.

Wait a minute - what did you just think there?

It had to be the dehydration. I was starting to lose my mind.

'Mr Ambrose!'

Even as a hallucination, she was darn persistent. I could have sworn her voice was coming closer...

The next moment, the figure of a muffled Arab appeared next to me. What the-

It took me a moment to realize that the face behind the white cloth was not the dark-skinned face of an Arab. Oh no.

'Mr Ambrose, Sir! Are you alive?'

'Go away,' he growled.

What were the chances of her actually doing what I told her, for once in her life?

'Why on earth should I?' she demanded.

As I thought. Zero.

Memories were slowly started to come back. She wasn't a hallucination. She had followed me into the storm – against my express orders, of course. And then... the rising winds, the fall from the camel... and then, blackness.

'It's not safe wandering around in this kind of tempest!' I growled up at her.

She raised an eyebrow. 'Oh, you've only just figured that out, have you?'

'I told you to stay where you were!'

'And I didn't listen. Now come, get over here.'

This was intolerable!

'Didn't you hear what I said? Go!' I tried to push myself up, tried to push her away from here, back where it would be safe – but my body seemed to have different ideas. It sank back down, sending a bolt of pain through me. An indistinct noise escaped the back of my throat. 'Go, I said! My lungs are being shredded! You have a camel; maybe you can make it out of here alive. Leave me to die in peace!'

Emphasis on *in peace*.

'Not a chance in hell! If you're going to die, I'm going to make sure your last minutes on this earth are as miserable as possible!'

'How very kind of you!'

Something tugged at me. Apparently, my dear semi-wife had decided that there was a better stretch of sand for dying on than the one I was currently occupying. I looked up at her – for the first time *really* looked and, underneath the stubborn mask, saw the fear flickering in her eyes. Fear for me. I tried to reach out to her – in vain. My hand wouldn't move. 'No! Leave me! Save yourself!'

In a flash, the fear was gone from her eyes. She stared at me suspiciously. 'Are you being unusually noble, or do you simply not want a girl to save your stony behind?'

Interesting question.

And the answer?

Both.

She seemed to take my silence as an answer, though. Her eyes flared hotter than the desert sand.

'So that's the way it is, is it? Well, I've got news for you, *Dick, my darling.*' She gave a firm tug on my arm again. Suppressing a groan, I slid a few inches in her direction. 'I've still got a wedding ring on my finger, and so do you, however temporary it may be. Do you know what that means? That means that right now I vow in the presence of God, a camel and a buttload of sand, to be your faithful partner in sickness and in health, in good times and in bad, in happiness as well as in sadness, and even when you behave like a bloody arrogant idiot!'

Well, thank you very much, darling.

'I promise to hate you unconditionally, to support you in your aspirations as long as you pay me for it, and to honour and respect you as long as I get a free day off every week. This–' she gave another violent tug, and I slid closer to the shelter of the camel, 'is – my – solemn – vow!'[31]

I cleared my throat, spitting out sand.

'How moving.'

'You think it's moving? Then move your behind! We have to get over there, pronto!' She pointed to the dark outline of her camel, which was lazily snoring through the sandstorm a couple of yards away. 'At least Ambrose will give us some shelter from the storm!'

'You,' I rasped, somehow managing to stagger to my feet and stumble over to her mount, 'are going to change that camel's name!'

'Oh, I am, am I?'

'Yes!'

'We'll see about that.'

Exhausted, we slumped to the ground next to the erroneously named camel. My dear wife started rummaging in the camel's saddlebag and, a second later, pulled out – of all things! – a headscarf, pouring some of the remaining water from her flask over it.

'Here!' She held the thing out to me. 'Put that over your mouth and nose!'

I gave her a look – the same kind of look with which I had sent gunslingers, highwaymen and aristocrats running for the hills.

'That is Arabian *women's clothing*! I will most certainly not–'

Smack! The rest of my words were drowned in wet cloth. I choked, trying to pull the thing from my face – then stopped. Somehow, even with the cloth over my face, it was suddenly easier to breath.

'Leave it on if you do not want to choke to death!' came the voice of my beloved wife from beyond the moist barrier. 'If you do, be my guest and remove it.'

'What was that about honouring and respecting me?' I enquired from behind the wet cloth.

'You remember the conditions, don't you? I haven't gotten a day off since we started on this accursed trip!'

'Well, then I have good news for you.' Reaching up, I pulled the infernal effeminate cloth off my eyes. But, as discreetly as possible, I left it over my mouth and nose. To some degree, she appeared to be right. It was easier to breathe with the thing on.

'Oh yes?'

'Oh yes, indeed.' I swept my arm around, gesturing at the storm raging around us. 'I give you the rest of the day off.'

'Thanks *so* much, Sir!' Her voice was dripping with sarcasm. For some reason, in the safety of the wet headscarf, I felt one corner of my mouth twitch the tiniest bit in some kind of muscle spasm. 'I'm going to the nearest café right away to enjoy a nice cup of tea and a piece of apple pie!'

'You're welcome!' I rasped. 'And don't forget–'

---

[31] WARNING! Do not use this vow in real life if you are planning to get married, no matter how much you may be tempted.

Whatever I would have said was cut of by a bellow of storm wind. Darkness descended around us, closing in from all directions, cutting off the sunlight as efficiently as a guillotine cutting the heads off the French aristocracy.

Hm.

Interesting.

'What in God's name...!' I heard my dear wife's voice out of the darkness. 'What is going on?'

It is going dark, my dear. You can tell that from the lack of light everywhere.

'Holy Moses and macaroons!'

'Ha!' Sometimes, she had quite an interesting way with words.

'What is happening?'

I decided that her limited female mental capacity could probably use some help in assessing the situation. 'The sun is dying,' I rasped.

'What?'

'Look.' I stretched out my arm. It hadn't moved far before its end disappeared in a dark fog, thicker than the smoke from the biggest of my factories. And that was saying something.

'This... this can't happen! A storm can't block out the sun like that! It would have to be...'

I nodded. 'Several miles high.'

'No! No, that can't happen! It simply can't!'

Females! Impressively talented when it came to ignoring reality.

'Apparently, it can.'

I felt her shifting around in the darkness. 'Bloody hell! No!'

Was she still in denial? Women!

She moved again. I felt her slide closer, and then–

'Ouch!'

A hand grabbed hold of my ear – and not gently either. This was intolerable! It was the second time on our journey she was trying to rip my ears off. Was she going to make a habit of this kind of thing?

Grabbing her arm, I pulled her up against the camel. If she wanted to grab hold of something to sooth her feminine fears, she could just as well use it, and not me. Particularly not parts of me that I still intended to use for the purpose of hearing.

'I would advise you,' I told her, keeping my voice cool and calm, 'to let go of my ear immediately.'

'Ah.' To her credit – in the non-banking sense – she did sound apologetic. 'Sorry.'

She let go, and I pulled her farther up against the camel, where she would have the best company and comfort available. It didn't seem to work as intended, though. After only a few moments, I heard a low whimper out of the darkness.

I felt a sudden tug in my chest, and before I knew what was happening, I found myself asking, in a half-shout, half-whisper: 'What's wrong?'

What the.... Why on earth would I want to know?

'I... I'm alone.'

The voice coming out of the darkness didn't sound at all like her usual voice. It didn't sound at all like a little fiery *ifrit*. It sounded soft and... scared?

I felt that tug in my chest again. What was the matter? Had I pulled a muscle?

'No, you're not,' I told her briskly. 'The camel is here.'

That should clear up the matter.

'The camel hates my guts!'

'Intelligent animal.' Though I couldn't see how personal feelings entered into the matter under discussion. I thought we had been talking about aloneness versus company.

'You... you're doing this on purpose!'

'Doing what?'

'Making me angry!' Came a growl out of the darkness. It sounded much more like her usual self. 'So I won't be afraid.'

In the safety of the darkness, I felt my lips tremble, wanting to shift into an almost-smile. I clamped down on the urge, hard.

'Is it working?'

'Yes, blast you!'

'Indeed?'

'That's all you've got to say? You are a bloody bank-vault-like, close-mouthed bastard!'

Ah, yes. Now she sounded very much like her usual self. Why was it that her insults made me want to reach out and pull her closer? Usually, when people insulted me, they didn't live past the next dawn. But she... she was a different matter.

How to respond?

'I see.' I paused, again struggling against the incomprehensible urge to reach out into the darkness. 'Or rather, I don't see. Anything, in fact.'

'Ha, ha! That's so funny!'

Silence fell between us. Or, at least, the absence of words. The whirling darkness battered against us, making the lack of words painfully loud in my ears. I had never minded silence. But right now...

'Mr Ambrose?'

Her voice broke the roaring quiet, tentatively.

'Yes?'

She hesitated. What in God's name would make my dear, temporary wife hesitate? This had to be good. Or, more likely, very, very bad.

'I... feel alone.'

Bad. Worse. Terrible. I felt an iron fist clench around my heart. Definitely a pulled muscle!

'Do you?'

'I don't want to be alone right now.'

Her words hit me like a fist. No, that wasn't right. I was very adept at dodging fists. But this I couldn't dodge. It hit me like a bullet. Fast. Hard. Unavoidable.

And before I could think of anything to say, there was her hand, brushing over the sleeve of my tailcoat. My whole body stiffened under her touch. She had touched me before – more than just touched, in fact – but this was different.

There was meaning in every tiny movement. A meaning that I didn't entirely comprehend. I wasn't even sure whether I wanted to.

Her fingers slid down my arm. When they reached the bare skin of my hand, I sucked in a quick breath, lost in the storm. Cautiously, almost tenderly, she brushed away a few grains of sand and stroked the skin underneath.

What in the name of all that is profitable...!

I wanted to say something, wanted to order her to stop, to never stop, but something was lodged in my throat, blocking any words from escaping. When I finally managed to squeeze a few syllables past the blockade, I didn't recognize my own voice: 'I thought that sort of thing between us was reserved for the dark of the night.'

Her voice came out of the storm, sweet and soft. 'It looks pretty dark to me.'

A pause. Then... 'Yes. You're right, it does.'

My arms came up, and, without asking for my permission, reached out towards her.

~~**~*~*

During the course of my life-long struggle for economic world-domination, I had visited a number of considerably dark places. The fur-hunting grounds of Alaska during the polar night, the catacombs of Rome, even the coal mines in my own native country—they all ranked quite high on the darkness scale. However, not one of them, it was my studied opinion, could compete with the utter and oppressive darkness that was now pressing in on us from all sides, battering us with sharp whiplashes of sand. If I were able to bottle this darkness, I could make a fortune selling it to countries suffering under prolonged heatwaves.

The something in my arms shifted, and I wondered if similar thoughts were going through its mind.

It. Yes, definitely *it*. I didn't dare think of it as 'her'. Not now that my arms were around her, and she was pressed up against me in a way that was... very distracting. Intolerably so.

'What's that?' a soft voice asked from somewhere below my chin. A voice that most definitely belonged to a 'her', not an 'it'. Damn!

A cautious hand touched my neck.

'That's me. My neck.'

Was it only the sand that made my voice sound so rough? I tried to believe it, but...

The cautious hand stopped being cautious. With soft fingers it took hold of my neck and pulled me down, demandingly. I didn't resist

'No, I mean that smell,' the it that was a she whispered. 'Has the camel had something bad for breakfast?'

I felt a nose tickle my armpit, and had to fight the instinct to... what? Flinch away? Grab hold of her and pull her closer? This was infuriatingly illogical! How could one thing motivate you to wish to take two different kinds of actions?

'I don't think so,' I stated, shoving those enervatingly illogical thoughts aside. 'That smell might come from the fact that you have your nose buried in my armpit.'

'Oh.'

Oh? Oh! What's that supposed to mean?

A pause. The storm roared on. She didn't remove her nose from my armpit.

You just thought 'she'. 'She', not 'it'. You're done for!

'Um...' Her voice was softer than ever before. I could hardly believe this was the same creature that had harried me like a little devil since the moment she had first stepped into my office. Like a little *ifrit*. My little *Ifrit*.

'It's a nice armpit.'

My breath caught—and not because of the sandstorm. Her words stirred something inside of me. For a long moment, I couldn't figure out why. They were not particularly impressive words, after all, whether seen from a contentual, poetical or linguistic point of view. But then I realized that those words, spoken by that soft voice, were the first compliment I had received in years.

Oh, people had complimented my wealth, my achievements and even, if they felt like risking their lives, my noble parentage. But no one, as far as I could remember, had ever complimented anything that was essentially me. Granted, my armpit was perhaps not my most stunning feature, but still...

Instinctively, I felt my arms tighten around the creature in my arms that I could not think of as a 'she', and that still was so soft, so feminine...

'Thanks.'

'Feels good.' The soft voice from the dark hesitated for a moment. Then, lower, so low I almost couldn't hear it anymore, it added in a whisper: 'All of you does.'

I felt like all the breath had left my body. But that didn't matter, because plenty of blood was still there, pumping hot and hard, shattering the ice in my veins.

What is the matter with you? What is happening?

I tried to remove my arms from around *it*, but they wouldn't let go, instead closing tighter around *her*, for yes, she was a *her*, all softness and curves in my arms that pressed into me all over my body, setting me on fire. I had to let go! Had to! Had to! Had t–'

'So do you.' The words were out of my mouth before I could stop them.

Suddenly, the black wind around us slammed into us hard. There was a cry from the dark and something soft and warm slammed into me. No – not something. Someone!

Dear, merciless King Midas...

Once more, my arms tightened instinctively and, inwardly, I cursed. God had really made an abominable construction error when he invented instincts.

'Oh God...' The sound of her voice, trembling, hardly audible in the roaring dark, tore at something deep inside me. 'I... I'm scared!'

'So am I.'

What the...?!

What had I just said? I was never scared, as a matter of principle. *Never!* And, even if by some insane fluke of nature I were at some future point in time to become scared of something, I would never be so gormless as to actually *admit* it!

But that wasn't the worst of it.

'Come here,' I heard my voice say. 'Let me hold you.'

What?

Had I completely lost my faculties for logical reasoning? We were trapped in a sandstorm, not a snowstorm! Pressing closely against each other would not increase our chances of survival by one single iota. What was I thinking?

That's the problem. You aren't. Period.

'Yes! Please!'

There was that soft voice again, all scared and lonely, and yet, underneath all that, still strong, still fiery, still my little *Ifrit*. Without thinking twice (or even once, to tell the truth) I pulled her up against me until our faces were pressed against each other, hard jaw to soft cheek, black strands to brown locks, lips to hungry lips.

I felt dazed. Was this really happening? Were the two of us really...? Could it be that...?

'Rick?'

That voice...

'Yes, Lilly?'

'I'm glad you're here.'

Don't say anything! Don't say anything! Don't say any–

'I'm glad you're here, too.'

Damn!

'Really?'

I felt that irrational tug at the corner of my mouth again that I only ever felt when she was around. 'Not glad that you're here in the sandstorm, in imminent danger of suffocation, obviously. I meant here *with me.*'

'Yes. I meant that, too.'

'Good.'

'Yes.'

A moment of silence. A moment of roaring storm winds. If only she would speak again. If only I could hear her voice, listen to that spark of fire!

'Lilly?'

'Yes?'

'If we don't survive, I want you to know that I...'

At that precise moment, the storm gave another roar, cutting me off mid-speech. Just as well. Because I actually had no idea what kind of wild, foolish thing I was about to say.

...THE MIDDLE...

236

ABOUT THE AUTHOR

Robert Thier is a German historian and writer of historical fiction. His particular mix of history, romance, and adventure, always with a good deal of humour thrown in, has gained him a diverse readership ranging from teenagers to retired grandmothers. For the way he manages to make history come alive, as if he himself lived as a medieval knight, his fans all over the world have given him the nickname 'Sir Rob'.

For Robert, becoming a writer followed naturally from his interest in history. 'In Germany,' he says, 'we use the same word for story and history. And I've always loved the one as much as the other. Becoming a storyteller, a writer, is what I've always wanted.'

Besides writing and researching in dusty old archives, on the lookout for a mystery to put into his next story, Robert enjoys classical music and long walks in the country. The helmet you see in the picture he does not wear because he is a cycling enthusiast, but to protect his literary skull in which a bone has been missing from birth. Robert lives in the south of Germany in a small village between the three Emperor Mountains.

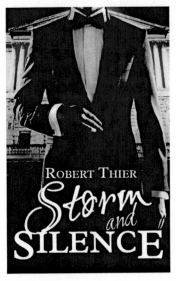

Storm and Silence

Freedom – that is what Lilly Linton wants most in life. Not marriage, not a brood of squalling brats, and certainly not *love*, thank you very much!

But freedom is a rare commodity in 19th-century London, where girls are expected to spend their lives sitting at home, fully occupied with looking pretty. Lilly is at her wits' end – until a chance encounter with a dark, dangerous and powerful stranger changes her life forever...

The award-winning first volume of the Storm and Silence series! Winner of the *People's Choice Award* and *Story of the Year Award* 2015.

ISBN-10:   3000513515
ISBN-13:   978-3000513510

The Robber Knight

When you are fighting for the freedom of your people, falling in love with your enemy is not a great idea.

Sir Reuben, the dreaded robber knight, has long been Ayla's deadliest enemy. She swore he would hang for his crimes. Now they are both trapped in her castle as the army of a far greater enemy approaches, and they have only one chance: stand together, or fall. Welcome to "The Robber Knight"—a tale full of action, adventure, and romance.

Special Edition with secret chapters revealed and insights into Sir Reuben's mysterious past.

ISBN-10:   1499251645
ISBN-13:   978-1499251647

UPCOMING TITLES

At present (2016) *The Robber Knight*, *Storm and Silence* and *In the Eye of the Storm* are Robert Thiers's only books published in English. However, book two of the Robber Knight Saga, *The Robber Knight's Love*, is being edited for publication. Keep updated about the book's progress on the internet.

Website: www.robthier.com
Facebook profile: www.facebook.com/robert.thier.161
Facebook page: http://de-de.facebook.com/RobThierHelmHead
Twitter: http://twitter.com/thesirrob
Tumblr Blog: http://robthier.tumblr.com
Goodreads: www.goodreads.com/author/show/6123144.Robert_Thier

CPSIA information can be obtained
at www.ICGtesting.com
Printed in the USA
LVOW08s1730160317
527463LV00004B/972/P